By Mark Ellis

Princes Gate
Stalin's Gold
Merlin at War
A Death in Mayfair
Dead in the Water

ABOUT THE AUTHOR

Mark Ellis is a thriller writer from Swansea and a former barrister and entrepreneur. He grew up under the shadow of his parents' experience of the Second World War. His father served in the wartime navy and died a young man. His mother told him stories of watching the heavy bombardment of Swansea from the safe vantage point of a hill in Llanelli, and of attending tea dances in wartime London under the bombs and doodlebugs.

In consequence Mark has always been fascinated by WW2 and in particular the Home Front and the fact that while the nation was engaged in a heroic endeavour, crime flourished. Murder, robbery, theft, rape and corruption were rife. This was an intriguing, harsh and cruel world – the world of DCI Frank Merlin.

Mark Ellis is a member of several writers organisations including the Crime Writers' Association and Crime Cymru. The third novel in his historical detective series, *Merlin at War*, was on the CWA Historical Dagger Longlist in 2018.

MARK ELLIS
DEAD IN THE WATER

ACCENT

First published in 2022 by Headline Accent
An imprint of HEADLINE PUBLISHING GROUP

3

Cataloguing in Publication Data is available from the British Library

ISBN 978 1 7861 5988 5

Typeset in 10.5/13pt Bembo Std by Jouve (UK), Milton Keynes

Printed and bound in Great Britain by Clays Ltd, Elcograf S.p.A.

MIX
Paper from
responsible sources
FSC® C104740

HEADLINE PUBLISHING GROUP
An Hachette UK Company
Carmelite House
50 Victoria Embankment
London EC4Y 0DZ

www.headline.co.uk
www.hachette.co.uk

To Geoffrey Haig Barclay

Note on Currency

As a rule of thumb I have taken a pound in 1942 to be worth roughly 40 times what it is today. The wartime exchange rate was around £1=$4.

Prologue

November 1938
Vienna

The apartment was in a fashionable residential building just off the Ringstrasse, the grand boulevard that encircled the centre of Austria's capital. Daniel was the fourth head of the Katz family to live there. Samuel Katz, his great-grandfather and founder of the eponymous family bank, had been the first. Daniel's wife Esther and the younger of their four children, Sarah and Rachel, shared the apartment with him. His son and older daughter were away studying at the Sorbonne in Paris.

Daniel had taken over the running of the bank in 1920, after the sudden death of his father. Under his assured management, it had weathered the economic storms of the twenties and early thirties and had emerged as one of the soundest finance houses in Vienna. All should have been good in the Katz world. It was not. For the Katzes were Jews, and since March, Adolf Hitler had ruled their country. Daniel's younger brother, Benjamin, had been quick to sniff the wind years before, when Hitler had first come to power in Germany. He had moved to London, where he had rapidly built up his own successful financial business. He had pestered Daniel for years to follow him, but Daniel had stubbornly resisted. An eternal optimist, he continued to believe, against all the evidence, that Hitler would make allowances for Jews who had brains

1

and skills to offer society. The German annexation of Austria had at last put paid to this optimism. It was now crystal clear that all Jews, clever or not, were to be pariahs. The authorities had begun to strip him of his business interests. There was no prospect of escape, and it had become only a matter of time before everything was lost.

Now, on this fine autumn morning, that time had come. The family was breakfasting together in the dining room. The servants had long gone, and mother and daughters had prepared the meal. A letter had just arrived from their son, Nathan, and Esther was reading it aloud. As she turned to the final page, there was a sudden fierce pounding at the door, and a voice screamed, 'Open up, Jewish scum!'

Daniel hurried to the hallway to see the front door already splintering under the pounding of rifle butts. Snarling soldiers pushed through. One of them dragged him down the corridor to where his petrified wife and daughters were cowering.

'I am Sergeant Vogel. You will all do as you are told. Where is your sitting room?'

Daniel inclined his head to the left. 'Second on the right. But . . . what is this about? This is a private dwelling. On what grounds . . .'

The sergeant struck him hard on his right cheek. 'Shut up and move along.'

'But gentlemen, please. You have no right. I must ask you to leave.'

The sergeant smiled and looked at his men. 'Gentlemen, eh? Very polite, ain't he, lads?' He waved his gun. 'Move.'

The party entered the larger of the apartment's two parlours. Vogel, a fat man with the purple nose of a serious drinker, had a quick look round, then instructed the other soldiers to search the rest of the flat. He turned his attention back to the family. 'Everyone get over there by the window.'

They did as they were told. Looking down into the street,

Daniel saw a fleet of military vehicles. 'May I ask what is happening?'

The sergeant grinned. 'What is happening is that we are taking some of you rich Viennese Jews on a nice little vacation. We've got a holiday camp waiting for you, a place called Mauthausen. You'll love it.' He moved to the window and looked down himself at the action on the street. He emitted a satisfied grunt, then turned his attention to the girls. 'You have two fine-looking daughters, Katz. I think I might steal a kiss before we go. Maybe a little more. What do you think, eh, my lovelies?' Sarah cringed as he reached out to touch her. Then a peremptory voice sounded.

'Vogel! What the hell are you doing?'

Another soldier was at the door. A younger man than Vogel but apparently of higher rank. His collar sported the insignia of the SS.

The sergeant stepped back. 'I was just .... just about to start searching everyone, sir.'

'Starting with the prettiest, I see.' The officer considered for a moment. 'You may check to see if Herr Katz is armed, but I think it unnecessary to search the ladies.'

A clearly disappointed Vogel nodded and frisked Daniel roughly. 'He's clean, sir.'

The SS officer flashed a shark-like smile. 'I'm forgetting my manners, Herr Katz. My name is Spitzen. Colonel Ferdinand Spitzen. Heil Hitler.' His hand rose in more of a wave than a salute. 'What a fine-looking family you have, Herr Katz.' He stared at the women for a moment, then looked down at his highly polished boots. 'Such a pity.'

'I beg your pardon, Colonel?'

Spitzen's face darkened. 'You may beg my pardon indeed, Herr Katz. However, it will sadly not be forthcoming. The time has come for Jews to pay the price for the crimes of their race.' He turned back to Vogel. 'Go and see how the others are getting on. Make sure no one damages anything, or there'll be hell to pay. Understand?'

3

'Yes, sir.' The sergeant disappeared into the corridor and the colonel began to walk around the room, voicing his admiration for the paintings, the opulent furniture and the numerous fine *objets d'art* dotted all around. Eventually he settled himself in a large leather armchair by the fireplace. 'So, Herr Katz. You will not be surprised to know, I'm sure, that the Reich has a full file on your long career as a crooked Jewish banker.' He flicked a speck of dirt from his trousers. 'Have you anything to say?'

'I have been a straight and honest businessman all my life. I do not recognise your description.'

After considering this reply for a moment, Spitzen eased himself to his feet, strolled over to Daniel and punched him hard in the face. Daniel collapsed to the floor, blood spurting from his nose. Esther and his daughters burst out crying, and rushed to help him to his feet.

'You lie, Katz!' shouted the colonel. 'You and your race have connived for years to defraud the great German people. The Führer has now, thankfully, decided to put a halt to this abuse once and for all. Justice will be served.' He returned to his chair. 'As it happens, the name of Daniel Katz is surprisingly well known among the ruling circles of the Reich. Not because of your criminality, but for another reason. You are something of an art collector, are you not?'

Daniel realised for the first time that his tie had come loose. He attempted to retie it, but found that his hands were shaking too much. He shrugged.

'We were under the impression that the greatest pieces in the collection were kept in your headquarter offices in Schottengasse. However, when we searched them, we did not find what we were looking for.' Spitzen glanced around the room. 'I see some attractive paintings here, but, unless I'm very much mistaken, these are again lesser works. *Am* I mistaken?'

Vogel appeared at the door before Daniel could answer.

'Yes, Sergeant?' Spitzen said irritably.

'We've found a lot of stuff. Paintings, drawings, sculptures, ornaments. Some jewellery in the bedrooms. Oh, and a safe that needs opening.'

'What about those particular items I listed for you?'

'Haven't found them yet.'

Spitzen frowned, then turned back to Daniel. 'You will open the safe for Sergeant Vogel. And you will show him any other hidden safes or receptacles for items of value in the flat. Don't bother trying to conceal anything. There is no point. Once you are out of here, everything will be pulled apart.'

Daniel closed his eyes, then nodded.

'I have what I believe to be a comprehensive list of the finest works in your collection. If they are not here, you must tell me where they are.'

'I . . . I sent some works abroad.'

'There is no record of transfer in official export records.'

'I did not . . . did not use official channels.'

'I see. Yet another crime to be added to your long list. It may interest you to know that we've already had valuable assistance from some of your employees. According to them, you have stored a good portion of your collection in this country. They remember items being packed and dispatched to Austrian destinations. Unfortunately, there is no written record of these destinations. No doubt if I put a team on the matter they will track the works down, but things might go a little better for you and your family if you provide the addresses now.'

Daniel glanced nervously at his wife but said nothing.

Spitzen indicated the two girls. 'You know, I made a point of protecting your daughters earlier.' The shark-like smile reappeared. 'Such protection could easily be removed.'

With a look of despair, Daniel conceded. 'All right, all right. I'll tell you.'

'How sensible of you. Vogel, find Herr Katz a pen and paper.'

5

Chapter One

Detective Chief Inspector Frank Merlin and Detective Sergeant Sam Bridges sat silently and patiently in their car. It was parked on the south side of Soho Square, facing east. The time was just after three in the afternoon. Forty yards or so distant, Detective Constable Tommy Cole was in position under a shop awning on the corner of Greek Street. Detective Inspector Peter Johnson was standing a similar distance behind them, on the square's junction with Frith Street. Ahead of Cole, on the south-eastern corner of the square, was Chez François, the French restaurant they'd been told to watch.

The tip-off had come in a phone call to Bridges two hours earlier. A gravelly voice had told him the names of the two men responsible for a string of recent armed robberies – Sinclair and Duvalier, both Canadian army deserters. The informant had said the men were currently staying in an upstairs room of the restaurant, whose owner was an old friend of Duvalier's. They had gone out in the morning to case another robbery target but ought to be returning to the restaurant soon. They'd most likely be coming from a pub they favoured just off Piccadilly Circus. Merlin and his team had been in position since 1.30.

Bridges broke the silence. 'Good job they're Canadians, not Yanks, eh, sir? Otherwise we'd be bound to hand them over.'

Merlin nodded. Under new legislation, the American forces administration were being ceded jurisdiction over all crimes involving members of their own military. He remembered with mild irritation that he had a meeting fixed the following week at the American embassy to discuss the new arrangement.

'You're convinced they'll be armed, sir?'

'Bound to be, Sam. They've used guns on all their jobs so far. We should probably have brought a couple more men with us. I'm sure they won't come quietly.'

'We'll just have to time our approach well, that's all. Catch them unawares.'

Merlin noticed movement ahead. Cole had raised a hand. The two men got out of the car and hurried across to him. The shop awning was not large enough to shade them all, and Merlin felt the full force of the August sun beating down on his head.

'Two likely customers down at the far end of Greek Street,' said the constable. 'It's safe to have a peek around the corner. They're still some way off.'

Merlin saw the men straight away. They were weaving their way slowly down the street. He pulled back. 'They look half-cut to me. One tall, burly fellow; one thinner, bald and a few inches shorter.'

Cole nodded.

'According to our informant, Sinclair would be the larger one,' added Bridges. 'If they're drunk, perhaps it'll be easier to reel them in.'

'Or harder if they panic and start letting off their guns.' Merlin stroked his chin. 'I think it's too risky to try and take them in the street. There's a chance of civilians getting hurt.' He turned to wave Johnson over.

'On their way, are they, sir?' Johnson's Geordie accent had softened a little during his years in London, but was still unmistakable.

'Looks like it, Peter. I suggest the sergeant and I position ourselves a couple of doors down from the restaurant. You two stay here. As and when the suspects enter the restaurant, we'll give it a few seconds, then pile in.'

As he crossed the road, Merlin noticed that the men had stopped halfway down the street to talk to a couple of girls. He paused on the pavement and watched. One of the girls suddenly slapped the bigger of the pair. Another man intervened. Merlin hoped they weren't going to get involved in a street brawl, and was relieved when the shorter man pulled his friend away.

It took the Canadians another six or seven minutes to reach the restaurant. After hovering outside for a moment, they went in.

Merlin waved Johnson and Cole over. 'The state they're in, chances are they'll want more to drink before going to their room.' He patted Cole's arm. 'Take a little stroll past the front window and try and see what's what.'

Cole did as he was told, then reported back. 'The restaurant's almost empty. I could only see one table occupied: two men – not ours – drinking coffee. There were some shadowy figures at the back of the room. I'd guess the bar area.'

'Having a couple of brandies, perhaps? If the customers are on their coffee, they should be gone soon. Let's wait.'

Sure enough, a few minutes later two foreign-looking young men emerged into the sunlight and went their separate ways.

'Take one more stroll, Constable,' said Merlin.

Cole returned to say he'd seen a man in an apron clearing the table of the recently departed customers, and as far as he could see, the shadows were still at the bar.

'Presumably the man in the apron is François. Any other waiters around?'

'Not that I saw, sir.'

Merlin nodded. 'Come on then. Let's do it.'

He led his team through the front door and towards the back of the room, flourishing his warrant card and shouting, 'Nobody move!' Notwithstanding, from the corner of his eye he saw the man in the apron melt out of sight. The drunken Canadians were slow to react

9

but eventually started flailing fists in all directions. Merlin avoided a couple of punches from the smaller man, Duvalier, then grabbed him in a bear hug before throwing him to the floor, where Johnson contained him. Bridges and Cole took on the other man, Sinclair. As they tried to get hold of him, the Canadian pulled a gun, but Bridges was able to slap it out of his hand. Then a punch from Cole caught Sinclair full on the nose. There was a nasty cracking noise.

Meanwhile, Duvalier somehow managed to wriggle out from under Johnson and drew a knife. Merlin had turned his back momentarily to check on Bridges and Cole.

Johnson shouted, 'Watch out, sir.'

Merlin turned and raised his arms defensively. Johnson launched himself at Duvalier but wasn't quick enough to stop him slashing one of the chief inspector's hands. As Merlin pulled away, blood spurting, Johnson kneed the Canadian in the groin. The knife clattered to the ground, but Duvalier again managed to squirm free and started for the door. Merlin, however, barred the way and struck out with his good hand, sending a winded Duvalier once more to the floor. As he fell, he hit his head on the base of a bar stool, and this time he stayed down.

Sinclair was still groggy from Cole's blow but roused himself to lunge at the constable. As the two men grappled, Bridges grabbed a whisky bottle from behind the bar and brought it down on the Canadian's head. Sinclair crumpled to join his partner in crime at the policemen's feet, and both men were cuffed in short order.

'Are you all right, sir?' Bridges asked his boss.

'I'll live. I just need a few stitches.'

'The big fellow's coming round,' said Johnson. 'Thought for a moment you'd done him in, Sergeant.'

Bridges grinned sheepishly as he helped Merlin to tighten the handkerchief he'd applied to his wound. 'I think you'd better go and see the nurse back at the Yard, sir, and quickly at that. We can tidy up here.'

'You're right, Sam. I'll grab a taxi. Tell everyone well done.'

Chapter Two

'Frank, there you are. Another success to note down in your little book then?' Assistant Commissioner Gatehouse smiled up from behind his desk.

'I don't have a little book, sir.'

'Don't be a pedant, Chief Inspector. Take a seat, please.' The two men were in the AC's Scotland Yard office, which was directly above Merlin's and had an equally fine view of the Thames and Westminster Bridge. In appearance, the only thing the two men had in common was height. Both were over six feet, though Merlin shaded it by a whisker. The chief inspector was a fine-featured, good-looking, green-eyed man in his forties, with the sleek black hair and dark complexion of his Spanish father. The AC was lankier in build, older and greyer. With small eyes and an excess of teeth, he was not good-looking and never had been. He was dressed soberly as always, in a plain dark suit, wing-collared shirt and neutral tie.

He nodded sympathetically at Merlin's bandaged hand. 'Painful?'

'A little sore. I've had a couple of stitches. Be tickety-boo in a day or two.'

'Good. So let's hear all about it.'

Merlin ran over the details of the Soho stakeout. When he'd

11

finished, the AC nodded sagely. 'A difficult job well done. Where are the two men now?'

'Downstairs spilling their guts to my men, with luck. They wouldn't say a dicky bird last night, but I understand they're in a different frame of mind this morning.'

'The usual game?'

'Yes, each man's been told the other has peached on him.'

'Quite a run of success they had. Any sign of the robbery proceeds?'

'Only a hundred and sixty quid found in their room.'

'A small portion. Could they have spent the rest?'

'They could have drunk a lot of it, given the state they were in yesterday.'

'What about the man who was harbouring them? The restaurant owner?'

'Monsieur François did a runner but was nabbed by a vigilant copper at Waterloo station this morning. He's downstairs too.'

The AC fiddled with his tie. 'What firearms did they have?'

'Smith & Wesson revolvers. Standard Canadian issue filched from army stores.'

'Any match with that Hackney cinema usherette who got shot?'

'Waiting on forensics, but I'm sure there will be.'

'So the noose for them, then.'

Merlin nodded.

'At least we can deal with them in our own courts. If they were Americans, now . . .'

'Indeed, sir.'

'You haven't forgotten the embassy meeting next week?'

'No, sir. Has the final legislation been signed off yet?'

'I think Parliament will formalise everything on Thursday.'

Merlin sighed. 'Will there be anything else?'

'Going back to the robbers, d'you think the tip-off came from Billy Hill?'

'He's the most likely source. Bound to have been upset at independent operators working his patch.'

'Yes.' The AC leaned closer. 'I had an interesting lunch with the head of our military police yesterday.'

'The provost marshal?'

'The same. I was shocked by what he told me about the astonishing amount of crime being perpetrated by military personnel.'

'I'm already aware, sir. We've come across some of it ourselves.'

'But the scale, Frank. I didn't realise. I knew that pilfering from army stores had become widespread, but what some people are getting up to is quite frightening. Everything appears to be fair game. Food, cigarettes, alcohol and petrol, naturally. But the other stuff. Soap, light bulbs, timber, heavy construction equipment. An amazingly long list.'

'There was a story the other day about Hill's gang stealing a huge cargo of army blankets and bed linen.'

'There you go! But you'd expect someone like Hill to have his fingers in many pies. What particularly surprised me was the number of supposedly honest citizens involved. And in the military, it's not just the other ranks. A number of senior officers have been caught red-handed.'

Merlin brushed a bead of sweat from his brow. The AC was notoriously averse to draughts, and usually kept his windows closed. 'Mind if we have a bit of air, sir? It's getting pretty steamy in here.'

'Oh, all right,' the AC allowed grudgingly.

At the window, Merlin looked down and watched a couple of attractive girls saunter along the Embankment. One, who had flowing auburn locks, reminded him of his pretty new wife. He suddenly jumped as he realised the AC had slid up quietly to join him.

'River's looking lovely today, eh, Frank?'

'It is, sir, yes.'

'Sparkling and glistening in the sun. You must know some apposite quotation?'

13

Merlin was known to his friends and colleagues as a great poetry-lover. A vast compendium of verse rattled around inside his head. 'How about this, sir?

Never did sun more beautifully steep
In his first splendour, valley, rock;
Ne'er saw I, never felt, a calm so deep!
The river glideth at his own sweet will.'

'Wonderful, Frank, though I'm sure the poet had a more countrified river than Old Father Thames in mind when he wrote those words.'

'Not at all, sir. Those lines come from Wordsworth's "Composed Upon Westminster Bridge".'

The AC chuckled. 'I stand corrected. I wish I had half your poetic knowledge. Never had much of a memory for verses and lines. I was hopeless in the last school play I did at Eton.'

'Who did you play?'

'The Player King in *Hamlet*. There were other things I did well, though. I was a wet bob, which means I rowed. Got in the first boat in my final year. Right build for it. You'd probably have been quite good at it yourself.' He flashed a gummy smile before heading back to the desk.

'I'd better get on, sir.'

'I know you're busy, Frank, but humour me for a couple more minutes. It's good to have a general chat once in a while.'

Merlin resumed his seat reluctantly. He decided he might as well use the opportunity to get something off his chest. 'Regarding the Americans, sir. Obviously it's great that they're over here, on our side, but these new jurisdictional regulations don't seem right to me. American police, American courts, American judges and American lawyers operating free of any British involvement. It's almost as if they're setting up a state within a state.'

'I tend to agree with you, Frank, but if that's what they want, we're not in any position to deny them, are we? We need them to help save our country.'

14

Merlin sighed. 'I presume they'll set up their own prisons?'

'I should think so.'

'What about executions? Who'll do the hanging?'

'I understand capital punishment abounds in the United States. They'll have plenty of qualified practitioners.'

'Albert Pierrepoint won't be happy with people invading his turf.'

'Mr Pierrepoint appears to have plenty to keep him busy at present.'

Merlin had attended a Pierrepoint hanging once. It was a dreadful experience, although the prisoner, who'd murdered several young women, had fully deserved his punishment.

'Where will the Americans have their courts?'

'All over the country, no doubt. In London, I believe they're renovating an old office building near Grosvenor Square. They'll probably use the embassy or local barracks until that's ready. I suppose it might be interesting to pop along one day and see how they handle things.'

'If we're allowed.'

'Of course.' The AC paused to blow his nose rather noisily, then asked, 'And the family, Frank. How's Sonia getting on? Happy to be back at work?'

'She is, and thank you again for your help.'

Almost a year earlier, Merlin had married a pretty Polish refugee called Sonia Sieczko. They now had a baby son named Harry. After a few months at home looking after Harry, Sonia had begun to yearn for something more challenging to do. In April, her brother, a pilot with one of the RAF Polish squadrons, had informed her that the Polish legation in London was in desperate need of translators. Sonia was keen, but it wasn't immediately clear how they'd manage. By happy coincidence, Sergeant Bridges' wife, Iris, who had a young child of her own, had just become involved with a group of young mothers who ran a day nursery in Battersea, just across the river from Merlin's Chelsea flat. The nursery agreed to take Harry, and Sonia was able to take the translating job. The AC had been good enough to help her obtain all the necessary security clearances.

'Young Harry is happy enough with the new arrangements?'

'He is, sir. Iris helps cover Sonia out of nursery hours as well, and he loves her.'

'Good, good.' The AC suddenly jerked forward in his seat. 'Heavens, I've forgotten to tell you the news.'

'What news, sir?'

'Your American friend, Goldberg, is returning to London.'

Detective Bernard Goldberg was a New York policeman who had been seconded to Scotland Yard the summer before. He'd worked closely with Merlin on a major case and the two men had developed a close friendship.

'That's good. In the forces now, is he?'

'I don't believe so. His name was in a hush-hush list I was copied in on.'

'Hush-hush? You mean he's a spy?'

'His proposed role was not spelled out.'

'Hmm. That's intriguing. When does he get here?'

'Some time in the next two weeks.'

The AC's eyes wandered off to the right. Merlin followed his boss's gaze to the golf putter Gatehouse liked to practise with on the office carpet. He guessed the little chat had run its course.

A couple of miles upriver, Leon Van Buren stared gloomily out of the window of his rented Chelsea house. The sight of the sun-dappled Thames did not arouse poetic thoughts in him. He was contemplating his finances, the subject that occupied most of his time these days. While not exactly on his uppers, he had big problems that needed to be resolved.

Van Buren was fifty-nine years of age, a tall, burly man who still possessed some of the rugged good looks of his youth. He had a square dimpled jaw and a full head of fine silvery fair hair. He was an Afrikaner by birth, born to a notable Dutch family who had been among the first to colonise the Cape in the seventeenth century. As early backers of the Dutch East India Company, the Van Burens had become very wealthy. Leon had wanted for nothing as a child, and had been provided with a fine education in South Africa, then England. He had avoided involvement in the Boer War, and on return to his homeland in 1904 had joined the family enterprise. Unfortunately, eleven years later, he'd had a major falling-out with the head of the family and decided to strike out on his own, moving to Holland in 1915 and starting his own business. The Great War had passed him by, as Holland had remained neutral. His business, an electrical manufacturing operation, grew and grew over the years, and by 1939 was second only to the Philips company in Holland.

The war had brought about a huge change in his circumstances. In 1941, the Germans had swept into Holland. Despite taking pains to cultivate a pro-Nazi reputation, and notwithstanding the many assurances given by German officials, his business empire was taken over lock, stock and barrel as an enterprise essential to the war effort. Leon had managed to escape to England to join his English wife and their children, but brought with him only a relatively small amount of his money. He was no longer a rich man. His difficulties were further compounded by expensive doctor's fees as his wife gradually succumbed to cancer.

He turned away from the window. If only he'd listened to his wife, he thought yet again, and transferred some of his wealth abroad on the outbreak of war. Now, available funds were running precariously low and he had been forced to borrow. His wife had had money of her own, but maddeningly, he had no access to it, while his spoiled children had increasingly unrealistic financial demands that he found difficult to resist.

He settled behind his desk and pondered. Fortunately, things were not completely bleak. Among the few possessions he'd brought from Holland were two of particular value. If he could liquidate them for anything like a realistic price, his situation would be transformed.

He reached into his pocket and took out the letter. He'd already read it several times today. It was from a Mr Augustus Ramsey, confirming the meeting at the gallery the following morning. It was wartime and market circumstances were difficult, but Leon had been advised that Ramsey was the likeliest man to get the job done. Expensive though the dealer's commission would be, this had to be his best route.

Estoril, Portugal

The casino was busy for a Tuesday night. The restaurant was humming and the gaming tables were almost at capacity. A group of regulars had settled at Antonio's roulette table. The Portuguese croupier with the thick moustache was the quickest and slickest of the operators.

'*Faites vos jeux, cavalheiros, s'il vous plaît.*'

The players reached out to place their bets, or communicated their wishes to Antonio with a nod. Then the croupier spun the wheel with a practised flourish and the dozen gamblers, all male save for one bejewelled Italian contessa, held their breath.

The young man had a good view of the table from his vantage point at the bar. Three of the players were of interest to him. One was the elegantly dressed middle-aged businessman, dark hair flecked with grey, who was facing him. Another, to the business-man's right, was the burly bald man he knew to be a senior Abwehr officer. The third, with his back to him, was a young curly-haired man who was one of MI6's Lisbon team. Neutral Portugal was one of the few places in wartime Europe where enemies could mix like this at close quarters. Lisbon teemed with scheming spies, agents and chancers of every hue. Many of them homed in on the casino for their nightly pleasure.

The observer was a Spaniard who went by the Portuguese alias of Tomas Barboza. He'd arrived in Lisbon only five months before

18

and had been quick to find his feet. Within a month, he'd acquired full-time employment and a small, comfortable place to live. There were dangers attached to his new job, but these were as nothing compared to those he'd just escaped. As a soldier on the losing side in the Spanish Civil War, he'd been lucky to survive. His brave efforts in the Republican cause had caught the eye of some powerful people and helped him to his new position.

The roulette wheel stopped spinning. Most of the players remained poker-faced. The businessman, however, allowed himself a brief smile as Antonio pushed a large pile of chips towards him. Then he rose, tossed a couple of chips to the croupier, nodded to his fellow gamblers and withdrew. The German and the Englishman proceeded to quit the table as well.

Barboza looked across the room, where he saw his boss waving at him discreetly. It was time to get moving. He finished his beer, deposited a few notes on the counter, then set off in pursuit.

Chapter Three

'Welcome, Mr Van Buren.' Augustus Ramsey rose from his French rosewood desk and shook hands with his guest before ushering him to a seating area with a white marble coffee table and two large leather armchairs.

Ramsey was a short, plump, white-bearded man whose congeniality was legendary in the London art world. He had a keen eye, a comprehensive knowledge of the art market, and an excellent reputation.

At a knock at the door, he waved a studious-looking young man into the room. 'This is Martin, my grandson. He's learning the ropes before the military get hold of him. Do you mind if he joins us?'

'Not at all.'

'Sit over there at the desk, Martin. If anything in our conversation needs to be noted, do it. Now, sir, how can I be of assistance?'

Van Buren cleared his throat. 'You may be aware of me as a collector of art?'

'I am. Before the war, I dealt with a man in Amsterdam called Janssen. Your name came up in conversation a few times. As I recall, he said you were a collector of taste and resource, with a particular interest in the Renaissance.'

'I dealt with Mr Janssen from time to time.'

'Have you heard how he coped with the invasion?'

'No, but I should think he'll be all right. There are plenty of Nazis with an interest in fine art.'

'So I understand. I heard that Goering, for example, is an eager accumulator of quality works.'

'One of many. I know that . . .' Van Buren looked down and left the sentence unfinished.

There was an awkward silence before Ramsey picked up the conversation.

'So. You are a keen collector. Are you perhaps looking to add to your collection? I must tell you things are very slow at present. Most people are determined to see out the war before they contemplate entering the market.'

'I'm here as a prospective seller, not a buyer, Mr Ramsey.'

'I see. What do you have to sell?'

'I possess two remarkable companion pieces. Renaissance masterpieces. I do not have them with me, but I have photographs.' Van Buren removed an envelope from his briefcase and passed it to Ramsey.

The dealer found his spectacles and began examining the photographs. As he did so, his eyes widened and he gasped. After several minutes, he set them down on the coffee table. 'I can't say I recognise the particular works, but the style looks very familiar. If you don't mind, I'd like to see if Martin can tell who the artist is.'

'Be my guest.'

Ramsey waved his grandson over and handed him the photographs. His response was quick.

'They look rather like da Vinci cartoons.'

'He's right, isn't he, Mr Van Buren?'

'He is.'

'And they are the real thing?'

'They are. I have them at my house.'

'Personally, I would be inclined to keep them in a bank vault.'

Van Buren shrugged. 'I am . . . rather attached to them.'

'And you really wish to sell them?'

'For the right price, yes.'

'As I said earlier, the market is not in good shape. However, I would be happy to try and assist. I have already thought of a few candidates. Some are abroad, which inevitably poses problems, but we shall see.'

'Very well.'

'You are aware of my terms?'

'I am. I understand that they are standard in the London market.'

'And you are happy for me to work exclusively?'

'I shall not use any other dealer. However, you should know that I have already been in touch with some interested parties. Those men aside, you will have a free hand.'

Ramsey frowned. 'Well, it's irregular, but all right, let's proceed on that basis. When can I see the drawings? I am available at your convenience.'

Van Buren leaned forward to retrieve the photographs. 'I have some other appointments this morning. I'll call you later to arrange a time.' He rose from his chair.

'Before you go, sir, could I trouble you to tell me a little about their provenance?'

'I shall be happy to do so when next we meet. I can assure you everything is above board.'

'I'm sure. However, I shall need to call in an expert for purposes of authentication. I'm sure you understand.'

'Do you have someone in mind?'

'A fellow called Clark. You may have heard of him. A very precocious young man. Hardly out of short trousers and already a knight of the realm. Runs the National Gallery. A world expert in da Vinci and the Renaissance.'

'I've heard of him. Fine. Now if you'll excuse me . . .'

'Of course. I shall eagerly await your call.'

★

The offices of the Fenchurch Street Discount Bank were not, despite the name, located in Fenchurch Street. They were in fact half a mile away, in a small lane off Bunhill Row, on the northern edge of the City of London. The chairman and managing director of the firm, Benjamin Katz, had arrived in England from Austria in 1933. Within only a few years, and against the odds, he had managed to establish a thriving and respected financial institution. As a Jew, of course, he had faced significant prejudice, but had always risen above it. Other Jews had acquired vast wealth, knighthoods and peerages, and he was intent on doing the same. It might be a while yet before he donned ermine, but anything was possible with hard work and dedication. For now, people knew that his word was as good as his bond, and more than enough financial institutions of substance were happy to deal with him.

Katz was a neat little man who wore his hair unfashionably long. He was more than comfortable financially, but avoided all shows of excess. His office was modest, and it was here he was to be found this lunchtime, re-reading his nephew's latest report. It was, as he'd expected, an impressive piece of work. Thirty pages of astute, detailed analysis of a company Katz was thinking of acquiring. He came again to the elegantly drafted final paragraph. Nathan Katz recommended the acquisition be proceeded with, but on completion the company be completely reorganised and refocused. This was exactly the conclusion Benjamin had reached himself. He sat back contentedly, smoothed his waistcoat then called out to his secretary. 'Get Nathan here, please, Sylvia.'

His nephew appeared promptly. Nathan was short like his uncle, but wirier, with intense dark eyes and curly raven-black hair. He looked nervously at Benjamin.

'Excellent work, Nathan, and I'm not just saying that because you've reached the same conclusion as me. And I marvel at your command of the English language. Considering you've only been here a couple of years, it's amazing.'

A flicker of a smile crossed the young man's lips. 'I've always had an aptitude for languages, sir. You agreed with my comments regarding cash flow and income management, then?'

'I did, my boy. Most perspicacious.'

'And in point six, I hope I made it clear that—'

Benjamin raised a hand. 'You made everything clear, Nathan. We can talk about implementation later. Meanwhile, I have something of a more personal nature to discuss.'

'Personal, sir? Have I done something wrong?'

'Not at all, my boy. It's just that Ruth and I have not forgotten that today would have been your mother's birthday.'

Nathan looked down at his feet. 'Not "would have been",' he mumbled.

'Very well then. Today is your mother's birthday.'

'Until there is firm confirmation of her death, I shall continue to believe she still lives.'

Benjamin sighed. 'But my boy, all the odds are that the Nazis have killed her, and the others.'

'Odds can be wrong, sir. I prefer to keep my hopes up.'

'Even if that means they're living hellish lives in a prison camp?'

'Even so.'

He sighed again. 'In any event, we thought it would be good to celebrate Esther's birthday with a dinner at our house. Ruth reminded me this morning that she hasn't seen you for a while. She's managed to get hold of some eggs, potatoes and a couple of chickens, along with some other scarce delicacies. You know how good her shakshuka and kugel is. You must come.'

'Of course, Uncle. Thank you.'

'Shall we say seven thirty?'

Merlin was contemplating, as he often did, the bronze Eiffel Tower paperweight on his desk. He'd acquired it on a pre-war weekend jaunt to Paris with his late first wife, Alice. He wondered what Alice would have thought of Sonia. What she would think

24

of him as a father. Poor Alice. The cancer had taken her so quickly. With an effort, he managed to push the bad memories away and returned to the forensics report in front of him. There was conclusive evidence that one of the Canadians' guns had killed the cinema usherette. There were only a few minor items now required to wrap up the case. After reading the last page again, he closed the file, then reached into a desk drawer, searching for his Everton mints. These sweets had taken the place of the more pungent Fishermen's Friends as his modest addiction. Sonia, who detested the smell of eucalyptus, had finally drawn the line. He popped a couple of mints into his mouth. As he did so, DC Claire Robinson appeared at the door, weighed down by a thick file. Robinson was the AC's niece. When he'd been asked to take her on in the early days of the war, he'd been reluctant, but she had become a valued member of his team. He waved her in.

'Sit down, Constable. We've missed you.'

Robinson fell heavily into the chair facing her boss. 'Sorry, sir. This Hammersmith case has been taking all my time. There's been a pile of evidence to compile and coordinate.'

'I understand. It's a complex case.'

'How's your hand, sir? I gather you caught a nasty blow.'

'Stings like hell, but I'll survive.'

Robinson smiled. She might have been burning the midnight oil, Merlin thought, but she looked none the worse for it. Her face was as fresh and attractive as always and her strawberry blond hair gleamed in the sunlight streaming through the window.

'How's it all looking, then?'

'Prosecuting counsel seems reasonably confident he has enough to secure convictions.'

'When is the case coming to trial?'

'It was originally set down for September, but a gap has opened and it may come on as soon as next week.'

'Where?'

'The Bailey. They want to give it the highest profile possible.'

25

'Quite right too. That's why it was handed to us in the first place.'

DI Johnson had been lead officer on the inquiry, but with Merlin's agreement, he had left most of the case management to the increasingly competent and effective young constable. It was not in the usual category of cases handled by Merlin's serious crime department. A council-owned building in Hammersmith had been hit by a bomb in May 1941, in the last days of the London Blitz. Inside it was a new air-raid shelter completed only a few months before. The shelter had collapsed, and forty-three people, men, women and children, had perished. Initially the event had been written off as a terrible but routine mishap of war. However, a year later, a young accountant, new to the council's financial department, had taken an interest and discovered that the file relating to the collapsed shelter had gone missing. After much persistence, he finally managed to track down a copy. Concerned by what he found, he drew his superiors' attention to the file, but was fobbed off. Then a clerk in the contracts department decided to confide in him and confirmed his suspicions.

It transpired that a building firm with family connections to the Hammersmith town clerk had been given the contract to construct the shelter. The clerk had received a substantial kickback and the builders had enhanced the profitability of the already well-padded contract by using sub-standard materials. Forty-three innocent lives appeared to have been lost due to fraudulent venality. The police were called in, and the AC had asked Merlin to take on the case to demonstrate the seriousness with which the authorities would now treat such crimes, which were becoming more and more common throughout the country.

'Remind me, Constable,' said Merlin. 'How many defendants in the trial?'

'Six. The town clerk, two other council officials, and the three principals of the building company.'

'And the charges finally decided on?'

'Fraud and manslaughter.'

Merlin shook his head. 'Not murder? That's what it really was.'

'You're welcome to look at the file, sir. It sets out all the thinking as regards the legal case.'

'Perhaps another time. I'm not going to second-guess anyone at this late stage.'

Robinson brushed a stray hair from her face and nodded.

'How's everything generally, Claire?'

'Fine, sir.'

'And that young barrister friend of yours?'

She blushed. 'We aren't . . . we aren't seeing each other any more, sir.'

'Oh dear. I'm sorry to hear that. There I go putting my foot in it.'

'It's all right, sir. I'm over it now. He met someone else in his chambers. A secretary.'

Merlin resisted the temptation to comment. The man was clearly an idiot. Before the barrister, Robinson and DC Cole had been an item for a few months, until the AC had decided Cole wasn't good enough for his niece and engineered a split.

'I've decided to give men a break for a while, sir. I'd rather devote my energies to the job.'

'Well, maybe that's for the best.' Merlin decided to change the subject. 'The AC tells me we may be seeing Detective Goldberg again soon.'

'That's good, sir. Is he being seconded to us again?'

'I don't think so. The AC was a little cagey.'

'Well, he certainly won't want for American company. The Yanks seem to be everywhere these days.'

'Yes, but we should be grateful. Where would we be if they hadn't entered the war?'

'You're right, of course, sir.'

Merlin laughed. 'And we've got the Russians as well. Who'd have thought eighteen months ago that Stalin would be our friend and we'd be counting on him and the Russian army to thwart Hitler in the east?'

'My uncle . . . sorry, sir . . . the AC said the other day that Mr Churchill might be visiting Stalin soon.'

'Did he now? I'd love to be a fly on the wall when that happens.' Merlin popped another mint in his mouth. 'All right, Constable. I suppose we'd better get on. Keep up the good work.'

Six people were crowded around the small table in the basement of the old terraced house in King's Cross. The lunch party had been going for over four hours and everyone was the worse for wear. A sprightly wild-haired man of seventy presided, juggling in his hands a glass of wine, a roll-your-own cigarette and a small notebook.

A blowsy-looking woman with untidy grey-brown hair banged on the table. 'Order, please. Roderick's going to read one of his latest poems.'

The wild-haired man smiled benignly at his audience, then proceeded to recite an interminable ode about the Industrial Revolution. When he had finished, he was greeted with an enthusiastic round of applause, whether in appreciation of the poem or gratitude that it was over was not clear.

'Bravo, Roderick Havering! Whither Tom Eliot now?' cried the blowsy woman.

Havering bowed his head. 'Thank you, Gwinnie.'

'Another gem,' opined a smartly dressed young man with slickly Brylcreemed orange hair. A dowdy middle-aged female and a younger raven-haired woman to Havering's left nodded their agreement.

Havering turned expectantly to his sixth guest, a robust-looking young man wearing a striped red and white blazer. He had strikingly blond hair, thick eyebrows, expressive brown eyes and a wide, sensual mouth. 'Did you like it, Robert?'

'Rather! Absolutely wonderful. I must learn from you, Roderick. You are an inspiration. I wish I could write as well.'

28

'But Robert, you have a wonderful poetic style. I'm so looking forward to reading your contributions to the magazine.'

'I can't understand why that poseur Connolly wouldn't take the poem for his pretentious little rag,' said Gwinnie.

Havering seemed slightly put out that she had revealed this upsetting fact to the company. 'There is little love lost between us, I'm afraid. And he's no doubt heard of our new venture.'

'Cyril Connolly is a jealous old queen,' said the dowdy woman.

'Jealous undoubtedly, Maeve, but hardly a queen. The man is a priapic gargoyle unaccountably surrounded by a harem of youthful enchantresses, of whom he takes full advantage, as we all well know.'

The red-haired man, a journalist and putative author called Crabbe, grimaced. 'That poor Lys Dunlap. She tends to the little toad hand and foot and he treats her terribly.'

Havering turned again to Robert Van Buren. 'I'm sorry, Robert. You must find this insular literary gossip of ours boring.'

'Not at all, Roderick. I've met Connolly actually. He was a friend of my mother's. I was invited to one of his *Horizon* soirées a while back.' Robert omitted to mention that Connolly had been brutal about a couple of poems he'd shown him.

'Did you meet anyone interesting?'

'Eliot, Thomas.'

'An interesting duo. I hope you didn't allow the Welshman to sponge off you. He tries it on with everyone, you know.'

'I'm afraid I did lend him a couple of quid.'

'You'll never see that again.'

Van Buren shrugged, then smiled at the raven-haired woman opposite him. Caroline Mitchum wore no make-up and apparently cared little about clothes, but he found her bohemian look strangely attractive. The two of them had recently become an item.

Roderick Havering was a noted man of letters. In some literary quarters, he was held in high regard. He'd never, however, been able to convert high regard into meaningful financial reward. His whole career had been spent scrabbling around for money. On one occasion only, when he'd produced a well-received novel, had the prospect of decent cash loomed. Sadly the publishers of the book had gone bust before paying him a single penny.

Havering's latest idea had been to establish a new literary magazine in competition with Cyril Connolly's very successful *Horizon*. He'd met Robert Van Buren in a pub a few weeks before and smelled money. Van Buren had literary ambitions and was excited by the prospect of involvement in Havering's new venture as a publisher and financial backer. The money, though, would have to come from his father, who might take a little persuading.

There was more banging on the table. This time it was Havering. 'So, Robert, I have informed the ladies here and Mr Crabbe of your kind offer to fund our new journal, *Athena*, to the extent of six monthly issues commencing at the end of next month. I'm sure everyone would like to register their gratitude.' Various complimentary comments ensued. 'I have asked Mr Crabbe, who is the most financially minded of our group, to work up a detailed budget, which he's promised to do by next week. Maeve has already set to work on securing contributors, and Gwinnie is developing design ideas. Caroline will have a go at finding advertisers to add some additional resources. We should meet again shortly to discuss that budget and the contents of the first issue. Once we have agreed those items, we shall require funds to flow. Will that be in order, Robert?'

'It will, Roderick. And it's agreed that some examples of my work will be included in the first issue?'

'Of course, my dear boy. Of course.' Havering patted Robert's hand and smiled unctuously. 'Shall we open another bottle?'

Van Buren looked at his watch. 'I think I'll pass. It's getting late. Thanks all the same.'

'Oh dear boy, you disappoint me. Come now, I'm sure you have time for a little more. A celebratory bottle, in fact. Gwinnie, dear, get another, will you? One of the finer reds. And I'm sure

Robert won't object to our luncheon expenditure being incorporated in the budget, will you, my boy?'

Berlin

The field marshal had gone to take an urgent telephone call in a neighbouring room. This gave his dining companion welcome time to reflect. Lieutenant Colonel Berndt von Wald had to hand it to the old man. Hermann Goering certainly knew how to drink and eat. Goering was von Wald's godfather, and he had commandeered a private room at the Adlon for their little get-together. Despite the many demands on his time, the field marshal was an attentive and dutiful patron. He had been a fellow officer and close friend of the young man's father during the Great War. Von Wald's rapid rise through the ranks of the Abwehr owed much to Goering's sponsorship, but his exceptional ability had also played its part.

Von Wald took out the old photo he always carried in his jacket pocket. His father and Goering together on the Western Front in 1917. It was difficult to reconcile the slim, dashing pilot in the photograph with the corpulent figure in the next room. Like von Wald senior, Goering had been one of Germany's top flying aces. However, unlike his old friend, the field marshal seldom referred to his heroic exploits. Hermann Goering was surprisingly modest about his combat achievements.

For much of the first half of 1942, at the request of Admiral Canaris, head of the Abwehr, von Wald had been engaged in a review of the Reich's intelligence assets in Britain. Interdepartmental friction had thrown up many obstructions, but he had battled on to complete his report and had submitted it in June. A week later, he'd received a reply from one of Canaris's closest aides: *'The Admiral and I have read your report. We do not concur. We have another important task for you shortly. Meanwhile, you will revert to*

31

your previous duties.' He was surprised and disappointed by this response. After mulling the matter over for a few day, he'd decided to discuss it with his godfather – hence the dinner. He'd not raised the subject yet, but he planned to on Goering's return.

The field marshal eventually reappeared, and made things easy for his godson by asking as he resumed his seat, 'So, don't you think it's time to tell me whatever it is you want to get off your chest?'

'It is, sir.'

'Very well.' Goering summoned the waiter and asked him to refill their schnapps glasses and leave the bottle. This done, he smiled and indicated that von Wald proceed.

'You are aware of the report I worked on for Admiral Canaris?'

'I am. I also know that it was quickly shelved. Despite Canaris's resistance, I was able to discover the contents of the report and the conclusions you drew. In summary, you were of the opinion that most of our agents resident in England had been compromised and turned or liquidated.'

'I was . . . I am.'

Goering downed his drink, then poured himself another. He looked expectantly at von Wald, who reluctantly did the same.

The field marshal continued. 'Canaris disagreed with this conclusion and sent you back to training agents, and that is the end of the matter.'

'Er . . . not quite.'

'What do you mean?'

Von Wald licked his lips nervously. 'I have initiated a plan. A plan to check whether I was right. Canaris knows nothing about it.'

Goering's thick eyebrows rose. 'Is that wise?'

'It is my duty to watch out for the interests of the Reich.'

The field marshal loosened his tie. 'Go on then. I'm listening.'

'Last year there was an aborted job in Ireland. A reliable agent of ours was left in the country. It was intended he be extracted, and I was charged with the job. My superiors apparently forgot about him, so I decided to leave him in place as a sleeper. When my report was dismissed, I thought of this man. His code name is Archer.'

Goering frowned. 'You reactivated this agent?'

'Yes.'

'Without telling anyone?'

'Apart from a few people on the ground in Dublin, yes.'

'I see.' Goering took a cigar out of his pocket and lit it. A trail of blue smoke was sent up to the ceiling. 'Look, Berndt, I share the Führer's reservations about Canaris. He is not one of us. However, with everything that's going on in Russia and elsewhere, he is currently unshakeable in his position. If he finds out you're going behind his back, there will be little I can do if he chooses to punish you.'

'I understand, sir. I'm not telling you this to seek cover. I'm telling you so you know why I'm in trouble if that should happen.'

Goering took another puff of his cigar. 'So tell me the details.'

'I got Archer on an Irish vessel to Liverpool. He's half-German, half-English. Completely loyal to our cause, I assure you. He spent a couple of years in an English public school and can blend in perfectly. I used one of our Republican friends in Cork as a handler. He set him up with the appropriate papers, and communication instructions.'

'He has a radio?'

'No, too risky. As I observed in my report, there are grounds to suspect our communications have been compromised.'

'There I shall take issue with you. Our codes are highly advanced and solid. There is no way the British can have broken them.'

'The British military have had a number of what might be called lucky breaks recently. Too much luck worries me.'

'Hmm. So this Archer has no radio with him. How are you communicating with him?'

33

'Standard tradecraft. Correspondence with micro-dots. News-paper adverts.'

'And what exactly have you asked him to do?'

'We have a number of supposedly operational agents, some based in England, some travelling back and forth between England and neutral countries. I picked out one or two and asked him to observe them. He's already managed to come up with some interesting information.'

'If he identifies a traitor, what are his instructions?'

'If no other option presents itself, to liquidate.'

'And his cover?'

'A building surveyor for an Irish construction company scouting British business opportunities.'

Goering fell silent. He knocked back his drink and stubbed out his half-smoked cigar before he spoke. 'You're a good man, Berndt, and your heart is in the right place. I can't condone what you're doing, but naturally I'll be interested to know of developments. You are sticking your neck out a long way. I hope it proves to be worth it.'

'It must be worthwhile to expose traitors.'

Goering reknotted his tie, then slowly rose from the table. 'Of course it is, my boy. But if you succeed and prove that our system is compromised, it will be devastating. Devastating! God knows what the Führer will do.'

Chapter Four

The Chelsea mansion flat that had been spacious accommodation for a single man was less so now it housed man, wife and baby. In the living room, Merlin was struggling to find a place to sit and enjoy his morning tea. One armchair was covered with freshly laundered baby clothes, the other with dirty. Various other baby paraphernalia were scattered on the settee and elsewhere. He couldn't really blame Sonia. She had been late back from work at the Polish legation the previous evening, and then she'd had to rush off back there first thing. Merlin couldn't think of leaving the mess for her to tidy later, so he set to. By the time he'd finished, his tea was cold, so he made a fresh pot. Harry appeared to be sleeping soundly. Sonia had arranged for Iris to pick him up at a quarter to nine. Merlin checked his watch. He had half an hour to wait.

The porter had posted some mail through the letterbox a little earlier, and Merlin began to go through it. Among the bills he found one item of interest. It had a Spanish stamp and he recognised the handwriting as his sister's. There was also a date imprint from Thomas Cook in Lisbon, which told him it had taken over three months for the letter to reach him. Before the war, Maria had been a frequent correspondent, but this was only the third letter he'd received from her since 1939. He suspected several had gone missing, as no doubt had a few of his.

Merlin was half-Spanish. His father had been a merchant seaman from Corunna who'd married a Cockney wife and settled down as a shopkeeper in the East End of London. Born Javier Merino, his name had been anglicised in due course to Harry Merlin, and his three children, Francisco, Maria and Carlos, had become Frank, Mary and Charlie. Mary, however, had reverted to Maria when she'd gone to Spain and married her second cousin, Jorge. She and her family had managed to get through the civil war relatively unscathed and were, last time Merlin had heard, still happily running a café in a small Galician village.

The letter was in Spanish. His was a little rusty, but he managed to make sense of it. In the last letter he'd received from her, in the autumn of 1941, she'd been pregnant with her fourth child. Now he learned that she'd been safely delivered of a son called Manuel. She was full of questions about Sonia and Harry, and she also provided the usual gossip about their Spanish relations. She finished by urging him to leave England and join her in the safety of neutral Spain, as she'd done in every letter since the outbreak of the war.

'Never gives up trying, does she?' he muttered to himself. Spain might not be at war, but Franco's dictatorship held no allure for him. And anyway, what the hell would he do there?

There was a postscript to the letter. *'Francisco, I should mention Jorge's nephew Pablo. He had a rough time in the recent troubles and spent some time in prison. You may remember I told you he was a bit of a hothead. After he got out, he disappeared, but recently Jorge got a postcard from him in Lisbon. He said he might be going to England. I've no idea how he would manage that, but he's a resourceful young man. I thought I'd better warn you, as he mentioned you in the card and it's possible you might get a call from him out of the blue.'*

Merlin got up stiffly and wandered over to the window. As he looked down on the street, he remembered Maria telling him a

36

while back that Pablo, of whom she was very fond, was a communist. This meant he'd joined the losing Republican side in the civil war. It wasn't surprising he'd ended up in prison. It was more surprising to learn he'd got out alive. When Merlin had met him at Maria's wedding, Pablo had been a sweet boy in his mid-teens. It would be good to see him if he managed to make it to London.

Merlin was watching the milk cart down below making late deliveries when he heard a cry. He turned and went to the baby's room, where the crying stopped as soon as he opened the door. He switched on the light and saw two small eyes keenly examining him from the cot. '*Buenos días* Harry Merlin. How are you this fine morning?'

Harry responded with a happy gurgle. Merlin heard a knock at the front door. 'That'll be your Auntie Iris. Come on, let's get you out of there and go and say hello.'

Lisbon

It was another sweltering morning. At only just after nine, the Figueira da Foz beach was already packed. Family parties carrying parasols, towels, and picnic baskets were swarming over the sands. The sound of children's laughter could be clearly heard in the Hotel Aviz, an opulent first-class establishment on the Rua Doutor António Lopes Guimarães, some ten minutes' walk from the beach. It did not, however, reach the hotel's largest and most sumptuous top-floor suite, whose windows had yet to be opened.

The suite's occupant, a small, balding seventy-four-year-old with a white brush moustache and matching eyebrows, was seated in an armchair working his way intently through a pile of art catalogues. Calouste Sarkis Gulbenkian was thought by some to be the richest man in the world. Only he knew if this was true, as only he knew the exact details of the labyrinthine network of assets and liabilities that constituted his fortune. He guessed the Rockefellers might have a little more, but whether they did or not, there was no doubt that Gulbenkian was a very, very rich man.

Born to a family of successful Armenian merchants, he had been educated in England and spent his formative years there. As a young man, he'd become involved in the early development and exploitation of the Middle East's vast oil reserves. Blessed with a brilliant business mind and a driven personality, he had been instrumental in the commencement of serious oil production in countries like Iraq, Persia and Turkey. In return for his efforts, he negotiated huge recurring commissions. In due course, he became known in the business world as Mr Five Per Cent. Over the years, as his wealth accumulated, he devoted much of his time and resources to the creation of what was now thought to be the world's greatest private art collection. He owned over six thousand works of art. His interests were wide-ranging, from Rembrandt to Gainsborough, from da Vinci to Degas, and from Egyptian antiquities to the creations of Lalique.

Gulbenkian had been living in Lisbon for the past six months. A year or two before the outbreak of war, he had moved from London to Paris. There he had acquired honorary Persian diplomatic status, which had afforded him advantageous tax treatment and, when the Nazis invaded, protection. However, having been obliged to move from Paris to Vichy, the new capital of unoccupied France, the subsequent overthrow of the Shah had deprived him of this diplomatic status. It had also become a matter of concern to him that his presence in what was now enemy territory would prejudice his British interests, and he began searching for an alternative base. He had settled on neutral Portugal.

He set down one catalogue and picked up another. It was from a major 1935 New York auction. As he looked at the photographs of the Egyptian bronzes he'd bought there, he sighed. He'd not seen any of his huge collection for some time. Most of the Egyptian pieces were on loan to the British Museum, numerous paintings had been lent to the National Gallery in London, and he'd had to leave a huge number of works behind him in Paris. The thought of what might be happening to his French 'children', as he thought of them, was a source of constant worry. There were rumours that his collection had aroused great interest among the Nazi establishment. He could only hope that his large holding of Reichsbank shares, and his powerful contacts in those global industries of most importance to the German state would prevent any hostile move on his art.

A door opened. His devoted private secretary, Isabelle Theis, a stylish dark-haired woman in her mid-thirties, entered. 'The British embassy just sent over a cable for you, sir. It's from Sir Kenneth Clark.'

Gulbenkian's mood lifted. Clark was a trustworthy and likeable man. He was also a man with his finger on the pulse of the international art world. He contemplated the cable with a pleasant feeling of anticipation. Might it contain news of some opportunity? Good ones had been notably scarce since the outbreak of war.

'My spectacles are filthy, Isabelle. Could you find me another pair? And while you're about it, could you order me a coffee and an orange juice? And a pastry of some sort. One of those local ones I like.'

'Of course, Mr Gulbenkian.' Isabelle always addressed him formally, despite the fact that they often shared a bed. Gulbenkian smiled. 'It's such a joy to be away from wartime privations. I should send Sir Kenneth another food parcel. I bet he hasn't seen any decent fruit for a while. Please arrange to put a hamper for him on the next London flight.'

'Sir.' Isabelle disappeared.

He turned his attention to the cable. '*OLA CALOUSTE STOP POSSIBILITY OF INTERESTING ITEMS COMING ON MARKET SHORTLY STOP WILL AWAIT FURTHER DETAILS BEFORE COMMENTING FURTHER STOP MEETING PROSPECTIVE DUTCH VENDOR SOON*

STOP ASSUME NO QUESTION OF YOUR FLYING OVER BUT MIGHT BE USEFUL IF YOU HAVE A MAN OF BUSINESS HERE WITH WHOM I COULD LIAISE STOP HOPE ALL WELL REGARDS KC'

An intriguing message. What might these interesting items be? Did the mention of a Dutch vendor provide a clue? There had been a rumour not so long ago of a lost Rembrandt cropping up. And a year before, there'd been talk of a Vermeer coming onto the market, though Gulbenkian had not thought it likely. Whatever the items were, if he wanted them, he'd have to turn his mind to a financing mechanism. Despite his vast asset wealth, the war had placed serious limitations on his liquidity. He had no problems funding his luxurious Portuguese life-style and that of his wife, Nevarte, who maintained a separate lavish establishment at the Palace Hotel in Estoril. However, to finance substantial art acquisitions he needed to be able to move his money around, and the British, Swiss and American authorities were currently making it difficult for him to do so.

Isabelle reappeared with a waiter in tow. The man laid out Gulbenkian's breakfast on a small table by the window, then departed.

Gulbenkian moved to the table. 'It's getting very stuffy in here, Isabelle. Those fans aren't working properly again. Open the French doors, please.'

She did as she was bid. A mild sea-breeze blew into the room and ruffled the hairs of the Armenian's moustache. He motioned to his secretary to sit down, then started nibbling on a pastry.

'Am I having a drink with Mr Vermeulen as usual tonight?'

'You are.'

'He must be making one of his regular trips to London shortly.'

'I believe he's planning to go tomorrow, sir.'

Gulbenkian wiped his lips with a napkin. 'That's excellent timing. He can do a little job for me.'

When he'd finished his breakfast, he walked out onto the balcony. The sun was already high in the sky. A flock of seagulls squawked above him. He clapped his hands and they flew off. When they'd gone, he became aware of the distant sounds of pleasure from the beach.

London

Nathan Katz's morning had been a busy one, and he was relieved to get away for a late lunch. He had eaten well at his uncle and aunt's the night before and his appetite was modest, but it was good to get out of the office for a while. At the nearby Lyons Corner House, he ordered a cup of tea and an iced bun and found a quiet corner where he could relax with a book. When he'd arrived in London in 1939, his English had been limited, but he'd worked hard, and now his grasp of the language was excellent. He'd educated himself by reading the classics. He had finished all of Dickens, Eliot, Thackeray and Austen, and was now ploughing through Trollope. He was completely gripped by his latest read, *'The Way We Live Now'*. The book's swindling financier villain, Augustus Melmotte, was a compelling character. A far cry from his scrupulously honest uncle.

His reading was interrupted as someone squeezing past jostled the table, spilling some of his tea.

'I'm frightfully sorry. These places are so chock-a-block,' said the culprit.

Katz looked up and was surprised to realise he knew the man. 'Martin?'

Martin Ramsey did a double-take. 'Why, Nathan! How are you, old chap? Sorry again about your tea.'

'Don't worry. On your own?'

'I am. This isn't my normal neck of the woods. I just ran an errand round the corner and thought I'd grab a quick bite to eat.'

'Why don't you join me?'

'If you're sure, I'd be delighted to.'

41

Katz smiled and nodded and his friend sat down at the table.

'Well, this is a pleasant surprise, Nathan. You work around here, don't you? I remember Jacob mentioning it.' Jacob Katz, Benjamin's son, had been a friend of Ramsey's at Cambridge.

'The office is just around the corner.'

'Any news of Jacob?'

'He's still in Palestine. My uncle had a letter the other day. He wrote that he's finding everything very interesting. And he seems to be doing well. Promoted to lieutenant already, apparently.'

'Good for him. The fellow always had something about him, I think.'

Ramsey dug into his Woolton pie. This was a cheap vegetable dish named for the current Minister of Food. Katz thought it inedible, but Ramsey seemed to be enjoying his.

'What are you up to, Martin? Last time we met, you were about to join up too.'

Ramsey sighed. 'Failed the medical, I'm afraid. Poor eyesight and two left feet. Still keen to do my bit, of course. My grandfather is trying to pull a few strings and get me a posting in the War Office. Meanwhile I'm helping out at his gallery. Learning the ropes. I hadn't quite realised what a big fish he is in the art world. And it's a very interesting business.'

'He's grooming you to take over?'

'I don't know. We'll see. He's in very good nick, so his retirement is probably quite a way off.'

'Does he have any particular specialities in his business?'

'No, he'll turn his hand to anything. He's just acquired a couple of paintings by a young man called Freud. Thinks he has a lot of promise.' Ramsey chewed the last piece of pie.

'My father collected art. In quite a big way.'

'Did he, now?' There was an awkward silence until Ramsey spoke again. 'I understand your father had some trouble with the Nazis before the war. I never learned exactly what happened. When I asked Jacob, he clammed up.'

Katz studied his now empty plate for a moment. 'He was taken away by the Nazis. My father, my mother and my two younger sisters. I like to think they are alive somewhere, but my uncle says I should accept they're dead.'

'I'm very sorry, Nathan.'

Katz looked at his watch. 'Goodness. Time is moving on. I should get back to the office.'

'Yes. Me too. Can I get this? I spilled most of your tea, after all.'

Katz shook his head and put some coins on the table. 'Of course not, Martin, but I'll leave you to handle payment, if I may?'

'If you insist, old chap. Perhaps we could get together for a drink and a proper talk some-time? I'm away for the weekend, but how about Monday? I hate Mondays. It'll be something to brighten up the start of the week.'

'Yes, fine. Where?'

'I'm based in Kensington at the moment, at my grandfather's house. You?'

'I have lodgings in Hammersmith.'

'I know a jolly little riverside pub thereabouts. It's called 'the Dove'. Does seven suit?'

'I'll be there.'

Chapter Five

Frederick Vermeulen stared at the patchwork quilt of English fields beneath him, so different from the landscape of the country he'd just left behind. The aircraft would be on the ground soon. It was time to collect his papers and put them back in the briefcase. When they landed, there should be a car waiting, and with luck he'd be in London by five. It had been a smooth flight, apart from the usual bumpiness over the Bay of Biscay.

The Douglas DC3 banked above the fluffy clouds, then levelled out on course for their destination, Whitchurch aerodrome, a few miles outside Bristol. BOAC Flight 777-A had left Sintra airport, twenty miles north of Lisbon, that morning with a full complement of thirteen passengers. The captain and his crew were Dutch. The plane had previously been owned by the Dutch airline KLM, but after the Nazis overran Holland in 1940, the Dutch government in exile had lent plane and crew to the British airline for use on the Lisbon run. The Nazis had agreed to respect Portugal's neutrality and allow the aircraft undisturbed passage. So far, though flights were often buzzed by German fighters, the arrangement had held.

Today's flight consisted of a typical mix of travellers, some of

44

whom the captain recognised. Three businessmen, an American, a Belgian and a Dutchman, were regular customers. The dour representative of a Jewish refugee charity was also a frequent traveller, as were the two British diplomats seated at the front of the plane. Unfamiliar to the captain were a young Portuguese man, three uniformed Frenchmen and a couple of English schoolgirls, who were accompanied by an older Portuguese woman.

The control tower came into view and the radio crackled to life. The captain left it to his wireless operator to respond to the landing instructions and relaxed. Outside, it looked to be a perfect English summer's day. He thought of the cottage he and his wife rented, a stone's throw from the River Severn. With luck, the farmer next door had made good on his promise to deliver a nice plump chicken for their dinner.

When the aeroplane finally drew to a halt outside the customs hut, the captain waited for the passengers to disembark, then followed the rest of his crew down onto the runway. His wife was waiting for him with their reliable old Austin. They embraced and got in the car. Before they drove off, he saw the young Portuguese man step out of the customs hut and look anxiously around. The captain idly wondered what had brought him to wartime England.

London

In 1934, at the preposterously young age of thirty-one, Kenneth Clark had been appointed director of the National Gallery. Now a world-renowned art historian, Renaissance expert, administrator, academic, and knight of the realm, Clark was as busy as ever. He had successfully organised the removal of the gallery's paintings from London to safe storage in Wales for the duration. He had established the War Artists Scheme, under which many of Britain's artistic community were supported with commissions of work.

45

And he had just completed a spell as head of the Ministry of Information's film department.

As he sat at his desk, elegant as always in a crisp Savile Row suit, Turnbull & Asser shirt, silk tie, and Lobb shoes, he contemplated the two files his secretary had just placed on his desk. The thicker of the two contained the records of his dealings with Calouste Gulbenkian. Much of the file related to his lengthy ongoing discussions with the Armenian about the provisions of his will. For years the British nation had been the intended beneficiary of Gulbenkian's collection after his death. However, despite Clark's best efforts, this arrangement had yet to be formalised, and he was beginning to suspect it never would be. In recent correspondence, Gulbenkian had been keen to postpone further discussion of the matter until after the war. However, the man was getting on. Who was to say he'd survive that long?

Clark stubbed out his cigarette, pushed the first file aside and picked up the slim second one. It contained two photographs, copies of his latest exchange of cables with Gulbenkian and a handwritten note of the meeting he'd had with a man called Leon Van Buren. The meeting had taken place on Wednesday evening at Augustus Ramsey's gallery. First impressions had not been good. Ramsey had told him Van Buren was Dutch, but that had been only partially true. He'd turned out to be an Afrikaner. Clark did not care for Afrikaners. He'd had some dealings with the world's most prominent Afrikaner, General Jan Smuts, in Churchill's Other Club. They had not got on.

After some time in Van Buren's company, however, Clark had warmed to him. He'd been impressed by his evident knowledge and appreciation of art. Eventually they had got round to the reason for their meeting, and Van Buren had shown him the photographs of the da Vinci drawings. He had originally agreed to bring the originals to the meeting, but for some reason had changed his mind. The photographs alone were, however, sufficient to excite Clark. As one of the world's leading da Vinci authorities, he immediately recognised the works pictured. They had disappeared from view in the mid nineteenth century, supposedly hidden away in the private collection of a wealthy German family called Horath. However, when the last count of that line had died in the 1850s, the drawings were nowhere to be found among the possessions he left.

Clark picked up a magnifying glass and bent to examine the photographs more carefully. Van Buren had been a little shifty about when the originals could be produced. He said he had promised to show them first to some other interested parties. Clark took this prevarication to be a clumsy attempt to improve his negotiating position. Van Buren had finally promised to get the originals to him within the week. Price had not been mentioned, and Clark had confined himself to agreeing with Ramsey's observation that there were unlikely to be many buyers around for such works in the difficult wartime market.

He set the photos aside and reread Gulbenkian's latest cable in response to his own: *'GREETINGS SIR KENNETH AND THANKS STOP LOOKING FORWARD TO HEARING MORE ABOUT YOUR INTERESTING ITEMS STOP FREDERICK VERMEULEN A TRUSTED ASSOCIATE WILL BE IN LONDON FROM THIS WEEKEND STOP HE CAN ASSIST AND HAS MY COMPLETE CONFIDENCE STOP HE WILL CONTACT YOU STOP REGARDS G'*

Then he turned his attention back to the other file and found a recent letter that had further concerned him. It was from James Lees Milne, a highly regarded architectural historian and leading light of the recently established National Trust. The man was also a great gossip. He'd heard from some friends that Gulbenkian had recently become very angry with the British government, who he said were giving him difficulties in a variety of areas. Further on in the file, there was a letter from William Delano, the intended architect of the hoped-for Gulbenkian annexe to the National Gallery. Delano wrote that he'd had heard rumours that many of the treasures Gulbenkian had left in Paris would shortly be on their way to Berlin. He'd speculated as to whether they'd survive the destruction of the city that must inevitably come.

As he closed the file, Clark wondered whether it might be advisable for him to get on a plane to Lisbon to tackle the old man directly about his intentions. He swiftly discounted the idea. Flights were supposedly safe, but he knew the government wouldn't allow him to risk the journey. No. His best way of getting Britain back into Gulbenkian's good books would be to help the man add two marvellous new pieces to his collection.

Cairo

After his long journey, Bernie Goldberg luxuriated in the hot shower of the comfortable quarters he'd been allocated in the grounds of the American embassy. After towelling himself down, he flopped onto his bed and watched as an ancient fan creakily stirred the room's sultry air. He resisted the temptation to close his eyes. Harriman had told him he'd only an hour before he'd be required.

Goldberg was a stocky man in his thirties with intense brown eyes, a broken nose and a prominent jawline. As he lay back, he pondered again the strange sequence of events that had brought him to Cairo. Averell Harriman was an exceptionally influential and powerful man, who served President Roosevelt as his special envoy to Europe. Six months previously, Goldberg had been running an NYPD investigation into apparent irregularities at the investment bank he had co-founded, Brown Brothers Harriman. The two middle-ranking executives who'd been defrauding the bank were in due course successfully exposed and prosecuted. Hearing of Goldberg's sterling work, Harriman had invited him to dinner at Arden House, his palatial family house in upstate New York. For some reason the distinguished New York aristocrat and the feisty Jewish policeman from the Lower East Side had hit it off. A few days later, Goldberg had been surprised to be informed by his precinct captain of an unusual request.

'God knows why, but this guy Harriman seems to have taken a shine to you. He's going travelling and wants to take you as his security man.'

'You mean like . . . like his bodyguard?'

'I suppose so, yeah.'

Goldberg had shaken his head. 'Well that's fine and dandy and very nice of him, but I've got some important—'

'Hold it right there, Detective. If you're going to decline this offer, let me give you a little advice. Sure, you did good work on the Harriman bank case, but you managed to blot your copy-book again by exceeding your authority in the Vincent inquiry and by ignoring orders in the Pearson murder case. Once again you are in bad odour with the powers-that-be. I think a little time out of the office would give things a chance to settle down.'

'Captain, you know I was fully justified in both instances. I—'

'There's no need to go over it all again. You know my sympathies lie with you, but that's irrelevant. Take my advice. Go with Harriman. He's a very interesting man and you'll probably have some worthwhile experiences.'

A few days later, Goldberg had set off on his travels. An uncomfortable military plane had conveyed him across the Atlantic to a US Air Force base in East Anglia. Then he'd been whisked to Northolt airport, where he'd met up with his new employer. Once Harriman had briefed him about his duties, they'd boarded a plane to Gibraltar and another to Cairo.

Now he was exhausted, and would have dozed off to the soothing rhythm of the ceiling fan but for a whining mosquito that roused him. He went to stand briefly under the shower again, then dressed for dinner. He understood he might see Churchill and

other British notables tonight. What would his friend Frank Merlin make of his new status?

London

Malta had been under siege from the Germans since 1940, and
escape from the island was almost impossible. Teddy Micallef,
however, had managed it, at great risk to his life. On his arrival in
London, he had been shocked to find that his principal contact in
the city, his godfather, Joseph Abela, had recently died. Abela had
been the leader of one of London's biggest gangs. After his death,
with the approval of Billy Hill, the capital's criminal kingpin, the
Abela operation had been absorbed by the Messinas, another Maltese gang. There was little love lost between the Messinas and the
Micallefs, and Teddy found himself out in the cold. However, at
the suggestion of Abela's widow, he'd managed to get a meeting
with Hill. Hill had been impressed by the story of his gutsy escape
from Malta and by his obvious intelligence. He had also liked Joe
Abela, and in an uncharacteristic spirit of generosity, he decided to
take the young man on. Micallef proved himself a handy operator,
and with his share of the Hill gang takings, he was soon able to set
himself up in a smart Bayswater flat.

Micallef was a handsome man, with dark, aquiline features,
sparkling teeth and shiny jet-black hair. He'd been educated at
Valletta's top English private school, and accordingly, as Hill put
it, spoke like a bit of a toff. Women found him extremely attractive, and his lunch companion today at the Caprice was the latest
of his conquests. Elizabeth Van Buren was a full-figured natural
beauty with an elfin face, bright green eyes and long, flowing
golden hair. She had arrived late, and as she sat down, he could tell
something was wrong.

'What's up, darling?'

'Oh . . . nothing.'

50

'You look like you've been crying. Something must have upset you.'

'Just order me a drink, will you?'

Micallef waved to a waiter and ordered champagne cocktails. When the drinks arrived, Elizabeth took a large gulp.

'Better?'

'Yes. That's heavenly. If you must know, it's Daddy. He's being mean. You know the lease is up on my flat?'

'Yes. You said you could renew it but you'd prefer to find somewhere else.'

'I've found somewhere else. Still in Chelsea and not far from Daddy's house. It's larger, and much nicer, with a decent view, but Daddy says it's far too dear.'

'Oh.'

'He says things are tight at the moment and he needs to reduce his expenses. I just . . . I don't understand it.'

Micallef sipped his drink thoughtfully. 'Maybe you caught him at a bad time. Try him again in a couple of days. I bet you he'll come round.'

She shook her head. 'I can't wait a couple of days. Someone else is interested in the flat. I need to commit by tomorrow, the agent says.'

'Agents always say that sort of thing. Tackle your father over the weekend. He'll change his mind, I'm sure.'

A waiter appeared with menus, and Micallef ordered two more cocktails. When the man had gone, Elizabeth spoke again. 'He was mean about you too.'

'Me? What have I done?'

'You haven't done anything. He just said that he doesn't like you and I should give you up.'

Micallef gave a wry smile. 'And are you going to give me up, my darling?'

She leaned over and pecked him on the cheek. 'Of course not, sweetheart.'

51

'What did he say exactly?'

'He said you were a shifty man on the make and I could do better.'

Micallef laughed. 'I don't object to being called a man on the make. There's nothing wrong with ambition.'

'Of course not. I told him you're a very successful businessman and will only become more successful. I was right, wasn't I?'

'You were.' So far as she was aware, he dealt in expensive cars and antiques. Of course, she had no idea of his real profession.

She picked up his hand and gave it a squeeze. 'Anyway, it's none of his damned business who I see.'

The waiter reappeared and they both ordered the sole. Micallef picked out an expensive Chablis from the wine menu. When they were alone again, Elizabeth returned to the subject of her father. 'I really don't understand why Daddy won't fork out. I'm sure he can afford it.'

Micallef knew something of the Van Buren family history. 'I gather he lives in comfort here. I presume he managed to bring quite a bit with him from Holland?'

'He'll never talk properly with me or Robert about his finances, but I can't believe he didn't. Apart from anything else, he has some very good art-work. He was quite a collector in Holland, you know.'

'Really?'

'Yes, he acquired some wonderful stuff over the years and I know for a fact that he brought some of it to England, although he had to leave a good part of the collection behind.'

'Oh? Where does he keep it?'

'Some is in the house and some in a bank, I think.'

The waiter brought them bread and, and water, and poured two glasses of wine.

Micallef toyed with a bread roll. 'Well, if he ever wants to sell any of his pieces, you know I'm in that line. Paintings, sculptures, whatever.'

Elizabeth giggled. 'I'm sorry, Teddy, but if Daddy did want to sell anything, I don't think he'd use you.'

'Why not? I have a very good clientele.'

Elizabeth sipped some wine. 'Mmm, lovely. Well, why don't you ask him yourself when you next meet?'

'I shall. When I met him that one time before, we had a perfectly pleasant chat. Until your brother rather rudely interrupted us, that is.'

Elizabeth sighed. 'Hah. My idiot brother. All he wants to talk about is that stupid magazine. Daddy's quite right not to want to throw his money away on it.'

'Oh, dear. Families, eh?' Micallef sampled the wine and nodded his approval. 'I'd love to know a little more about your father's taste in art.'

Sonia Merlin greeted her husband excitedly at the front door. 'You did it, Frank! You managed to get home early on a Friday evening for once.'

They embraced and kissed. Then Sonia laughingly pushed him away. 'I've got a nice treat for you. Go and make yourself comfortable in the living room. Or perhaps you'd like a bath?'

'Are you suggesting, dear wife, that I'm a bit smelly?'

She giggled. 'Well you have been cooped up in that stuffy office all day, and it's been pretty hot.'

'All right, I'll have a quick bath, but I'll take a beer with me.'

'What luxury. Is your hand all right?'

'In good enough shape to hold a beer bottle. How's the boy?'

'Fast asleep when last I looked. I'll get your drink.'

An hour later, Merlin was on his third beer and Sonia her second glass of red wine. The remains of a rabbit stew sat before them on the kitchen table. While rabbit wasn't on the ration, it was usually hard to find, but the butcher nearby on the King's Road had a soft spot for Sonia, and whenever he got supplies, he would put one aside for her.

'This is delicious as always, darling. Plenty of meat, too. A big rabbit. What did the baby get up to today?'

'Iris and some of the mothers went for a long walk. Did you know there's a piggery in Battersea Park now? That caused a lot of amusement, apparently.'

'I'm sure it did.' Merlin mopped up some gravy with a piece of bread. 'You never told me what was so pressing yesterday that you had to go in at the crack of dawn.'

'It's secret, but I'll tell you. There were some documents for the British Foreign Office that required urgent translation. They concerned the mysterious disappearance of a large number of Polish soldiers and civilians.'

'Can you tell me more?'

'As you know, when the Germans invaded my country, the Russians poured in from the east as part of their filthy deal with Hitler. Thousands of Polish men were rounded up and sent off to Russian prison camps. When the Nazis broke their treaty with the Russians last year and became our allies, General Sikorski and the Russian ambassador here, Maisky, agreed that Poles and Russians would work hand in hand against the Germans. Our top general, Anders, who'd been imprisoned by the Russians himself, was asked to form a new Polish army to fight alongside the Red Army. An order was given for all Polish prisoners to be released from the Russian camps. The Russians claim that that has happened, but the Polish government in exile says a substantial number remain unaccounted for.'

'A substantial number?'

'Over twenty thousand, according to one document I translated yesterday.'

'*Madre de Dios!*'

'The Russians say our records are wrong. General Anders asked one of his senior officers to liaise with the Russians and investigate the matter. There was no real cooperation and he got nowhere.'

'Isn't Anders in England now?'

'Yes. Not surprisingly, in light of this, he decided he couldn't work with the Russians and managed to get his men here. The only available option now is for the British government to pursue the matter. To that end the Poles have collated all their records and evidence for submission to the Foreign Office. That's what I was working on.'

'Was it the Russian army that held all these men?'

'No. It is believed it was NKVD.'

'The security services? That doesn't bode well. Are there detailed lists of those missing?'

'I have seen some.'

'Recognise any of the names?'

'No, but I bet my father would. There are a number of senior engineers on the list.'

Sonia's parents were, like their daughter, refugees who'd got out of Poland just in time. Her father had been a highly regarded mechanical engineer in Warsaw. He'd struggled for a long time to find employment in England, but had recently obtained a good job in a Lancashire munitions factory.

Sonia started to tidy the plates away.

'Let me help you.'

'No, you stay put, Frank Merlin. I have another of your favour-ite treats. Stewed plums and custard.'

'You're spoiling me.'

'Do you have to work this weekend?' asked Sonia as they ate their dessert.

'I could be in the clear. The Canadian case is pretty much wrapped up.'

'They will hang?'

'Yes.'

She shuddered, then reached out to wipe some custard from her husband's chin. 'You're like a big baby, sometimes, Frank.' She poured herself a little more wine. 'So. If we have a free weekend, what shall we do?'

'What would you like to do?'

'Just normal family stuff. Go for a nice walk with Harry. Go out for lunch.'

'Battersea Park?'

'He's there all the time. We should give him a little variety.'

'How about Regent's Park Zoo? He'll have more than piglets to excite him there.'

Sonia laughed. 'That's a wonderful idea. Is the zoo open, though? Didn't it get bombed in the Blitz?'

'Yes, but I heard everything's up and running again.'

'Were there casualties?'

'No people were killed that I heard of. I did hear that the management chose to put down all of their venomous animals. They were worried about snakes and the like getting loose after a raid.'

Sonia wrinkled her nose. 'Snakes aren't really my favourite animals, but that's very sad. Poor things.'

There was a loud cry from down the corridor. Sonia grinned. 'He must have heard us talking about the zoo. I'll try to get him back to sleep. Perhaps I'll tell him he'll be seeing lions and tigers tomorrow.'

'Does he know what those are yet?'

It was Tommy Cole's first proper West End night on the town for ages. A dinner date in Soho, followed by dancing at the Paramount Hall in the Tottenham Court Road. His companion was a petite red-haired Irish girl called Shona, whom he'd met at one of his history evening classes just before Christmas. He wouldn't quite say she was his girlfriend yet, but things seemed to be heading in that direction. It had taken him until April to pluck up the courage to ask her out. They'd had several dates since then, mostly going to the pictures. This night was a definite step up in their relationship.

Over dinner, they chatted about what they'd been up to during the week. Cole described the show-down with the Canadian robbers.

Shona sighed. 'As usual, your week's been a hundred times

56

more exciting than mine.' She was a secretary in a City bank. 'I suppose the high point of my week was seeing Mr Attlee in the office. He came to lunch with some of our directors.'

'Well, that's quite something, seeing the deputy prime minister.'

Shona laughed. 'I can't really see that having a grey old politician walk past my desk is in quite the same league of excitement as taking on a couple of murderous gangsters!'

'Perhaps not, but I have to say I admire Clement Attlee. Seems a dry old stick, but he's giving Mr Churchill good support.'

'Speaking of Churchill, one of the directors let slip after lunch that the PM might be off to Russia shortly.'

'Makes sense. Joe Stalin is very important to us now.'

'Mr Attlee also told my boss that he's very optimistic about the course of the war.'

'I suppose he's bound to try and keep our spirits up. Things don't look so good to me, though. Mr Merlin was talking about it in the office the other day. The Germans are giving the Russians a hell of a bashing on the Eastern Front, the British army's still not making much progress in North Africa and the Japs are running riot in the Far East. He was very worried.'

'From what you've told me, I wouldn't have your boss down as a pessimist.'

'He'd just had an ear-bashing about the war from the AC, I think, which had got him down.'

'Now that the Yanks are with us, though, we're bound to win in the end.'

'You're right, but we're going to have to go over a lot of bumps in the road before we get to that point.'

They finished their meal and Shona got to her feet. 'I'll just pay a quick visit to the powder room. You get the bill and we'll split it like last time.'

'Shona, please let me—'

'No. Remember my old dad was a copper over here for a while.

I know what British policemen get paid. We'll split it. You can pay the dance-hall entrance fee, if you like. It'll not be much, but if it soothes your male·pride . . .'

The route to the dance hall took them through Soho Square, and Cole pointed out the now boarded-up Chez François. At the dance hall, they found a huge crowd besieging the entrance. The majority of the men appeared to be servicemen, and a good many of those were American. The United States had entered the war in December 1941, and thousands of American military personnel had been flowing into the country ever since.

It took Cole and Shona quite a while to get in. Cole immediately grasped Shona's hand and headed through the crowd towards the bar. Halfway there, he suddenly turned and smiled awkwardly at her. He'd realised it was the first time they had held hands.

At the bar, Shona asked for a half of Guinness and Cole ordered a pint of the same. They found an empty table in a far corner of the cavernous room. The place was too noisy for conversation, so they sipped their beers and, listened to the music. Eventually, the band struck up with 'In the Mood' one of Cole's favourites. He patted Shona's hand, then pointed to the dancers. She smiled and followed him out onto the dance floor.

Cole was not a particularly experienced dancer, but he had a good sense of rhythm. Shona, he realised from the outset, was a natural. They danced to five tunes before moving to the side for a rest. As Cole was recovering his breath, he became aware of a commotion to his left: a group of American GIs getting noisily angry. The focus of their attention appeared to be two couples who were happily jitterbugging away. The men dancing were soldiers too. Black soldiers. The girls were pretty and white. They were clearly oblivious to the attention they were arousing.

The music ended and the bandleader announced that there would be a short break. As the dancers left the floor, a couple of the angry GIs pushed their way through the crowd and confronted the black soldiers. Several more GIs quickly waded into the fight.

Cole tapped Shona's shoulder, 'I'd better try and stop this.' He set off towards the melee, but hadn't gone far when a hand gripped his shoulder. He turned to see another American military man. From the pips on his collar, Cole knew he was an officer.

'I wouldn't get mixed up in this if I were you, sonny.'

'I'm a police officer.'

'Policeman you may be, but I'd still stay out of it. This is an American matter. Those stupid cotton-pickers asked for it when they danced with those white girls.'

'What's wrong with that?'

The officer shook his head and smiled before releasing his grip and melting back into the crowd. Cole continued to push his way through, getting a nasty elbow in the face in the process. When he reached his destination, though, he found things had calmed down, for the good reason that both black soldiers were laid flat out on the floor. They had clearly taken a heavy beating. There was a sudden shout of 'Snowballs!' followed by a chorus of whistles. A group of white-helmeted American military police were barging their way towards Cole, who decided he might as well leave things to them.

When he found Shona, she was upset. 'That was horrific. Those poor boys.'

'I know. Sorry, but I think we'd best get away from here.'

On their way out, he was surprised to see that the two black soldiers were now on their feet in handcuffs. There was no sign of their attackers.

'That can't be right. Excuse me, Shona.'

He found the officer who appeared to be in charge. 'I'm sorry, sir, but you're arresting the wrong men. These lads you've cuffed are the victims.'

The man looked at him sourly. 'What's it to you, pal?'

'I saw everything. I'm a policeman.'

'Are you now? Well, as you know, the criminal behaviour of American soldiers is our business now, not yours. Besides, from what I hear, these boys had it coming. Now butt out.' He turned away and issued some orders, and the two black soldiers were hauled off.

Cole was seething when he got back to Shona.

'This is so unjust.'

'I guess the Yanks have different ideas about justice to us.' She raised her hand to his cheek. 'What's that bruise?'

'I took a knock when I was pushing through the crowd.'

'It looks quite nasty.' She raised herself up on her toes and lightly kissed his cheek. 'Maybe that'll make it better.'

Chapter Six

Saturday August 8ᵗʰ 1942

The man known to his controllers as Archer emerged cautiously from the station into the glare of the bright summer morning. He had tracked his target from a Knightsbridge café to South Kensington Tube station and then onto a District Line train to Richmond. He saw his man heading off down Richmond High Street and quickly set off in discreet pursuit. The target proceeded through the town and then down to the riverbank, where he took the towpath in the direction of Ham. The lovely weather had brought out the weekend crowds and it was relatively easy for Archer to avoid detection. There was more danger of him losing his man than being spotted.

About a mile and a half further along the path, in sight of Ham House, he saw his target step into the small ferry that travelled the short distance back and forth to connect the Richmond side of the river with the Marble Hill side. Archer considered for a moment. If he ventured into the boat himself, he might be exposed. Then again, the man hadn't evinced any sign that he suspected he was being followed. He decided to risk it and jumped into the ferry on its return. On the other side, he saw his man queuing to come back. Perhaps he'd had his suspicions after all? Archer decided to wait for a while. Wait and watch. He walked along the path and found a tree-shaded spot from which he would be able to observe the man when he was back on the other side.

A few minutes later, he saw the man disembark and head off in the same direction as before. Four hundred or so yards on, he suddenly sat down on a bench set a little back from the river. Archer cursed himself for not bringing his binoculars. He couldn't see the bench very well, but he could see enough to tell that soon someone joined the man and appeared to engage in conversation. The pair sat together for about ten minutes, at the end of which Archer thought he saw them exchange something. Then they got up and went off in opposite directions, with Archer's man heading back towards Richmond.

Archer realised he'd have to get his skates on to catch the ferry back over. Then he relaxed and lit a cigarette. It wouldn't be the end of the world if he lost the target for now. He'd seen something interesting this morning. It wouldn't be difficult to pick him up later in town.

He savoured his cigarette for a moment, standing in the shadows, and watched as his man receded into the distance. Suddenly another figure burst from the undergrowth not far from the bench the two men had sat on. He looked anxiously from left to right, then seemed to spot what he was looking for and headed off down the path in the Richmond direction. Archer couldn't make out his face, but he had the impression it was a young man. It occurred to him that someone else might share an interest in his target. Or perhaps protection was being provided by the target's side, whichever side that might be. He sighed and stubbed out the cigarette on the bark of a tree. With this type of job, he knew from long experience, one suspected everyone and everything.

Chapter Seven

Monday August 10th 1942

Merlin picked up a newspaper at the booth by Westminster Tube and paused to read the headlines. The main story was about a British general called Gott who'd been killed in an air crash in North Africa. At least, Merlin thought ungenerously, this war was taking some casualties from the top end of the military. In the previous one, the generals had mostly stayed well away from the action.

Gott's death was not news to him, as it happened. The AC had phoned him at home on Sunday and mentioned it. The pretext for the call had been a thin one. Another reminder about the big American meeting on Monday morning, of which Merlin was well aware. Perhaps Gatehouse had been feeling lonely. He had told Merlin recently that his wife's work for the Women's Voluntary Service was requiring an increasing amount of travel, with weekends away becoming quite common. Whatever the motivation behind the call, the AC had waffled on for almost an hour, much delaying the walk on which Merlin, Sonia and Harry had been just about to embark.

When he arrived at work, Bridges and Cole were in his office.
'Tea, sir?'
'That would be nice, Sergeant.'
Bridges nodded to Cole. 'And make it strong like the chief

inspector likes it. The last one you made for me was as weak as a baby's handshake.'

Cole went off to the cubbyhole down the corridor that served as his and Constable Robinson's office. It also housed the kettle. Merlin noticed that he had a vivid purple bruise on his cheek.

'Anything to report, Sam?' he asked. Bridges manned the office over the weekend.

'Been very quiet. The Canadian High Commission got in touch to say they'd like to have a chat with our two robbers, and I arranged that yesterday. Otherwise, I was able to catch up with a lot of paperwork.'

Merlin saw that Bridges had obviously tidied his desk, and gave him an appreciative smile.

'Good weekend, sir?'

'We went to the zoo on Saturday. Harry's a bit young for it, I know, but I think he enjoyed it.'

'Bet the wife was happy to have you to herself for two whole days.'

'Yes, I'll be in her good books for a while. So how did Cole acquire that nice shiner?'

'He was just telling me about it, sir. A worrying story, in fact. I hope it's not a sign of problems to come.' Bridges proceeded to tell Merlin about the fracas at the dance hall. He was most of the way through the story when Cole reappeared with the tea.

'I'm just hearing about your unfortunate Friday night, Constable.'

'It was terrible, sir. Those poor black soldiers were almost killed.'

'Was drink behind it, d'you think?'

'No, sir. I'm sure a few of the people involved had sunk a few, but it wasn't just that. The white GIs clearly hate the black ones. I've never come across anything quite like it.'

Merlin stroked his chin. 'I'm aware that there are major racial divisions in the United States, but I have to say it never really occurred to me that the American forces would bring those divisions with them. Naïve of me, I suppose.'

'Was I wrong to try and intervene, sir?'

'I'm sure I'd have done the same, but that said, I don't think there's much we can do. However, now that I know what happened, I shall make a point of mentioning it at my meeting with the Americans this morning. It'll be interesting to see what they have to say.'

'Sir. If you'll excuse me, I've a couple of chores to do.'

'Of course.'

Merlin sipped his tea thoughtfully as Cole went out, then looked at Bridges. 'So what's on the schedule for you today, Sam?'

'I said I'd help Sergeant Mason follow up some leads on that cigarette robbery in Acton.'

'How's the warehouseman doing? I heard he took a very nasty knock.'

'Things don't look good. There's a chance he might not make it.'

Merlin frowned. 'I wonder if this is another bunch of independents like the Canadians. Billy Hill encourages his men to keep violence to a minimum.' He sighed. 'To kill a man for a few cigarettes.'

'Thirty thousand packs, sir.'

'All right. For a lot of cigarettes.' Few people didn't smoke in wartime Britain, and tobacco was a huge business. Cigarettes were not subject to rationing but were often in short supply. The haul from Acton could be worth around £2,000 on the street. A lot of money.

'How is Mason these days?'

'Busy, sir. Robbery and theft numbers are going through the roof.'

'I know. Well, you help out as best you can. What's Inspector Johnson up to?'

'He's gone to the Scrubs to tie up a few loose ends with the Canadians.'

Merlin looked up at the Swiss cuckoo clock on the wall behind him. It was a souvenir of one of his pre-war cases. It was coming up to ten o'clock. 'I'd better get off to this meeting with the Americans. I'm not looking forward to it at all.'

Merlin was directed to a grand room on the first floor of the embassy. Portraits of American worthies filled the walls. He was one of the first arrivals, and as he waited for the room to fill, he examined some of the paintings. His attention was caught by a stern-looking bewigged man with a round face, thin lips and long nose. He recognised the name at the bottom of the frame but struggled to remember his role in American history.

'John Adams,' said a voice from behind his right shoulder. 'One of the Founding Fathers. A great man.' Merlin turned to find a rugged, hawkish face looking down on him. Merlin was tall, but the American had a good three or four inches on him.

'Thank you. I couldn't quite recall Mr Adams' part in the scheme of things. Forgive my ignorance of American history.'

'Not at all, Detective Chief Inspector Merlin. I'll bet your knowledge of British history far exceeds mine.' The man spoke with a distinctly Southern accent.

'You have the advantage of me, sir. You know my name but I don't know yours.'

'Captain Max Pearce at your service. Max is short for Maximilian. My father was a great admirer of the first and last emperor of Mexico.'

'Another area of history I'm not so strong on. Pleased to meet you, Captain.' They shook hands.

Pearce looked back at the portrait. 'John Adams was one of the prime movers in the American Revolution. After the War of Independence had been won, he was twice vice president under Washington, then America's second president. He was also the first American ambassador to Great Britain and father to another president in John Quincy Adams.'

'A man of signal achievements, then.'

'Indeed.' He nodded towards the long table, where places were rapidly filling up. 'Shall we?' They took two chairs at the window end. Shortly afterwards, the meeting was called to order.

The chairman, a fat, bullet-headed man with an intense air, announced himself as Joshua Kissin, the embassy's chief of mission. He then asked everyone else to introduce themselves. There were six American diplomats in addition to Kissin himself. The British administrative contingent also numbered seven, and was led by a dry Home Office civil servant called Dunne. Complementing the diplomats and civil servants were four policemen. Captain Max Pearce of the American military police was one of them.

Merlin could tell at the outset it was going to be a long meeting. After some lengthy introductory remarks from Kissin, Dunne replied in kind, speaking for half an hour without saying anything much. When Kissin spoke again, he went through the new legislation on American military jurisdiction in fine detail. The minutiae were then debated by the bureaucrats for over an hour and a half. At last, in a brief lull, Merlin managed to attract attention.

'You have a question, DCI Merlin?' asked Kissin.

'Yes, sir. My question relates to an incident witnessed by one of my officers at a London dance hall on Friday night. There was a brawl among some American soldiers. Eight or nine men, of whom two were black. The white soldiers started the fight, according to my man, and attacked the blacks. Of course, as they were significantly outnumbered, the black soldiers came off much the worse. A group of American military police arrived and made arrests, but only of the black soldiers. My officer pointed out that he thought an injustice was being perpetrated, but was told it was none of his business. My question is, if British police are witnesses to American criminal activity, will their views be taken properly into account?'

A bout of muttering broke out. Kissin engaged in a whispered consultation with two colleagues before replying. 'Thank you, Chief Inspector. Before I answer, may I say what a pleasure it is to have you with us. Your reputation is high in this building. Some of my colleagues recollect your sterling efforts to investigate the unfortunate staff . . . difficulties we had back in the early days of the war. Now, to your question, I am naturally disturbed to hear of any possible failings on the part of our military police. Of course, police everywhere make mistakes from time to time. I would say that if any of your officers observe such mistakes by our men, they must feel free to inform us. However . . .' he paused to look round the table, '. . .henceforth the ultimate judgement on such matters must rest with American officers. Now, in the spirit of friendly mutual cooperation, if your officer would care to provide more details of this brawl through the appropriate channels, I assure you it shall be looked into.'

Max Pearce pre-empted Merlin's response. 'There'll be no need to look into it, Mr Kissin. I was present myself at this so-called brawl. There was no miscarriage of justice. A couple of uppity negroes were dancing with white girls. Completely out of order, as I'm sure you'll agree. Some of our boys decided to give them what for. When my Snowballs arrived, the negroes spoke offensively to them and resisted arrest. They were quite correctly handcuffed and taken away.'

'Ah, I see' said Kissin. 'Well, there you have it, Chief Inspector. Apparently no further investigation is required.'

Merlin's cheeks flushed and he struggled for a moment to find his voice. When he did, he asked, 'Am I the only person in this room to be shocked by the captain's comments? Unless there's been a change in the law of which I'm not aware, it is not illegal in Britain for people of different races to dance together. Even—'

Captain Pearce cut back in. 'Back home, many states prohibit the mixing of the races. These boys knew what they were doing was wrong. Intervention was necessary.'

Merlin looked at Kissin. 'Am I to take it then that one

consequence of the new legislation will be the application in Britain of some of your more barbaric laws? Didn't you Americans fight a civil war about the rights of the black man?'

'I don't believe Mr Lincoln thought he was fighting about the right of a black man to copulate with a white woman,' Pearce growled.

Kissin brought his hand down on the table. 'Gentlemen, please!'

'Damn it, Kissin, I'm not going to have some Limey—'

'That's enough, Captain.' Kissin glared at Pearce. 'Perhaps it's for the best that this subject has been raised early. It is a useful reminder that there are some serious cultural differences between our countries.' He looked through his papers and produced a little brown book. 'We anticipated that such differences might provoke friction and took the precaution of preparing this pamphlet to explain them. You've seen it, Chief Inspector?'

'I have, and I've read it, but I don't recall seeing anything about black soldiers not being able to dance with white girls.'

'Yes . . . well, if you have any suggestions for the modification of the pamphlet, I'm sure we'll be happy to consider them. Meanwhile . . .' he consulted his watch '. . .time is moving on and we are all busy men. May I suggest we look at some of the broader issues raised by some members of my team. I . . .'

Merlin tuned out as Kissin droned on. He couldn't wait to get out of the room, but had to suffer another hour of the meeting before he could do so.

As he at last made his way to the door, he felt a tug on his arm. Pearce pulled him to one side. 'As you're probably aware now, Merlin, I'll be one of the most senior American police officers on the ground in London. I hoped to develop a friendly relationship with the guys at Scotland Yard. I'm guessing that's going to be difficult in your case.'

'You guess correctly.'

Pearce shrugged. 'Then we'd best hope our paths don't cross too frequently.'

'Or at all.' Merlin turned and hurried down the stairs, desperate for some fresh air.

Vermeulen was late returning to the cosy little mews house he kept in Knightsbridge. He hoped his friend hadn't given up on him. As he stepped through the door, he was delighted to see she had not.

'Darling Ursula! I'm so sorry to have kept you. I've had a hectic day. Please forgive me.'

Ursula Dunne was a tall brunette in her late thirties. Vermeulen had enjoyed much success with women in his life. Experience had taught him that happiness was more likely with those not in the first flush of youth.

She smiled and set down her martini. 'No need for apologies, Frederick. I know you're a busy man.' They kissed, then moved to a settee in the small, brightly-furnished living room.

'Tell me what you've been up to, Frederick. What have you got on the go this trip?'

Vermeulen maintained a mixed business portfolio. He represented a number of important Portuguese exporters as well as being involved with Calouste Gulbenkian.

'This and that, but let's not talk about it now. It's just so wonderful to see you!'

'Let me get you a drink.'

He relaxed back in his seat as his lover mixed him a cocktail. 'You're looking very well, Ursula. You have some nice colour in your cheeks. Have you been in the country?'

'Yes, we had some of Charles's colleagues and their wives out to stay for the weekend. It was a long-standing commitment I couldn't get out of. Otherwise I'd have been here earlier to see you.'

'No matter. You're here now.'

She brought him his drink and they clinked glasses.

'Cheers, darling. And how *is* Charles?'

'Busy as ever. The Home Office takes up most of his time. And then there's the golf club.'

'And the boy?'

'Holidaying with friends in Scotland.'

Vermeulen sipped his martini. 'So you've been alone a lot?'

'I have, which you know I enjoy. But now I've got you for a little while. How long are you staying this time?'

'At least a week. Maybe two. Apart from my normal business, I have a particular errand from Mr Gulbenkian.'

'That sounds intriguing. You must tell me more.'

'Oh, just some art he wants to buy.' He suddenly realised he'd not shut the blackout curtains, and rose and crossed the room to do so. When he returned, he asked, 'So what's keeping your husband so busy at work?'

Ursula shrugged. 'You know Charles. He seldom tells me anything. I heard him talking on the telephone about some business with the Americans. And he's involved in some rationing review. The usual tedious stuff, but he thrives on it.' She reached up a hand and stroked Vermeulen's neck. 'And how is Portugal?'

'Salazar and his government continue to interfere in the wine business, which makes life a little more difficult for my port producers. Otherwise life goes on pretty much as normal.'

'You're still . . . still doing that other work you mentioned?'

He got up without answering. 'Come on, darling. Let's sort out dinner. I was thinking of that little French place behind Harrods. I'll telephone them now.'

'Do you think we'll be able to get in at such short notice?'

'I'm a good customer. I think I have enough pull. Shall I try for eight thirty?'

'Make it nine thirty. There's something I'd like to do first.' She stood and smiled. 'I'll be waiting for you upstairs.'

The Dove was a charming old pub in Hammersmith. 'Been here since the 1700s, you know,' said Martin Ramsey as he and

Nathan Katz sat down at a riverside table with their pints. 'Supposedly Charles the Second dined here with Nell Gwynn. The Fuller's brewery is only a short walk away. We're drinking my favourite beer – London Pride. They produce another, stronger brew called Extra Special, which I only drink very occasionally. It gives me the most terrible hangover but tastes wonderful. I'm avoiding it for now. I don't want to blot my copybook with my grandfather.'

'I am gradually developing a taste for your bitter beer,' said Katz. 'It is of course very different from beer on the Continent. When I was a student in Paris, I mostly drank pilsner.'

'Never had it. Must give it a try some-time. Anyway, cheers!'

Despite its being a Monday night, the place was crowded and they'd been lucky to get a table. The pub business was one of the few to be benefiting from the war.

'They say the man who wrote "Rule Britannia" wrote it in this very pub,' said Ramsey.

'Really? I must say, Britannia doesn't seem to be ruling enough at the moment. The Allies could do with a victory somewhere.'

'You're right. Any sort of victory would be a great boost for morale. Everyone cheered up when the Yanks came into the war, but the effect has worn off somewhat. We don't seem to have seen any real progress on the ground for quite a while.'

'Perhaps there will be good news out of North Africa soon.'

'Maybe, but that Rommel fellow is no pushover.'

They were momentarily distracted as a pretty young girl squeezed past the table.

Ramsey smiled. 'Got anything brewing on the female front, Nathan?'

'I'm . . . I'm afraid not. Too busy with work. You?'

He gulped some beer. 'I had a girlfriend, but . . . but she bought it in the Blitz, I'm afraid. She was renting a room in a house not far from here. Place took a direct hit.'

'I'm very sorry.'

Ramsey shrugged. 'Haven't had the heart to start looking for someone else. We'd known each other since we were fifteen.'

Katz could think of nothing helpful to add, so concentrated on his beer.

Ramsey eventually roused himself. 'Your cousin Benjamin mentioned you had a sister who managed to get out of Austria with you.'

'Yes, Rebecca. We were both at the Sorbonne. She met a Swedish man there, Anders, married him and went to live in Stockholm.'

'A safe enough place to be these days. Good for her. Do you keep in touch?'

'I had a letter a few months ago. She has a job in the British embassy. She gets on well with her husband's family. Her father-in-law edits a newspaper and Anders works for him as an investigative journalist.'

'I bet he's got plenty to keep him busy. They say the neutral countries like Sweden, Switzerland and Portugal are hotbeds of espionage and general skulduggery.'

'Skulduggery?'

'Sorry. Old English word. Means underhand dealing, crookedness.'

Katz shook his head and sighed. 'I don't think I'll ever get on top of your language.' He realised their beer glasses were empty and went off to buy a round. When he returned, he took something out of his pocket. 'You remember I said my father was a keen art collector?'

'I do.'

'This is a list he gave me a while ago. I made a fresh copy as the original is a little torn and ragged. It details the works in his collection. Generally speaking, he was very short-sighted about the dangers posed by the Nazis. However, this was one precaution he was prepared to take. He wanted me to have it just in case.'

'In case the Nazis came for the Jews?'

73

'Yes. Not that I can really do much with it for now. Perhaps when the war's over and Europe is open again, I'll be able to investigate.'

'Your presumption is that the Nazis took the art?'

'It's more than a presumption. I know they did.'

'May I see?'

'Of course.'

Ramsey put on a pair of reading glasses and took the list from Katz. As he read, he gave several gasps of surprise and recognition. When he finally handed it back, there was a look of amazement on his face. 'Poussin, Degas, Rubens, Velasquez, da Vinci . . . my God, Nathan, your father was certainly one hell of a collector. His art must have been worth an absolute fortune. You're sure the Germans took it?'

'Some of the collection was in plain sight, of course, and thus easy pickings. As regards what wasn't, my uncle received a letter from an old friend of my father's who'd managed to escape to America just before the war. He said he understood the Nazis had coerced family friends, employees and associates and managed to track down pretty much everything else that was in storage or in bank vaults.'

Ramsey shook his head. 'That's a damned shame.'

'Yes.' Katz drank some more beer, then realised the alcohol was going straight to his head. 'Are we going to eat something, Martin?'

They agreed on sandwiches, and Ramsey insisted on doing the honours. As he got up, Katz asked, 'I was wondering, Martin, if you could do me a small favour?'

'Mustard on your sandwich? Chutney?'

'No. No. Nothing to do with food. It's the list. Could I leave it with you? As I said, I have the original.'

'Of course, but to what end?'

'You work in the art world. It's a long shot, I know, but it's always possible you or your grandfather might hear of one or other of these items coming onto the market.'

74

'Well, yes, I'll be happy to keep an eye out, but it's most unlikely the Nazis will be sending anything to the London market. The pieces are more likely to be gracing the home of some German bigwig.'

'I agree, but . . . well, you never know. It would be a comfort to me to know someone was . . ."on the case", as a crime writer might put it.'

'Not a problem, old chap.'

Katz put the list back on the table and Ramsey went off for food.

'Cheese and onion was all they had, I'm afraid' he said on his return.

'Not to worry, I love cheese and onion.'

Ramsey picked up the list and took another look as he bit into his sandwich.

'I have to say, there are a few artists I'm not familiar with. Klimt, for example. Who's he?'

'An important early twentieth-century Viennese painter. My father was a great supporter of his.'

'Ah.' Ramsey took another look at the list. 'And not everything is described in detail. These da Vinci pieces at the bottom are unspecified.'

'I'm sorry. My mistake. My father didn't spell everything out, as he knew I had particular knowledge of some of the items, and I just copied his list verbatim. The da Vinci pieces mentioned were a couple of religious drawings – cartoons, as they are sometimes called.'

Ramsey's eyebrows rose. 'Religious drawings, you say? Drawings of what exactly?'

'One is of St Paul and the other the Virgin Mary. They were particular favourites of my father's. He kept them in his study and I saw them often. 'Why do you ask?'

Van Buren's housekeeper, Mrs Macdonald, cleared the remains of the simple meal she'd served to her employer and his son, then left the two men to their port. Robert Van Buren returned to his favourite subject.

'You know, Father, I've given my word to Roderick. You indicated that if I did what you wanted, everything could proceed. I've arranged to see the fellow again as you asked.'

'I appreciate that, Robert. That can only be to the good, but . . .' Leon sighed. 'Let's leave it there for now. I'd like to accommodate you, but things are still not clear as regards my finances. I can't commit to your magazine until there are further positive developments.'

'But you promised.'

'No I didn't. I said I'd think about it if you did what I requested. I'm still thinking about it.'

Robert let out a groan of frustration. 'But I don't understand. I know the Nazis didn't do you any favours, but you're living in this big house in comfort. I know you managed to bring some valuable art with you from Holland. Then there's Mummy's money and property, which—'

"You know I can't touch a penny of Mummy's until the litigation is successfully concluded. As is the case with anything involving lawyers, that will take some time. Art is illiquid. The chances of my realising proper prices for what remains of my collection are slim. Meanwhile, I have the substantial expenses of this house, and of you and your sister. As things currently stand, it would be foolhardy of me to commit substantial funds to your damned magazine.'

'You say that, but you've just agreed to Elizabeth's moving to a more expensive apartment. Why have you done that if things are so dire?'

'She's told you about that, has she?'

'Yes, and I think it's damnably unfair.'

'You have a nice flat of your own, which I finance, do you not?'

Robert shrugged.

'And you don't have noisy neighbours, or plumbing problems like Elizabeth currently has in hers, do you?'

'Well, no, but that's not the issue.'

'The fact is that I do my best to see you are both well set up. Pouring money into some rag for literary hangers-on is another matter. Now let's change the subject. When is your next meeting with that fellow?'

'In a couple of weeks,' snapped Robert.

'Good. I'm grateful.'

Robert looked down at his glass. 'It's just that I do so want to get on somehow in the literary world.'

'I know.' Leon topped up their port glasses, then decided to take a more conciliatory approach. 'Have you prepared a proper budget for this magazine of yours?'

'Roderick's got a financial chap putting something together now.'

'And you really think there's a chance of it making money?'

'Connolly's *Horizon* makes money.'

'Reputedly, but who knows for certain. He has a very rich backer – Watson, isn't it?'

'So I believe.'

'A chap with money to burn, unlike myself. I understand he gives a lot of money to that awful Spanish dauber. What's his name again?

'Picasso. Many think he's a genius.'

'Genius or not, not my cup of tea.' Van Buren senior stroked his chin. 'And this Havering fellow you want to get into bed with . . . he doesn't seem to have made a great success of his life so far, does he?'

'He's very highly regarded in the literary world.'

'Is he now? Well, all right, I'll have another think, my boy. Perhaps something will be possible if my finances take a turn for the better. Now, didn't you say you were meeting someone around now?'

Robert looked at his watch. 'Yes, I'm seeing Caroline.'

'Off you go, then.'

After his son's departure, Van Buren lit a cigar and pondered. If Ramsey and this Clark fellow managed to do the business, his finances would take a monumental turn for the better. However, whether that happened or not, he'd insist on the boy knuckling down to the bar exams as he'd always planned. He'd be damned if he would waste a penny on his son's stupid magazine.

Chapter Eight

The sun was pouring straight through the window into their eyes, and both men were obliged to raise their hands against the glare. 'I'm so sorry, Mr Vermeulen,' said Sir Kenneth Clark. 'I'll draw the curtains.' He did so, then sat back at his desk. 'So you were saying that your business interests bring you often to London?'

'Yes. It is something of a miracle, but trade between Portugal and England happily continues.'

'And long may it do so. You have known Mr Gulbenkian long?'

'Since he arrived in Lisbon.'

'He appears to repose considerable trust in you.'

'We have developed a good relationship and I have done a good deal of negotiating in my time.'

'You have negotiated art purchases?'

'No, but are art purchases so different from others?'

'I would think so, but it's Mr Gulbenkian's decision, and of course, I'll be happy to advise.'

Vermeulen leaned forward. 'The fact is, Mr Gulbenkian has some particular requirements.'

'Yes?'

'You know, I believe, about his problems with the British and American financial authorities.'

79

'I'm aware of his complaints.'

'Those problems inevitably have liquidity implications.'

'Really? For such a rich man?'

'A considerable proportion of the Gulbenkian wealth is held in countries now controlled by Germany. Put that together with the official constraints on accessing his assets in Allied countries, and you will understand the problem. Of course, he still has access to significant resources, but in the circumstances, he would prefer to negotiate an element of credit. He recently acquired a Rubens in South Africa on extended terms. He expects me to agree any proposed purchase on a similar basis.'

A flicker of irritation crossed Clark's face. 'He did not tell me about the Rubens.'

Vermeulen shrugged.

'I'm not sure the seller will deal on terms.'

'Has he any other interested parties?'

'He claims so. The dealer, Ramsey, and I are of the view that they are straw men. We may be wrong, but there are very few collectors in the market at present with the inclination or resources to pursue this level of acquisition.'

'Have you looked into the man's financial position?'

'Ramsey has done a little checking. There is a mixed picture. Van Buren lost a fortune when the Nazis took over in Holland. However, he lives here in reasonable comfort. Apparently there's some litigation in progress regarding his deceased wife's estate. Ramsey understands that if that goes his way, he'll receive a decent windfall.'

'So he's not down and out?'

'Ramsey thinks he's in a position to hold out for a fair price. But then again, Ramsey has a commission to earn.'

'Have you seen the drawings yet?'

'Only photographs. This will be the first time I see the originals.'

There was a knock on the door and Clark's secretary informed them that Van Buren and Ramsey had arrived. After introductions had been made, the four men sat around a large coffee table by the window. Van Buren had with him a battered-looking leather portfolio case. Sir Kenneth offered tea, but there were no takers. 'To business, then, Mr Van Buren. As I'm sure Augustus has told you, Mr Vermeulen here represents a prospective overseas purchaser.'

'So he has, Sir Kenneth.'

'I presume the drawings are in your case? May we?'

Van Buren nodded and opened the case, removed the cloth in which the drawings were wrapped and set them down on the table.

Clark produced a magnifying glass and leaned forward to examine the nearest drawing, that of St Paul. He pored over it for several minutes, then took a measuring tape out of his jacket pocket. 'Sixteen by eight to the nearest inch,' he pronounced before relaxing back into his chair. 'I congratulate you, Mr Van Buren. I believe this is indeed what you claim it to be. A beautiful piece.' He leaned forward again and repeated the procedure with the drawing of the Virgin Mary. 'This second work is a little smaller, but equally exquisite.' He frowned and thought for a moment. 'I'm pretty convinced of their origin, but as belt and braces I would like to confirm my opinion with colleagues. I wonder, Mr Van Buren, whether you'd be prepared to leave the drawings with me for a day or two?'

Van Buren shifted uncomfortably in his seat. 'Is that really necessary? I'm not comfortable at the idea of the pieces leaving my possession.'

'Remember, Mr Van Buren,' Ramsey chipped in, 'you are talking here to Britain's pre-eminent art expert. A former Keeper of the Royal Collection. I'm sure the drawings will be perfectly safe with him for the short period he requires.'

'You forget I have other parties interested in seeing the works.'

'I assure you we'll be as quick as we can,' said Clark.

'You'll provide a receipt?'

'Of course. Now, how about provenance? Can you tell us a little more on that subject? I have done some research but not found much. As we discussed, the drawings were last seen in the possession of the Horath family nearly a century ago. Then they disappeared. Have you any idea of where they were before you acquired them?'

'I'm afraid I don't. I bought them from a small art shop in The Hague. The owner said he'd got them in a country house clearance. He was not aware of what he had. I know a lot about Renaissance art, and I felt reasonably certain they were da Vincis. I acquired them for not much, then took them to an expert to see if I was right.'

'Which expert?'

'Visser of the Rijksmuseum.'

'I know him. Is he still in place?'

'Unfortunately not. I understand he fell foul of the Nazis soon after the invasion. He complained too loudly about the liberties some soldiers took with his daughter. He was shot.'

'Goodness! I'm very sorry to hear that.'

'That's all by the by, Sir Kenneth. Let us get to the point. I wish to sell the drawings. If you agree they are genuine and Mr Vermeulen's friend wants them, the issue becomes simply one of price.'

'No doubt you have a price in mind?' asked Vermeulen.

Van Buren turned to him and switched from English to Dutch. 'Where are you from in Holland, *mijnheer*?'

'Rotterdam.'

'Were you an exile before the war, or did the Nazis chase you out?'

'I have lived abroad for many years.'

'In Portugal?'

'Yes.'

Van Buren nodded. 'These gentlemen have not named the man you represent yet, but I believe I know who it is. A great collector with the deepest of pockets. Some would say that with such a prospective purchaser, I could name my price.'

82

'English, please, gentlemen,' muttered Clark irritably.

Van Buren laughed, then complied. 'We were talking about Mr Vermeulen's friend in Portugal. His name is Gulbenkian, I believe.'

Vermeulen nodded.

'As regards price, I am happy to go by what poor old Visser told me. He said I would be a fool to sell the St Paul's drawing for less than three hundred and fifty thousand pounds sterling, and the Virgin Mary for less than three hundred. Six hundred and fifty thousand in total. I'm amenable to payment in certain other currencies. In dollars that would be around two point six million.'

His words were met by shocked silence. Clark and Ramsey waited for Vermeulen's response. Eventually he smiled. 'Naturally, *mijnheer*, I reject your suggestion. Six hundred and fifty thousand would stretch credulity in peacetime. It is a fantasy figure in the current market.'

Van Buren smiled in turn. 'That's the price, Mr Vermeulen. Take it or leave it. There are other interested parties. If no buyer meets my expectations, I'll sit back and wait until happier times. I suggest you consult your man in Lisbon. Meanwhile, if I could just have that receipt?'

Since his arrival in England, Nathan Katz had developed a keen interest in English history. As he turned into Cheyne Walk, he remembered reading somewhere that Henry VIII had once had a manor house somewhere nearby. He'd have liked to explore and see if anything remained of it, but he had more important things to do. On reaching the address Martin Ramsey had given him, he took a deep breath before firmly rapping on the door. A plump middle-aged woman in an apron appeared.

'Is Mr Van Buren in?'

'I'm sorry, he's not.'

Katz looked at his watch. It was just past five. 'Any idea when he'll be back?'

'No, sir. He had a number of business engagements and a lunch and left no instructions as to his return.' The housekeeper spoke in what he recognised as a Scottish accent. 'Would you like to leave a message?'

'No. Thank you. Good day.' The door closed and he crossed over the road towards the river. He'd left work early on the premise of having a dental appointment and wasn't expected back, so he could wait as long as he liked for Van Buren's return. Around twenty minutes later, he saw a solid-looking greying man approach then enter Van Buren's house. He quickly hurried back over the road and banged on the door again. The housekeeper acknowledged her employer's presence but said he'd given instructions that he didn't want to be disturbed.

Katz persisted. 'Tell Mr Van Buren that it concerns the da Vincis. He may want to speak to me then.'

Five minutes later, Katz found himself waiting in Van Buren's study, sipping a cup of tea the housekeeper had kindly provided. He was trying to maintain a calm demeanour, but his heart was thumping hard.

'Mr Katz?' Van Buren appeared wearing a blue silk dressing gown. 'Please forgive my attire, but I was just about to bathe when told of your call. It's been a long day and it would have been preferable if you'd telephoned to arrange an appointment. However, you're here now and I can give you a few minutes.'

'My apologies. I had your address but not your telephone number.'

'I see.' Van Buren sat down and examined his visitor. 'How can I help you? Mrs Macdonald mentioned something about da Vinci?'

Katz spoke in a rush. 'You're trying to sell some da Vinci drawings. One of St Paul, the other of the Virgin Mary. They are not yours to sell. The Nazis stole them from my father. They are rightfully my family's.'

Van Buren's face darkened, but he made no reply.

'Well, sir?'

He got slowly to his feet and walked over to a drinks cabinet, where he poured two straight Scotches. He handed one to Katz. 'You look like you could do with this.' He held up his own glass. It glittered in the late-afternoon sunlight beaming through the window. 'A fine oak eighteen-year old Macallan. Hard to beat. Expensive, of course, but which of the good things in life are not?'

'I can think of many.'

Van Buren laughed. 'I'm sure you can, Mr Katz. May I ask what you do for a living?'

'I work for my uncle's bank in the City.'

'You have done well then, for a Jewish refugee from the Reich. That's what you are, I take it?'

'It is.'

Van Buren looked at him thoughtfully. 'So. My da Vincis. I know nothing about your family and its problems, Mr Katz. I acquired the works to which you refer legally and in good faith from a Dutch vendor in Holland before the war. The transaction was properly documented and I know I shall have no problem proving proper title in the event of a sale. That is all I can or need to say. I am sorry if your family suffered at the hands of the Nazis. As it happens, I am likewise a victim. They also stole from me. Millions of guilders down the drain. I managed to bring just a few of my possessions with me to England, the da Vinci drawings among them.'

'Clearly your Dutch vendor must have bought them from the Nazis.'

'I can't stop you speculating, but the fact is, the drawings are mine. You will not be able to prove otherwise.

'Surely you asked your vendor where he got them?'

'I did, and he did not give me the answer you would like.' Van Buren sighed. 'You know, Mr Katz, I really don't appreciate being cross-examined like this in my own house. You have said your piece and I have responded. Now drink up, please. I'm going to have that bath.'

'May I see the drawings?'

'You may not. They are not on the premises.' Van Buren

finished off his drink in one gulp and got up. 'Mrs Macdonald will show you out.'

As Van Buren made for the door, Katz grasped hold of his arm. 'Even if you know nothing of how the drawings came to be in Holland, surely you wouldn't wish to benefit from such a vile crime. My parents didn't just lose their possessions. They went to the camps where they've most likely perished. Have you no shame?'

Van Buren stared at him icily, then removed the young man's hand from his arm and left the room.

Billy Hill was enjoying an early-evening drink with some cronies in the office above the West End club he used as his principal base. He was laughing at a dirty joke someone had told when he saw Edward Micallef hovering at the door. 'Well, well, if it isn't Maltese Edward,' he shouted. 'Come on in, mate. Where've you been keeping yourself?'

Jimmy Miles, a red-headed tank of a man seldom to be found far from Hill's side, sniggered. 'Probably been busy poking that posh bit of stuff of his. Elizabeth something, isn't it?'

Micallef replied coldly. 'That's her name, but no, that's not where I've been.'

'Got bored with her already, eh?'asked Hill.

'Not yet, no. I've been a bit busy selling some cars.'

'Oh? Good for you. Someone pour the lad a drink. Beer or spirits, Teddy? I'm on the whisky.'

'Beer'll do fine, thanks.'

A pint of bitter found its way into his hands.

'I heard you wanted to see me, Billy?'

'That's right, son.' Hill was a dapper looking man in his early thirties. His jolly, bright-eyed countenance seemed out of place on a violent gangster. 'Jimmy here's got a job on the go. He's been casing a jewellery shop in Mayfair. There's someone on the inside. Should be a good earner. I suggested you join the team.'

From the look of Miles, Micallef guessed he wasn't over-enthused by the suggestion. 'Of course, Billy. Happy to help. When's the blag?'

Hill laughed. 'Getting the jargon down nicely, aren't you, Teddy?'

'Always looking to improve myself.'

Micallef sipped some of his beer. It was far from his favourite drink, but he thought it'd help him fit in with Hill's crew better.

'Job's set for ten days' time. We have to wait for Jimmy's insider to return from the seaside.'

'Aren't all the beaches closed for the duration?'

'Figure of speech, son. He's gone on holiday somewhere.'

Miles sighed wistfully. 'All the holiday camps are closed too. Government's taken most of 'em over. Me and Peggy used to go to Butlin's in Skegness before the war. Great fun it was.'

'All right, all right,' said Hill. 'That's enough memory lane.' He lit a cigar, then waved a hand at Miles. 'Take everyone downstairs for a mo', Jimmy. I'd like a private word with young Teddy here.'

Miles grudgingly acquiesced and the two men were soon on their own. Hill leaned close.

'There's probably some other jobs coming up the pipeline for you,' he said. 'I'll fill you in shortly. Meanwhile, I asked you to keep your eye open for opportunities. Anything doing?'

'Well, yes, as a matter of fact, I might have something.'

'Let's hear it then.'

'It's Elizabeth.'

'Your bit of fluff? What about her?'

'Her father's a Dutch businessman who's had a few ups and downs recently. Lost his business to the Nazis but he's still worth a few bob, according to his daughter. More specifically, she told me the other day that he'd managed to bring some valuable pieces of art with him from Holland.'

'He did, did he? Where's he keep them?'

'Elizabeth says he has a few in his house in Cheyne Walk.'

'Cheyne Walk, eh. A fancy address.' Hill took a few puffs on his cigar. 'As it happens, I've knocked off a little art in my time and done quite well out of it. That said, most of the high-end fences have gone to ground. Are we talking pictures?'

'Mostly. Some very valuable, apparently. Might be some other worthwhile stuff.'

Hill considered for a moment, then nodded. 'All right. Sounds worth a punt. You don't have any problems knocking off your girlfriend's old man's place?'

'She's a nice girl, Billy, but business is business.'

Hill grinned. 'Spoken like a man after my own heart. Give me a little more detail.'

'Father's name is Leon Van Buren. He's a widower. Has a housekeeper but she doesn't live in. There's a lot of knick-knacks in the house, along with old prints and portraits. All probably worth a few bob. The really valuable stuff's not on show, Elizabeth says. She also mentioned that ever since the Germans froze his bank accounts in Holland, her father's not comfortable with leaving funds in banks. Likes to have a bit of cash around.'

'Sounds good.' Hill blew a stream of cigar smoke up to the ceiling. 'Is there a safe?'

'Behind one of the paintings on the wall in the drawing room. Elizabeth mentioned it.'

'She's a very helpful girl, I must say. You'll need one of my best men. You're not a safe-cracker, are you?'

'My dad did a bit in his time.'

'That's fine and dandy, but we can hardly ship him over from Malta for the job. I've got a man in mind. I'll put you in touch and you can work out a detailed plan with him.'

'Right you are, Billy.'

Hill contemplated his whisky thoughtfully. 'Going back to the subject of art, there's one fence I know for certain's still in business. He shifted some quality paintings for me a few years ago.

Course, if you're aiming to nick something like the *Mona Lisa*, he might find flogging that a little challenging.'

'Funny you should mention the *Mona Lisa*, Billy. Van Buren's better pieces include some stuff by da Vinci. Or so Elizabeth says.'

Hill almost choked on his drink. 'Christ, Teddy. Are you serious?'

'Some drawings apparently.'

'He keeps them in the house?'

'So she says.'

'Well, that would be the dog's bollocks if we got hold of something like that. Hard to fence, as I said, but still . . .'

'So the job has your blessing?'

'I'll talk to Jimmy and some of the others, but yeah, I think so.'

'Thanks, Billy. Am I all right to go now?'

'Yeah, hop it, son.' Micallef got up. 'And Teddy . . .'

'Yes, Billy.'

'If you don't like beer, don't drink it. It's no skin off my nose, you know.'

Lisbon

Calouste Gulbenkian was cradling a cup of hot milk in bed and listening to a pretty voice singing fado on the radio when his secretary knocked on the door.

'I know it's late, and I'm sorry to disturb you, sir, but I thought you'd like to see these.' She had some cables in her hand. 'There are two from New York, one from Chicago, one from Brazil and two from London.'

Gulbenkian set down his drink with an irritated grunt. 'I'll look at the British ones. The rest can wait until tomorrow.'

The first was from Kenneth Clark. *NOW SEEN DV ITEMS STOP BELIEVE GENUINE BUT CHECKING WITH*

89

COLLEAGUES STOP AIMING AT DEFINITIVE JUDGEMENT BY THURSDAY STOP THINK SELLER KEEN BUT WILL STICK FOR FAIR PRICE STOP CLARK.

The second was from Vermeulen. *DRAWINGS LOOK REAL THING STOP ASKING PRICE STEEP STOP TWO POINT SIX USD STOP WE CAN DO BETTER STOP VERMEULEN.*

'Of course we can do better,' Gulbenkian muttered to himself. But the price was not so silly. Another da Vinci drawing had sold at Sotheby's for a million and a quarter dollars a few months before the war. An opportunity missed.

There were three questions he had to answer. If the drawings were genuine, did he want them? The answer? Yes, of course. The second question was the price, and the third, how to pay. After a little thought, he decided he'd authorise Vermeulen to go to a million and a half. In the long run, such a price would prove to be a bargain. As regarded payment, he would have to be careful given his present liquidity restraints. He resolved to sleep on the matter.

After Isabelle had gone and he'd turned out the lights, a thought came to him. He remembered an old friend who owed him a favour. Someone in London. He made a mental note to refer Vermeulen to him in the morning.

Chapter Nine

Tuesday had been a long and draining day for Hermann Goering. He had been working intensively with his senior officers on the Luftwaffe's support strategy for the march on Stalingrad. It had been a late night, but he was up early. With his well-known fondness for the good life, he'd acquired a reputation for laziness, but this was quite undeserved. He worked hard when he worked and he played hard when he played. His bravery had never been in question, nor had his loyalty to the Führer. In addition to his love of fine food and drink, beautiful women and hunting in the forests of his estate, Goering was mad on art. Partly at his direction, the Nazis had undertaken a systematic wide-scale looting of art treasures following their invasions and occupations of France, Belgium, Holland, Denmark, Poland and the other European countries now subject to German domination. The field marshal had made sure he was at the head of the line, even before Hitler, when it came to the housing of the choicest masterpieces. To his delight, he'd taken possession of many of the works on his own personal hit list, but the ones that had evaded him continued to rankle. A Rembrandt here, a Raphael there, a Titian, a Canaletto. He was thinking about some of those when his wife Emmy joined him at the breakfast table. He acknowledged her with a nod, then gazed out at the immaculate lawns running from the house to the tree-line over half a mile away. He turned back to his newspaper with a sigh. There he saw something that improved his mood. He smiled.

'Something amusing, dear?' asked Emmy.

'I don't know that "amusing" is the right word. I recognised a name in a list of prominent casualties on the Eastern Front.'

She frowned. 'Oh? Who?'

'Fellow called Spitzen. Colonel Ferdinand Spitzen. You may recall he dined with us once or twice a while back.'

'Yes, I do. A dashing young man. He's dead?'

'Yes, strafed in a Russian fighter attack.'

'Oh dear.' Frau Goering, a statuesque former actress who loved her food almost as much as she loved her husband, bit greedily into a large piece of toast. 'But why does news of his death make you smile?'

'The man did me a disservice. I'm pleased that he's now paid the penalty.'

'What kind of a disservice?'

'He deprived me of a couple of artistic masterpieces.'

Frau Goering looked askance. 'Oh Hermann, really. As if we don't have enough artistic masterpieces already.'

'The items in question were two priceless da Vinci drawings.'

'And how did this fellow Spitzen deprive you of them?'

'I instructed him to keep an eye out for me in Austria after the Anschluss. I was aware of several wonderful collections in the hands of Jews. One had been put together by a banker called Katz. When we started arresting people, Spitzen was responsible for pulling him in. He said he'd managed to track down a good part of his collection, but not all. He claimed the da Vinci drawings were among those missing.'

'You think he wasn't telling the truth?'

'I know he wasn't. After the invasion of Holland, one of my officers found out that the drawings had ended up in the hands of a Dutch businessman called Van Buren. There was evidence that Spitzen knew him. Unfortunately, Van Buren escaped to England and it would seem he took the drawings with him. There was no sign of them in the possessions he left behind.'

'Surely you confronted Spitzen about this?'

'I did. He denied selling them.'

'So what did you do?'

'I had him posted to the Eastern Front.' Goering allowed himself another smile. 'And now he's dead.'

Emmy Goering rose and stood behind her husband, wrapping her arms around his shoulders. 'No one should ever cross my Hermann.' She pecked his cheek. 'Never mind, my darling, you'll be able to get hold of these drawings when we take control of England.'

Goering grasped his wife's hand. 'Perhaps there is something I can do before that. My godson controls one of our undercover agents in England. I could ask him to get his man to take a look at Van Buren. Maybe . . .' He stopped and got to his feet. 'But enough of that for now. I must get back to work. The Battle of Stalingrad is imminent. I'll see you later, my dear.'

'Yes. Have a good day, Hermann. Heil Hitler!'

London

It looked like Merlin was going to have a quiet day at the Yard. Johnson was in charge of wrapping up the Canadian case. The two men had made full confessions and the Canadian military authorities were now investigating other soldiers for assisting in the theft of weapons. The restaurant owner, François Tavernier, had been charged as an accomplice and was under lock and key with his friends in Wormwood Scrubs. Preparations for the Hammersmith fraud trial had been completed and all was ready for trial. Bridges was out helping out with the cigarette robbery investigation, and Cole and Robinson were busy attending to duties elsewhere. For now, Merlin's cupboard was unusually bare.

He had thought of arranging to meet up with a friend for a pub lunch. Unfortunately, the friend in question wasn't available. Jack Stewart was a station commander in the Auxiliary Fire Service, and Merlin was told when he called that he had just hurried out to investigate an unexploded German bomb in Pimlico. He'd probably be away for quite a while. Merlin decided to get out of the office anyway. It was another fine day, and he would pick up a sandwich and go to St James's Park.

Now, at just after 1.30, he was sitting on a shaded bench watching two ducks squabbling over the small piece of Spam he'd thrown into the pond. He was thinking it was time to head back to the office when he became aware of someone standing close behind him.

'Room for two on there?'

He turned to find a very large man smiling down at him, brown paper bag in hand.

'Things must be quiet at the Yard if you've time to feed the ducks, Frank.'

'Ditto at MI5 too, I presume. How the devil are you, Harold?' Merlin tried to get to his feet to shake hands, but Harold Swanton pushed him back down.

'No need for ceremony, Frank. Just budge up, will you.'

Swanton, a sturdy, heavy-boned man in his mid-fifties, settled himself on the bench. He had a head of thick greying hair, a square chin, a bulbous nose and a neat little moustache.

'I was meant to be meeting some Whitehall grandees, but the lunch was cancelled at the last minute. Like you, I suppose, I looked out of the window, saw the sun was shining and thought I'd have my lunch in the park.' Swanton opened his paper bag and took out a cheese roll.

Harold Swanton had been a chief inspector at the Yard when Merlin had been a young sergeant. In 1936, he'd been transferred to Special Branch, and then, in 1938, to MI5. He took a large bite out of his roll. 'It's been a while, Frank.'

'A year at least, I think.'

'That long, eh? How time flies. The unpleasantness with De Gaulle's Free French, wasn't it? A lot of water's passed under the bridge since then.' Swanton sat up and slapped his forehead. 'But what am I thinking of? I should be offering you my congratulations, shouldn't I? On becoming a father, I mean. Well done, Frank!'

'Thanks, Harold.'

'A little boy, someone told me. Mother and son well?'

'In the pink. The boy's name is Harry. Not in your honour, I'm afraid, but after my father.'

Swanton chuckled. 'No offence taken. And how's Mrs Merlin coping with motherhood?'

'Pretty well. We've got some help and she's managed to get a part-time job as an interpreter at the Polish legation. Knowing how you like to keep tabs on everyone, I'm surprised you don't already know.'

'I think I need to shake up my sources.' To the disappointment of the gathering ducks, Swanton finished his roll without leaving a single crumb. 'So what's new, Chief Inspector?'

Merlin proceeded to give him a quick summary of recent cases. When he'd finished, Swanton nodded sagely. 'You've got a well-oiled machine working for you at the Yard and no mistake.' He wiped his mouth with a handkerchief. 'Fancy a cuppa at that kiosk on the other side of the pond?'

'Sounds good.'

The two men strolled over and bought their drinks, then found an empty bit of grass. Swanton groaned as he lowered himself to the ground. 'I'm afraid these old joints have seen better days. It's a good thing my job is mostly sedentary these days. Are you keeping fit?'

'I walk as much as I can. It's the only exercise I have time for.'

'I remember watching you play football for the Met team when you were a youngster. A very elegant and balanced player you were.'

'Kind of you to say so. Perhaps young Harry will take to the game when he's older.'

'You'd like that, I'm sure.' Swanton became thoughtful. 'You know, Frank, when your father cropped up in conversation earlier, something else came to mind. He anglicised the family surname, didn't he, as well as all the Christian names?'

'He did.'

'And the original surname was . . . Merino, wasn't it?'

'Yes.'

'Is that a common surname in Spain?'

Merlin shrugged. 'He used to say it had something to do with sheep. There are a lot of sheep in Spain, so maybe it is common.'

'Hmm.' Swanton lumbered to his feet.

'Why does my surname interest you, Harold?' asked Merlin as he followed suit.

'Well, it's just that we were alerted to a person of interest travelling from Portugal under false papers in the name of Tomas Barboza, but his real name we know to be Merino.' Swanton brushed some grass from his trousers. 'But as you say, it's probably a very common name.'

'What's his first name?'

'Pablo.'

'What age?'

'Early twenties. Twenty-two or three, I think.'

Merlin frowned. 'As it happens, I do have a relative that name and age.'

'You do? Well . . . look, have you time to come back to my office to look at our admittedly thin file'

'I'd be happy to, but you must realise I only ever met the boy once, when he was a kid.'

'Come anyway. You never know.'

'All right. I did get a letter from my sister mentioning that

96

Pablo might be in London soon. I do hope the boy's not in any trouble.'

After a disturbing breakfast meeting at the Reform Club, Vermeulen made his way straight to the City, his destination the offices of Warwick Petroleum, a British oil services company in which Calouste Gulbenkian had a controlling interest.

He was shown into the office of Cedric Calvert, the company's managing director. The two men eyed each other warily. They had never really got on. At Gulbenkian's instruction, Vermeulen was on Calvert's payroll as a consultant. Calvert clearly found it irritating to have the Dutchman on his books but not subject to his authority.

Calvert, a tall, lean man whom Vermeulen found stiff and over-bearing, had a comfortable office overlooking the courtyard of St Paul's Cathedral. Thanks to the Luftwaffe, the view was more expansive than it had been on Vermeulen's first visit two years before.

'I am very busy this morning, Vermeulen. The accounts department is cutting a cheque for you as we speak. Is there anything else you require?'

'I thought you'd be interested in how Mr Gulbenkian is keeping?'

Calvert smiled awkwardly. 'Why yes, of course. How is the old gentleman?'

'Very well, though I don't know that he'd be particularly pleased to be referred to in that way.'

Another awkward smile. 'I'm sorry, but he is in his seventies, isn't he?'

'He is, but his intellectual faculties remain at their peak. He has been perusing your latest accounts keenly and has concerns about profitability. Things seem to have been tailing off since the beginning of the year. He found the comments you made to accompany the figures rather unilluminating. Have you more I can pass on?'

97

Calvert flicked a speck of dirt from his trousers and pursed his lips. 'I don't know that I do. Mr Gulbenkian knows that the war continues to have a negative impact on our specialised areas. It is in fact quite an achievement that we remain profitable.'

'What prospects for improvement do you see?'

'None, I'm afraid. Not in the short term, at least.'

'I have a copy of the accounts with me. Perhaps we could go through them line by line.'

Through gritted teeth, Calvert agreed, and they spent forty minutes doing so.

When they had finished, Vermeulen thanked him. 'I'll pass on your observations to Mr Gulbenkian. As you know, he continues to believe that oil is the key to success in the war. Whoever has best access to it will win. Companies must be quick on their feet to take advantage of the global shifting sands. The Allies currently have sufficiency of oil supplies, Germany and Japan do not. The Axis powers are only able to gain greater access to oil through conquest. Corporate strategy should reflect these facts.'

He put the company accounts back into his briefcase. 'By the way, I presume you heard that terrible story about Transglobal? Quite a mess. Fraud, fiddled accounts, even trading with the enemy, or so I heard.'

Calvert tapped his watch. 'Look, I haven't got time to gossip. You've already had an hour of my time. I have an important meeting shortly. I'm sure your cheque will be awaiting you outside.'

Vermeulen dipped into his briefcase again. 'I'm sorry, but there's one more item we need to discuss.' He set a new file on the desk. 'A very important item.'

'Oh really! This is too much. Whatever it is can be dealt with another day.'

'I'm afraid the contents of this file cannot wait. It concerns you.'

Back on the street, Vermeulen put Calvert out of his mind and concentrated on the next business. There had been no reply as yet to his cable to Gulbenkian, and he had decided to take the bull by the horns and see Van Buren again. He knew Gulbenkian's thought processes well, and guessed that they would be on the same wavelength. It was time for a little softening-up.

When he got to Van Buren's house, the housekeeper showed him immediately to the study, where he found his host at his desk, poring over some papers.

'An unexpected pleasure, Mr Vermeulen. Take a seat. You've been offered refreshment?'

'Yes, but I'm fine, thanks.'

'I see. I presume you wish to discuss the drawings. We seem to have started in English. Shall we continue, or would you prefer Dutch?'

'English will be fine.'

'Very well. I believe the ball is in your court, as they say.'

'Indeed. I thought it might be best to get on with things, as my time here is limited. I have passed on some of my thoughts to Mr Gulbenkian.'

'You have? And is he prepared to pay my price?'

Vermeulen clasped his hands on the desk in front of him. 'Mr Van Buren, you know very well that no one is going to pay two point six million for the drawings in the current environment.'

'The price is a fair one based on comparable recent sales.'

'The last comparable sale was in 1939. Since then, the world has been plunged into a terrible war. A 1939 price is inappropriate in 1942. If you want anything approaching that figure, I suggest you hold on to your drawings until the war is over.'

'Perhaps I'll do that then.'

'Your choice. However, before going down that route, you should hear what I have to say. First of all, you should know that I have taken the trouble to look more closely into your financial situation. I shall not beat about the bush. Your finances appear to be . . . shall we say precarious.'

Van Buren's face reddened. 'Who the hell do you think you

99

are? I do not take kindly to people rummaging around and digging up half-arsed stories about my affairs. My finances are fine, thank you very much, and I have no intention of selling these drawings for a song.'

'Mr Gulbenkian does not expect to acquire them for a song. He proposes to buy them for a fair price in current market conditions. A price that would incidentally comfortably resolve the financial problems you say you don't have.'

Van Buren calmed a little. He noticed a loose thread in his jacket and took the time to carefully extract it. Then he looked up at Vermeulen. 'What price, pray, does Mr Gulbenkian consider to be fair in current market conditions?'

'I can't say yet. I need to consult further with him before naming a price. The purpose of this meeting was to let you know that Mr Gulbenkian definitely wants the drawings and is prepared to be very reasonable.'

'Very reasonable, eh? I wonder what that means. Please remember that there are other interested parties.'

'Yes, of course. Other interested parties.'

'You said your time in England was limited?'

'I shall be here until early next week. We are due to receive final confirmation of authenticity from Clark and his experts tomorrow. Assuming all is well, I suggest we meet again on Friday. We can talk real figures then.'

Van Buren stroked his chin thoughtfully. 'Very well. Friday it shall be. Meanwhile have you time to talk a little about Holland? Perhaps we have friends in common?'

Pablo Merino sat in a café in a street off the King's Road, contemplating the little he'd learned from his efforts to date. He had located his target's residence and learned a little about his personal life. He'd seen what looked like a secret exchange of information with an unknown party in Richmond. He'd followed his man to various addresses in and around central London without being able to identify the purposes of the visits. He should be further along in his mission and was beginning to worry it would end in failure. Then there was the strange, concerning fact that someone else seemed to be following his man as well. Who the hell was he and which side was he on?

He took out his notebook and read again where his travels had taken him. Fulham, Knightsbridge, Chelsea, Pimlico, Westminster, Kensington, Putney, the City of London, Trafalgar Square and, of course, Richmond. Trafalgar Square was where he'd met his own main contact in London. This man was supposedly the organisation's top man in Britain, but Merino hadn't found him very impressive, nor particularly supportive. The man hadn't appeared to think much of Merino's masters back in Lisbon, nor indeed of the mission with which he'd been entrusted. The only positive had been the man's kind words about the young man's service in Spain. Pablo Merino had seen staunch service as a Republican soldier in the civil war. He'd been wounded twice, and had ended up in prison under sentence of death. Thanks to incompetent warders, and the bravery of a couple of fellow prisoners, he'd managed to escape and, with the help of the underground Republican network, get to Portugal.

During his time in the Republican army, he had been recruited for intelligence work by the Russian GRU. On his arrival in Lisbon with scant funds, he'd made the Russian embassy his first port of call. A junior diplomat had checked him out and received a glowing report back from the GRU. He'd been referred to the local intelligence chief, Major Goncharov, who'd been happy to take him on as an agent. In due course, after settling into the job, his good English had helped to make him first choice for his current mission.

The main reason his London contact had been dismissive of Goncharov and the task he'd set Merino was that he had a feeling the major was motivated by some sort of personal vendetta against the target. Pablo found that hard to credit. He liked Goncharov and believed what his superior told him. If he thought the target might be a triple-crosser, he must have valid reasons for doing so.

A uniformed policeman passed the window. Pablo was reminded that his aunt's brother was a London policeman. A pretty senior one too. He knew his family would expect him to contact Francisco Merino if he had a chance, but that might not be wise while engaged on such a mission. Perhaps he'd do it when the mission was over and he was about to return to Lisbon.

The target suddenly appeared from around the corner, his latest meeting obviously ended. The young man hurried to the counter to pay his bill. When he got out of the café, Frederick Vermeulen was around forty yards ahead of him, walking towards the King's Road. Pablo Merino set off in pursuit.

Micallef had seen the inside of Van Buren's house. Today he wanted to get a good look at the outside. He parked his car on the Royal Hospital Road, strolled along to Cheyne Walk and walked past the house three times. The third time, he continued westward until he reached a narrow alleyway on the right. He turned in. Tall walls bordered the alley, which ended at a small courtyard surrounded by three cottages. Over the wall on the right lay the gardens attached to the row of properties on Cheyne Walk. He made sure no one was around to see him, then hoisted himself up onto the wall. Van Buren's house was the fifth property along. In its garden was a tall tree rising close to the house. It had an abundance of branches. Pleased with this newly acquired knowledge, he jumped down from the wall and made his way back to the Royal Hospital Road.

Instead of getting back into the car, he dropped into a nearby pub, ordered himself a glass of wine and considered his plan. Half an hour later, at seven o'clock, he walked to Elizabeth Van Buren's flat. He'd booked Quaglino's for eight and was looking forward to a good dinner. In the flat, he found packing cases strewn everywhere.

'So you're definitely on the move? Daddy didn't change his mind again?'

Elizabeth was wearing a diaphanous sky-blue evening dress and had a glass of champagne in her hand. 'He's still not come up with the deposit, but the agent said the place is mine so long as the money arrives on Friday. He's promised to send it by then, so I decided to be positive and start getting prepared.' She took the champagne bottle from its ice-bucket and poured Micallef a glass.

The bottle was almost empty. Micallef hated drunkenness in women. It revived unhappy childhood memories. His mother had drunk as a way of coping with the violence of his father. As Elizabeth put an arm around him, he pulled away a little too abruptly. This provoked a pout of annoyance, but before she could say anything, the telephone rang and she hurried to take the call.

When she returned, any irritation with Micallef had been subsumed by her annoyance with her brother. She sat down on a sofa and patted the space beside her. Micallef took his place and reached for her hand. This was not the time to fall out with her.

'That was bloody Robert on about money again.'

'Still hasn't got his magazine money?'

'No.'

'What are his chances?'

'I don't know. Perhaps they've improved a little. Daddy mentioned to me today that he had some deal on the go that might provide a little windfall.'

'That sounds good.' Micallef took care not to appear as interested as he actually was in her family's financial affairs.

'Yes, some rich man in Portugal might be interested in buying those da Vinci pieces I told you about.'

'Really?'

'Daddy thinks he might get a decent chunk of cash. He didn't say how much.'

'Here's to da Vinci and cash, then!' They touched glasses. Micallef realised he might need to get a move on with his plan.

103

'Robert will go bonkers if Daddy does come into some money but still refuses to fund the magazine.'

'Poor Robert.'

'No need to feel sorry for him, Teddy. He's done very well over the years. Daddy's funded his polo and other sporting activities. Paid off his debts. Doctor's bills. Legal bills. You have no idea.' She shook her head. 'Let's not spoil our evening by talking about Robert and his problems.'

'As you wish. If your father's going to be in funds, any idea what he'll spend the money on?'

'Me, I hope, but that will have to be after he's settled his debts, I suppose. I know he owes quite a bit to his litigation lawyers.'

'Litigation lawyers?'

'Haven't I mentioned the litigation before? My mother changed her will before she died. Instead of leaving the bulk of her wealth to Daddy, she left most of it to her sister and brother-in-law. Robert and I received decent bequests too, but we aren't allowed to touch the money until we're twenty-six, unless Daddy dies before then.'

'Did your mother have a large fortune of her own?'

'Not by comparison with Daddy's in Holland, but a tidy sum and some valuable property. There's a family estate in Wiltshire. My aunt and her family live there but it was in Mummy's name. Daddy's challenging the will.'

'Not very nice for your uncle and aunt. On what grounds?'

Elizabeth lit a cigarette 'Mummy was very ill at the end. Daddy claims she wasn't in her right mind when she made the new will.'

'Will your father move house if he comes into the money?'

'Who knows? The Chelsea house is only rented, you know. If he does stay there, I imagine he'd take on a few more staff. We had hordes of staff in Holland. Here there's only Mrs Macdonald.'

'Does she live in?'

'No. She goes home to her husband every night. But why on

earth are you asking about the housekeeper? Let's get going.' Elizabeth jumped to her feet. 'How do I look?'

'Wonderful, darling. Simply wonderful!'

Benjamin and his nephew were as usual the last people in the office. Nathan was scribbling away on a notepad when his uncle appeared at his office door. 'You are looking very tired, Nathan. It's gone eight. I think you should go home now. I'm sure whatever you're working on can wait until tomorrow.'

'I just wanted to finish this page. It's the paper you wanted on the currency movements.'

'Ah. I look forward to reading it, but it can wait a little while. From the hollows under your eyes, I can tell you could do with a good night's sleep.'

The young man sighed and reluctantly tidied up his desk.

'Nothing worrying you, is there, my boy?'

Nathan had yet to tell his uncle about the da Vinci drawings. Benjamin Katz had worries enough of his own with his son away on active service in the Middle East. Suddenly, however, he could keep it to himself no longer. Despite himself, he began to blurt everything out.

When he had finished, his uncle shook his head sadly and sat down. 'Let's discuss this rationally. This is shocking and upsetting news, of course, but we need to be realistic. I doubt there's anything we can do about your discovery. This Van Buren fellow claims he acquired the drawings in good faith. Before the war, Holland had a reputable art market. We have no proof of family ownership. Any documentary evidence your father had relating to the acquisition of these works disappeared long ago into the ashes the Nazis have made of Europe. We are powerless.'

'I have my father's list.'

'A scrap of paper of little or no evidentiary value in a court of law.'

'There are witnesses who can vouch for his ownership of these works. You, me, my aunt. Your word must carry weight as a respected City financier.'

'Respected only insofar as a Jew can be in a Gentile world. And even if we say we know these works were in your father's collection, who's to say he didn't sell them to raise cash before everything turned sour in Vienna?'

'But we know he didn't. He'd have told me.'

Benjamin shrugged. 'You get my point, though.' He could tell Nathan was on the brink of tears and reached out to pat his shoulder. 'I have a friend, a King's Counsel in the Temple. A clever fellow called Aikens. I'll speak to him and tell him the story. See if he has any ideas. All right?'

'Yes. Thank you, Uncle.'

'But don't get your hopes up. The odds are very much in Van Buren's favour, and in any event, litigation is seldom more than an expensive waste of money.'

Merino remembered hearing Aunt Maria talk occasionally about the rowdy London pub next door to her parents' chandlery shop. The noise used to keep her awake, she said, but it had had its good points. The landlord's son had been her first sweetheart.

He had not yet been into a traditional English pub, but he'd decided that tonight was the night. There was a place within yards of his hotel, and after a day of tramping around London, he was weary, thirsty and hungry.

The King's Head was busy, but he managed to find a small table by the window. A young woman was sitting alone at an adjacent table, and he asked her if she'd mind keeping his place while he went to the bar. She smiled sweetly and nodded.

When he got back with a glass of lemonade and a cheese pie, he saw the woman talking to a sharply dressed man with slicked-back hair.

'Got to clear off now, Barbs,' the man was saying 'Got some business to attend to. Here's some money for the taxi. I'll see you out.'

'I've not finished my port and lemon yet.'

'I don't want you hanging around in here on your own. People might get the wrong idea.'

'I won't be long.'

The man glared at her for a moment, then shrugged. 'Suit yourself.' He turned on his heel and left the pub with a couple of other men.

Merino bit into his pie. It was stale and tasteless and he made a face. The woman giggled. 'Food's not much cop here, I'm afraid. You'd be better off with a bag of crisps.'

'I wish you'd told me that before.'

'That's a nice accent you got. Where are you from?'

'Um . . . Portugal.'

'Portugal, eh? My gran was from Portugal. Some people say I have a bit of a Latin look about me.'

Pablo scrutinised the woman properly for the first time. She was right. Short black hair, dark brown eyes, a neat little nose, and bow lips plastered with bright red lipstick. 'I can see that. I'm Tomas, by the way.'

'Barbara. Pleased to meet you, I'm sure. What brings you to London?'

'I'm a salesman. I work for a leather company in Lisbon. I'm over here to see clients.'

'Are you indeed? How's that possible? Isn't Portugal in the war?'

'No, it's neutral, like Spain and Switzerland.'

'I didn't know that. Forgive my ignorance. Lucky you, then. No soldiering to worry about.'

'No.' Pablo sipped his drink. 'Your friend who just left hasn't been called up yet?'

'Vince? No. He's got a medical condition. Him and his mates. They've got a good doctor, if you know what I mean.' She tapped her nose with a finger.

He didn't know what she meant but pretended he did. He noticed she'd emptied her glass. 'Would you like another?'

'Don't mind if I do, thanks. Only if you join me in a proper drink, though.'

'All right. Perhaps I'll try some English beer.'

Archer called it a day just after nine. An hour earlier, the woman who was obviously Vermeulen's mistress had arrived, and he'd decided they were probably having a quiet night in. He hadn't eaten all day and headed for the little Hungarian restaurant in Soho he'd been to once before. He blocked out thoughts of work as he enjoyed his meal, and it was only as he cradled his glass of post-dinner Tokay that he allowed his mind to turn to Frederick Vermeulen.

The Dutchman had certainly had a busy week since his early suspicious foray to Richmond. Various office buildings in the City, the National Gallery, a big house in Ealing, a large riverside house in Chelsea, a block of flats in Fulham, others in Pimlico and Lambeth, more offices in Soho and Kensington. He had covered a lot of ground.

The information provided to Archer on Vermeulen's legitimate business interests had been a little sparse. A variety of commercial activities relating to Anglo–Portuguese trade and the oil industry was all he'd been told by his controllers. All that really mattered to them was his status as an agent. Was he a loyal double agent exploiting his important British contacts and running a small network of other German agents, or had he somehow been turned?

Vermeulen clearly knew a lot of people in London, a fact that was supposedly an important part of his value to the Abwehr. Archer had come to recognise, though, that he would have to be more enterprising about piercing the man's carapace. Hence, the day before, his bribing of the porter at the Fulham apartment block. Through him, he now knew who Vermeulen had visited there: Arthur Davidson, a War Office civil servant. Tomorrow morning he planned to intercept Davidson on his way to work and find out his exact relationship with Vermeulen. Things might go awry, of course. If so, he would simply have to liquidate the official.

His mind now turned to the man he thought of as a companion. The other man trailing Vermeulen. Archer had found out his name and where he was staying. He'd also observed him shaking hands with a burly foreigner in Trafalgar Square. He wasn't sure if Tomas Barboza was aware of him yet, but he thought it was bound to happen. Of course, if he decided Barboza presented a threat to his mission, firm action would become necessary.

USAF 97th Bombardment Group Polebrook

They were almost finished. It was nearly midnight. The three American mechanics in the hangar were attending to one of the newly arrived Flying Fortresses. The hour was late because a base visit from some senior British and American Air Force officers earlier in the day had disrupted their schedule. The mechanics were all of equally low rank, but Airman Virgil Lewis was the longest-serving and had responsibility for signing off the service check-list. He was standing beneath the cockpit ticking off various items for the second time when John Withers appeared from the other side of the fuselage. 'Tyres all done, Virg.'

'Check, Johnny.'

Thirty seconds later, Ramon Sanchez exited the aircraft door and clambered to the ground. 'Been over everything one more time, Virg. All fine.'

Lewis entered a few more ticks in his notebook, then gave a weary sigh. He was not keen on night-time maintenance work. Mistakes were more likely under the dim hangar lights, and anyway people tended to be less focused and attentive later in the day. The aeroplane was due out on a test flight at eight in the morning. He had toyed with the idea of another last check before that, but had ultimately ruled it out. Withers and Sanchez were good, experienced men, and he knew himself to be a competent supervisor. 'All right, guys, let's call it a night,' he said.

'I could murder a beer,' said Sanchez.

'I don't know about beer, but I know where to find some soda,' said Lewis.

Withers hung out his tongue and panted.

'I take it that means you're thirsty too, Johnny?'

'I could drink a barrel of anything at the moment.'

Lewis signed, timed and dated the checklist with a flourish, then led the way to a far corner of the hangar, where a table and chairs were to be found. There were also some filing cabinets. He reached behind them and dragged a cardboard box to the table.

'That your stash, Virg?'

'Nope. It's Miller's, but since he still owes me ten bucks from a poker game four weeks ago, I reckon I'm entitled to take possession.' He lifted three bottles from the box. 'Sorry, boys, it's only English soda. Two lemonade and one ginger beer.'

'I'll take a lemonade. I hate that ginger beer stuff,' said Withers.

'You, Ramon?'

'Anything, I'm so parched.'

'You have the lemonade then. I like ginger beer. There are cookies too.'

The three men settled down to their simple repast.

'All set for tomorrow, are we, Virg?' asked Sanchez.

'Tomorrow? What's happening then?'

'Get this guy.' Withers laughed. 'What's happening tomorrow? We've got our first furlough, that's what's happening. Our first chance to have a look at the great city of London and sample its delights.'

Lewis finished his Rich Tea biscuit, then shrugged. 'It's no big deal. Remember, I've been here longer than you guys. I've done the sightseeing thing.'

'Daytime and night-time, Virg?'

Lewis laughed. 'You know that night-time stuff don't interest me.'

'Hooey!' cried Withers. 'That's a son of a preacher speaking right there, Ramon. Those Southern Baptist churches are strong on hellfire, ain't that so, Virg? Black man so much as looks at a woman, he's headed straight for damnation.'

'Look, you all go ahead tomorrow. I'll have a nice rest here on base and catch up on my reading.'

'Oh come on,Virg,' said Sanchez. 'Don't be such a spoilsport. You can be our guide and show us ignorant country hicks around.'

'Yeah, Virg. Don't duck out.'

Lewis slapped his knee. 'You guys! Oh all right. I suppose I'd better come along and make sure you don't get into trouble. What time does furlough start?'

'Eleven a.m.,' said Withers.

'I'll come with you then, but I'll be heading back here at six. I don't intend to end up sleeping in some London slop-house.' Lewis got to his feet. 'Now drink up. It's hard work being a tourist, and we're going to need some beauty sleep.'

Chapter Ten

The wizened old man wore a frock coat, striped trousers, wing-collared shirt and black tie. A few wisps of black hair struggled to make it across his sizeable cranium. He bowed to Vermeulen. 'Welcome, sir, to the humble offices of Anatolian Enterprises. Please take a seat.'

The office was far from humble. It was large and sumptuously decorated. The Dutchman took his place as directed in a high-backed armchair patterned in a strikingly colourful oriental design. His host seated himself in a smaller, more orthodox leather chair.

'May I offer you some coffee? I'm afraid the English version is mostly undrinkable, but thankfully I have plentiful stores of the Turkish variety.'

'No thank you, Mr Tatar.'

'I see. No refreshment required. You are an important man of business, and wish to get straight down to hard tacks, as the English say. Am I right?'

'Forgive me for appearing rude, but yes. I'm sure we are both busy men.'

Tatar pulled a large fob watch from his waistcoat and checked the time. 'Ten thirty-eight. I have another meeting at eleven thirty. I am yours until then.'

'It was very good of you to see me at such short notice.'

Tatar smiled. 'The name Gulbenkian opens many doors, Mr Vermeulen. You have seen him recently?'

'Only a few days ago, in Lisbon. I pride myself that we have become friends.'

'You are lucky. Calouste Gulbenkian does not make friends easily. Perhaps it is inevitable in a man of such genius.'

Vermeulen shifted in his chair. Beautiful though it was, he found it distinctly uncomfortable. He'd heard tales of Hollywood producers who seated their visitors on chairs lower than their own to establish their superiority. Perhaps Tatar was employing a variation of that practice.

'In his last communication, he spoke of *you* as a friend.'

Tatar nodded thoughtfully. 'We were indeed friends, long ago in another world. Our families knew each other in Istanbul, or Constantinople as it was then. When we came of age we were both sent here for education. In due course, Calouste chose to strike out into the oil business. I stuck to our family's more traditional lines.'

'As you still do?'

'To the best of my ability. The war does not make business easy. Our main activity remains metal trading. That and a few other enterprises serve to put food on the family table.'

Vermeulen looked around at the surrounding opulence. 'Quite a lot of food, I would guess.'

Tatar's shoulders shook with laughter. 'Ha! I like a man with a sense of humour. Now, to business, if you please. Time is moving on.'

'Mr Gulbenkian would like to ask a favour. A financial favour.'

Tatar's bushy eyebrows rose. 'A financial favour? For the richest man in the world? You surprise me.'

'He wishes to make an art purchase from a vendor in this country. The purchase is substantial, and he believes an element of cash would help secure a favourable deal. For various legal reasons, he

113

cannot access his assets in England at present. He has similar difficulties elsewhere.'

Tatar held up his hand. 'Stop, please.' He chuckled. 'You are telling me that Calouste is short of cash?'

'Let's just say he has a temporary liquidity problem.'

Tatar got up and crossed the room to his desk. He reached into a bright red wooden box. 'Cigarette, Mr Vermeulen? Turkish, of course but of the very best quality. I find smoking them helps my thought processes.'

'No thank you.'

'As you wish.' He lit up and returned to his chair. 'So for some reason, Calouste can't touch his money here at present. Why can't he just get a loan from one of the many British banks who have profited from him over the years?'

'As you may be aware, Mr Gulbenkian spent some time in Vichy after leaving Paris, serving as an accredited diplomat to the Vichy government. While this had its advantages at the time, it had disadvantages too. One such unfortunate disadvantage is that he has been designated by the British government as an enemy alien. As you would expect, he has lawyers working diligently to rectify this situation. At present, however, British banks are not allowed to lend to him.'

'I read about that diplomatic appointment. Persia, wasn't it? Sometimes Calouste is too clever for his own good. The appointment may have secured his protection in France, but now it means he's not creditworthy here.' Tatar smiled. 'You have to admit, it is rather amusing.'

Gulbenkian's cable had told Vermeulen that if Tatar seemed unreceptive, he should mention one word to him. He decided to do so. 'Mr Gulbenkian told me I should remind you about Medallion.'

A bright red spot appeared on Tatar's right cheek and he looked away for a moment. He took a long draw on his cigarette and slowly exhaled, filling the room with that sweet Turkish cigarette aroma Vermeulen had always disliked.

114

'I should have known Calouste would rely on more than our friendship in seeking assistance.' He stubbed out the cigarette in the ashtray at his side. 'Medallion was a little venture of mine in which he assisted me. It was more than twenty years ago and some would say I had repaid the debt with various kindnesses over the years.'

Vermeulen shrugged. 'I'm sorry. I know nothing of the detail.'

Tatar sighed. 'How much does he require?'

'A hundred thousand is the figure we have in mind.'

He drew in his breath. 'A lot of money. This is to be a loan?'

'Yes. Mr Gulbenkian would be happy to pay interest of five per cent and a modest arrangement fee.'

'Very generous of him. And what security?'

'He cannot offer security. He said you know he'll be good for it.'

'Term?'

'One year, or whenever his UK assets are unfrozen if earlier.'

Tatar gave the matter a good deal of thought before finally acquiescing. 'Very well. I'll get my solicitors to draft something. Presumably you have power of attorney?'

'I do. Is it possible that the cash could be provided by tomorrow lunchtime?'

'That quickly, eh? I'll ask the lawyers to try and get the paperwork ready by close of business today.' He consulted his watch, then got to his feet. 'And may I ask what exactly my money will help buy?'

'A couple of Renaissance drawings.'

'Drawings, my God! I always knew Calouste was mad.' He smiled to himself. 'You will please leave your telephone number with my secretary. Someone will call you when the loan papers are drafted. And . . . and could you tell Calouste that I would have lent the money purely out of friendship. There was no need to reference ancient deeds.'

'I'll tell him, Mr Tatar.'

★

115

Humphrey Butterfield was a bag of nerves. A skinny, long-legged man, he stared anxiously across the desk at his solicitor. 'Damn it, Wilfred, as I've said many times before, this is quite ridiculous. The idea that Mary was not in her right mind when she signed that will is poppycock. She may have been ill, but her brain was as sharp as ever.'

Butterfield's lawyer, Wilfred North, was the physical opposite of his client. Short, tubby and rosy-cheeked, he was normally relentlessly cheerful. Not today, though. Forty-five minutes with his client had worn him down.

'I know, Humphrey, but saying it over and over again doesn't make your brother-in-law's case go away. He will have found medical experts to support his view, and their opinions will have to be weighed in the balance against those of our own experts. His lawyers have sent me Dutch paperwork suggesting Mary had some kind of nervous breakdown after receiving her cancer diagnosis. Not very helpful, and nor was this week's affidavit from her British GP.' North consulted a document on his desk. 'To quote, "apparent moments of forgetfulness, aphasia" et cetera.'

'The man's an idiot, but forgetfulness is not insanity.'

'I thought the doctor was a good friend of yours?'

'He is, but he's also one of those holier-than-thou fellows who insists on telling things as he sees them. No allowance for nuance.'

'I see.'

'But look, we have several other friends and acquaintances who can vouch for Mary's sanity in her final days.'

'Well you'd better put them in touch with me, and soon.'

Butterfield extracted his legs from under the desk and stretched them out to his side with a little grunt of relief. 'So what exactly does this Dutch paperwork say?'

'Apparently, in May 1939, Van Buren's Dutch doctor, a man called Bakker, referred Mrs Van Buren to a sanatorium in a place called Alkmaar. She spent three weeks there. This report was produced after her departure. The words "nervous breakdown" are used specifically. Symptoms described include depression, severe mood swings, loss of appetite . . . There's plenty there for Leon's lawyers to make a meal of.'

Butterfield started kneading his hands together. 'Dear, dear. She never said anything about this to me or Audrey. What treatment did the sanatorium provide?'

'Psychiatric care, counselling and medication. There were a number of drugs she was meant to continue with after her discharge, but there appears to be no reference to them in her English medical reports. If she didn't keep taking the drugs, your brother-in-law could argue that her mental problems might have got worse. He might also raise the matter of other mental instability in the immediate family. You know of what I speak.'

'I can't imagine he'd sink so low.'

'Oh come, Humphrey, you know how ruthless he is.'

Butterfield sighed. 'Is there any good news you can give me, Wilfred?'

'Well, clearly Leon won't be able to produce any Dutch doctors in court here to attest to their reports. It's possible we may be able to exclude their evidence.'

'That's something.'

North retied the pink ribbon on the case file. 'I know you've rejected the idea of talking to Van Buren, but perhaps you could reconsider. Stay in London overnight and fix a meeting for tomorrow. If there's any chance of an amicable settlement, you must take it. If litigation proceeds, it will be protracted and the costs will be substantial, as I've told you.'

Butterfield looked aghast. 'You don't know what you're asking, Wilfred. The man seems determined to bankrupt me. I really can't bear to speak to him.'

'Be sensible, Humphrey. Swallow your pride and contact him. Some meeting of the ways may still be possible.'

Butterfield looked up at the ceiling and groaned. 'You know how things stand, Wilfred. The estate is losing money, and will lose more if, as seems likely, we have a brigade of soldiers billeted on us. It was because Mary recognised how tough things were that she changed her will, not because of mental derangement. As far as she was aware, despite the disaster in Holland, Leon had kept hold of a significant part of his fortune. It's his own fault really. He never deigned to discuss his finances openly with her. In consequence, she made incorrect assumptions.'

'I know all that, but at least try and have a conversation with him. You never know.'

Butterfield sighed. 'Very well. I'll see if something can be arranged. I bet he won't agree to see me anyway.'

'Just have a go, Humphrey. Just have a go.'

Virgil Lewis knew he'd made a mistake. They'd visited most of the tourist hot-spots: Buckingham Palace, the Houses of Parliament, Trafalgar Square, Piccadilly Circus, St Paul's Cathedral, Tower Bridge, the Tower of London, Covent Garden. There had been no good reason why he couldn't catch the six p.m. train back to High Wycombe. However, parched after walking several miles in the heat, he'd foolishly succumbed to the suggestion of a drink near Piccadilly Circus. One beer had become several, and it was now well past nine.

They were on their third pub, this one in the heart of Soho. John Withers had just returned from the bar with a fresh round.

Virgil took a small sip of his beer, then slammed the glass down. 'All right, guys. That's it. I've had more than enough. I'm going to love you and leave you. I think there are still a couple more trains going back to base, and I'm aiming to be on the first of them.'

'At least finish your beer,' urged Withers.

'No. I'm going, Johnny.'

'I think you'd better hear what we're going to do next, Virg, before you make up your mind. Tell him, Ramon.'

'When you were in the can, Virg, we heard tell of a great club round the corner with naked ladies. Place called the Windmill. Thought it might be worth a visit.'

'Naked ladies? You know that's not my kind of thing.'

'Just come for half an hour. You'll still be able to make the last train. It'll be fun!'

Virgil protested some more, but somehow soon found himself in a crowd of raucous, expectant males waiting for the curtain to rise. When it did, the audience was presented with the spectacle of four buxom young ladies standing stark naked in a mocked-up Roman setting. Two held pots in front of their bosoms, while the other two held wreaths above their heads. Virgil couldn't believe what he was seeing. He sat wide-eyed through three more similar tableaux before he needed to answer a call of nature.

After he'd used the facilities, he paused for a moment in the empty foyer. He suddenly felt ashamed of himself. What would his parents think of him visiting this sleazy joint? He decided to take his opportunity and leave.

As he walked by the pub where they'd been drinking earlier, he heard the call of last orders and realised to his horror that it was too late to catch the last train home. What could he do? He was very drunk, and began to wander aimlessly through the dark streets. At one street corner, he vomited copiously, to the loud disgust of some passers-by. He realised he'd better find a place to lie down. Not long afterwards, he found one. Someone briefly pulled back a black-out curtain, and the flash of light revealed a small garden square over the road. He ran across and climbed over the metal fence. Once in the garden, he tripped over what turned out to be a bench. Exhausted and dizzy, he collapsed onto it. His eyes closed almost immediately.

119

Chapter Eleven

'Anything happening, Sergeant? I could do with something to get my teeth into.'

Bridges was just putting the telephone down at Merlin's desk. 'Better sharpen them then, sir.'

'Oh yes?'

'A body's just turned up in a Soho alley. A man. Looks like he's had his throat cut.'

'We'd better get going then.'

Twenty minutes later, they found themselves back in Soho Square. The alley where the body had been found was only a short distance from the restaurant where they'd arrested the Canadians the week before. Waiting for them were two uniformed policemen and an elderly lady with a small pug dog at her feet.

The senior of the two officers introduced himself as Sergeant Brooks, and the other as Constable Swift. Merlin nodded and looked down at the dog, which immediately started yapping.

'Poor little Charlotta,' said the animal's owner as she lifted it into her arms and stroked its excuse for a nose. 'I'm afraid it was an awful shock for my baby to discover that . . . that poor man.'

'Ah. It was the dog who found him, was it? No doubt it was an awful shock for you too, Mrs . . .?'

'Gordon. Miss Gordon. But no. I've witnessed far worse things.

I was a nurse in the first war. Saw all sorts there. Heads blown off, arms, legs, privates. It takes a lot to shock me.'

'I see. Well, if you don't mind waiting, you can tell us what happened in a moment. Sergeant Bridges and I need a word with these two officers first.' Merlin turned to Brooks. 'Has anything been touched, Sergeant?'

'We went through his pockets, and then the ambulance medics made a relatively quick examination. Otherwise the body is exactly as it was found, on the other side of that large bin on the left.' Brooks nodded down the alley.

'The medics have been and gone?'

'They used the police box round the corner to check in and were sent on another call. They knew the man couldn't be moved until you'd been here. They said they hoped to be back within the hour.'

'What did you find in his pockets?'

'Not much. A few coins and a key. It's a large key and looks like it might be for a hotel room, but there's no name attached.'

'No personal identification?'

'No, sir.'

'You and the constable better go round all the local hotels to see if anyone recognises the key.'

'Sir.'

'But let's take a look at the body first.'

A few yards into the alley was an industrial black drum bin overflowing with rubbish. The stench of rotting food was powerful. The body beside it had been covered with a white sheet by the ambulance-men. Merlin bent down and pulled it back to reveal the face of a strangely peaceful-looking dark-haired young man. There were bruises on his chin and cheeks.

'Looks like he put up a bit of a fight.' Merlin pulled the sheet down further. The cause of death was immediately apparent – a thick bloody gash across the man's neck.

'I'd say whoever did this knew his business, eh, Sergeant?'

'A professional job, you mean, sir?'

'Yes. We'll see what the pathologist says.'

The man's shirt, tie and trousers were spattered with blood. 'Any sign of a jacket, Sergeant Brooks?'

'We've had a good look, but no, sir. The key and coins were in his trouser pockets.'

'Hmm.'

'It's been warm lately,' said Bridges. 'Maybe he didn't bother with a jacket.'

'Maybe. Or perhaps the murderer took the jacket away with him to go through its contents safely away from the scene.'

'You have this down as a robbery, sir?' asked Constable Swift.

'I don't have it down as anything yet, Constable.' Merlin straightened. 'Let's see what the old lady has to say.'

Miss Gordon and her dog were still waiting patiently at the entrance to the alley.

'Could you tell us what happened, please,' Merlin asked.

'I live in a flat on the other side of the square.' The old woman had a deep voice that could easily have been a man's. It seemed out of place in her diminutive frame. 'Every morning after rising, I have a cup of tea then take Charlotta around the square so she can perform her ablutions.'

'At what time did you go out today?'

'Just after half past seven. I always listen to the news on the radio with my tea. That finishes at a quarter past seven and I normally set out then. Today, however, after the news there was a short programme of Paul Robeson songs. I adore that man's voice, so I listened to him before departing. Charlotta made a few stops as normal as we made our way around the square. When we got to where we're standing now, she started pulling on her lead towards the alley. Once upon a time she discovered a juicy piece of steak by the rubbish bin, and the memory lingers, so this is not unusual. I was obliged to follow. She went past the bin, then turned and burrowed behind it. It was then that I saw the body. I immediately bent to check the man's pulse. It was clear that he was dead, so I went to the public telephone box on Dean Street and rang the police. In due course, these two gentlemen arrived.'

'So would you say you found the body at around seven forty-five?'

'Perhaps a little after.'

'The lady's call was logged at seven fifty-six,' said Brooks. 'We got here at eight twenty and Constable Swift called the Yard about twenty minutes later.'

Bridges spoke. 'I know you live on the far side of the square, Miss Gordon, but did you happen to hear any unusual noises during the night? People arguing, shouting, fighting?'

'We are right in the heart of Soho, Sergeant. Revellers roam the area every night. It's seldom that I don't hear some night-time fracas.'

'All right, but did you hear anything last night?' asked Merlin.

Miss Gordon gave the question some thought. 'There was the usual racket at closing time. I went to sleep around eleven fifteen or eleven thirty. It was uncomfortably warm last night and I had the window open. I believe I did hear a few strange shouts just before I dropped off.'

'Did you hear any of the words shouted?'

'I'm afraid not, no.'

'Very well. I think that's all. If anything else occurs to you, here's my card.'

As Miss Gordon headed off, Merlin issued some instructions. 'Go to the police box, Sam, and check that forensics and the police doctor are on their way. And you, Sergeant Brooks, Constable, start canvassing the square to see if anyone else heard or saw anything odd. When you've done that, start checking the hotels.'

Gulbenkian was about to depart on his regular pre-lunch walk when the two cables arrived. The first was from Clark confirming that he and his other experts were in concord about the authenticity of the drawings. The purchase could be proceeded with if a price could be agreed. The second cable was from Vermeulen. The Dutchman believed that a price of $1.6 million, or approximately £400,000, could get the deal over the line. As to terms, he proposed the £100,000 cash down-payment already discussed, with the balance payable in six months. He also confirmed that Tatar had agreed to lend the cash for the down-payment. Gulbenkian found this all very satisfactory. The only potential fly in the ointment was the news in Vermeulen's cable that he might have to return to Lisbon earlier than anticipated. No reason was given for this potential change of plan. Gulbenkian was keen that he stay in London until the deal was finalised. It was always possible that things could go wrong or get delayed, and he didn't want to have to rely on Clark alone. He pressed the button on his desk, and his secretary appeared promptly, pencil and paper in hand.

'Cable to Vermeulen. "PRICE AND TERMS AGREED IF YOU CAN GET STOP WELL DONE STOP VERY CONCERNED THOUGH TO HEAR OF POSSIBILITY EARLY RETURN STOP BE GRATEFUL YOU REMAIN LONDON UNTIL DEAL COMPLETED STOP REGARDS G." Send it off straightaway, Isabelle. Then come back in with a bottle of the Krug 1932. I believe it's time for a celebration.'

'Remember what Dr Soares said, sir.'

'One little glass of champagne won't do me any harm. My London doctor used to say it was good for me, as long as I drank only the best.'

The secretary raised an eyebrow but hurried off to do as she was bid. She soon returned with bottle and glasses and poured out two small measures.

Gulbenkian smiled. 'Come now, my dear. I think my old bones can manage a bit more than that.'

'If you're sure, sir.'

He nodded, and she topped up both glasses.

'*Kenadz*, my dear.'

'*À votre santé*, Monsieur Gulbenkian.'

They drank.

'When do you think you'll be able to take possession of the new purchases?'

'I'm hoping Vermeulen will bring them back with him. If not, I suppose Clark will have to look after them until Vermeulen's next trip.' He turned towards the open French window. 'Madame Gulbenkian will not be enjoying this heat. How is she doing, do you know?'

'All is well, I understand. And remember, sir, there's always a decent breeze out there in Estoril.'

'So there is.' He tugged at his beard and a twinkle came to his eye. 'You know, Isabelle, I think we can skip the walk today. There are other ways of exercising. What say we have another glass and then perhaps a little siesta together?'

'I serve at your pleasure, sir.'

London

Merlin and Bridges got back to the Yard at midday. The forensics team and the police doctor had been a long time coming. Eventually, once the doctor had examined the body, he gave a provisional time of death of between ten p.m. and three a.m. Forensics were still on the job when they'd left, but had yet to discover anything of note. The body had been removed to St Pancras morgue by the returning ambulance men. Additional local officers had also arrived to help Brooks and Swift in their canvassing work.

The telephone rang as soon as they were through the door, and

Bridges hurried to answer it. Merlin went to look out of the window and remained oblivious to the conversation until Bridges waved him over. 'It's the West End station, sir.'

'Is it Sergeant Brooks?'

'No, sir. Another officer. Apparently some of his constables picked up a drunk American airman early this morning. They want advice.'

'We're running an advice bureau now?'

'The officer said he'd called earlier and been put through to the AC by mistake. When he explained his problem, the AC told him to speak to you as the resident expert on the new American rules.'

Merlin groaned. 'Thank you, Mr Gatehouse. What does this fellow want to know?'

'Whether under the new rules he's allowed to just release the arrested man or whether he's obliged to notify the American military police and hand him over.'

'He was arrested for being drunk and disorderly?'

'Seems so. The officer says the man was a bit out of order when they picked him up, so he could charge him with assault as well. They're snowed under, though, and he would be inclined just to let him off with a caution but is concerned not to break any of the new rules.'

Merlin sat down at his desk and pondered for a moment. 'On balance, as it's early days with all this, I think he should err on the side of caution and contact the US military police in Grosvenor Square.'

Bridges passed on the message and was about to put down the phone when Merlin said, 'Hang on, Sam. I'll have a word. What's the officer's name?'

'Inspector Gibbs, sir.'

He took the receiver. 'Inspector Gibbs. Good day to you. As a matter of interest, on what part of your patch was this American chap picked up?' His eyes widened. 'Soho Square, you say? That's very interesting. Around what time? A quarter to five in the morning.' He got to his feet. 'Forget what my sergeant just told you, Inspector. Keep the man in your cells and we'll be with you in a trice.'

Vermeulen picked up the telephone in the hallway of his Knights-bridge house and dialled the offices of Anatolian Enterprises. It took a while, but Mustafa Tatar eventually came on the line. 'Good day to you, Mr Tatar. I was wondering if you'd managed to put the loan together yet?'

'I am not King Midas, you know, Mr Vermeulen, with a crock of gold resting by my side. The amount required is a large one. I am working on it.'

'May I know how much you have at the moment?'

Vermeulen heard Tatar shout in Turkish to someone else in the office. There was a pause before he came back on the line. 'I have approximately seventy-five thousand pounds in hand.'

'Will you have the balance shortly? It's just that I'm planning to see the vendor this afternoon and would like him to have sight of the deposit.'

There was another moment's silence before Tatar replied. 'It will take a while, yet. It occurs to me, Mr Vermeulen, that you might be able to cut a deal for this lesser amount and have no need of the balance.'

'That may be possible, but I would prefer to have the full amount with me before proceeding to final negotiations.'

'Then I'm afraid you'll have to wait.'

Vermeulen had been a little spooked by his earlier conversation with Kenneth Clark. The art expert had told him that as Surveyor of the King's Pictures, he had felt duty-bound to mention the potential sale to His Majesty the King. The Royal Collection contained several da Vinci drawings and the artist was a favourite of the king's. Vermeulen had begun to worry that the king's interest might somehow throw a spanner into the works of his deal. Clark had doubted His Majesty would have serious interest in acquiring the drawings, as it would not look good if the royal family were to splash out a large sum on art while the nation was almost bank-rupted by war. However, Vermeulen could not take anything for granted. There was also the fact that close intelligence contacts had warned him to leave the country quickly for his own safety. He needed to get the deal over the line as soon as possible.

'Look, if you like, Vermeulen, you can come and pick up what I have. If it's short, it's short. The balance will come as soon as I can lay hands on it.'

'When are you available?'

'Come after lunch. Two thirty.'

'I'll be there.'

Nathan Katz had found it impossible to get the da Vinci drawings out of his mind. He knew his work was suffering, and when his uncle called him to his office after lunch, he was fully expecting a reprimand. To make things worse, he had taken his lunch in a pub and drunk two pints of beer. He knew his uncle would be able to tell, and he wasn't wrong.

'Have you been drinking, Nathan?'

He nodded shamefacedly.

'I see. I notice your work has not been up to scratch this week. Why is that?'

'I . . . um . . . I haven't been sleeping well, sir.'

'Is this to do with those damned drawings?'

Nathan looked down and shrugged.

Benjamin Katz sighed. 'Sit down, please. You really must move on from this, you know, Nathan. You must look to the future. You have exciting prospects with me and this firm. You are an exceptionally capable man. The past is the past. Your mother, father and sisters have gone to a better place. You must not become eaten up by the evil that took them.'

'I know you're right, sir. However, I was just wondering whether . . . whether you'd heard from your lawyer friend. The KC you said you were going to consult.'

128

'Yes, I have spoken to Mr Aikens. He was not encouraging.'

'What did he say?'

'What I expected. Insufficient hard evidence to mount a case.'

'My father's list?'

'Not enough. I'm afraid, my boy, you must forget the idea of legal redress.'

'Something might be possible after the war?'

'Perhaps, but we both know that's a long way off.' Benjamin Katz reached into a drawer. 'Now, I have a new project for you to review. Cast your eye over this file for me and give me your views. Since the Luftwaffe have other fish to fry in Russia, and the Blitz seems to be a thing of the past, I have been thinking about the property market. One of our clients is looking for a co-investor in this portfolio of London plots. Some are vacant bomb sites, others are damaged properties.'

'Of course, Uncle,' said Nathan unenthusiastically.

Benjamin Katz sat back and studied his nephew carefully. Then he glanced at the old clock by the door. 'It's getting on. Most people in the City will already have quit their desks and decamped for the weekend. I suggest you do the same. And take Monday off too. Try and get some exercise. You have a bicycle, don't you? Go for a few long rides. I spent many a happy weekend cycling along the river and in Richmond Park when I was younger. Get some good meals inside you, and have some proper sleep. Clear your head and come back a new man on Tuesday. All right?'

'Yes. Thank you.'

'And drink in moderation, Nathan. I don't think it agrees with you.'

'I'll try.'

A dishevelled and severely hung-over Virgil Lewis awaited Merlin and Bridges at the West End Central police station in Savile Row. Before entering the interview room, the two officers spoke to Gibbs, the young inspector who'd called the Yard, and he explained

129

the circumstances in which Lewis had been found. 'A couple of constables discovered him sleeping off a bender on a bench in Soho Square. He had a grey suit jacket draped over him. Inside it they found a wallet containing money and a Portuguese passport.'

'In what name?'

'Tomas Barboza.'

The name gave Merlin a jolt. He looked at the passport, then closed his eyes briefly. There was no doubt the photograph inside was of the dead man. A dead man whom Swanton's file had persuaded him was his nephew.

'One other thing,' said Gibbs. 'One of my sergeants jumped the gun while I was on the phone to you. Without waiting for my orders, he went ahead and contacted the Americans to tell them about Lewis. I'm sorry, but you may only have a short time with him. They said some MPs would be here to pick him up shortly.'

Merlin sighed. 'We'd better get on then.'

They found Lewis scratching his head vigorously, as best he could with hands manacled to the table. The station building was relatively new, but bed-bugs had clearly taken up early occupation. Gibbs made the introductions.

'So, Mr Lewis,'started Merlin.

'Airman Virgil Lewis, Second Class, sir.'

'So Airman Lewis, Second Class. What's the story?'

Lewis stared at Merlin through bloodshot eyes. 'The story? Well, I made a mistake, didn't I? We had some leave and came into town for some sightseeing. I didn't want to stay, but my buddies insisted I join them for a drink at the end of the day. I ain't a drinking man, sir. Alcohol don't agree with me. I got pretty drunk. I wandered away on my own at some point and realised I'd missed the last train home so I found somewhere to crash out. Next thing I know, there's a couple of bobbies manhandling me.'

'The bench was in Soho Square?'

Lewis shrugged. 'If you say so.' He rubbed his eyes. 'Look, what's this all about? If you're going to book me for being drunk and disorderly, go ahead. I'm truly sorry if I cut up rough when I was arrested, but I was in no fit state and didn't know what I was doing. Back home I'd get a night in the slammer and a fine for something like this. I've done the night, so just tell me what I owe and I'll head back to base.'

'Unfortunately, things are a little more complicated than that. When you were found, you had a man's jacket with you.'

'Yeah, sure, my uniform jacket.'

'No. Another one. A grey suit jacket.'

'I don't remember no grey jacket.'

Merlin looked at Gibbs. 'Can you fetch it, please, Inspector?'

Gibbs did as he was asked, then showed the jacket to Lewis.

'Remember it now?' asked Merlin.

'Nope. It clearly ain't mine. It's way too small.'

'You were using it as a blanket. Looks like you stole it.'

Lewis looked indignant. 'No, sir. I ain't no thief. I was brought up not to break the Commandments.'

'How do you explain having it, then?'

He stared down at his cuffed hands. 'Look, my head is pounding like I got the Duke Ellington band inside. You gotta give me a moment to think.'

'All right, but don't take too long.'

A flicker of recognition eventually registered on Lewis's face. 'Yeah . . . I think it's coming back to me. So I dozed off on the bench. Then a while later, I don't know exactly when, some noise woke me.'

'What sort of noise?' asked Bridges.

'Can't rightly say. Whatever it was, I got up, climbed over the fence and went for a wander. It was pitch black, of course, and I couldn't see much. Then I stumbled into something.' Lewis nodded to himself. 'Yeah, that was it. My feet ran into something soft on the pavement. Bent down and found a coat. That coat there, sure to be. I realised I was shivering. Either from the drink or there was a night chill. I must've taken the jacket back with me to

131

the bench to keep warm. Then I went back to sleep.' He nodded to himself again. 'Yeah, that's what happened, I think.'

'You're sure?'

'As sure as a man with a pounding hangover can be, yes.'

Merlin studied Lewis's face carefully. 'The thing is, Airman Lewis, this jacket belonged to a man who was murdered within yards of where you spent the night.'

Lewis's mouth opened wide. 'Whoa there! I ain't got nothing to do with no murder. I found a lost jacket in the street in the middle of the night. I didn't kill no one.'

'You deny involvement in the murder, then?'

'I sure as hell do.' He raised his cuffed hands and brought them down hard on the table. 'My daddy raised me to heed the Bible: "Thou shalt not kill." Whoever murdered that man, it weren't me!'

The door suddenly opened and a uniformed constable appeared. 'Sorry to disturb you, Inspector, but there are some American military police here.'

Gibbs looked at Lewis, who had slumped back into his chair, eyes closed, then at Merlin. 'What should I do, Chief Inspector?'

'I think I should make a call. May I?'

'Of course. Follow me.'

In the inspector's office, Merlin picked up the phone and placed an urgent call to Captain Max Pearce at the American embassy.

Vermeulen had been caught in a sudden heavy summer shower while waiting on the Cheyne Walk doorstep. It was Van Buren himself who opened the door, his housekeeper hovering nearby.

'Why, Mr Vermeulen, you're drenched. Mrs Macdonald, get the gentleman a towel, will you, please?'

She returned quickly and Vermeulen mopped himself down in the hallway. 'That came rather out of the blue. I'd got used to the sun on this trip.'

'Can I interest you in a medicinal Scotch, perhaps?

'That would be nice.'

The two men went into Van Buren's study and were soon comfortably seated by the fireplace, neat whiskies in hand.

'My daughter always nags me to add water to my drink,' Van Buren commented. 'Says it's better for the system, but I prefer it straight.'

'Me too. Are you in good health?'

'Tolerably so for a man in his fifties. You?'

'The same.'

Van Buren leaned back in his chair and crossed his legs. 'So. What news from Portugal?'

'Good, I believe.'

'You should know that one of my other interested parties is keen to see me over the weekend.'

Vermeulen tilted his head to one side and smiled. 'Come now, my friend. Can we not now drop these silly games? We both know that Gulbenkian is the only game in town.'

Van Buren raised an eyebrow, but said nothing.

'That said, as I indicated at our last meeting, Mr Gulbenkian wishes to make a fair offer, and we take you at your word when you say you are not a forced seller.'

'Very well. Let's hear it.'

'This offer will be valid until midnight tonight. If you have not agreed by then, it will lapse and Mr Gulbenkian will turn his attention to other opportunities. The terms are a total payment of four hundred thousand pounds or dollar equivalent, of which seventy-five thousand will be paid up front in cash and the balance sent to an overseas account of your choosing within six months.'

Van Buren's expression remained unaltered. After a moment, he stood up and wandered to the window, where he remained looking out at the river for several minutes. When he eventually returned to his chair, he said, 'The price is some way below what I asked for.'

'You know very well it's a good price. It is almost sixty per cent of the sum you were asking. Only a forty per cent discount for wartime conditions is a very generous one on Mr Gulbenkian's part. You would be, forgive me, a fool not to take it.'

'And why does such a rich man require terms?'

'There is a war on, Mr Van Buren. There are exchange controls everywhere. This is a huge sum of money. You cannot doubt that Mr Gulbenkian will be good for it, but in the current difficult situation, even a man of his wealth needs time to arrange large transfers.'

Van Buren picked up the two almost empty whisky glasses and went to the drinks cabinet to top them up. 'When exactly would I get the cash advance?'

Vermeulen had a pleasant warm feeling. He sensed Van Buren was buckling. 'Whenever the paperwork is complete. Presumably it could all be sorted by Monday?'

'Monday. I see.'

There was a long silence. Vermeulen thought he knew a way to push the deal over the line. He reached down to his briefcase. 'In this case, Leon, I have seventy-five thousand pounds in cash. As a sign of good faith, you can have twenty thousand of it now, in advance of completion, if you accept the offer.' He took out a thick bundle of crisp notes and held them up.

Van Buren couldn't help licking his lips.

'Is it a deal, Leon?'

Another long silence. Then Van Buren took a large gulp of whisky and nodded. 'It is.'

Sergeant Brooks had left a message at the Yard to say Pablo Merino's hotel had been identified. Bridges turned on his heel and went back out to join him there. The police doctor's preliminary report was sitting on Merlin's desk. He read it carefully and realised it had nothing new to tell him. He popped a mint into his mouth and thought sadly back to his one and only meeting with Pablo in Spain before the war. He remembered a bright, cheerful lad who seemed eager to please.

Momentarily, the balmy August weather had abated, and the afternoon was overcast and cool. He went to close the window and looked out onto a stream of military vehicles passing over Westminster Bridge. Mostly American, so far as he could tell.

The telephone call with Max Pearce had not gone well. He'd tried to be conciliatory, and put the initial unpleasant encounter with the captain out of his mind. The Americans clearly had the right to take Lewis into their custody under the new rules, but in the particular circumstances, he requested he at least be allowed to complete his preliminary interrogation of the suspect. Pearce's response had been blunt. 'You can butt out now, Chief Inspector. The man is ours to hold and the case is ours to investigate. All I need from you is a summary of your investigation so far.' This Merlin had unhappily provided.

Back at his desk, he reran the Lewis interview in his mind. For some reason he felt very strongly that the man had been telling the truth. Over his many years as a policeman, he'd developed a fairly reliable sense of when people were lying. Eye movements, facial expressions, physical tics all generally told a story. In Lewis's case, Merlin had noticed none of the usual signals. It was nothing more than intuition, of course, and his intuition was not infallible. Perhaps his new awareness of American prejudice against black soldiers had provoked unjustified sympathy for the man? Still, for whatever reason, he couldn't see him as a violent murderer.

A while later, Bridges came on the phone. 'Been speaking to the lady on hotel reception. The young man checked in with his Portuguese passport a week ago today. She says he was pleasant, polite. She was quite upset when I told her he was dead. I've made a quick preliminary search of the room. I found some business cards that had him as a sales representative of the Oporto Fine Leather Company. Also some leather samples. Quite nice stuff as it happens. And three language dictionaries.'

'What languages?'

'Portuguese to Spanish. Spanish to English. Then surprisingly, Russian to English.'

'Hmm. Anything else?'

'Not at present. Brooks and I are waiting for forensics to come and do the full works. I'll talk to them before coming back to the Yard.'

Not long after Merlin had put the phone down, Inspector Johnson appeared.

'Take a seat, Peter. You've heard the latest?'

'About the Soho knifing? Yes.'

'Did you hear that the victim was a distant relative of mine?'

'Very sorry, sir. Anything you want me to do?'

'Yes. You remember the number for MI5 in St James's?'

'By heart, sir.' Johnson had been seconded to MI5 for a while the previous year to help with the investigation of Rudolf Hess's strange flight to Britain in May 1941.

Merlin pointed at the telephone. 'Dial them direct for me, will you, please. Ask for Harold Swanton. He'll want to know about our victim.'

Van Buren had drunk some more whisky after Vermeulen's departure and had been moved to organise a little celebration of his good news. He'd sent Mrs Macdonald out to the shops for food and drink, then made two calls, one to Elizabeth and one to Robert. Both were otherwise engaged for the evening, but he'd insisted they cancel and join him for a family supper. In the circumstances, he'd had to agree to their bringing their respective partners.

His guests all arrived promptly as requested at half past six. Van Buren met them in the drawing room, chilling bottles of Pol Roger and glasses by his side.

'There you all are.' He warmly embraced his daughter and son and gave perfunctory greetings to Micallef and Caroline Mitchum. 'Mrs Macdonald, will you please do the honours?'

The housekeeper poured the champagne.

'Everyone got a drink? Yes? Good. Well, pip-pip, as my dear wife used to say. Here's to it!'

The four young people gave slightly subdued responses, then sipped their champagne.

Van Buren propped a hand on the grand piano, which had a central position in the room, and beamed. 'I'm very sorry about the short notice and the disruption to your plans. It's just that something very wonderful has happened and . . .' he paused to look at Elizabeth and Robert, 'like the good father I am, I wanted to share the news straight away with my children.'

Elizabeth responded a little irritably. 'That's all marvellous, Daddy, but I was so looking forward to hearing Jessie Matthews singing "Whip-Poor-Will" in the flesh. It's one of my favourite songs.'

'Don't worry, my darling. I'll get you tickets for another night.'

'How can you bear that rubbish, Lizzie? It's dreadful,' sneered Robert.

Elizabeth glared at her brother. 'We're not all snobbish high-brow culture fiends like you.'

'What sort of music do you like, Robert?' asked Micallef, in an attempt to lower the temperature.

'I'm partial to German music, actually. Not so much Beethoven and Bach, but more modern composers like Schoenberg.'

'I see.' Micallef did not recognise the name and hoped for a change of subject. He was nervous, his adrenaline running high. He hoped it didn't show. He'd only had a short time after being told of Van Buren's invitation to set things up. Luckily Billy Hill had been available to give the go-ahead, and Jake Penny, the crack safebreaker Hill had picked for the job, was in town and had been ready to act at short notice. He'd agreed to be in place in the back alley from 9.

Van Buren allowed a little more champagne to be drunk before banging the piano top and calling for silence. 'So, everyone, the news is that I have reached agreement for the sale of my da Vinci drawings.'

137

'Bravo, Father!' Robert exclaimed.

'Marvellous news, Daddy,' said Elizabeth before getting up on her toes and kissing her father on the cheek. Micallef smiled, while Caroline Mitchum looked bemused.

'Are you getting a good price?' asked Robert eagerly.

'Not bad. I'd rather not go into detail at this point.'

'I should think there'll be enough to get the magazine off the ground with ease, eh?'

Van Buren frowned. 'Now is not the time to discuss such things, Robert.'

Caroline Mitchum addressed Van Buren for the first time. 'Any chance of seeing the drawings, sir? They must be beautiful to be of such importance.'

'It's not really convenient now, my dear. They've been stored safely. Another time, perhaps.'

As he said this, Micallef couldn't help noticing Van Buren's little glance towards the spot where he understood the safe was hidden. He raised his glass. 'Congratulations on your good luck, Mr Van Buren'

Van Buren's eyes narrowed. 'Luck has nothing to do with it, young man. I've always had a good eye for art. From the moment I acquired these works, I knew I'd be able to turn a good profit on them one day.'

'I congratulate you on your business skills then.'

After the announcement, the party gravitated towards the window. The earlier clouds had disappeared and the weather had warmed up. Beyond the Albert Bridge to the west, a glowing red sky was illuminating the river. Van Buren stood off for a moment and was pleased to see his children chatting pleasantly together. They were not the closest of siblings and were frequently prone to jealous spats, mostly these days to do with money. His eye fell on Caroline Mitchum. She was an odd-looking girl. He was sure Robert could do better. As for Micallef, Elizabeth knew his views, but tonight was not the time to air them again.

Presently, the gong sounded and Mrs Macdonald announced supper.

Van Buren thought the meal went off quite well. Cold cuts, fish, and sticky toffee pudding. Simple fare, as he preferred it. Conversation flowed and everyone seemed to enjoy themselves. When Mrs Macdonald began to clear the dessert plates, he decided it was time to have his private chat with the children. He excused himself to Micallef and Caroline and suggested they wait in the drawing room. 'Mrs Macdonald can serve you coffee there before she goes home. Or something stronger if you like.' Then he, Elizabeth and Robert adjourned to the study.

In the drawing room, coffees served, Caroline Mitchum prattled on at length about her hopes for Robert's magazine. As she did so, Micallef contemplated his next steps. He heard the front door slam and thus knew the housekeeper had left. Caroline then excused herself to powder her nose. He took the opportunity to double-check the safe was where he'd told Penny it was.

'I think I'd better powder my nose as well,' he said when Caroline returned. 'Where . . .?'

'The loo on this floor is out of order, apparently. You have to use the one on the first floor. It's on the left at the top of the stairs.'

He made his way up, but instead of stopping on the first floor, he kept going all the way to the top of the house. He was fortunate to quickly find the room he wanted, the one closest to the tall tree he'd spied from the lane. It was a small bedroom that looked as if it hadn't been occupied for a while. Beside the unmade single bed was a sash window. It was stiff, but he managed to open it without making any noise. He put his head out and whistled once. A single whistle came in reply. Then he whistled twice, the signal confirming that the job was on. A double whistle came back: Penny was ready to proceed. Finally he gave another double whistle, the timing signal. They'd agreed one whistle for ten p.m., two for half past, and three for eleven. Van Buren had said several times over

139

dinner that they'd all have to be out of the house by ten, as he had an appointment elsewhere. Ten thirty seemed the best time.

On his way back down, he took time on the first floor to pull the chain in the toilet. When he reached the ground floor, he found everyone congregated in the hallway.

'There you are, Teddy darling. I'm sorry we were away so long,' said Elizabeth.

'Not to worry, darling. Caroline and I had a nice chat.'

Van Buren already had his coat on and seemed eager to get moving. 'It's been a lovely evening, but all good things must end, eh? Chop-chop. If you'll all go out ahead of me, I'll lock up. And a very good night to you all.'

As he reached the pavement, Micallef checked his watch. It was ten exactly.

When Vermeulen finally got home, he collapsed exhausted into an armchair. It was late and he should have gone straight to bed, but he decided to have a night-cap. Apart from his success with Van Buren, he had accomplished a number of other tasks, some pleasant, some not. There had been no time for Ursula, but he hoped to make up for that over the weekend.

Before pouring himself a glass of port, he opened the secret drawer in his desk and deposited some documents. Then he flopped back into his chair. It took a while for him to properly relax. He had begun to realise that he would not be able to keep up this fraught way of life for very much longer.

Gulbenkian quite understandably wanted him to stay in London until the da Vinci deal was completed. Vermeulen had agreed and now planned to return to Lisbon with the drawings on Tuesday. This ran counter to the advice he'd received, but so be it. He would have liked to know exactly why they'd given him this advice, but his controller had not been forthcoming.'

He got up to pour himself a second drink and on his way back turned the radio on. He recognised the dance tune that was playing and tried, unsuccessfully, to remember its name. When the music programme finished a quarter of an hour later, he suddenly felt very hungry and went to his small kitchen to make himself a snack. He found some cheese and biscuits and was reaching for a plate in one of the cupboards when he heard the doorbell ring. It could only be Ursula at this late hour, coming on the off chance that he'd finally returned home. She had her own key, of course, but must have forgotten to bring it. Tired as he was, he was delighted at the prospect of seeing her and went to the hallway with an expectant smile on his face. A smile that swiftly vanished when he opened the door.

Chapter Twelve

Sonia was reading the newspaper when Merlin joined her at the breakfast table. As she got up to make some toast, she pushed the paper across to him. 'Yours?' The headline blared out in large capitals: '*BLOODY KNIFE ATTACK IN SOHO. FOREIGNER MURDERED.*'

'Yes and no.'

'What do you mean?'

'I'll explain when I've got some food inside me.'

Sonia put the bread under the grill. 'You got in late last night, and seem a bit grumpy this morning. Did you have a little too much at the pub with Sam?'

'Not the pub, and not Sam but I did end up having a few too many drinks with Harold Swanton. Sorry if I'm not myself.'

'I forgive you. I hope Mr Swanton isn't getting you involved in something terrible like that French spy business last year.'

'It's me involving him rather than the other way round.'

'Oh. Anyway, what about this murder?'

'Well, first off there's a personal angle.' He sighed. 'The victim was Pablo, Maria's nephew, who I was telling you about the other night.'

'Oh Frank, I'm terribly sorry.'

'I only ever met the boy once, so I cannot pretend to great emotion, but . . .' He shrugged.

'Was he robbed?'

'It looks that way. I interviewed a potential suspect, but then the case was taken off me.'

'Because of the personal connection?'

'No, because that suspect is American and the Yanks now have jurisdiction over criminal matters involving their own people.'

'But shouldn't you at least work together on this? What if this suspect turns out to be innocent? What if the real culprit is English?'

'That's a good point, and I think there's a chance the American suspect isn't guilty.'

'Why?'

'Just a hunch. I didn't think he was a liar.'

'The famous Merlin intuition at work again, eh? Oh. Your toast is ready. It's a little burned, I'm afraid.'

'That's all right. I like it that way.'

Sonia spread butter and honey on the toast and handed him the plate. 'Is it this case that you were discussing with Swanton?'

'Yes. He thinks Pablo was engaged in spy work for the Russians.'

'Spying's a dangerous business. Perhaps that's what got him killed?'

'Indeed. However, when I said I should inform the Americans, he wouldn't have it. Said something about protecting his sources.'

'Maybe MI5 themselves had something to do with Pablo's death and Swanton's covering up.'

'But if that's the case, why would he tell me his suspicions in the first place?'

'There is that. Maybe some other part of the organisation was involved? Anyway, I see you've made short work of your toast. Do you want some more?'

Before Merlin could answer, the telephone rang. It was Bridges. 'We've got another one, sir. Body, that is. Mews house in Knightsbridge. A shooting.'

143

'Someone upstairs must have been listening when I complained of lack of action. You're there now?'

'Yes.'

'Where exactly?

The mews house was a hive of activity. The body lay by a desk in the living room. One slippered foot poked out from under the white sheet with which it had been covered. Officers from Denis Armstrong's forensics team were busy down on the floor around the victim. Across the room, Merlin saw Robinson talking to an unhappy-looking woman on a settee. He heard the sound of footsteps behind him and turned to see Johnson descending the stairs with a young police doctor he recognised from a recent case.

'Morning, Inspector. Where's Bridges?'

'Going through the bedrooms, sir.'

Merlin pointed at the body. 'Who is he?'

'Name of Frederick Vermeulen. That's his girlfriend over there with Constable Robinson. She was the one who found him.'

'What sort of name is Vermeulen?'

'Dutch, apparently.'

'I see. Well, I suppose I'd better have a proper look at him.' Johnson handed over some protective gloves and he bent down to pull back the white sheet. Vermeulen's lifeless eyes stared up at him. In the centre of his forehead was a single bullet hole.

'Just the one shot, is it?'

'Yes, sir.'

Merlin tilted the head and found the exit wound, then stood back up.

'Have you found the bullet?'

'Not yet, sir. It's a forensics priority, of course.'

'Any sign of forced entry?'

'No.'

'So he most likely knew his killer.'

144

'Or perhaps he opened the door and found himself facing a gun, sir?'

'And was obliged to let his killer in? Maybe. Anything taken?'

'We're checking, but at first sight it doesn't seem so. There are a couple of half-open drawers in that desk. Perhaps something was removed from there, but hard to tell what.'

Merlin looked towards Robinson. 'What's the name of the woman the constable's interviewing?'

'Ursula Dunne. She discovered the body when she arrived around eight this morning. She has her own key. She was in floods of tears earlier, but seems to have calmed down a bit.'

'Good job you brought Robinson. She's very good in these situations.'

'Apparently the lady and Vermeulen were meant to go out for dinner last night, but he rang in the afternoon to cry off. Pressure of business. They arranged that she'd come round first thing today.'

'Any idea what he did for a living?'

Bridges suddenly appeared at the bottom of the stairs and answered his boss's question. 'There's another desk in the bed-room and I found some business cards there. On one he's a senior trade representative of a port company in Oporto. On another he's the managing director of a Lisbon consultancy business. And on a third he's senior consultant to a British oil company. There's some other paperwork that suggests he travels back and forth between London and Portugal a lot.'

'No doubt the lady will be able to provide more detail.'

'I told Robinson to be careful with her. I believe she should be regarded as a suspect at present.'

'Quite right. Where's the doc gone?'

'He had to hurry to another case, sir,' said Johnson.

'What did he have to say?'

'His preliminary take was that the man died somewhere between ten p.m. and two a.m. Cause of death . . . well, that's clear.'

Merlin heard the sound of sobbing. He turned and saw that

Robinson had placed a consoling arm around Ursula Dunne's shoulder. 'If she was the shooter, I have to say she's a great actress. I suggest we leave her to Robinson for now. Make sure she's tested for gunpowder residue before she's allowed to leave. Anything else to tell me?'

'I found some cables in the upstairs desk,' said Bridges. 'It seems Vermeulen was involved in a major transaction of some sort. The figures being bandied around were very big. The exchanges were between Vermeulen and someone called Gulbenkian. An unusual name.'

'It's Armenian' said Merlin. 'I recognise it. There's a very rich oil tycoon of that name. I remember reading somewhere that he's a big art collector too, so chances are it's him. What was Vermeulen doing for Gulbenkian?'

'I've only had the opportunity to have a quick look at the cables, but it seems he was acting as Gulbenkian's agent in an art purchase.'

'I wonder what Miss Dunne knows of this.'

'It's Mrs Dunne, sir,' said Johnson.

'Widow, or is there a husband somewhere she's been cheating on?'

'The latter, I think.'

'The plot thickens.' Merlin looked at his watch. 'Right, there's something important I need to do back at the Yard. I'm sure I can leave everything here in your capable hands, gentlemen. I'll catch up with you later.'

The something important Merlin needed to do was to have another go at Max Pearce. When his call was put through, the American seemed in high spirits. 'And what can I do for you this fine morning, Chief Inspector? I thought you'd be at home taking advantage of the leisure I've afforded you by taking over your knifing case.'

'I've other things on the go, Captain.'

'You do? Well, don't let me detain you.'

'I wanted another word about that case.'

Merlin could hear a long sigh. 'What word is that?'

'Look, Captain, there's a very good chance Virgil Lewis isn't your killer.'

'Really? Seems pretty open-and-shut to me, but I'm in a good mood, so I'll indulge you. Why do you say that?

Merlin knew he could not disclose what he knew from Swanton. What he could say was weak, but he said it anyway. 'In the short time I had with the man, his story seemed to have the ring of truth. Like you, no doubt, Captain, after many years in the game, I've developed a good nose for lies.'

'I have indeed been in this game a long time. I've been a police officer in Alabama for over twenty years and I've dealt with plenty of scum like Lewis. I've listened to his story and I smell lies. The man is guilty as hell.'

'There . . . there are other factors in play here.'

'Other factors? Please enlighten me.'

'I'm afraid I'm not at liberty to discuss them. It's beyond my authority.'

'What the hell does that mean? You know what I think, Merlin? I think you've got a soft spot for Virgil Lewis because he's black. You British haven't got the experience we have of black people. I tell you, violence, thieving and lying are second nature to them. You should keep your sympathy for the poor victim, a relative of yours, I'm told. His throat slit for small change.'

'It's very possible someone could have had another motive for killing him. I'm sorry, but I can't go into any detail.'

Pearce chuckled. 'You know that's not good enough, Merlin. If you've information relevant to my investigation, spit it out. Otherwise stop wasting my time.'

'Do you not think, Max, in the circumstances, that it'd be better if we worked together on this case? After all, if it turns out Lewis is innocent, the reason for you having jurisdiction falls away.'

'Lewis is guilty, and I don't need your help bringing him to account. Now, I'm a busy man. Good day to you.'

As the line went dead, Merlin felt like kicking himself. He'd been dealt a poor hand but had played it terribly. He'd have to persuade Swanton to intervene somehow or other.'

He still hadn't been able to put the matter out of his mind when Johnson returned to the Yard an hour later. 'I've left Bridges at the scene, sir. He wanted to do a little more rummaging. Forensics should be finished shortly. They still haven't been able to find the spent bullet, unfortunately.'

'And Robinson?'

'Is here. We dropped Mrs Dunne off at her flat on the way back. She was still in a bit of a state. We've arranged for her to come here tomorrow to make her formal statement.'

'I'd like to know what the constable has got out of her so far.'

'I'll go and fetch her.'

Johnson returned with Robinson a few minutes later and they both took seats at Merlin's desk.

'So, Constable, Ursula Dunne?'

Robinson consulted her notebook. 'Mrs Ursula Dunne. Married to Mr Charles Dunne, a Whitehall civil servant. Had known Frederick Vermeulen for about a year. He was an international businessman with varied interests. Main residence in Lisbon, but a frequent traveller to London. Kept the mews house for when he was in town. Rented.'

'How often was frequent?'

'Approximately once every five weeks. His previous visit had been at the beginning of July. His trips usually lasted around five or six days. Sometimes a little longer. On this trip he arrived here on Friday August the seventh.'

'Same day as Pablo Merino. They must have been on the same plane,' Merlin observed.

'Mrs Dunne and Vermeulen had apparently been in a relationship since they met. She says they were very close and shared a few secrets.'

'Such as?'

'The most striking in her view was that he told her he was a spy.'

'*Madre de Dios*, not another one. A spy for whom?'

'He never went into detail, but she naturally assumed for us.' She wanted us to know in case it had anything to do with his death.'

'I'll get on to Swanton and see what he can tell us. The inspector told you about the cables from a Mr Gulbenkian?'

'He did, sir.'

'Did you put the name to Mrs Dunne?'

'I did. She said Vermeulen was negotiating the purchase of some da Vinci drawings from another Dutchman, a Mr Van Buren, who has an address in Chelsea.'

'Da Vinci, eh? Blimey. No wonder the figures involved are big. We'll need to have a word with this chap Van Buren. What about the husband? Did he know she was having an affair?'

'She wasn't completely straightforward about that, but I got the sense he did and just put up with it.'

'Has there been any talk of divorce?'

'I didn't ask her and she never mentioned the subject. They have a son. Fifteen years old.'

'The doc estimated time of death between ten p.m. and two a.m. Does she have an alibi for those hours?'

'No. She says she was at home on her own in their London flat. Her husband was at their country place, somewhere near Oxford, and the son's on holiday in Scotland.'

'Did forensics do a gunpowder test?'

'They did. It doesn't seem as if there was a trace, but they haven't ruled definitively yet.'

'I see. Those tests aren't foolproof, of course, especially if someone's had a chance to have a good scrub-down.'

'I have to say, sir, she didn't strike me as the type. To kill I mean. Also she seemed genuinely distressed.'

'Maybe she's a good actress? What if she discovered Vermeulen

149

had another woman? You don't think her capable of a crime of passion?'

'Not really. She seemed sensible and organised.'

'Very well, Constable. Your opinion is duly noted. And well done handling a difficult situation.'

'Thank you, sir.'

Merlin turned to Johnson. 'You or the sergeant can take Mrs Dunne's statement tomorrow. Meanwhile I need to speak to Swanton and see if he knew our victim. We also need to speak to Mr Van Buren and explore whether this art deal might have had anything to do with Vermeulen's death. And we should find out more about his work. One of his employments was with a British oil company, wasn't it?'

'Yes. The card listed a London office. Warwick Petroleum.'

'I presume the office will be closed until Monday, but get someone to check. Will the sergeant be bringing such personal papers as he finds?'

'I believe so, sir.'

'And we'll have the full forensics report when?'

'Tomorrow morning.'

'Am I right in thinking Cole is off, today?'

'You are, sir. He'll be in tomorrow,' said Robinson.

'Good.' Merlin's mind had gone back to the Merino case. 'I think I have a job for him.'

Moscow

The event was taking place in a cavernous room in the heart of the Kremlin. As a concession to his guests, Stalin had invited the entire visiting party to the dinner. Thus Goldberg, to his great surprise, found himself at the table, sitting between Walter Thompson, Churchill's main bodyguard, and a burly crew-cut Russian who worked for Marshal Voroshilov, one of Stalin's

150

long-time cronies. It was past eleven and the feast had already been going for three hours. The table still groaned with vast quantities of food and drink. Every so often, at Stalin's command, conversation was halted to allow for toasts. Goldberg had counted ten so far. Conscious that he remained on duty as Harriman's security officer, he was trying his best to limit his alcoholic intake. It was a losing battle.

His Russian neighbour was called Kutuzov. 'Just like the general who beat Napoleon,' he'd said with a proud smile when introducing himself.

When Kutuzov disappeared to relieve himself, Goldberg turned to Thompson. 'Do you think Mr Churchill is enjoying himself?'

'Oh yes. Likes his food and drink, he does, as everyone knows. As to politics, whether the dinner gets him further along with Stalin, who can say? However, we ought to find out one important thing tonight.'

'Oh yes?'

'Which of the two leaders is the better drinker.'

Goldberg laughed. 'Comrade Kutuzov tells me Stalin can hold his liquor better than anyone.'

'We'll see.'

Goldberg glanced down the table towards where the principals were sitting and had the unnerving experience of catching Stalin's eye. The Russian dictator held his gaze for a moment, then raised his glass. Goldberg blushingly returned the gesture.

Thompson noticed this and moved closer. 'Looking into the eye of a man who's murdered millions,' he whispered. 'A little unsettling, eh?'

Goldberg decided it was best to remain silent on the subject of Stalin's crimes. He changed the subject. 'You've always been a policeman?'

'Most of the time, yes. Briefly, however . . .' Thompson picked up a pickled cucumber and examined it closely, 'I was a grocer.'

'Really? Quite a different line of business. When was that?'

'Not so long ago. I'd been with Mr Churchill for fourteen years. In 1935 I escaped his clutches and set up shop. He got me back when war was imminent.'

'So on and off you've worked for him for a very long time?'

'Indeed I have, and at some cost. My first marriage, for instance.'

Goldberg reached out for some sort of savoury pastry topped with what looked like fish paste. He took a tentative bite, grimaced, then set it aside.

'Why did you rejoin him?'

'Force of nature, ain't he? Hard to say no to someone like him.' Thompson sipped his lemon vodka. 'Quite passable, this stuff, isn't it?'

'I suppose.'

'So is this a temporary job you've got with Mr Harriman, or are you in it for the longer term?'

'Oh, temporary. I've just heard that something's been lined up for me in London once this trip's over, if I'm interested. Some sort of liaison job.'

A waiter bustled up and deposited a platter in front of them. On it lay a whole suckling pig covered in a thick, pungent sauce.

'Don't think I'm quite up to that, Detective,' Thompson said.

'Me, neither.'

'You've been to London before?'

'I had a few months' secondment to the Met. Very interesting and enjoyable.'

'Who were you with?'

'DCI Frank Merlin.'

'A fine officer. The boss has a very high opinion of him.'

They turned at the sound of a commotion further down the table. Another toast seemed to be in progress, and people were getting to their feet yet again. Stalin said a few words in Russian, raised his glass to Churchill and drank. After a brief round of cheers, everyone sat down again except Stalin, who began to make a tour of the table. Kutuzov had returned and made a point of refilling Goldberg's glass. As he contemplated the drink, he became aware of a presence at his shoulder. His stomach lurched and he turned and managed a nervous smile. Up close, he could see that Stalin's face was heavily pockmarked. The Russian leader muttered something to Kutuzov. Goldberg heard the word *'Ameri-kanskiy'* in Kutuzov's reply. A broad smile slowly broke beneath Stalin's bristling grey moustache, and he spoke some more Russian, this time directly to Goldberg. Kutuzov translated. 'He says to touch glasses. Then you have to down drink in one.' Goldberg knew he had no option. The liquid burned his insides and tears came to his eyes, but he managed it. Stalin nodded approvingly and spoke again.

'Another, he says,' said Kutuzov.

Chapter Thirteen

As he left the flat that morning, Merlin faithfully promised Sonia he'd be back home by two for a family afternoon. When he got to the Yard, he found Cole waiting as arranged.

'Pleasant day off, Constable?'

'Yes, sir. I went for a nice long walk with a friend.'

'Your Irish lady friend?'

Cole blushed. 'Yes, sir.'

'And how was your trip to Swindon on Friday regarding Charlie Mason's cigarette case?'

'I picked up some useful information. Would you like me to run over what—'

'No. Not now, thanks. As you probably know, quite a lot has happened in your absence.'

'Inspector Johnson filled me in, sir. How are things going?'

'We haven't got far yet. I know it's the weekend, but I had hoped to have made a little more progress.'

'Anything you want me to do?'

'I do indeed have a task for you.' Merlin proceeded to brief Cole on the Merino case: his misgivings, the information provided by Swanton, and the constraints imposed on the sharing of that information with the Americans.

'So what exactly do you want me to do, sir?'

'I want to try and run a parallel investigation. A low-key one, of necessity. You are to get on the ground and find out everything you can about Pablo Merino and what he got up to in England.'

'That'll be hard to do without the Americans getting wind.'

'Just do your best. They may not notice. They think they've got their man and for that reason won't be putting themselves about.'

'When do you want me to start?'

'How about now?'

Wiltshire

Audrey Butterfield looked with concern at her husband. 'Are you feeling quite all right, Humphrey?'

They were working together in the kitchen garden of their elegant but dilapidated farmhouse. Butterfield had said very little since his return from London, and though he was generally taciturn by nature, she sensed something was wrong.

'I'm fine. Could you pass me the secateurs, please.'

Audrey did as he asked and he started pruning the rose bushes.

'Are you ever going to tell me what happened with Leon? You saw him, didn't you?'

Butterfield mumbled something inaudible.

Audrey Butterfield was a plump, busy lady with a kind and bubbly disposition. She was almost the complete opposite in temperament and character to her husband. When they'd got together all those years ago, everyone had agreed they made a very unlikely couple. Despite this, they'd had a successful marriage and raised three bright and balanced children. For most of the time, Humphrey had proved an efficient and successful manager of the family farm. Just before the war, though, things had begun to get on top of him. As tenants rather than owners, he obsessed about how they would survive. The bequest of the farm by Audrey's sister, Mary, had seemed a life-saver. Then, Leon had commenced his litigation, and a permanent dark cloud had settled over them.

'I beg your pardon?' Audrey said.

'Just let me get on with my gardening, will you,' Humphrey snapped. 'We can talk over lunch. Shouldn't you be in the kitchen by now?'

'I'll be going there shortly, but we won't be able to discuss Leon over lunch. Have you forgotten? The colonel and his wife are coming.'

Butterfield stepped back abruptly from the bush. 'Damn it all, Audrey. Call them and cancel. Say I'm not feeling well.'

'I can't do that. Marjorie's already been in touch this morning to confirm the arrangements. She specifically asked about you and I said you were fine. Cancellation is not an option.'

Butterfield threw the secateurs angrily to the ground. 'Damnation!'

'What on earth is wrong with you? They'll be here at two. I suggest you have a little lie-down. Whatever happened with Leon can wait until this evening.'

'Very well! I shall,' he barked.

As she watched the French doors close behind him, Audrey sighed and bent down to pick up the discarded secateurs. Then she looked up at the cloudless sky. There was a warm sun and a pleasant breeze. A perfect day, and she was determined not to allow Humphrey's foul mood to ruin it.

London

Archer was in two minds. Should he notify his handlers of Vermeulen's death via newspaper advertisement, secret ink or microdot? He had all the paraphernalia for the latter set out on the kitchen table in his London bed-sit. Outside, he could hear the

156

puffing, groaning and clanking of the steam engines in the shunting yard behind the house, sounds he found strangely soothing. Eventually he decided to advertise. The *Irish Daily News* was the regular conduit to the Abwehr in Dublin. Before the start of his mission, they'd worked out a variety of newspaper formulae for possible events. There was one to register confirmation of the Abwehr's suspicions, one to say Vermeulen was in the clear, one to notify them of his demise, and so on. He had more to tell his controllers than the fact of the man's death, but that could wait until he was out of England. He grabbed pencil and paper and scrawled out the relevant formula. *'Congratulations to Mr Alfred Youngman of Howth on your 80th with love from all the family in Clapham.'* He'd call it in first thing Monday morning.

He took a nip from the bottle of Bushmills on the table and grunted with relief. Another difficult job completed. A job well done? Others would determine that, but he could see no grounds for complaint. Where would he go next? There'd been talk of a job in the United States. He had always wanted to go to America.

Merlin took a call from Bridges shortly after Cole had set off on his new mission. 'I'd meant to come in today, sir, but I'm sorry, I'm not feeling great.'

'What's wrong?'

'Dicky stomach. Iris decided to try a new recipe on me last night. Some sort of oriental stew with pig's trotters. It didn't agree with me. I think I'd better stay put for the moment. I feel—'

'Fine, Sam. You needn't burden me with the details. Are Vermeulen's papers with you at home?'

'No, sir. My neighbour the plumber has an emergency job this morning at the Yard. I asked him to drop them in. Probably in the hands of one of the desk sergeants already.'

'Thanks. I'll check.'

'The inspector had a personal matter to deal with and asked me to take Mrs Dunne's formal statement.'

'Don't worry, Robinson's in and I'll get her to do it. She tells me that the scientists confirmed the gunpowder residue test was almost certainly negative. Put together with the constable's intuition that Mrs Dunne is not a killer, I think she must be an outside prospect.'

'Very good, sir.'

Merlin got the Vermeulen papers from the desk sergeant and began to go through them. There was a good deal of correspondence relating to Vermeulen's Anglo–Portuguese trading activities, none of which seemed useful. There were the cables Bridges had mentioned and a few other items relating to the art deal. There was a card from an art gallery in Mayfair, and a handwritten note referring to someone called Sir Kenneth Clark, a name that seemed familiar to Merlin. Then there were various bills. He was surprised to find nothing to do with Warwick Petroleum, which he had assumed to be an important part of Vermeulen's business life.

When he'd gone through everything, he grabbed a sheet of paper and scribbled a few notes on his new case.

Possible motives:
Espionage
Revenge
Art deal
Robbery
Business connections
Personal relations

There were other things he'd have to add, no doubt, but this was a start. He bent over his desk and considered the list. His eye lingered on the word *Espionage*. As if on cue, the telephone rang and the desk sergeant told him Harold Swanton was on the line.

'I gather you were trying to get hold of me, yesterday, Frank. I'm sorry, but I was tied up on some business in Woodstock.'

Merlin knew that he meant the Duke of Marlborough's huge

Oxfordshire pile, Blenheim Palace, where MI5 maintained an operational presence. 'A good outcome?'

'Too early to say yet. I'm letting our clients kick their heels for a while before I question them again. Anyway, what can I do for you?'

'There are a couple of things. First, can I ask you to reconsider your reluctance to put the Americans fully in the picture about Pablo. They won't listen to me otherwise.'

'Sorry, Frank, I did have another chat with the powers that be, but nothing doing.'

'Then an innocent man is for the gallows, I fear.'

'Surely the Yanks will give him a fair trial?'

'How can they if we're withholding material evidence?'

There was a long, awkward silence before Swanton asked, 'And the second thing?'

'Name of Frederick Vermeulen mean anything to you?'

There was another long silence, then, 'Why do you ask?'

'We found his body yesterday. Bullet in the head.'

'Shit!'

'No trouble then, Teddy?'

'It all went smoothly.'

Hill swung his feet up onto the desk. 'The mark disappeared in good time as expected?'

'Bang on ten. Him and everyone else left the house, yes. All was clear for Jake to come in through the open window as planned.'

'I've not yet seen Penny myself, but I understand he's happy. Managed to open the safe without blowing it. He's a real artist, no mistake. And it appears we hit the jackpot. Twenty grand in nice clean notes, a few hundred more in dirty. The da Vinci drawings. A number of other valuables. Congratulations are in order, son.'

'Thanks, Billy. Where are the goods now?'

'Here, safely under lock and key. I'll sort out your cut tomorrow morning.'

'How quickly do you think you'll be able to shift the non-cash items?'

'Well, as you know, the drawings will take a while. As to the rest, two or three weeks, I should think.'

'Van Buren had agreed a sale of the da Vincis, by the way. Around four hundred grand, Elizabeth said.'

Hill whistled. 'Had he now? Well, we're not going to get anything like that.'

'What if we offer them under the counter to the man who agreed to buy them?'

Hill smiled. 'That's a thought. Not sure how we'd go about it, but happy for you to give me your ideas. Meanwhile, let's have a celebratory drink, shall we?' He poured out two whiskies. 'What's cheers in Maltese?'

'Sah-ha.'

'Sah-ha to you then, lad, and here's to a job well done!'

After drinks, Micallef left the club. There was a telephone box nearby in Rupert Street and he knew he'd better call. Elizabeth immediately burst into tears, then started gabbling. He eventually managed to interrupt her. 'I can't understand a word you're saying. Please pull yourself together and start again.'

She calmed down a little. In more measured tones she said, 'Daddy's definitely gone missing. I told you earlier I was sure something had happened. I went to the house and there was no answer. I rang several times.'

'You still can't find your key?'

'No. I think I must have left it there on Friday.'

'Where's the housekeeper?'

'No idea. I suppose she's got the weekend off, and I don't have her address or anything.'

'Hasn't Robert got a spare?'

'Yes, but he's gone off somewhere for a dirty weekend with his girlfriend.'

'Look, darling, as I said before, your father's probably done the

160

same with that lady friend of his. He'll turn up today or tomorrow, you'll see.'

'He's definitely not with her. Much as I detest the woman, I steeled myself to call her an hour ago. She's not seen him since Friday night.'

'Oh.'

'And another thing. I couldn't get into the house, but I had a look round outside. From that lane in the back I could see there was a bedroom window open.'

'Er . . . I don't think that's anything to worry about. With all the fine weather, the housekeeper probably gave the rooms a good airing and just forgot to close it.'

'I don't know . . . it seems dodgy to me. Look, have your meetings finished? Are you coming back here now?'

'I'll be there in half an hour. Just stop worrying. Everything will turn out fine.' He put the phone down and stepped out onto the pavement. The pleasant buzz from Hill's whisky had worn off. It looked likely he was in for a tedious afternoon. Another drink would not go amiss. There was a nice pub just round the corner, and it was nearly opening time.

Chapter Fourteen

Merlin found Swanton sitting as arranged on the bench where they'd met the other day. The sun shone down brightly on the pond, which was, as usual, a hive of avian activity.

'Frank. Morning. Hard to believe on such a glorious morning that we're a nation at war, eh?'

Merlin nodded towards a couple of soldiers manoeuvring a field gun in the distance. 'Not so hard.'

Swanton chuckled. 'I didn't see them.'

Merlin stretched his legs out in front of him. 'So, Harold. Frederick Vermeulen.'

Swanton sighed. 'A very effective MI6 agent. One of the best.'

'Can you tell me any more?'

'I shouldn't, but as it's you . . . The Germans thought he was their agent and that he ran a ring of Nazi spies in London.' Swanton pronounced the word 'Nazi' with a soft 'z', just like Churchill. 'However, he was a double. Our double.'

'Do you think the Germans discovered the truth and took him out?'

'You said the murder looked quite professional. Single shot to the head. No sign of a bullet?'

'Yes.'

'Hmm.'

'Are there enemy agents in the country? Real ones, I mean.'

'The Germans have tried to establish networks here, of course, but we believe we've caught, turned or eliminated every single agent.'

'You believe?'

'One can never know for certain.' A curly-haired little girl suddenly ran up to the bench and beamed at them. 'Look what I've got.' She held out a rag doll. 'Sarah wants to say hello.'

A harassed-looking young woman in a nanny's uniform hurried up and grasped the child's hand. 'Come away, Emily! You shouldn't be bothering these gentlemen with your silly dolly.'

Emily stamped an angry foot on the ground. 'Sarah is not a silly dolly. She's a very nice and clever dolly.'

The nanny smiled apologetically and pulled the child away.

'Never had kids myself,' said Swanton, with a wistful look. 'The missus couldn't. Wouldn't have minded a couple of nippers. You're a lucky man, Frank, having young Harry.'

'I know.'

'But back to Vermeulen. What to do?'

'I've just lost one of my cases to the Americans, as you know. Am I now going to lose one to you?'

'Maybe. Maybe not.' Swanton looked down and contemplated his shoes. Then he decided. 'I think for the moment we can work together. You carry on as normal with your investigation while we do some digging on our side. In a couple of days, we can reconvene, share our findings, then decide where to go from there. Does that suit?'

'You know it does. So we meet again Wednesday?'

'Yes. Unless there are any important developments. Make it five p.m. here.'

Bridges was back at work.

'Tummy better now, Sam?'

'Yes thanks, sir. Something interesting has occurred.'

'Oh?'

'This Van Buren fellow involved in the art deal with Vermeulen. I picked up on a missing person report in Chelsea. His daughter contacted the local station early this morning to say her father hadn't been seen since Friday.'

'Friday? That's not such a long time.'

'She's convinced something's happened to him. Furthermore, she thinks his house has been burgled. I've called and she's waiting for us there.'

'Let's get going then.'

'And one other thing. The AC called. Asked me to tell you the Americans have set down Virgil Lewis's trial for Friday of this week.'

'This Friday? That's no time at all. What are they thinking?'

'That they've got him bang to rights, I suppose.'

They approached Cheyne Walk via Flood Street. As they passed Rossetti Garden Mansions, Merlin thought of the murder committed in a flat there the year before. An army officer called Powell had managed to survive the bloody military evacuation of Crete only to suffer an ignominious death on his return home.

When Bridges drew the car up at Van Buren's house, they saw the front door was wide open. There was no one in the hallway when they went in, but they could hear the faint sound of crying above. Then a woman wearing an apron appeared and looked anxiously at them. 'Police?'

Merlin nodded.

'I'm the housekeeper, Mrs Macdonald.'

'Good morning. Are there any other officers here?'

'There's a Constable Higgins upstairs with Miss Van Buren. She's in a bit of a state. You know why, I presume?'

'We know only the barest of facts. Do you live here?'

'No. I work here every weekday and occasionally at weekends.'

'But not this weekend?'

164

'No. I left Friday night. When I returned this morning . . .'

They heard the sound of a male voice above. 'Any sign of the Yard yet?'

'They've just arrived, Constable.'

'We'll get more from you later, Mrs Macdonald. We'd better see Miss Van Buren first.'

The housekeeper led them up four flights of stairs to the top floor. From the landing she turned into a small room that Merlin noticed looked out onto the back garden. There they found Higgins standing by a bed on which sat a tearful young woman.

Introductions were made, then Higgins deferred to the lady. 'You'd best hear everything directly from Miss Van Buren. If you're up to it, that is, miss?'

'Yes, of course.' She mopped her eyes with a handkerchief and took a deep breath. 'I'd been trying to get hold of my father all weekend. I made numerous telephone calls. I came to the house but didn't have a key. It seemed empty. Daddy and I are close and he nearly always tells me what he's up to. I phoned again early this morning. Thankfully Mrs Macdonald was here. When I arrived, it was clear Daddy hadn't been here all weekend. His bed is made. He wouldn't have made it himself, so it's fair to presume it hadn't been slept in since Thursday night. I checked to see if any of his luggage was missing, in case he'd gone away on a sudden trip, but it's all here. He's . . . he's disappeared.'

'There was mention of a burglary?'

'The window in this bedroom was open. Mrs Macdonald is sure she closed all the windows before leaving on Friday night. And there are other signs of entry.'

Constable Higgins spoke up. 'There are what look like dried-out muddy footprints in here and on the stairs.'

'I think there were a couple of heavy showers on Friday afternoon,' said Bridges. 'But no rain since.'

'And there's the dog.' Higgins pointed at a broken china figurine beneath the window. 'I haven't had a proper look downstairs

165

yet, but Miss Van Buren and the housekeeper think there are a few items missing.'

'There are certainly a couple of candlesticks gone, and some valuable small ornaments. That's without having a thorough check.'

'What would be the likeliest target for a burglar?'

'There's a combination safe in the drawing room. I looked and it's still locked.'

'That doesn't mean it hasn't been opened, I'm afraid. Do you have the code?'

'Only Daddy knows it, I think.'

'We'd better go down and have a look,' said Merlin.

As they went down the stairs, Higgins pointed out the muddy marks on the carpet. When they reached the ground floor, Miss Van Buren led them into the drawing room. She went straight to one of the pictures hanging on the wall, an agreeable landscape painting of English-looking rolling hills and downs. Higgins helped her to lift it off its peg and set it down. A large wall safe emblazoned with the name CHUBB was revealed. She demonstrated that it was locked.

'Quite an old model, eh, Sergeant?'

'Sir. Any idea as to the contents, miss?'

'Normally, I wouldn't know, but from what Daddy said on Friday night, it might have contained some very valuable items.'

'I see.'

Miss Van Buren caught her breath. 'I've been thinking so far that a burglar might have come here when the house was empty. But what if he was here when Daddy returned home on Friday night. What if Daddy decided to take him on? It's the sort of thing he'd do. What if the burglar injured him and . . .' Tears began to flow again and Mrs Macdonald hurried over to comfort her.

'If it's any consolation, miss,' said Merlin, 'the professional British burglar is seldom a man of violence.'

Miss Van Buren made no reply as Mrs Macdonald settled her down in the nearest chair.

'You said the safe might have held some very valuable items,' said Merlin. 'You didn't, perhaps, have in mind some drawings by a master of the Renaissance?'

The young woman gasped in surprise. 'Why yes! How . . . how on earth do you know that?'

'I'll explain in due course.' Merlin turned to the housekeeper. 'I take it you don't know the combination?'

'No.'

'The house is owned by Mr Van Buren?'

'No, he rents it.'

'Do you, so to speak, come with the property?'

'Yes. I've worked here for several years and a number of tenants.'

'You must know the landlord, then. Presumably he would know the combination.'

'I would assume so, but I'm afraid Mr Stuyvesant lives in America and moves around a lot. He's not easy to get hold of. There is a letting agent, but I'm not sure he'd know.'

'Best I get on to Charlie Mason, sir,' said Bridges. 'He'll be able to get it open for us somehow. If he can't do it himself, he'll know people at Chubb.'

'You do that, Sergeant. And get forensics round here as soon as possible. May the sergeant use the telephone, miss?'

'Of course.'

'Thank you. Now, I'd like to learn more about your father and his recent movements. I think, however, that we should move to another room, as this may well prove to be a crime scene.'

'No one's been in the kitchen,' Mrs Macdonald said. 'I'd know if they had.'

'Very well. Let's go there.'

Although most of the senior US military police officers continued to operate for the moment from the US embassy, a new MP headquarters was being established in a modified office building just off Grosvenor Square. This was where Virgil Lewis had spent his

167

weekend, in a tiny sweltering cell that could not have been much more than a broom cupboard in its previous life. Lewis, who had been asthmatic as a child, had found breathing increasingly difficult. This wasn't his only physical discomfort. He still ached from the pummelling Pearce's men had given him soon after his arrival. A careful going-over that had elicited the confession they wanted.

If he lay as still as possible on the couple of planks that formed his bed, he found he could breathe a little easier. He ran over again in his mind Pearce's words to him the day before. 'Virgil boy, you're going to swing nice and easy on that rope. The only thing that's worrying me is whether one of our own hangmen is available to do the job. There's one supposedly on the way from the States, but if he don't get here in time, we'll have to make do with a Limey. The main man here is very good, I'm told. Got a pretty fancy name on him, that's for sure. Albert Pierrepoint. It's all very scientific, you know. Executioner has to calculate your weight and the length of fall. Get it wrong and death can be drawn out and excruciatingly painful. Let's hope that doesn't happen, eh?'

The only source of hope he had was that he had been allocated a decent defence counsel. An officer from the air force legal department was coming to see him at two. He hoped he'd be able to persuade him that the confession had been beaten out of him. Pearce's men had been careful to avoid too much visible bruising. There was one uncomfortable thought which worried him, though. On the night of the knifing, he'd clearly been off his head with drink. Was it possible, in that terrible state, that he'd somehow got hold of a knife and killed the man?

Merlin and Bridges spent some time with Elizabeth Van Buren going over her father's background, what she knew of the pending sale of the drawings, his recent movements and activities and the Friday-night supper when she'd last seen him. They had planned to go over the same ground with Mrs Macdonald, but there was a call to say her husband had been taken ill, and they'd allowed her to rush off. When they left the house, forensics were continuing their examinations. The safe remained as yet unbreached.

Although they'd tried to be upbeat with the young woman, both Merlin and Bridges were not optimistic. The signs of a break-in, Van Buren's disappearance and the strange coincidence of Vermeulen's death suggested serious grounds for concern.

Back at the Yard, Bridges wondered, 'If Vermeulen was a spy, does that mean Van Buren was in the espionage game as well?'

'It must be a possibility, Sam.'

Merlin called out for Cole, who he'd seen hovering in the corridor minutes before.

'I forgot to tell you, Sergeant, but I asked the constable here to do a little poking around on the sly regarding Pablo Merino.'

'You do surprise me, sir.'

'Anything yet, Constable?'

'His hotel room was occupied yesterday, so I couldn't do anything. I thought of having the guest temporarily turfed out, but decided that was likely to draw unwanted attention. Happily, the room became vacant this morning and I was able to have a good look. As forensics had already gone over it, I wasn't optimistic, but I struck lucky.'

'You did?'

'As I was looking around the bed, a floorboard squeaked. I pulled back the carpet. The board was loose and I lifted it. In the gap beneath, I found this.' Cole held up a small notebook. 'It's Merino's, and it contains a couple of interesting names.'

'Whose?'

'For one sir, there's yours. With your home address.'

'Oh dear.' Merlin shook his head. 'Poor boy must have been hoping to get in touch. And the other?'

'Frederick Vermeulen's.'

Merlin reacted with amazement. '*Madre de Dios!*'

Bridges was equally nonplussed.

'What else is in the book, Cole?'

'You'd better have a look for yourself, sir. Most of it's in Spanish.'

Merlin took the notebook. Merino's notes covered four pages in a neat, easily readable script. He read swiftly through them, then looked across the desk at his officers. 'I'll translate. It's a record of his movements in England. The heading is "English Mission". Beneath it reads: '" Friday August 7th. My first aeroplane flight. Vermeulen sitting a couple of rows behind. V picked up by big car at the airport. As promised, car also waiting for me. Drive to London took nearly four hours. Exhausted when got to small hotel in centre of London. Quick walk round. To Trafalgar Square where first meeting with senior man from embassy as arranged. Gave me V's address which was told not more than half an hour's walk away. Said he was getting me more English clothes so I could blend in better. Didn't seem to think much of my mission or my boss. New clothes arrived later. Good fit. Went to café near hotel for meal. Food terrible!

' " Saturday August 8th. To V's house early. Came out around nine, went to café then caught train to a nice place by the river called Richmond. Tracked him along river path and saw him meet and do some sort of exchange with an unknown man. Couldn't tell whether other man English or something other and couldn't get close enough to hear conversation. Strange feeling I was not alone trailing him."

'There's no entry for the Sunday, so it continues the following day. " 'Monday August 10th. V stayed in all day. Attractive woman visited. Definitely feel someone else watching.

' "Tuesday August 11th. Busy day. Vermeulen many appointments. Went to a grand building in Trafalgar Square which learned was National Gallery. Missed him for next couple of hours as had safe house meeting with G. Picked him up again after lunch when left home for apartment building in area called Pimlico. Later another apartment block in Fulham. In evening took his woman to restaurant near his house. Turned in at eleven.

' "Wednesday August 12th. Vermeulen to office building in City of London. One of outside nameplates was for oil company which, according to my briefing, is one he represents. After to riverside house in Chelsea. Saw him home then packed in at nine. Went to pub. Had interesting time!

' " Thursday August 13th. Vermeulen to City again to two offices. Back to Fulham again then Pimlico." '

Merlin closed the book. 'And that's it. He was dead the following day.' He popped an Everton mint into his mouth and sucked it thoughtfully. 'So Pablo's mission was to follow Vermeulen. If Swanton's right, he was following him on Russian orders. Why? The Russians are supposed to be our allies now. Why would a Russian agent be following a British agent?'

'And, if Pablo was right,' added Bridges, 'who was the other man on Vermeulen's tail?'

'Perhaps MI6 got wind that their man was being followed and arranged to put someone on him as a form of protection?'

'If that's the case, they didn't do a very good job, did they, sir,' said Cole.

'No. I guess the "G" referenced on the Tuesday must be Pablo's Russian contact in London. The fellow he met in Trafalgar Square.'

The three officers brooded in silence for a while. Cole was the first to speak. 'Any idea how Pablo got mixed up with the Russians, sir?'

'The Russians backed the Republicans in the Spanish Civil War. Pablo fought on the Republican side. He could easily have come into contact with Russian officers then.'

'Perhaps his mission was more than just to observe Vermeulen. Maybe he was meant to take him out.'

'As far as I can see at the moment, with all these spies running around, any scenario is possible.' Merlin started toying with his Eiffel Tower paperweight. 'He mentions his contact not thinking much of his mission and his boss, presumably the chief Russian spy in Lisbon. It could be there was some in-service rivalry going on that Pablo fell foul of.'

'You mean the Russians might have killed him, themselves?'

'As I said, Sam, anything is possible. At some point I'll consult Swanton and see what he thinks of this new information, but I'll wait to see if anything else turns up first. Have you managed to glean anything more about Pablo, yet, Constable?'

'No, sir. Most places were closed yesterday, of course. My plan today is to do a trawl around the shops, pubs, and cafés within a reasonable radius of the hotel.'

'Off you go then. And very good work finding the notebook.'

Johnson came in a little later, having been to the offices of War-wick Petroleum and seen Cedric Calvert, the managing director. Calvert had confirmed that the company had employed Vermeulen as a consultant. His role was to provide insights into developments in the world oil markets and to act as liaison with Calouste Gul-benkian, the principal shareholder and presumably the same man who'd wanted to buy the da Vinci drawings. He had claimed to know nothing of Vermeulen's other business activities or his per-sonal life, and had no idea as to who might have killed him.

Bridges returned later with the news that Van Buren's safe had finally been breached. 'If there was anything in there, sir, I'm afraid it's all gone.'

'You'd better let Miss Van Buren know.'

'One other thing. Miss Van Buren mentioned that her father was dealing with an art expert called Ramsey.'

'And that name cropped up in Vermeulen's papers.'

'Someone should pay him a visit, sir.'

'You're right. I'll go with the inspector. You can put your feet up a bit and man the fort. Let's hope someone calls in with a sight-ing of Van Buren.'

At Ramsey's gallery, the receptionist informed the officers that the proprietor had not yet returned from lunch. Merlin looked at his watch. It was gone four and he decided the man couldn't be that much longer. They waited. Twenty minutes later, Augustus Ramsey rolled through the front door with a young man. It had clearly been a very liquid lunch. The officers were shown into Ramsey's office, where they learned that his companion was his grandson, Martin. The younger man seemed considerably more compos mentis than Augustus, and thus it fell mostly to him to relate the tale of the gallery's dealings with Van Buren, Vermeulen, Kenneth Clark and Gulbenkian.

It was gone six when they got back to the Yard. Merlin decided it was time to call it a day. 'We have a lot to consider, Peter. Let's go over everything tomorrow morning, when our minds are a bit fresher.'

He decided to walk home and enjoy the warm summer evening. Later, after dinner, he sat by the radio sipping a pale ale, Sonia across from him reading a book. 'Any further news on your missing Poles?' he asked.

'Afraid not, and the senior people at the legation aren't very optimistic.'

'Sorry to hear that, though I can't say I'm surprised.' He relaxed back into his chair. 'Did I tell you Bernie Goldberg was coming back to London?'

'No, you didn't.' Sonia's face lit up. 'Such a lovely man, and you and he got on so well. He's arriving from New York?'

'Well, no. The AC told me he's been in Russia with the prime minister.'

'Churchill has been in Russia?'

'I believe it will be in the newspapers tomorrow.'

'I wonder if the subject of our missing men was raised?'

'Perhaps it was, but what chance of a straight answer from Stalin?'

'You're right, of course. So what is Bernie doing on such a trip?'

'I don't know. Hopefully he'll be able to tell us when he gets back.'

Sonia looked back at her book, then stifled a yawn. 'I think that's it for me. I'm off to bed. Don't be long. You must be tired too.'

She was right. He ought to be tired. He was not, however. From being underemployed, all of a sudden he had three cases on the go. The adrenaline was flowing. This was what he lived for!

Chapter Fifteen

Tuesday August 18th 1942

Davy Stamper was not feeling his best. He'd been celebrating a friend's twenty-first the night before at his Wapping local, and had sunk at least seven pints of Courage bitter.

'I told you to go easy, you silly bugger.' His father, Ivor, was at the wheel of the family-owned tug, which plied its trade among the cargo ships moored in and around the Port of London. Reilly, the mate, sniggered. 'I told you before the lad can't take his booze.' He cast a sly glance at the skipper and muttered under his breath, 'Like father, like son.'

'What's that, Sean?'

'Nothing, Ivor.' The Irishman shrugged and returned to his chores. A slight breeze was blowing from out of a cloudless sky. The boat was on its way to Surrey Docks for some lightering work.

Ivor Stamper handed his son a mug of strong tea. 'Drink it up, lad. It'll settle your stomach.'

Davy felt it was more likely to do the opposite, but he obediently took a gulp. Immediately he rushed to vomit over the rail..

'For Christ's sake, son!'

His head stayed over the rail for a while longer. He eventually straightened when he heard his father sound the horn and the boat begin to slow in anticipation of its turn into the dock. Then something in the water caught his eye. Something bobbing a short distance off the port side.'

'Watch out, Dad. There's a log or something in the water.'

Ivor slowed the boat almost to a halt. 'Where? I can't see anything. Can you see it, Sean?'

Reilly moved to Davy's side, shading his eyes from the sun. 'Yes. A timber spar, looks like. Pull the boat a little to port, Ivor. Oh . . . oh my God.'

'What?'

'It's a stiff. I can see hands.'

The skipper brought the boat alongside the object, then brought it to a complete stop and stepped out of the cabin. 'Shit! You're right. Just our luck. This is going to royally bugger up our morning. Come on then. Let's haul it in.'

The corpse landed face down on the deck. It was a man in a suit. The head was entangled in the suit jacket, and they couldn't see it properly. Reilly bent down to pull the material away. When he did so, the sight was enough to send young Davy back to puking over the rail.

Merlin was perusing Vermeulen's papers when Bridges interrupted him. 'According to the duty sergeant, Harold Swanton's waiting out front in a car. Wants you to pop down for a quick word.'

He soon found the car on the other side of the Embankment. Swanton was reading the *Times* in the back while his driver stood guard on the pavement. The driver opened the door and Merlin slid in.

'Thanks for making the time, Frank. I'm on a rather tight schedule. I'm due at Blenheim at eleven.'

'Happy to, Harold, though I thought the plan was to meet tomorrow.'

'It was, but something's cropped up.' Swanton pointed to the newspaper. The front page had a photograph of the prime

176

minister, Stalin and Harriman under the headline *Mr Churchill in Moscow*. 'Did you know?'

'The AC mentioned it.'

'Sometimes I worry about that man's loose tongue.'

'Don't. The only person he gossips to at work is me.'

'But what about outside work?'

Merlin shrugged and Swanton put the paper away.

'You say something's cropped up?'

'Yes. We received some interesting but worrying information from our most secret source.'

Merlin knew this to mean the code-breakers at Bletchley, of whose amazing work he was one of the few to be aware, courtesy of Swanton.

'They have evidence that a hitherto undetected German agent has been active here for several weeks. When I said the other day that we'd closed down all secret German operations in the country, I was wrong.'

'Did your source identify him?'

'No. They picked up some chatter that showed the Abwehr in Lisbon knew of Vermeulen's death. It seems they got this from Berlin. As you know, the story has been kept out of the papers and knowledge is confined to a handful of people. The natural conclusion to be drawn is that someone transmitted the information to Berlin from London.'

'And that that someone might be Vermeulen's murderer?'

'Very possibly.'

'Does your source think this agent is still in the country?'

'There's no information. But if his sole mission was to take out Vermeulen, he's either gone already, or is about to. Naturally we've alerted the ports, et cetera.'

Merlin considered for a moment. 'So let me get this straight. Vermeulen was a spy for us but pretended to the Germans in Lisbon that he was spying for them. Someone on the German side, someone in Berlin perhaps, might have suspected that he was not what he claimed to be and sent an agent to observe him in London. Is that what you're thinking?'

'Yes, Frank. And perhaps Vermeulen did something that showed his true colours, which prompted the agent to eliminate him.'

'But . . . Well, you're the spy expert, Harold, but if the Germans found out they were being deceived, wouldn't they prefer to get him back to Lisbon and debrief him before executing him?'

'Good point, Frank, but perhaps circumstances dictated that the agent take matters into his own hands. Perhaps Vermeulen realised he'd been compromised and . . . Well, there are many unanswered questions.'

'Is this the point where I have to stand down?'

Swanton looked out of the car window. 'Not quite, Frank. Despite everything I just said, I have to concede there's still a chance Vermeulen's death was unrelated to espionage activities. A slim chance, but a chance nevertheless. Because of that, I'll allow you to keep going for a while longer.' He grasped Merlin's arm. 'I hope you realise that if I were dealing with any other police officer, I wouldn't be saying this, but I know your value.'

'Thanks, Harold. I'll make sure you're on my Christmas card list.'

After a solid night's sleep, Augustus Ramsey had just about recovered from his over-indulgence of the previous day. However, it would take more than a good sleep for him to get over the disastrous news of the likely theft of the da Vinci drawings. Thus he was in a sombre mood as he presided over his gallery that morning. He glanced through his desk diary. He had some new prospective customers coming in at eleven. Then he had a meeting regarding a couple of English eighteenth-century paintings that were coming to market. They might generate some interest. Now that it seemed his substantial Van Buren commission had gone up in smoke, he needed to get on with business and generate other fees. It was no use crying over spilled milk.

Before his first meeting, he knew he should tackle the distasteful task of informing Sir Kenneth Clark of developments. He asked his secretary to put a call through. The news initially stunned Clark into silence. Eventually he found his voice. 'Is it absolutely certain the drawings were in the safe?'

'Not certain, no, but the police consider it very likely on the basis of what Van Buren's daughter said.

'What a catastrophe! For those exquisite works to suddenly emerge from the darkness after so long and then . . . and then vanish within days again. It is too upsetting. And poor Mr Van Buren has vanished as well and Vermeulen is dead. It's a horror story.'

'It is, Sir Kenneth.'

'Do the police suspect foul play with regard to Van Buren?'

'I understand they're open to all possibilities.'

'How about Gulbenkian. Has anyone put him in the picture?'

'I don't know. I haven't.'

'His London lawyers must know about Vermeulen, but they might not know about the drawings. I'll cable him to make sure. What was agreed in the end, by the way? Last I heard was as of Thursday.'

'They agreed a price on Friday afternoon. Four hundred thousand with terms. Everything was supposed to be formally completed yesterday.'

'A very full price in the end, but what does it matter now? I'd better tell His Majesty what's happened as well. He was so looking forward to seeing the drawings. Well, thank you for your call, Ramsey. Good day to you.'

After Ramsey put the phone down, his grandson came into the room. 'I hope you're feeling better today, sir.'

'Not really, Martin. Not with this Van Buren disaster.'

'Any news about the man?'

'Not that I've heard.' Ramsey studied his nephew. 'You don't look so well either. Something worrying you, my boy? You don't seem quite your normal cheerful self.'

'Actually, sir, there is. I'm worried that I have some information relating to the Van Buren case that I ought to pass on to the police.'

'You do? What sort of information?'

Ramsey looked down. 'I . . . I bumped into an old acquaintance. Chap called Nathan Katz. His cousin Jacob was up at university with me. Nathan works for Jacob's father in the City. Unfortunately his immediate family has suffered at the hands of the Nazis. His parents and two of his sisters were arrested in Vienna before the war. They are most likely dead.'

'How awful.'

'Anyway, we bumped into each other in a café, then arranged to meet in a pub last week. He told me a little more about his family. Like Benjamin, Nathan's father was a successful financier. He was also a great connoisseur of art, and had built up a wonderful collection. And when I say wonderful, I mean . . . Well, Nathan showed me a list. It was more than wonderful. It was astonishing.'

'And what has happened to this collection?'

'The Nazis confiscated it, or as much of it as they could find.'

'That's terrible, but I still don't quite see what this has to do with Van Buren.'

'Nathan left a copy of his list with me. His father's collection included some works by da Vinci.'

'What type of works? Paintings, sculptures?'

'No.' Martin gave his grandfather a meaningful look. 'Drawings.'

Augustus did a double-take. 'You're not saying . . .'

'Yes. It looks as though Nathan's father once owned the drawings Van Buren put up for sale. Nathan assumes he acquired them from a Nazi vendor.'

'He knows of Van Buren's ownership?'

'On the basis of his list, I . . . I'm afraid I felt duty-bound to tell him.'

With a deep sigh and a shake of the head, the elder Ramsey

leaned back in his chair. 'My boy, my boy. I wish you'd kept your counsel and waited to discuss the matter with me.'

'I'm very sorry, Grandfather.'

Augustus picked up a pencil and examined it thoughtfully. 'Have you considered the possibility that Van Buren acquired these drawings quite innocently? He said he found them in a shop where the owner didn't realise the significance of what he had. Perhaps the shop owner bought them from the Nazi vendor?'

'That wouldn't change the fact that the drawings were stolen from Nathan's family. Nathan was very angry when he learned they were in Van Buren's possession. What if he decided to raise the matter with him in person? What if he was in a temper when he did so?'

Augustus Ramsey sat bolt upright. 'My God, you mean you think he might have raised a hand to Van Buren?'

'I wouldn't have thought Nathan a man of violence, but it must be a possibility.'

Augustus's head was starting to throb again. 'I shall not conceal my disappointment with you, Martin. I have told you many times that discretion is one of the principal requirements in this business. Discretion and judgement. On this occasion you have been lacking in both, with who knows what consequences.'

Martin bent his head. 'I'm terribly, sorry, sir. You cannot blame me any more than I blame myself. Clearly I must inform the police about Nathan. I'll go and do that now.'

The older man raised a hand of warning. 'Before you do that, I think you owe it to your friend to put your suspicions to him. Perhaps he can convince you he had nothing to do with this. Perhaps he never got round to seeing Van Buren. You should at least ask him before you contact Scotland Yard.'

'You're right, sir. I'll get on to him now.'

Bridges and Robinson were deep in conversation when Merlin returned from his chat with Swanton. They seemed very serious.

'All well here?'

'Oh . . . the constable was just bringing me up to speed on the upcoming Hammersmith trial, sir.'

'That was due to start today, wasn't it? Shouldn't you be down at the Bailey already, Constable?'

'It's been delayed a day, sir. The prosecuting counsel has been taken seriously ill. Heart attack, they think.'

'I'm sorry to hear that. It'll be a job to get a replacement up to speed in twenty-four hours. Have they got hold of someone?'

'They have. It's . . .' Robinson blushed. 'It's a little awkward.' She glanced towards Bridges.

'The new man is Geoffrey Rutherford, sir,' said the sergeant.

'Why, isn't that the young fellow you were stepping out with a few months back, Constable?'

'It is, sir.'

'Well . . . I suppose that's all water under the bridge. Is there a problem?'

'Not on my part, sir. However, he thinks there is.'

'How so?'

'As you know, I was to be the principal police witness, having done much of the case legwork. He says he's not comfortable with that. Sees some potential conflict because we had a personal relationship. Says he'd prefer DS Price from the Hammersmith station to take over from me. He has been on the case all along, but he hasn't been as deeply involved as me. Geoffrey says that if there are gaps in Price's knowledge, DI Johnson can cover those in the stand as my principal supervisor in the case.'

'I see. And as you've helped construct most of the case, you naturally want to see it through to the end. You are upset?'

'Yes.' Robinson lowered her head.

'I completely understand. If Mr Rutherford thought your being a lead witness would be a problem for him, he should not have taken the case on. I've got a good mind to call his chambers and tell him what I think.'

182

'Please don't do that, sir' pleaded Robinson. 'It's embarrassing enough as it is. I'd rather avoid any fuss.'

'Very well, if you're sure, but if I ever have dealings with that young man in the future, I'll be sure to tell him what I think of him.'

'Sir.'

'Looking on the bright side, however we can make good use of your skills elsewhere, eh, Sergeant?'

'Absolutely, sir.'

Robinson managed a weak smile. 'I'm here, ready and willing. What do you want me to do?'

'First off, I think Cole could do with a bit of assistance. As you probably know, he's trawling around Soho for information about Pablo Merino. He's already had some success, but chances are we'll get on quicker if you lend him a hand.' Merlin looked at Bridges. 'Has he already gone out ?'

'No, sir. He had a couple of things to do first.'

'There you are then, Constable. You can make your way to Soho together and draw up a plan of campaign.'

When they were alone again, Bridges asked about Swanton, and Merlin filled him in. Then he moved on to what needed to be done next.

'We need the same standard police work regarding Vermeulen and Van Buren, as Cole and Robinson are doing re Pablo. We need to find out their movements in the days leading up to the one's death and the other's disappearance. Let's make an action plan.' Merlin found pencil and paper and started scribbling. When he'd finished, he showed Bridges his notes:

Vermeulen:

Check movements since arrival in Britain
Talk to Ursula Dunne again
Get more on art transaction
Follow up questions raised in Pablo's notebook.

Review V's papers in light of any new discoveries
Have another look round his house
If possible, get further information on his MI5 activities
Identify enemies

Van Buren:

Find
Check recent movements (interview family, dinner party quests, friends)
Who else knew about da Vinci drawings and prospective sale?
Reasons for sale/financial position?
Skeletons in closet/enemies
Pablo Merino:
Movements and contacts since arrival in Britain (Cole/Robinson)
Find out more about his mission in London
Enemies
Find evidence to help delay/halt Virgil Lewis trial

'I thought you'd decided Ursula Dunne was in the clear? Did something new come up when she made her statement?'

'No, Sam, but I've got a niggling feeling about her and I'm not prepared to rule her out completely yet. I'd like one of you to have another go at her. Perhaps the inspector?'

'Fine by me, sir. I've got enough on my plate. One other thing regarding your list. We know Pablo was following Vermeulen. Isn't it worth considering whether Vermeulen realised that and took action?'

'Good point. Anything else?'

'On your final point under the Pablo heading. Just so we're clear, as I see it, the only way we are going to save Lewis is by proving another man murdered Pablo.'

'It is. Maybe not beyond all reasonable doubt, but as near as dammit.'

'Should I go and find the inspector so we can agree the plan with him as well?'

'Please.'

The telephone rang before the sergeant got to the door. He paused as Merlin took the call and heard him say, 'I see. Tell them we're on our way.'

Merlin looked at him. 'River police have a body down by the docks. A man. In quite a mess. One observant copper saw there were initials on his shirt cuffs.

'What initials?'

'LVB.'

Leon Van Buren's body lay under a grubby tarpaulin in the Wapping police station basement. Sergeant Hooper, an old footballing friend and colleague of Merlin's from years ago, was at its side. 'Sorry, Frank, but that's all we had to hand to cover him.'

'Don't think it matters much to him now, Vernon. Has he been here long?'

'Fifteen minutes or thereabouts. We waited ages for the ambulance at the docks, idle gawkers all around, then gave up and brought him here ourselves.'

'Where was the ambulance meant to be coming from?'

'The London Hospital. As it turns out, they had a good excuse. An unexploded bomb went off this morning in the Mile End Road and there were several casualties.'

'Have you tried anywhere else?'

'Yes. St Pancras. Said they'd be here in twenty minutes.'

'We'd better get on and have a look then.'

Merlin had seen a lot of horrors in his career, and as a soldier in the Great War, but even he was taken aback by the sight of Leon Van Buren's head. He noticed that Bridges had gone very pale.

Two long gashes formed a kind of jagged cross on Van Buren's face. In addition, there was only one eye, and no nose or upper lip.

185

A large flap of skin fell loose from the scalp when he moved the head back.

'Do you want to see the other side?' Hooper asked.

'No thanks, Vernon. Seems pretty fragile. I don't want it to fall to pieces before the pathologist's had a look.'

'We can only hope he was already dead when the boat hit him.'

'You think that's what happened?'

'Wounds seem most consistent with a boat propellor to me, Frank. Maybe the pathologist will call it different, though.'

Merlin replaced the tarpaulin. 'Any other sightings before the tug crew picked him up?'

'Not so far.'

'Any idea how he ended up in the water?'

'No. Where did he live?'

'On the Chelsea Embankment.'

'Right next to the river then. Probably a chance he went in there.'

'If he went in the river in Chelsea, wouldn't he be dragged westward rather than eastward?' asked Bridges.

'Not necessarily,' replied Hooper. 'The river is tidal. If you factor in the wind, objects can go all sorts of directions. That said, if he got tangled up in a boat's gear, he would have had no choice but to go where the boat took him.'

'Wouldn't a crew notice if something got snagged in their propellor?' Merlin asked.

'Not necessarily. Some of these barges, fully laden, are very, very heavy. A man's body might not make a noticeable impact on the motion of the boat. Not in the short term, at least.'

'I see. Find anything on him? Apart from his initials, that is.'

'A wallet with some cash. Keys. That was it.'

'All right. Let's wait and see what the pathologist has to say.'

Hooper turned and led the Yard officers up the stairs.

'Still turning out for the Met old-timers, Vernon?' Merlin asked.

'Once in a blue moon. Last game I played was in March.'

'I envy you. What I'd give to get on a football pitch again.'

'There's nothing to stop you, Frank. You're welcome to join us any time. I'd love to see your silken footballing skills deployed once more.'

'Flattery, flattery, Vernon.'

'If it gets you playing again, I'll flatter you as much as you like!'

Merlin patted his old team-mate on the back.

Liverpool

It was raining in Liverpool, a misty drizzle that Archer found welcome after the London heat. The MV *Artemisia*, a small, battered-looking cargo vessel, sat low in the water in an out-of-the-way dock. The ship was fully loaded and ready to depart on the tide. Archer picked up his suitcase and climbed up the gangplank. When he reached the deck, he was accosted by a squat bearded sailor.

'And who the hell might you be, pal?' asked the man in a thick Irish brogue.

'Barron. Arthur Barron. I've booked passage to Dundalk.'

'Have you now? I know nothing about it. Let's see your papers.'

Archer handed over his Irish passport and the letter confirming his passage.

'You've been through the customs shed?'

'I have.' There'd been a scare when one of the customs officers went off to consult another about the passport, but he had eventually been waved through. As arranged, his documents had been left for him in a locker at Lime Street station. They included fake correspondence supporting Archer's cover as an agricultural machinery salesman.

'Wait here.' The sailor disappeared briefly. On his return, he pointed behind him. 'Captain'll see you. Second cabin on the left.'

Captain Riordan sat at a small table beneath the cabin porthole, a bottle of Jameson's and two glasses in front of him. A burly, white-haired man with a cast in one eye, he rose to shake hands. 'Pleased to meet you, Mr Barron. You'll join me in a dram?'

Archer nodded and the captain poured. 'Everything all right when you came through?'

'The papers seemed to do the job.'

'And you didn't risk carrying anything um . . . provocative in that little suitcase of yours? No weapons or transmitters in secret compartments?'

'Do you take me for a fool, Captain?'

'No offence meant, Mr Barron. I just like to be sure, as that sort of thing has happened on occasion. Anyway, welcome. *Sláinte!*' They clinked glasses and drank.

'Successful trip, was it? Caused those English bastards a few headaches, I hope?'

'You could say that.'

'Not asking for details, mind. Just glad to know all went well.'

There was a knock at the door. 'Pilot's aboard, sir.'

The captain rose. 'Make yourself at home, Mr Barron. This is your cabin. Once we get going, I'll organise some food. And . . .' He pointed at the whiskey bottle. 'Be my guest.'

London

Before heading off to Wapping, Merlin had spoken briefly to Johnson about Ursula Dunne. 'Robinson did a good job, but she's young and perhaps there are some angles she missed. Mrs Dunne might also give different responses to a man. Get more on Vermeulen and her husband.'

Johnson had made straight for her London residence, a flat in a large modern block not far from Kensington High Street. The place was bright and airy, with tasteful modern furniture. Colourful paintings covered almost every inch of the walls. They were seated on a stylish blue settee in the drawing room. Through the window, Kensington Gardens was visible in the distance.

Johnson declined the proffered cup of tea. 'Thanks, Mrs Dunne, but I just had one at the Yard.'

'No doubt you're very busy and would like to get down to business. I have to say, I thought I'd given the young lady everything you needed.'

'We need to follow up in light of developments.'

'You're making progress, then?'

'Some. You mentioned that Mr Vermeulen had revealed to you that he was engaged in secret work?'

'I did, although he never said quite what.'

'You have to be a brave man to do that kind of stuff.'

'He . . . he was.' There was a small catch in her throat. 'He was wonderful in many ways.' She sighed and carefully smoothed the pleats of her skirt.

Johnson nodded sympathetically. 'Is your husband in, by any chance?'

Mrs Dunne looked a little disconcerted by the question. 'He's at work.'

'Of course. He's quite high up in the civil service, I understand. Did he know about you and Mr Vermeulen?'

Mrs Dunne looked away. It took her a while to answer. 'There are large areas of life my husband and I don't discuss, some of our friendships among them. It's possible he knew about Frederick but if he did, he never said anything. We have, what shall I call it, a laissez-faire attitude to each other's attachments. A modern attitude, dare I say. We are both devoted to our son. We would not allow anything to make him unhappy.'

'So divorce and remarriage to Mr Vermeulen was never on the cards?'

'No.'

'Was Mr Vermeulen married too?'

'No. Frederick lived most of the time in Lisbon and was

189

committed to his life there. I loved the man, but a long-distance relationship suited both of us best.'

'How long had you known him?'

'As I told Constable Robinson, I met him around this time last year. Charles took me to a cocktail party but was called away on business. Frederick came over to chat. Things went from there.'

'Mr Vermeulen's path never crossed with that of your husband? London can be a small place sometimes.'

'No. To tell the truth, Charles and I don't spend an awful lot of time together. Apart from his work, which is very pressured and time-consuming, he has his golf, and he loves spending time in our country home, on which I am less keen.' She reached out for a lacquered black box on the table in front of them. 'Cigarette, Inspector?'

'No thank you.'

'I shall, if you don't mind.'

'You said you have a laissez-faire attitude to each other's attachment. Do I take it therefore that your husband has a mistress?'

Mrs Dunne tilted her head back and sent a trail of blue smoke off towards the ceiling. 'If he does, he's been remarkably discreet about it.' To Johnson's surprise, she gave a short, throaty laugh. 'I could hardly complain if he did have someone, could I?'

'And . . . forgive me, but do you think it possible Mr Vermeulen had other women here or in Portugal?'

Her reply was swift and to the point. 'Absolutely not. He loved me and me alone.'

Johnson made some notes, then continued. 'Mr Vermeulen was clearly indiscreet with you about his involvement in espionage. Do you think he might have been indiscreet with others?'

'No doubt all spies like to have someone they can open up to. In Frederick's case, that was me. I'm sure he was utterly discreet otherwise.' She raised an eyebrow. 'I presume the secret services will be looking into his death too?'

'I believe so.'

Ursula Dunne blew more cigarette smoke above her, then smiled sardonically. 'From the rather abrupt tone you've adopted in this interview, Inspector, I have a feeling mine is one of the names on your suspect list. Perhaps you think I shot him in a fit of jealous passion? I did not. I had no cause for jealousy, and even if I had, I could never have harmed a hair on his head. Besides, I did a gunpowder paraffin test. That must have turned out negative?'

'It did, although those tests are not completely foolproof. Of course, if you didn't kill him, you might have arranged for someone else to do so.'

There was a repeat of the throaty laugh. 'You are now reaching the higher realms of fantasy, Inspector. You think I have a list of potential hit men in my diary?'

Johnson decided to change tack. 'Did Mr Vermeulen tell you much about his life in Lisbon?'

'He talked a little about his business activities, deals he was engaged in, competitors, the difficulties of dealing with the Portuguese authorities. He was friendly with a rich man out there for whom he did some work.'

'Calouste Gulbenkian. We know about him. We understand Mr Vermeulen was negotiating an art purchase on his behalf. Did he talk about that?'

'He told me he'd been appointed Mr Gulbenkian's agent in the purchase. He'd been busy with the vendor on Friday. That was one of the reasons his day became jammed and he called off our dinner.'

'Did he say anything about his other business in London?'

'No, not really, though I do remember him making uncomplimentary remarks about the man who runs Gulbenkian's oil company in the City. Don't ask me to repeat them. They consisted almost entirely of four-letter words.'

'How about his friends and contacts in London?' Did you meet any of them?'

'No, we were satisfied with our own company.'

'Did he have any particular vices of which you were aware?'

'He liked to gamble. He told me stories about casino life in Lisbon.'

'Did he gamble here?'

'Not that I know.'

'Did he seem out of sorts in any way on this trip? Worried about anything?'

'No doubt he worried about the various balls he had in the air, but with me he was nothing but his usual charming, urbane self.'

Johnson consulted his notes. 'One final question, Mrs Dunne. Do you have any idea as to who killed Mr Vermeulen?'

She stubbed out her cigarette. 'I'd put money on it being some foul Nazi spy, and I hope to God you or the secret services catch him quickly and string him up.'

When they got back from the East End, Bridges volunteered to break the bad news about Van Buren to his daughter. After he'd left, Merlin got a call from the St Pancras coroner's office to say that Van Buren's post-mortem would be conducted by Sir Bernard Spilsbury. Sir Bernard expected to be in a position to share his preliminary results by 5.30. Would the chief inspector care to receive them in person or over the phone? He agreed to go in person, and Bridges was back in time to drive him there.

'How'd it go?' Merlin asked in the car.

'Pretty bloody, as you'd expect. Fortunately she had a friend there, who said she'd stay to take care of her.'

'The brother wasn't around?'

'No, but Miss Van Buren said she'd tell him.'

Bernard Spilsbury welcomed the officers warmly into his office. He was the country's most eminent pathologist and had a high public profile. He had been the principal medical witness in a string of notorious murder cases, including that of Hawley Harvey Crippen, the notorious murderer who'd been the first to be apprehended with the help of wireless telegraphy. Other notable Spilsbury cases included the Armstrong poisonings, the Brides in

192

the Bath murders and the Brighton Trunk Murders. He and Merlin knew each other well from previous investigations.

'You remember Sergeant Bridges, Sir Bernard.'

'Plain Bernard will do, Frank, and yes, of course I do. The case of the Polish flyer, wasn't it, Sergeant?'

'It was, sir.'

'September 1940. Seems a long time ago now. Anyway, I'm sure you're busy, so let's get down to it.'

Spilsbury's large steel desk was piled high with paperwork, and he took a moment to tidy things away. Merlin thought the man looked a good deal older and more gaunt than when he'd last seen him. His son had died in the Blitz and this had clearly taken its toll.

'I was very sorry to hear about Peter.'

'A terrible tragedy . . . a very promising young man. He would have been a great doctor. I received your very kind note of condolence, Frank. Thank you. I'm afraid my wife has been badly affected.'

He placed the last couple of files in a drawer. One folder remained on the desk. 'So, the late Mr Leon Van Buren. Would you prefer to discuss my findings here, or in the presence of the corpse downstairs?'

'I think we've seen enough of the body, Bernard, unless you prefer . . .?'

'No, no. Here is fine.' He opened the file. 'These then are my preliminary conclusions. Cause of death was drowning. The dreadful injuries to the head are consistent with close contact with a boat propellor. These injuries were most likely caused postmortem. There is evidence, however, of some injury that I do not believe attributable to the propellor. There are contusions on the upper right forehead, most likely caused by blows to the head.'

'Caused by the boat itself, perhaps? Or other items in the water?'

'Possibly, Frank. Or a blunt object or fists.'

'There was perhaps a fight before he entered the river?'

'Very possibly.'

Merlin pulled his chair closer to the desk. 'What time of death, do you think?'

'Given the state of the body and the fact that it's clearly been in the water for a while, that's not so easy. On the basis of the usual tests, my best guess is sometime Friday or Saturday.'

'Van Buren was last seen after dinner on Friday night,' said Bridges.

'Well, that helps to narrow it down a little. Time of death then late Friday or some time Saturday, probably earlier in the day than later.'

'It's unlikely there was a fight and someone pushed him in the water in broad daylight,' Merlin mused.

'Where did Van Buren live?' Spilsbury asked.

'Cheyne Walk.' Just across the Embankment.'

'If I remember correctly, the river wall on the pavement there is only about four feet tall.'

'I think that's right, Bernard. Not that difficult to fall over. Clearly we should make that spot our first port of call.' Merlin checked his watch. It had gone six. With the wartime double summertime hours, the evenings did not stretch out as long as usual. It would be dark by eight. He looked at Bridges. 'I think it's too late to start a search tonight, Sam. We should go first thing in the morning. Anything else we should know, Bernard?'

'I'll take a second look at the body tomorrow, as I usually do. If I find anything new, I'll call you.'

Armed with copies of Pablo Merino's passport photo, the two constables had trudged separately around Soho and the immediately surrounding areas all day. They had made no progress. No one had seen or spoken to Merino, or at least would admit to doing so.

They met as arranged at eight at the pub near Merino's hotel. Robinson got there first, feet aching and feeling quite disheartened. As their last effort of the day, they would need to question the bar staff and the customers. She decide to await Cole's arrival before starting that, and ordered herself a lemonade.

Cole arrived soon afterwards. 'Any luck?'

'None at all. You?'

'Nope, and I'm really parched. That lemonade looks good, but I think I fancy something a little stronger. Can I tempt you?'

'No thanks.'

He went to the bar and ordered a pint of Courage. The barmaid, a buxom young blonde, smiled at him as she pulled it. 'That your girlfriend over there, love? Pretty little thing, ain't she?'

'No, she's . . . she's someone I work with.'

'Oh my. Footloose and fancy-free, are you then?' She winked.

He smiled awkwardly and returned to the table with his drink.

'Spoken to anyone here, yet, Claire?'

'Thought I'd wait for you.'

Cole took a gulp of beer. 'Let's take a breather to have our drinks, then we can start going round the room.'

'You'd best start with the barmaid. Her eyes were all over you.'

He made the mistake of glancing towards the bar. Sure enough, the barmaid winked at him again.

Robinson giggled. 'See what I mean?'

Cole surveyed the room. They were in the saloon bar. The public bar was behind a partition on their right. It wasn't a very big place. He counted eight customers in the saloon area. Maybe there were a similar number in the other bar.

Drinks finished, they went immediately to work. Robinson nudged Cole in the direction of the barmaid, and she herself approached an elderly male drinker at the nearest table. It took them an hour to canvass everyone. When they reconvened, they were both a little happier.

'So . . . Tommy?'

'No luck with any of the customers, but the barmaid had some useful information. Vera, her name is.'

'Did you get her number as well?'

'Ha, ha. No, but she recognised Pablo's photo straight off. Said she'd seen him in here a couple of times. Good-looking fellow, so she was bound to notice him, she said. She also saw him once coming out of his hotel when she was arriving for work.'

'And . . .?'

'One of the times he was in here, she saw him chatting to a woman. Chatting at length.'

'Which evening?'

'All she could say was some-time last week.'

'Description?'

'Young, attractive, short dark hair.'

'A prostitute?'

'Vera thought not. She's seen the woman in here a few times with friends of both sexes. She didn't think the men were punters.

'Sounds like a reasonable chance she'll be in again.'

'Yes. Vera'll keep an eye out. I've given her our number at the Yard.'

'Bet that pleased her.'

'Enough, Claire, please. She wasn't sure, but she thought Merino and the woman might have left together.'

'Did she now?'

'How did you get on?'

'I had a bit of luck too. See that old biddy?' She pointed towards the window. 'Skinny thing in a green cardigan. She also recognised Pablo. Says she saw him here once having a drink with a young woman, presumably the same one as Vera saw. She also thought the two of them left together.'

'Must be certain then. Anything she could add to the description?'

'Her exact words were "young dago and a tart".'

'Nice.'

'She was better on timing than Vera, though. Said it was last Wednesday they were here. She comes in every Wednesday and

Friday for a port and lemon, always at nine. Pablo and the young woman were together when she arrived and left together just before closing.'

'Last Wednesday . . . that's only twenty-four hours, give or take, before he was murdered. Had the old lady seen the woman in here before?'

'A few times, but she knows nothing about her.'

'But she thought she was a tart?'

'I think she's the sort of woman who calls any female under fifty a tart.'

'Huh!' Cole took time to scribble something in his notebook. 'Let's hope we can track her down.' He gave her a funny look. 'So, as the day hasn't turned out to be a complete disaster, I think we've earned one for the road. Will you have a proper drink now?'

Robinson hesitated, then smiled. 'Oh all right then. I'll have a gin and it.'

'Just like old times, eh, Claire?'

Chapter Sixteen

Wednesday August 19ᵗʰ 1942

Bernie Goldberg groaned as he reached out to turn off the alarm in his Piccadilly hotel room. He looked blearily at the clock. It was 6.45. He remembered with another groan that he had an early meeting at the embassy. The trip back from Moscow had been exhausting. There had been stops in Teheran, Cairo and Gibraltar before journey's end had finally been reached at Northolt aerodrome late the previous night. It was in Cairo that he had said his goodbyes to Averell Harriman. One temporary boss had asked him to pass on greetings to the new one, Lieutenant General Dwight D. Eisenhower.

Grosvenor Square was only a short walk away, and he made the embassy in good time. A pretty young uniformed woman showed him into a windowless meeting room on the second floor of the building. There were several easels at one end of the room facing a large table. On one was a map of occupied Europe, and on another, a map of North Africa. Fifteen minutes later, a tall, middle-aged officer with a Clark Gable style moustache entered the room, briefcase in hand.

'Mr Goldberg. Good to meet you. I hope you've recovered from your arduous trip?' Goldberg recognised a Bostonian accent.

'Still a little groggy, sir.'

'I'm very sorry then to have dragged you out of bed so early. Unfortunately, this was the only time I could make today.'

'That's all right, sir. I'm sure you're a very busy man.'

'I'm Colonel John McCluskey, by the way, and I'm not sure that in your new position you are required to call me sir. Colonel will do fine. Glad to meet you, Detective.' McCluskey reached out his free hand for Goldberg to shake, then sat down opposite him.

'You have been made familiar with your new role?'

'Mr Harriman said I am to act as liaison between the US military police here and the London Metropolitan Police while the new jurisdictional changes are bedded in.'

'That's exactly it.' McCluskey smoothed his moustache. He was a good-looking man and seemed keenly aware of it. 'Although, perhaps the word "trouble-shooter" should be added to the job description. With luck, however, there'll be very little trouble to shoot.'

'I hope so too. May I ask, Colonel, why I've been given this job?'

'You got the job because, according to your superiors in New York, you're a no-nonsense, highly effective, independent-minded police officer, and because Mr Harriman gave you a superb reference. Your recent successful secondment with the Metropolitan Police was also a key factor.' McCluskey reached into his briefcase and drew out a file. 'In here are details of all the cases that have been transferred or taken up directly by our officers in the short time since the new legislation took effect. As your first task, I suggest you familiarise yourself with them.'

Goldberg took the file and weighed it in his hand. 'Quite a number of cases already, it seems.'

'Indeed. Our police teams are very busy. And the list of crimes under investigation is quite varied. Murder, rape, robbery, fraud . . . a wide range.'

'And is it you I report to, Colonel?'

'It is, and I in turn report directly to General Eisenhower, who has asked to be kept apprised of your work. As regards an office, you have a comfortable little room just along the corridor from mine.'

'Thank you. I was wondering, Colonel, whether I am expected to be proactive in identifying difficulties, or do I just deal with them as they come to me?'

'A good question, which I don't think I can answer at the moment. Let's just take things as they come to start with. I trust experience will guide us as to best practice.'

'Very well. When will I get to meet your officers?'

'I'll try and arrange a start on that today.'

Goldberg opened the file. The first document detailed a rape case. The officer in charge was listed as Captain Max Pearce.

'Captain Pearce is one of your top men?'

'Indeed he is. A very good man with considerable experience as a police officer in civilian life.'

'May I ask where he was an officer?'

'Alabama, I believe.'

'Hmm. Policing down there can be a little different from that in big cities like New York or London.'

'He's accommodated himself, I assure you.'

Goldberg heard the door opening behind him, then saw McCluskey jump to his feet. He thought he'd better follow suit. The newcomer was General Dwight D. Eisenhower.

'Why, sir, I wasn't expecting you.'

'At ease, Colonel. I was just on the phone to Mr Harriman, who was briefing me about Moscow. He also took the time to tell me about Detective Goldberg here. Good to make your acquaintance, Detective.'

Goldberg grasped the general's extended hand. Eisenhower was a balding, wiry, genial-looking man who spoke with a faint Midwestern drawl. McCluskey pulled out a chair.

'No, no, Colonel, I won't be staying. I have an important operational meeting in five minutes. I just wanted to say hello to the detective.' Eisenhower patted the colonel's shoulder. 'McCluskey here is a good man, Detective. If you've any problems, he'll be able to help you out. I expect there'll be a few, as the British can be thin-skinned and small-minded from time to time. As can we all, of course. I wish you good luck.'

'Thank you, sir. I hope you'll remember I'm new at this sort of thing. I'm bound to make a few mistakes.'

'Naturally. Just do your best, that's all I ask.'

'I'll try, sir.'

Merlin, Johnson and Bridges were on their way to the Chelsea Embankment. Johnson was taking the opportunity to brief his two colleagues on his interview with Ursula Dunne. When he'd finished, Merlin said, 'It looks like we ought to have a word with Mr Dunne.'

'Think so, sir. I'd be interested to know what he really knew about his wife's affair.'

The car got stuck in traffic in Sloane Square. Merlin looked out at the bustling crowd outside the Tube station. A thin drizzle was falling and umbrellas were out in force.

'Vermeulen strikes me as a bit of a player,' observed Bridges as he manoeuvred the car through the line of vehicles. 'I'd be surprised if he didn't have one or two other women on the go.'

'You may be right. Easier in Lisbon than here, I'd have thought. Mrs Dunne strikes me as the possessive sort, eh, Peter?'

'Whatever the situation, I think she was telling the truth when she said she didn't believe he was playing the field. I didn't sense any undercurrents of jealousy.'

'Then you think we were right to discount her as a suspect?'

'I think so, sir. I gave her quite a hard time, but she didn't buckle.'

Bridges parked the car a few doors along from Van Buren's house. As the three men got out, Merlin saw the faint outline of a rainbow in the distance, above Battersea Power Station. They cut through the small public gardens outside Van Buren's house and crossed the road.

Merlin paused for a moment to take stock, then started to issue instructions. 'Sergeant, you head along the pavement in the

201

direction of the Royal Hospital. Go about a hundred and fifty yards, then turn and work your way back looking for anything out of the ordinary. You do likewise, Peter, from the other direction. I'll stay here and see what's to see.

As his men walked off, Merlin went to the river wall. It looked, as they'd thought, no more than four feet high, if that. Nearby was a pier that led out to a mooring. He counted seven houseboats tied up. It occurred to him that if Van Buren had been involved in a fight here, boat residents might well have seen something. He made a mental note to follow up that possibility later

Two glum faces greeted him when Johnson and Bridges returned.

'Nothing?'

The officers shook their heads in unison.

'Damn it. Looks like we'll have to get a full forensics team out here.'

'Do you think we can justify that, sir?' said Johnson. 'This seems quite a long shot, and Denis was telling me yesterday how stretched his department is at present.'

Merlin drew in a breath. 'You're probably right, Peter.' He cast his eyes down. As he did so, the sun poked through the clouds for the first time that morning and lit everything up. Merlin caught a flash of colour at the foot of the riverside wall.

'Got those handy tweezers of yours on you, Sergeant?'

'Of course, sir.'

The colour had been provided by two sodden red petals. Merlin bent to pick them up with the tweezers and dropped them onto his handkerchief.

'I seem to remember there being something in Van Buren's button-hole when we saw him in Wapping.'

'You're right, sir. The remnants of . . . oh, what's it called?'

'A corsage?' suggested Johnson.

'Yes, a corsage.' Merlin nodded. 'A carnation, wasn't it?'

'Not very well up on my flowers, sir' said Bridges. 'Something like.'

202

'I wonder if we could get a match?'

'The mortuary will probably have chucked the flower out by now, sir.'

'Maybe, Sergeant, but we should find out.'

'There's a police box in the Royal Hospital Road. I'll go and make a call.'

Humphrey Butterfield was in the estate office when he took the call from his solicitor. 'Humphrey? Wilfred here. I was wondering if you'd heard the news?'

'What news?'

'About Leon. I'm afraid he's dead. He was fished out of the Thames yesterday. His solicitor just telephoned to tell me.'

Butterfield said nothing.

'Humphrey? Are you there?'

'How terrible.'

'On the one hand terrible, but on the other hand pretty wonderful. For you at least. Chances are you'll be in the clear.'

'What do you mean?'

'Why, on the litigation.'

'Leon's children might continue with the case.'

'I'd be surprised if they do. They were never particularly supportive of it, I believe. And in any event, it's not as if they're going to be short of money after his death.'

'Why? From what I heard, they won't necessarily be getting much from him.'

'Perhaps, but you are forgetting the terms of Mary's will. There are significant bequests to the children that they receive at twenty-six or on Leon's death, whichever is earlier. And if the stolen goods are recovered, of course, they'll be sitting even prettier.'

'Stolen goods? What stolen goods?'

'Word is there was a burglary at Leon's house on Friday night. It's thought some valuable art and a stash of cash went missing.'

'Goodness.'

'Anyway, the fact is, whoever caused Leon's death looks likely to have done you a huge favour.'

'Is foul play suspected?

'According to Leon's solicitor, the police are open to all possibilities. Accident, suicide, murder.'

'I see. So what happens next? As regards the case, I mean.'

'If they decide to withdraw the litigation, it'll probably take a month or two for formalities to be completed, costs to be sorted, et cetera. Not long really. Then you'll have your life back.'

After he put the phone down, Butterfield sat back and considered North's parting words. *'You'll have your life back'*. After all the mental torture of the past year, had that time really come?

Nathan Katz had suffered another sleepless night. Now, standing at the wash-basin in his room, he looked at himself in the mirror. It was a sorry sight. There were deep hollows under his eyes, his hair was a mess, a couple of nasty spots had broken out on his nose, and he sported four days' worth of unattractive stubble on his chin. He had not benefitted at all from the time off his uncle had given him. All it had done was to give him more time to dwell on his terrible predicament. He had been due back at work the day before, but had been unable to summon the strength to go in. It had been the same today, but he had been stirred to action by the mid-morning arrival of a cable: *SURPRISED NOT TO SEE YOU IN OFFICE TODAY STOP ARRANGEMENT WAS RETURN TO WORK TUESDAY STOP ARE YOU UNWELL STOP HOPE TO SEE YOU SOON STOP YOUR UNCLE BENJAMIN STOP*. He was letting his uncle down and only making things worse.

He closed his eyes, but his father's face came to him again. A reproachful face. He could not get Daniel Katz out of his mind, nor Leon Van Buren. Those damned drawings! He should have listened to his uncle and moved on and forgotten about them. There was nothing to be done.

An hour later, after a supreme act of will, Nathan Katz was washed, shaved, dressed and ready for the office. Outside he found the pavements wet, but the sun shining. He'd decided to tell his uncle that he'd caught a bug and had been unable to get to a telephone. He would be forgiven, he was sure. Then he'd plunge straight into his work and thereby keep the demons at bay.

The two men faced each other across Billy Hill's desk. Hill didn't seem happy. Micallef thought he knew why.

'Where the hell have you been, Teddy? I've been trying to get hold of you since yesterday.'

'Out and about, Billy. Didn't get the message until just now and came here straight away. What's up?'

Hill's lip curled. 'What's up, Teddy old pal, is that a little birdie of mine in the Met says the geezer you burgled last week has turned up as dead as a dodo in the Thames.'

'Um . . . er, yes, I heard that too.'

'You did? Who told you?'

'Van Buren's daughter.'

'And when was that?'

'Yesterday.'

'Yesterday. And you didn't think to give poor Billy a little tinkle to put him in the picture?'

'Sorry, Billy. As you can imagine, Elizabeth was distraught. She required a . . . a good deal of attention.'

Hill's eyes narrowed. 'Did she now? And you played the part of the dependable boyfriend?'

'Er . . . yes.'

'Then how come one of my lads told me you were seen on the town last night with one of those Windmill tarts? Got bored with comforting Miss Van Buren, did you?'

Micallef looked down at his feet. 'Sorry, Billy.'

Hill glared silently at the young man for a while, then asked, 'You have anything to do with it? The man ending up dead, I mean?'

'Course not. God's honour. Why would I want to knock him off?'

'Perhaps, contrary to what you and Jake Penny told me, the burglary didn't go off quite so smoothly. Perhaps Van Buren caught Jake red-handed. Perhaps you were keeping an eye out for Jake and went to cover his back. Perhaps things got rough. Perhaps—'

'Nothing like that happened, Billy, I swear. There was no bother at all and Jake was never disturbed.'

'Yeah? Where's Jake now?'

'I don't know.'

Hill picked at his fingernails. 'Get me a stiff one from the bar over there, will you. And one for yourself if you like.'

Micallef did as he was told and returned with two large neat whiskies.

Hill took a sip, then leaned back in his chair. 'Thing is, Teddy, as I'm sure you're aware, with a corpse now involved, the police will be all over this caper like a rash. Has your girl said anything about what they're thinking?'

'No, Billy.'

'It's quite hard to fall into the Thames in the centre of London without someone giving you a helping hand. I bet the coppers are looking at it that way.'

'Perhaps they'll think it was suicide.'

'Did he seem the suicidal type?'

'No.'

'Anyway, they'll be buzzing over everything and we'll need to lie low. There's no chance of us hawking the drawings around at the moment. I had been thinking of your idea about contacting this Gulbenkian fellow, but if a man's been killed, we can't risk that. We're going to have to sit on the damned things for a long time.'

'The job was still worth it for all that cash we got.'

'Perhaps it was.' Hill looked warily at Micallef. 'Thing is, Teddy, now we have to have a little think about you.'

'How'd you mean?'

'You were at the Friday-night dinner.'

'Of course. Then I went with Elizabeth to her place.'

'So you say. The police are obviously going to take a particularly keen interest in everyone who was in the party.'

'I'm ready for them, Billy. I can handle it. I've got no record. I'm completely clean as far as the coppers know. And I've got a legitimate trade.'

'You've done some kosher deals, have you? If they check?'

'Sure. A few car deals for friends. Shifted some antiques. All above board.'

'But you've also shifted some stuff for me. Let's hope that doesn't come back to bite us. Thing is, lad, we're all going to have to be very careful, you more than anyone. Looks like you've got a decent alibi for after the dinner. That said, I'd like you to keep your distance for now. Stay away from here and the other lads.'

'But why, Billy? Won't that—'

Hill raised his hand. 'Don't argue, Teddy. I want you under wraps until this all blows over. Got it?'

Micallef nodded. 'All right.'

'And play sweet with the daughter. Do not run around with other women. Now is not the time to fall out with her.'

The answer from St Pancras was that the soggy Van Buren corsage did indeed remain in storage. Bridges reported back, then jumped in the car with the petals carefully folded in Merlin's handkerchief. Merlin, however, decided he couldn't wait. Was it really possible to match petals to a flower? The slim possibility of connection was enough for him. He was going to take the risk and call in forensics straight away. If it all turned out to be a waste of time, he'd get a rocket from above, but so be it. He turned to Johnson and sent him off to make the call.

On the inspector's return, Merlin said to him, 'I think I'll take this opportunity to have another chat with Miss Van Buren. Her flat's not far, I understand. Do you mind if leave you here to wait for forensics?'

'Not at all, sir.'

It took him just over ten minutes to reach the flat, which was full of packing cases. Miss Van Buren was clearly grieving but relatively in control of herself. She agreed to answer some more questions.

'I wonder, miss, did your father wear a flower in his buttonhole at the Friday dinner?'

'Yes. A carnation, as I recall. A red one, His favourite flower. Why?'

'We just found something on the Embankment, roughly opposite your father's house. Possibly the remnants of such a corsage.'

'But . . . what does that mean? Daddy was there at some point?'

'It's a long shot, but we're going to look into whether that's where he went into the river. I've called in forensics and there'll be a thorough examination of the surrounding area today.'

'I see.'

'Forgive me, but I have to ask this question. Do you think there's any chance your father took his own life?'

'Suicide? Not a chance.'

'There's no doubt in your mind?'

'He wasn't the type, to start with. If he had problems, he fought to solve them. He was no quitter. Over and above that, consider that he was just about to come into a fortune from the sale of the drawings. Any financial difficulties would be sorted and he'd be almost as wealthy as he was before. What on earth could prompt him to kill himself at such a time?'

'We shall discount suicide then. Moving on, I have some questions regarding the drawings. Was Friday night the first time you knew of the deal your father had struck?'

'Yes, course. It was only agreed that afternoon.'

'But you were aware before that something was in prospect?'

'All I knew was that he had some deal in progress that might

bring a significant improvement to his finances. He made no spe-
cific mention of the drawings.'

'Did your brother know more?'

'Robert was pestering him all the time for money he didn't
want to give, so I doubt it.'

'But your father did end up revealing everything at the
dinner?'

'He was obviously very excited and couldn't keep the sale to himself. But he didn't give the financial details to the whole party. He
only confided those to me and Robert when we met in private.'

'Did he just tell you the price, or did he mention the cash that
had already been handed over?'

'He told me about the twenty thousand when we had a moment
to ourselves. I don't know if he told Robert.'

'Where did he say the money was?'

'He said he had it to hand. I assumed that meant in the safe.'

'You gave us the names of the two other dinner guests.' Merlin
took out his notebook. 'A Miss Caroline Mitchum, a friend of
your brother's, and a Mr Edward Micallef, a friend of yours.'

'Yes.'

'Micallef's a Maltese name, isn't it?'

'Yes.'

'He has family here?'

'No. They're all in Malta. Very wealthy, apparently, and able to
set him up nicely in England.'

'When did he leave Malta?'

'Just before I met him.'

Merlin frowned. 'How did he do that? Malta's been under German blockade for the past two years.'

'He managed somehow. He's a very brave man.'

'You've known him long?'

'Since the beginning of the year.'

'He's a close friend?'

'We are, as they say, an item.'

'And what does he do for a living?'

'He's a dealer. Nice cars, antiques. Luxury items.'

'We shall need to speak to him, of course. I'd appreciate every-one's details.'

'I can give you Edward's and Robert's, but I don't have Miss Mitchum's. You'll have to get her number and address from my brother.'

Merlin checked his notebook. 'We didn't have a chance to speak properly to Mrs Macdonald. Is she back at work? Presum-ably she knows about your father?'

'She called me today. Her husband was taken ill, as you know, but appears to be out of the woods. She hadn't heard about Daddy and was naturally very upset when I told her. She asked whether we wanted her back at work and I said yes. She's paid for a couple of months in advance, so she might as well be there to look after the place. She'll be in tomorrow.'

'Good. One question we didn't ask when we saw you at your father's house. Did you notice any of the guests go upstairs during the Friday dinner party?'

'Upstairs? I'm not sure . . . Oh yes, I remember there was some problem with the downstairs toilet, so the one on the first floor was in use. I presume everyone used it at one time or another.'

'You weren't aware of anyone going up to the top floor?'

'No.'

'Presumably there was quite a bit of drinking at the party?'

'Certainly some champagne and wine was drunk.'

'Was anyone the worse for wear?'

'Not that I recall. Robert got rather bombastic, but that's normal.'

'How about your father?'

'He certainly had plenty to drink but it took a lot to make him drunk. A little merry, perhaps.'

'You went straight home after the party?'

'Yes.'

'With Mr Micallef?'

'Yes.'

'Forgive me for prying, but did he . . . did he stay the night?'

'He did, but I don't know why that's relevant.'

'He was with you the whole night?'

'Apart from when he went out for a breath of fresh air, yes.'

'How long did that take?'

'I'm not sure. I went to bed. Not long, I think.'

'The dinner party finished quite early by London standards. Any particular reason for that?'

This question seemed to make Miss Van Buren a little uncomfortable. 'I . . . I . . . er, I should probably have told you this before. Daddy had an engagement after supper. A lady friend he wanted to see. Apparently she was going away in the morning and he wanted to spend a little time with her before her departure. That was why he wanted the party to end at ten.'

'Are you telling me that your father had a girlfriend?'

'I suppose that's one word for it.'

'But she wasn't invited to the dinner?'

'The fact is . . . Robert and I don't get on with her. Daddy was being sensitive to that.'

'May I ask the reason you don't get on?'

She brushed back her hair. 'Daddy's relationship with the woman pre-dated my mother's death. It's true that my mother was almost completely incapacitated when it began, but we both found it very difficult to cope with.'

'Did your father support this lady?'

'I don't know for certain, but I suspect so. She lives not far from here. She doesn't have a job that I know of.'

'If your father went to visit her after the dinner, she might have been the last person to see him apart from his killer.'

Elizabeth Van Buren flinched at Merlin's choice of words.

'Assuming he made it to her house in the first place, that is. Where is it?'

211

'She lives in one of those chintzy little streets off the King's Road.

'Her name?'

'Frances. Frances Walters.'

Inspector Armstrong's forensics team were already hard at work when Merlin found his way back to the Embankment. The inspector himself was there to greet him. He wasn't happy. 'I hope this doesn't turn out to be a wild goose chase. Scores of people, if not hundreds, must have tramped the pavement here since last Friday. Then there's been quite a bit of rain. If we find anything useful, I'll eat my hat.'

'We found the carnation petals, though, didn't we?'

Armstrong shrugged and went off to supervise his men.

Merlin told Johnson about his talk with Miss Van Buren, then stayed to watch the forensics operation. Elizabeth Van Buren had given him her brother's address, also in Chelsea, and he decided after half an hour of standing around, to pay him a visit.

Johnson manned the fort again and was on the spot to hear someone shout, not long after Merlin had left, 'Over here. I . . . I've found something.' The officer was standing twenty feet or so from where the petals had been discovered, with one foot in the gutter and the other on the pavement. Armstrong, Johnson and a couple of others converged on him. In his gloved hand was a small object that gleamed in the late-morning sunlight.

'What have you got there, Willis?' asked Armstrong.

'A tie pin, sir. It was hidden under some leaves.'

Johnson bent to have a closer look. 'Silver or silver plate, I think. There's some sort of design in blue. Like an arrowhead.'

Armstrong took the pin from Willis and produced a small magnifying glass. 'I think the technical term is "chevron". It's a heraldic device.'

'Any chance of lifting some fingerprints, Denis?'

'Given its size and the probability that it's been out in the open

212

for a while, I doubt it, but we'll give it a go. Of course, there's nothing at all to suggest this has anything to do with your case. Any old Tom, Dick or Harry might have dropped it.'

'Maybe, but you never know.'

Robert Van Buren's flat was ten minutes away in the opposite direction to his sister's. It was in a mansion block close to the Royal Hospital where Merlin remembered attending a party years ago. The occasion had stuck in his memory because the elderly hostess had told him stories about Oscar Wilde, who'd lived nearby in Tite Street, and with whom she claimed to have been friends.

The door was opened by a young lady who turned out to be Caroline Mitchum. She told him that Robert Van Buren was out, but Merlin said he'd appreciate a few words with her. Smiling, she led him into a large, untidy drawing room with a partial view of the river. Papers and items of clothing were scattered everywhere and there were signs of a half-eaten meal on a table by the window.

'I'm so sorry. Robert is very untidy, and I have to admit I'm not much better. Please give me a moment.' She spent a few minutes clearing up and succeeded in bringing a semblance of order. 'Please, Chief Inspector.' She pointed at a black sofa and they sat down next to each other. 'I'm afraid Robert has gone out to a business lunch. I was meant to accompany him, but the man he's meeting is a dreadful bore, so I ducked out. Gave me a chance to get on with some writing. Anyway, it's so terrible what's happened. How can I help?'

A klaxon suddenly blared noisily outside. Miss Mitchum rolled her eyes. 'Those river barges do make rather a racket, don't they? I never realised until I came here.'

'You . . . er . . . live here with Mr Van Buren?'

'Goodness, no!' She laughed, blushed and tossed her hair, seemingly all in one movement. The features on her face seemed oddly out of proportion. She wore no make-up and was dressed in a

213

dowdy brown corduroy skirt and shapeless green jumper. She apparently cared little for her appearance. She had, however, Merlin thought, something about her. 'I share a place in King's Cross with a couple of other girls. I've just been staying here for the past few days to provide Robert with a bit of support. It's obviously been horrible. First the disappearance, then the discovery of the burglary, then finally yesterday's awful news.'

'Horrible indeed. Were Robert and his father very close?'

'I believe so.'

'You've known Robert long?'

'As it happens, no. Only a few weeks. We seem to have hit it off. I do part-time work for a man called Roderick Havering.' She picked at a loose thread in her jumper. 'He's the editor and publisher of the new literary magazine that Robert is involved with.'

'Miss Van Buren mentioned that. Robert is to be the principal backer of this magazine.'

'The only backer, in fact. It's all very exciting. Do you know the *Horizon* magazine, Mr Merlin?'

'I occasionally read new poetry in it.'

'You are keen on poetry?'

'I am.'

'Well, you must subscribe to Robert's magazine. It's going to be called *Athena*. The plan is to go into direct competition with Horizon. We're hoping to get some big names to contribute, and of course, there'll be room for exciting newcomers.' She smiled self-consciously. 'I write poetry myself. Robert has promised to put some of my work in the magazine.'

'I wish you luck. Now, you were one of the last people to see Mr Van Buren alive, Miss Mitchum. Please tell me about Friday's dinner party.'

'To tell the truth, I found it all a bit nerve-racking. I'd never met Mr Van Buren before, nor Robert's sister.'

'Nor Mr Micallef, presumably?'

'No.'

'And how did you find Mr Van Buren?'

'Rather forbidding.'

'He wasn't particularly friendly?'

'I wouldn't say that, but I had the distinct feeling that he'd much rather Mr Micallef and I had not been there. Quite understandable really, as he had important family news to deliver and he didn't know me from Adam.'

'Did the evening improve as it went on, from your perspective?'

'Well, inevitably I relaxed as things progressed. A few drinks helped, of course. I didn't really talk much to Mr Van Buren, but Elizabeth and her friend were reasonably friendly.'

'What did you think of Mr Micallef?'

'Very good-looking and knows it. Elizabeth seems quite smitten. He was polite, but . . . I got the impression he and I didn't have much in common.'

'Did you have a chance to look around the house?'

'No. Not really. I saw the drawing room and the dining room. And the bathroom upstairs. The downstairs WC wasn't working.'

'Did you notice Mr Micallef taking the opportunity to look around?'

'Well, I suppose he went upstairs to use the facilities at some point. Yes, I remember that he did.'

'Was he up there a long time?'

She laughed. 'I'm not in the habit of timing people's calls of nature, Chief Inspector, so I can't really say.'

'Did Mr Van Buren and his children get along well during the evening?'

'I think so. Of course, there are always undercurrents in family relationships that can pass others by.'

'What do you mean by that?'

Caroline frowned. 'Look, Mr Merlin, I'm happy to answer questions about the dinner, but I'm not really comfortable engaging in idle gossip. What does that have to do with finding out how Mr Van Buren died?'

'I'm sorry, but in any murder investigation, which this most likely is, it's important to have a complete understanding of the victim's circumstances. I know already, for example, that there was some tension between Robert and his father over money.'

'I see.' She sighed. 'Well, yes, it's true Mr Van Buren wasn't exactly jumping at the idea of funding Robert's magazine. There had been words, but as far as I am aware, Mr Van Buren had recently conceded the matter and given Robert to believe that some money would be forthcoming. This was before the drawings sale had been agreed.

'Are Robert and his sister close?'

'I've only been around a short time, Chief Inspector, and I don't know if I can really say. I've no reason to think not.'

'Is Robert an easy-going fellow?'

'I'm not sure exactly what you mean. He's certainly charming and good company.'

'And his character?'

'Resilient, I'd say. He's managed to get through difficult times, and no doubt he'll get through this.'

'You mean his father's business problems and his mother's death?'

'Obviously those, yes, and I understand as well that he had quite a difficult time when he was in his teens.'

'What happened?'

'I don't know the details, but I believe there was some kind of traumatic event and he was ill for a while because of it.'

'I didn't know that.' Merlin stroked his chin thoughtfully, then, deciding that he'd heard enough, he got to his feet and offered his thanks.

'Good luck in your investigations, Mr Merlin. I'll tell Robert you called.'

★

During the course of the day, Martin Ramsey had broken off several times from his cataloguing work to try and get hold of Nathan Katz. He had been unsuccessful. When he got back from lunch, he decided to give it another go and finally managed to get through.

'It's Martin. God, Nathan, you're a hard man to track down.'

'I've not been well.'

'Sorry to hear that. Are you all right now?'

'Just about. I'm very busy, though, Martin.'

'I'll be brief then. I'm ringing about Van Buren. You heard the news?'

'What news?'

'The man is dead. Washed up in the river. The police are investigating.'

There was no reply.

'Nathan?'

'Are they? Well, thanks for telling me.'

'The thing is, Nathan, I was wondering . . . After that discovery we made in the pub, did you ever follow up with Van Buren? Call him or anything?'

'I visited him at his house the day after and we had a talk.'

'What did he say?'

'What you'd expect. Denied the drawings were stolen. Said he owned them fair and square. Told me pretty much to get lost.'

'You . . . you argued?'

'Not really. I stated my case and he responded. Then we parted.'

'When was this?'

'The day after our drink. Tuesday of last week.' Katz's voice took on a sharper edge.

'Why are you asking me all this, Martin?'

'Oh . . . sorry, no offence meant. I was just wondering, that's all.'

'Wondering if I had anything to do with his death?'

'Of course not.'

'Look, Martin, I wish I'd never told you about the damned drawings. Forget I ever mentioned them. A very good day to you.'

The line went dead. Ramsey sat back in his chair and considered the conversation for a long while. Then he went to see his grandfather.

'I've finally spoken to Nathan Katz. He admits to seeing Van Buren early last week. Says they spoke about the drawings but Van Buren sent him packing.'

'That's it? There was no unpleasantness?'

'He says not. And he categorically denies having anything to do with Van Buren's death.'

'Well there you are then. You need do nothing.'

'The thing is, Grandfather, I don't know if I believe him. There was something about his attitude. He seemed rather unfriendly.'

'Perhaps that's understandable if he thought you were asking whether he was a murderer.'

'He did see it like that. I'm not really satisfied, though. I'm still inclined to contact the police. See what they make of him.'

Augustus Ramsey stroked his beard thoughtfully. 'Well, Martin, I'll not interfere. You must do what you think right.'

'I'll go and make the call now.'

When Merlin returned to the Embankment, he was buoyed to hear about the tie pin. He hung around for a while observing Armstrong's men at work, then left Johnson in place again and returned to the Yard. It was nearly five when he got there. Two messages were waiting. One was that Martin Ramsey from the art gallery had called and would like a word. The other was that Bernie Goldberg would be waiting for Merlin in the Red Lion pub around the corner at 5.30. The invitation was irresistible, and Merlin decided the call to Ramsey could wait until morning.

He spotted Goldberg through the crowd. The American had managed to get a table, on which sat two frothing pints of beer. He rose and the men embraced.

'Great to see you, Bernie. Sharp suit you've got there. Already made a quick trip to Savile Row?'

218

Goldberg stroked his lapels. 'This is fine American cloth, Frank. Bought in Brooks Brothers before I set out on my travels.'

'Well, it looks good on you.'

They sat down. 'All well with you, Frank? Life as a married man and father suiting you?'

Merlin laughed. 'It's all a bit different, but the lad is a joy. So is Sonia.' He took a sip of beer. 'So you've been to Moscow, I understand? How exciting. You must tell me all about it.'

Goldberg proceeded to do just that. Merlin was naturally impressed. 'Churchill, Stalin, Harriman. Quite a group! Good material for your autobiography when you write it.'

'You've met Mr Churchill, haven't you, Frank?'

'A couple of times. I have to say, I'd love to see Stalin up close.'

'I'm not sure you would. He gave me the shivers.'

'A champion drinker, I read somewhere.'

'Him and all his men. Even Churchill couldn't keep up with them.'

'What about your Mr Harriman?'

'He was about the only one on the trip who managed to remain sober throughout.'

'An impressive man?'

'Yes. Serious but likeable. It's good to know he's America's principal liaison with the British government.'

'The trip was a success?'

'Of course, I wasn't fully in the loop, but on the way home everyone seemed very happy. As I understand it, Stalin's big gripe was the delay in establishing a second front. Seems Churchill managed to convince him more time was needed.' Goldberg drank some beer. 'Anyway, enough of me. What about you? What's up at the Yard?'

Merlin told his friend his news. Mention of the Pablo Merino murder opened the door to discussion of Goldberg's new temporary job.

'I'm sure you'll be perfect in that role, Bernie, and it's great for me and my colleagues at the Met to have you in the job. Have you met any of the senior American police officers yet?'

'I met some today. The rest tomorrow.'

'You say you were given a file of the initial handover cases. Have you had a chance to go through it?'

'Not properly, no.'

'When you do, no doubt the Merino case will be there. Look at it carefully. The suspect in custody is called Virgil Lewis. It's my belief he's the wrong man.'

'Who's taken over the case on our side?'

'A man called Pearce.'

'I haven't met him yet, but I've heard a little.'

'Lewis is black. Pearce doesn't seem very keen on black people.'

'He's from Alabama. Things aren't good down there if your skin's not white.' Goldberg wiped beer froth from his lips. 'You've voiced your concern about the case to the American authorities?'

'I told Pearce, but he's not interested.'

'Seems to me you're generating my first case as liaison officer.'

'I guess I am. The thing is, Pearce is rushing to bring this to trial. If things can be slowed down a little, there's a better chance the real culprit can be identified.'

'But that'll be no use to you, since you're supposed to be off the case.'

Merlin smiled cryptically. 'There are many ways to skin a cat.'

'I trust you'll tread carefully.'

'You know me, Bernie.' He had a glint in his eye. 'Always a stickler for the rules.'

'No comment. So when do I get to see Mrs Merlin and your new addition?'

Chapter Seventeen

Gulbenkian was toying unenthusiastically with his breakfast of scrambled eggs and tomatoes when his secretary came into the room.

'Another cable from London, sir.'

He shook his head. 'What now? More disasters?'

In the last seventy-two hours, he'd had a steady stream of cables from his London lawyers relaying news of Vermeulen's death, the presumed theft of the drawings, and lastly Van Buren's death.

He steeled himself. 'All right then. You read it. I don't think I have the strength.'

Isabelle Theis put on the expensive bejewelled reading glasses Gulbenkian had given her for her last birthday. ' "GREETINGS CALOUSTE STOP UNFORTUNATE NEWS ABOUT DV DRAWINGS JUST REACHED ME FROM ONE OF MY SOURCES STOP WHEN CAN I EXPECT RETURN OF POUNDS DEPOSIT ADVANCED VERMEULEN STOP PROMPT ACTION ANTICIPATED STOP ALSO ARRANGEMENT FEE DUE AS PER DISCUSSIONS WITH V STOP SORRY FOR YOUR LOSS STOP

SAYGILARIMLA YOUR GOOD FRIEND MUSTAFA
TATAR STOP".'

Gulbenkian stared miserably down at his eggs. 'It's the stolen twenty thousand pounds he's talking about. The balance of fifty-five thousand he gave Vermeulen has been recovered and returned, hasn't it?'

'Yes. Vermeulen left it in the safe keeping of the lawyers. Do you want to reply?'

'I'll have to pay the wretched man, I suppose. We'll do it through one of my South African accounts, but take your time. Let's make him wait a bit. Compose an appropriate holding cable, would you, my dear, then run it by me.'

Isabelle removed her glasses and he looked up into those deep blue eyes of hers. She was no longer young, but she was still a fine-looking woman. Perhaps a little nap together later would help take his mind off the recent unpleasant train of events.

'I was wondering, sir, to whom the thieves could possibly sell the drawings?'

'Good question. Some unscrupulous dealer or collector might be interested in taking them off the thieves' hands for a fraction of their true value, but the pool of such people has been reduced by wartime conditions. The associated risk will obviously be very high. With a death on top of the burglary, Scotland Yard will be all over the case.'

He pushed away his half-eaten breakfast, got up and walked out onto the balcony. There was a welcome breeze today, which was ruffling the foliage of his numerous potted plants. He stared out towards the sea and took a few deep breaths before returning inside. Isabelle had not moved.

'You know, my dear, I have a funny feeling about those draw-ings. A good feeling. Although things look a bit bleak at present, I believe they will still end up in my hands. I feel it in my bones. I may have to wait a while, but I'm sure they will ultimately be mine.'

Swanton called first thing to convene another meeting in the park. As before, Merlin found him already in place. Swanton looked up at him and frowned. 'You look a little peaky, Frank. Not succumbing to anything, I hope?'

'I'm afraid I had a beer or two too many last night with an old friend. Just a little hung-over, that's all.'

'Oh well. These are difficult times. We're all entitled to let our hair down once in a while. Was the friend anyone I know?'

'You remember Bernie Goldberg, the American detective who was seconded to me last year?'

'Yes, of course. I heard on the grapevine he was in London and had been given an interesting job.'

'We had a jolly evening but did touch on a little business. I discussed the Merino case with him.'

'Did you now? Didn't tell him anything you shouldn't, I hope?'

'Of course not, Harold, more's the pity.'

Swanson had brought a bag of breadcrumbs for the ducks and began scattering them on the ground. A feeding frenzy inevitably followed and neither man said anything until it was over. Then Swanton spoke. 'So. Developments. I'm afraid we've not made much progress, but I've arranged to meet today with one of the local Russian spooks, a senior fellow called Grishin.'

'I know the man.'

'You do? Normally I wouldn't expect to get much out of a fellow like him. As it happens, however, we've done a few favours for the Russians recently. I'm due one in return.'

'I see.' Merlin remembered he'd not told Swanton about Pablo's notebook. Clearly Swanton was being as accommodating as he could, and he knew he ought to do the same. 'You should know, Harold, that we've turned up a connection between Pablo and Vermeulen.'

'What kind of connection?'

'I took the liberty of arranging for Pablo's hotel room to be searched again.'

'Without telling the Americans?'

'Yes. One of my constables found a small notebook under the floorboards. It was a diary of Pablo's stay in London. It seems that his mission was to tail Vermeulen.'

'Good God! You have it with you?'

'It's at the Yard. I'll get it sent over to you.'

'You might as well wait until this afternoon. I want you with me when I see Grishin.'

'Isn't that . . . um . . . contrary to MI5 procedure?'

'Bugger procedure. We're working this case together. If this Grishin fellow has anything to tell us, you should hear it too.'

'Well . . . thank you, Harold. Where and when?'

'The Russian embassy at three.'

A few late-arrival ducks pushed up against the men's legs, hunting for any remaining breadcrumbs.

'Unfortunately, our rogue German spy managed to get away. He escaped on an Irish freighter from Liverpool on Tuesday. He'll be sitting pretty in Dublin or thereabouts by now.'

'He left because he knew you were closing in on him, or because his mission was complete?' asked Merlin.

'Both most likely. He's the prime suspect for Vermeulen's murder as I see it.'

'Pablo mentioned in one of the diary entries that he thought he might not be alone tracking Vermeulen.'

'Did he now? Well there you are.' Swanton clapped his hands in a fruitless attempt to drive off the ducks. 'Have you found any evidence pointing to another killer?'

'Not so far.'

Both men fell silent before Swanton eventually lumbered to his feet. 'Time to get back to the grindstone, I think. See you later.'

★

Sir Bernard Spilsbury called when Merlin was back in his office. 'I've had another look at Van Buren's body as I said I would, Frank. I may have found something new. The damage to his head is extensive. However, I believe I've discovered another injury that may not derive from a boat propellor.'

'I see.'

'There's a slash wound on his neck that looks more likely to have been caused by a knife. I don't believe it was a fatal wound, but it is further evidence that Van Buren may well have been involved in a fight before he met his end. I've written up my findings and will send a copy round to you.'

Bridges entered the room as Merlin was putting the phone down.

'I have some new information, sir.'

'Me too, Sergeant, but you go first.'

'Martin Ramsey called. Said he'd left a message for you last night.'

'Oh yes. I was going to call him this morning. What does he want?'

'Thinks we should know about someone with a grievance against Van Buren. Fellow he knows called Nathan Katz. An Austrian refugee. Katz believes those da Vinci drawings are his. Says they were looted from his parents by the Nazis before the war.'

'Does he have evidence?'

'I don't know about evidence, but Ramsey seems to thinks the story is true.'

'Where are Katz's parents now?'

'Presumed dead or in a Nazi prison camp.'

'And Ramsey thinks Katz might be a suspect?'

'Katz visited Van Buren at his house to make his case. Van Buren dismissed it out of hand. Ramsey finds it hard to believe Katz is capable of violence, but the thought that he might have confronted Van Buren again has been playing on his mind. He thought it best we know and form our own judgement.'

'Do we have an address for Katz?'

'Ramsey gave me his work address. It's a bank in the City.'

'One of us had better speak to him, then. But first I'd like to see the housekeeper. Miss Van Buren told me she'd be back at work today. We'll go together.'

'Very good, sir.'

'And one other thing. We need to interview the occupants of the boats moored on the pier at Cheyne Walk in case anyone saw something that Friday night.'

'I'll add it to the list, sir.'

Goldberg was shown into the captain's office by a pretty uniformed redhead. Max Pearce greeted him with a warm smile and they shook hands. 'Detective Goldberg. I've been hearing a lot about you. Please sit down.' Pearce guided him to a cramped seating area by the window. Outside, the detective could hear the sound of children playing in the square.

'So, Bernie . . . You don't mind me using your first name, do you? Where I'm from, we don't like to stand on ceremony.'

'Not at all . . . Max.'

'Good. So how can I help?'

'I'm just doing the rounds. Getting to know people. I've already met most of your colleagues.'

'A good bunch all in all. Some pull their weight more than others, but that's life, I guess.'

'From all I hear, you're well ahead of the majority in terms of policing experience.'

'I've been round the block. Been a serving police officer since the early twenties.'

The redhead appeared with coffee. As she bent to set them down on a side table, Pearce patted her rear. The young woman behaved as if nothing had happened as she calmly departed. Goldberg could only presume she was accustomed to such behaviour.

Pearce chuckled. 'Nice little piece, eh, Bernie?'

Goldberg nodded uncomfortably, then asked, 'So, how do you think the new arrangements are working so far?'

'Pretty good. It's obviously better that we're able to take control if our own people transgress. Our way of doing things is far superior. But hell, I should think you know that better than anyone. I heard you spent time on secondment to the locals last year. Covered yourself in glory in some murder and espionage caper, the story goes.'

'I'm not sure I'd put it quite like that.'

Pearce leaned forward in confidential mode. 'To tell the truth, Bernie, one or two of my colleagues have been griping about you. Questioning your credentials for the job. Just so you know, I put them in their place. Told them you were a tough cop with a great record and certainly ripe for a job like this.'

'I appreciate that, Max. Thank you. So you're happy with the way things are going?' You've had no problems at all to date?'

'Inevitably there've been a few ruffled feathers, but nothing serious.'

'I gather you've had some dealings with Frank Merlin.'

Pearce's eyes narrowed. 'Merlin? You know him?'

'He was the officer I was seconded to last year.'

'Was he now? What a small world. Now how come I didn't know that?' Goldberg sensed the atmosphere in the room cooling. Pearce nodded to himself. 'I get it now. No sooner are you through the door of your new office than your pal Merlin's on the blower bending your ear. Am I right?'

'He's my best friend and closest contact in England. Naturally we've been in touch.'

'Of course you have. And I bet he couldn't wait to tell you that he and I didn't see eye to eye on something.'

'He told me he had concerns about the Merino case, which you took over from him.'

'I'm sure he did.'

'Look, Max, I've only a cursory knowledge of the case as yet.

227

The fact is, disagreements like this one with Merlin are exactly why I'm here. It's my job to help resolve them fairly. The fact that the chief inspector and I are friends doesn't come into it.'

'The suspect I have in the cells is undoubtedly guilty, Detective, and will hang. Merlin is barking up the wrong tree. It's my guess he has a soft spot for Lewis because of the colour of his skin.'

'Merlin's a bigger man than that. But if he presents a credible case for Lewis's innocence, we need to consider it.'

'There is no credible case for his innocence.'

'I understand the trial is set for as soon as tomorrow. Isn't that very hasty?'

Pearce leaned back in his chair and clasped his hands together. 'Detective, on the battlefield, justice should always be swift. My grandfather used to tell a civil war story about a friend who deserted his post. He was found, tried and shot within twenty-four hours. By those standards, I'd say the proceedings against Lewis are dilatory.'

'With respect, Captain, we're not on the battlefield.'

'Not yet, But we will be pretty soon. The maintenance of military discipline is of the utmost importance, whether here in London or across the Channel when we get there. Our men have to understand there will be no tolerance of criminal behaviour, and retribution will be swift.'

'Is there no way the trial could be postponed for just a few days, to allow time for Merlin to explain his concerns?'

Pearce jumped to his feet. 'Look, Detective, I've got a ton of cases on the go. I've listened to Merlin. He hasn't a leg to stand on, and neither has Lewis. The trial will proceed tomorrow. My job is to clear my cases swiftly and efficiently. That's my contribution to the war effort.'

'Will Merlin be allowed to give evidence at the trial?'

'We have statements from the English officers who found the body, from those who found Lewis, and from the medical examiners. That is sufficient. Merlin has nothing to add but vague supposition. There's no need for him to sacrifice his valuable time.'

'But—'

'That's it, Detective.' Pearce stuck out a hand. 'Good luck with the new job. I think you're going to need it.'

Mrs Macdonald looked tired and stressed when she opened the door to them. She led them through the hallway, down a corridor and into the high-ceilinged kitchen. There were piles of crockery and pots spread over the table.

'There's really not much work to do in an empty house, so I've been doing some reorganising to keep myself busy. I don't like not being busy.'

They settled at the table. From where he was sitting, Merlin could see the bottom of the tree up which the burglar was presumed to have climbed.

'What do you want to know?' Mrs Macdonald asked. 'I thought I'd told you everything.'

'We'd like to know a little more about what Mr Van Buren got up to in the days leading to his death.'

'Starting from when?'

'Monday the tenth.'

'I'll have to concentrate. So much has happened.' She screwed up her eyes in thought. 'Ah, yes. So on Monday, Mr Van Buren went out a few times but there were no visitors until the late afternoon, when Mr Robert came to see his father. He stayed for supper. My daughter had visited from the country at the weekend and brought me some eggs. I made omelettes. Mr Van Buren was very partial to an omelette. They passed a pleasant evening.'

'No arguments?'

'Not that I'm aware.'

'It's our understanding that father and son were in disagreement about his future. Did you hear any talk about that?'

229

The housekeeper pursed her lips. 'I'm not in the habit of eaves-dropping on my employers.'

'I'm sure you're not, but sometimes one can't help hearing.'

She looked down at her hands. 'I know Mr Van Buren was keen for his son to settle down and train for a profession, prefer-ably the law. I also know he didn't have much time for Mr Robert's magazine. However, I didn't hear any mention of the subject over supper. That doesn't mean it wasn't raised, of course, when I was in the kitchen, or earlier, before they ate.'

'All right. What about Tuesday the eleventh?'

'On Tuesday, Mr Van Buren was out when I arrived and didn't return until after lunch. In the late afternoon, he had one visitor. A young foreign gentleman. He wouldn't give me his name, but Mr Van Buren agreed to see him, even though he seemed quite tired. They were not together long. Half an hour maybe.'

'Did you hear any of their conversation?'

'No.'

'Raised voices?'

'I can't say. I was busy on the top floor while their meeting was going on.'

'Did they part on good terms?'

'Again I can't say. I just heard the front door slam from upstairs.'

'That's all from Tuesday?'

'Yes. Wednesday was the day the Dutch gentleman came. Mr Verm . . . something.'

'Vermeulen.'

'That's it. An elegant, business-like gentleman. He spent about an hour with Mr Van Buren. I didn't hear anything of what went on, but they seemed very cordial when Mr Vermeulen left. Then on Thursday, there were no visitors but Mr Van Buren went out for a while. He didn't say where he was going, but I was at the door when he hailed a taxi, and I heard him give the cabbie an address in Harley Street.'

'Was he unwell?'

'Not that I know. Seemed as fit as a fiddle to me.'

'We'll ask his daughter if she knows anything about it. Speaking of Miss Van Buren, she didn't visit at all during the week?'

'I know they spoke several times on the telephone, and he may have met up with her when he was out. Also remember, Chief Inspector, unless specifically requested otherwise, I finish at seven thirty. I can't speak for what goes on after then. Except for the Monday and Friday, of course.'

'Understood. So, Friday.'

'Mr Van Buren was out in the morning, I know not where. In the afternoon, the Dutch fellow came back and they spent a while together again.'

'All cordial, as before?'

'Yes. If anything, more so.'

'And then everyone arrived for the get-together.'

'Yes, at six thirty. I had to organise everything in a great rush.'

'What time did you go home that night?'

'Around nine thirty. Maybe a few minutes later. I served drinks to the young lady and gentleman in the drawing room while Mr Van Buren had a chat with his children in the study, then left.'

'What about telephone calls?' asked Bridges. 'Any that stick out from that week?'

'As you'd expect for a busy man, he had plenty. I don't know if I can remember them all, and anyway, I don't necessarily answer all the incoming calls. There are two telephones, one in the hall and one on Mr Van Buren's study desk. If he was in, he would often pick up before me. Of those I answered, there were several from Elizabeth and Robert. Twice, I believe, I picked up to a Mr Ramsey and once to Mr Vermeulen. There was also a quite regular caller called Frances. I don't know her last name, but she was a friend of Mr Van Buren's.'

'Her full name is Frances Walters. She was never a visitor here?'

'Not during my working hours, no.'

'Mr Van Buren never had any female visitors that you know of?'

'Only his daughter.'

'Any other telephone calls?' asked Bridges.

'No . . . Oh, yes, what am I thinking? There were several calls from Mr Van Buren's brother-in-law, Mr Butterfield. He seemed very keen to arrange a meeting, but Mr Van Buren wasn't having any of it and refused to speak to him. The man got quite irate.'

'When did he call?'

'I think he rang once on Thursday evening, just before I left, and then he tried perhaps four or five times on the Friday. The telephone also rang a few times during the dinner, but Mr Van Buren told me to ignore it.'

'Do you know from where Mr Butterfield was calling?'

'Various London telephone boxes. He left numbers each time should Mr Van Buren wish to return the call.'

'Have you ever seen Mr Butterfield here?'

'Never.'

'I presume Miss Van Buren would know how to contact him?'

'I should think so.'

'Our forensics people took away Mr Van Buren's private papers, didn't they?'

'They did.'

Merlin looked at Bridges. 'We should see whether they found anything.'

'Been meaning to follow up, sir, and have a look myself, but so much has been happening.'

Mrs Macdonald cleared her throat. 'Perhaps you're unaware that the papers are back here? Your officers brought them back in cardboard boxes this morning. They're in the study.'

'Are they now? We'll get on to them when we have a chance. Now, finally, let's go over the events of Friday night again, in case we've missed anything.'

Merlin asked a number of other questions, but discovered

nothing new, other than the fact that, like Elizabeth Van Buren and Caroline Mitchum, Mrs Macdonald had seen no one go beyond the first floor of the house that night.

When they stepped out onto Cheyne Walk, Merlin looked at his watch and realised he'd have to hurry to make his Russian embassy meeting. It was agreed that he would hail a taxi, and Bridges would take the car to the City to see Nathan Katz.

Katz was in the office bathroom, splashing his face with water and trying to calm his shaking hands. He'd been told that a policeman was waiting for him in the boardroom on the first floor. He couldn't help remembering the last encounter he'd had with a policeman, back in 1936 in Vienna. The vicious, ugly brute had given him a beating for no reason. It had become clear to him then, if not yet to his father, that the days of the Viennese Jews were numbered.

Benjamin Katz had been angry and affronted when he learned that an officer of the law wanted to see his nephew. It was only with difficulty that Nathan had persuaded his uncle that he should be left to handle the matter alone.

Five minutes later, he entered the boardroom. It had a gloomy, spartan air. The only view through the windows was of the wall of the neighbouring building, and little natural light reached the room. A single picture adorned the bare white walls, a battered print of Vienna. An old grandfather clock stood beside the print, and the table and chairs in the centre of the room were metal and purely functional.

Katz forced a smile as he sat down opposite Bridges. 'It's rather bleak in here, isn't it? I apologise. My uncle doesn't believe in shows of extravagance. Takes the view that when a customer comes in here, he can see that his money isn't being wasted on fripperies. So how can I help you, Sergeant?'

'I'm investigating the death of a Mr Leon Van Buren. Do you recognise the name?'

'I do.'

'Mr Martin Ramsey, a friend of yours, I believe, told us you'd had some dealings with him. He said there was an issue relating to some artwork owned by Mr Van Buren.'

'Some artwork stolen by Mr Van Buren,' Katz replied sharply.

'We heard the story. Mr Ramsey said you went to see him.'

'So I did. It was last Tuesday.'

'May I ask how the meeting went?'

'Not well. Van Buren rejected my claim to the drawings. Said he'd bought them fair and square. I knew he was lying.'

'How did that make you feel?'

'It was disappointing, but I expected no different.'

'Surely you felt more than disappointment?'

'The Nazis stole the drawings from my parents and Van Buren became party to the theft. Your assumption is correct, Sergeant.'

'He had no sympathy for you?'

'No.'

'Did your discussion become heated?'

'There was no shouting or loss of temper. I stated my case, he replied firmly but calmly. Then I left.'

'Did you meet again?'

'N . . . no.'

Bridges noted the hint of hesitation in Katz's reply.

'No telephone conversations?'

'No. I thought of seeing him again, but decided instead to explore what legal recourse there might be. I told my uncle about the drawings and he spoke to a lawyer friend of his.'

'And . . .?'

'The lawyer said that without access to Austrian and Dutch records, litigation would be futile at present. The prospects might be better after the war.'

'You know we believe the drawings were stolen the night Mr Van Buren died?'

'I did hear there was a burglary, yes.'

'Did you have anything to do with that?'

'Do I look like a burglar to you, Sergeant?'

'Burglars come in all shapes and sizes.'

Katz sighed. 'No, I didn't burgle Mr Van Buren's house. I wouldn't have the first idea how to go about it.'

'And you were nowhere near his house last Friday night?'

Again Bridges noticed some slight hesitation before Katz responded. 'No.'

'Do you have an alibi for that night? After ten?'

'I went for a late walk by the river where I live in Hammersmith. Then I went home to bed.'

'Anyone see you?'

'I doubt it in the blackout.'

'When did you go home?'

'Around . . . around midnight.'

Bridges leaned back in his chair. 'The thing is, Mr Katz, we believe that someone assaulted Mr Van Buren across the road from his house that night, some-time after ten. We believe that someone struck him, possibly slashed his neck with a knife then pushed him into the river. I have to ask if that someone was you?'

Before Katz could respond, the boardroom door flew open and Benjamin marched into the room accompanied by a thin, sallow man bearing a large briefcase. The latter introduced himself curtly. 'Eustace Pringle of Gray's Inn. Solicitor to the Fenchurch Discount Bank. Mr Katz apprised me of this meeting and requested I come round straight away.' He looked at Nathan. 'I advise you to say nothing further, young man. I'll handle this.'

Three stone-faced giants guarded the main entrance to the Russian embassy. Merlin waved his warrant card and was shepherded through the door and up a wide staircase to a cavernous high-ceilinged room crammed with heavy, ugly wooden furniture.

'There you are, Frank.'

'Sorry I'm late.'

'Don't worry about it. Last time I visited, they kept me waiting for over an hour. Did you bring that notebook?'

Merlin nodded and passed it over.

Their wait was in fact mercifully short. A sturdy female secretary came to escort them into Grishin's office. A grim portrait of Stalin stared down on them as they took their places at the ornate mahogany desk. Outside, the extensive scaffolding surrounding Kensington Palace was visible. The building had taken a pounding in the Blitz.

'Welcome, gentlemen.' Grishin rose and shook their hands. He was a solid-looking middle-aged man with a thick greying moustache much resembling that of his master in Moscow. 'To what do I owe this honour?'

'An occasional exchange of views with a respected close ally must always be a good idea.'

Merlin smiled inwardly at Swanton's choice of words. For the first two years of the war, Russia had been the Nazis' close ally, happily sharing in Hitler's carve-up of Europe. Betrayed by the German invasion of the year before, they had been obliged to complete a volte-face and switch sides.

'You know Chief Inspector Merlin, I believe?'

'Yes. Good to see you, Chief Inspector. The case of the stolen gold. I remember it well.' Grishin had good reason to remember the case. It had almost cost him his life. 'Tea?'

'No thank you, Colonel. We're all busy men,' said Swanton. 'Shall we cut to the chase?'

'Cut to the chase.' Grishin laughed. 'I like that. A useful English phrase. I learned where it supposedly came from only last week. The ambassador and I were shown the real tennis facility at Hampton Court. An incomprehensible game. Even harder to understand than cricket but . . .anyway, yes, please cut to the chase, Harold.'

'You will recall the assistance we gave you the other day with regard to your agent in Canada, Mr Sokolov?'

236

'Indeed. We are grateful.'

'One favour deserves another, don't you think?'

'Another useful English phrase.' Grishin chuckled. 'I suppose that must depend on what favour you want.'

'Does the name Pablo Merino mean anything to you?'

'Merino? No, I think not.'

'How about Tomas Barboza?'

Grishin shook his head slowly.

Swanton frowned. 'Your answer disappoints me, Colonel. You know as well as I do that Merino, or Barboza, was a Russian agent. He was carrying out a mission in London when he met his death.'

The Russian was poker-faced. Merlin couldn't tell whether the agent's death was news to him or not. The colonel stared thoughtfully out of the window and took his time responding. Eventually he said, 'I'm guessing the favour you have in mind will be disproportionate to the one you did us. In Sokolov's case, you provided diplomatic assistance. Here you appear to be trespassing onto operational matters.'

'Come now. Our help with Sokolov was more than just diplomatic assistance and you know it.'

Grishin said nothing.

'Look, Colonel, we're allies now. We should be prepared to help each other for the common good, without worrying about matching tallies.'

'Maybe your Mr Churchill sees it that way, but I doubt Josef Vissarionovich would. He keeps a mental tally going all the way back to his Georgian cot. 'However,' he continued with a hint of resignation, 'ask your questions and I'll try my best to answer them.'

'Thank you,' said Swanton. 'Can you please tell me the nature of Merino's mission?'

'Merino works for our Lisbon office and was sent here by them. We were asked to provide support. I met him. He seemed a little green, but I was told he'd done excellent work in Spain, and the Lisbon command clearly had a high opinion of him.'

'And his mission?'

'To tail a man.'

'That man being Frederick Vermeulen?' said Swanton.

'Yes.'

'Did you know Merino was dead before I mentioned it?'

'Yes.'

'And that Vermeulen was killed too?'

Grishin looked out of the window again. 'They seem to be taking forever with the work at the palace. If an important building like that was damaged in Russia, Stalin would make sure it was fixed quickly. Your king appears to be less efficient.'

'You know very well, Colonel, that Stalin and the king are two very different kettles of fish.'

Grishin smiled. 'More of your useful English phrases.' He turned back to his visitors. 'To answer your question, yes, we knew of Vermeulen's death as well.'

'Did you have anything to do with it?' asked Merlin.

'No, we did not.'

'So why was a Russian agent following him?'

'Our people in Lisbon initially understood he was a British double agent duping the Germans. Then something occurred to suggest that it was in fact the British who were the dupes.'

'You mean,' said Swanton, 'that he was a . . . a triple agent?'

'Yes. A Russian operative was compromised with the Germans and a finger was pointed at Vermeulen.'

'Why didn't they speak to MI6 in Lisbon?'

'They tried, but they say they were given the brush-off – another handy English phrase. But then it is not really surprising that our respective teams in different parts of the world are finding it difficult to bed in together. To get used to the fact that we are allies now. In any event, in the absence of an adequate response from your people, our Lisbon office decided to take the initiative.

238

It was known that Merino spoke excellent English, and he was tasked with following Vermeulen to London to see if he might somehow give himself away.'

'And did he?'

'Not so far as I'm aware, but Merino was only halfway through his job. He'd been given another week to find something before returning to Portugal.

'If he did discover anything, what were his instructions? To report or act?'

'To report. He had no brief to kill Vermeulen, if that's what you're getting at. Of course, he had full liberty to act in self-defence.'

'What you say about Vermeulen is news to me,' said Swanton. 'I'll pass it on to the relevant people, but I very much doubt that the suspicions of your people in Lisbon are valid.'

Grishin shrugged. 'Merino died before Vermeulen, hence he was not his killer. However, the reverse is a possibility you should consider. Perhaps Vermeulen discovered Merino was following him and decided to take the initiative.'

'Point taken, Colonel, but if that's what happened, it would have given you a reason to dispose of Vermeulen, would it not?'

Grishin's grey eyes twinkled. 'We had nothing to do with Vermeulen's murder, I assure you.'

Swanton eased himself back in his chair. Merlin saw his shirt buttons strain.

'I believe Merino was a relative of yours, Chief Inspector?' said Grishin.

'Yes, he was my sister's nephew.'

'My condolences. Naturally in this case you are particularly keen to find his murderer. A man has been charged, I believe.'

'Yes. He's about to be put on trial. He's not the right man, in my opinion, but they seem determined to press on.'

'The Americans do not listen much to the opinions of others in my experience.'

'It is of course not unknown for agents to be punished by their employers for making mistakes.'

'No indeed, Chief Inspector, but in this instance the young man hadn't yet had time to make serious mistakes. He appeared to be getting on diligently with his task. We did not kill him.' Grishin ran his finger along the edge of his desk. 'Have you considered the possibility that Vermeulen might have been the victim of a German agent? Perhaps they had a man on the ground checking whether he was playing straight with them. Such a man might indeed be a candidate for both killings, if he found Merino getting in his way. Or then again, perhaps a rogue element in your own service was culpable?'

'We live in a very devious world, don't we,' Swanton replied. 'Do you have any knowledge of German agents on the ground in London? Did Merino mention any suspicion along those lines?'

'I would guess we know as much as you.' Grishin smiled enigmatically. 'Merino said nothing. Now are we done?'

'Yes, I think so.' Swanton looked at Merlin, who nodded.

Grishin patted a weighty volume on his desk. 'Dickens, gentlemen. *The Pickwick Papers*. Very amusing, although I have to admit, some of his language goes over my head. Did you know that Comrade Stalin is a great admirer of classical English literature?'

'I don't believe I did,' said Swanton.

'Yes. He told me once he had committed many quotations from English literature to memory. One of his favourites is from Sir Walter Scott.'

'That's Scottish literature,' observed Swanton.

'Forgive me. It goes, I think, "Oh, what a tangled web we weave, when first we practise to deceive." It seems rather appropriate in the circumstances.'

Bridges found Cole taking a breather in the cubbyhole. 'Where's your partner in crime, Tommy?'

'Robinson?'

240

'No. The Metropolitan Police Commissioner. Who'd you think?'

Before Cole could reply, Robinson appeared at the door.

'Ah, there you are. How've you both been getting on?'

'I'm afraid there's nothing since the pub sighting, Sarge,' Robinson replied.

'I see. I'm beginning to think your talents are now needed elsewhere. Things are beginning to get on top of us.' Bridges sat down and filled the constables in on recent developments. Then he gave them their new tasks. 'I'd like you to go to the boat mooring in Chelsea. See if anyone saw or heard anything that night. When you've done that, Robinson, you go and see Van Buren's lady friend, Frances Walters. And Cole, see if you can track down Humphrey Butterfield.'

'What's the latest on the burglary?' asked Robinson.

'Good question. We need to follow up on that with Charlie Mason.'

'I can do that, sir,' said Cole.

'Thanks.'

'And who's following up on that mystery Harley Street appointment of Van Buren's?' asked Robinson.

'That's down to me and the boss.'

Wilfred North had occupied the same office in Gray's Inn for more than thirty years. Over that time, he had built up a vast collection of legal textbooks and reports, which filled the room's numerous bookshelves. He found their presence reassuring, but seldom consulted them. Inevitably, there was a lot of dust. North was used to this and wasn't troubled by it. Humphrey Butterfield, however, most definitely was. The solicitor waited patiently for his client's loud sneezing fit to subside, leaving Butterfield red-eyed and hoarse.

'You know, Humphrey, I've told you before, but you really should see a specialist. I know a very good man in Wimpole Street.'

241

'I'm all right, Wilfred,' Butterfield spluttered. 'It would help if you opened a window.'

North grudgingly slid one window open a couple of inches. He was not very keen on fresh air, even on the warmest of summer days. After pouring a glass of water for Butterfield, he opened the file in front of him. 'I'm afraid I haven't had a reply to my letter yet. As I said on the telephone, I thought it was premature to chase Van Buren's children so soon after the death. Perhaps we should show a little more sensitivity.'

'After everything Leon Van Buren put me and Audrey through, I'm hardly in the mood for sensitivity. I need to know where I stand. Please persist and try and get an answer as soon as you can.'

'Very well. I'll do my best.' North reached for the crystal decanter on his desk. 'I know you're still on the wagon, Humphrey, but I hope you don't mind me indulging. It's been a long day.'

'Feel free, Wilfred.'

North poured himself a large schooner of sherry and raised his glass. 'Here's to the end of your problems, my friend.' He took a large gulp. 'Have you any news of the police investigation?'

'I know no more than what's in the newspapers.'

'The police haven't been in touch with you?'

'Why should they need to be in touch with me?'

'You're a close family member, even if things were difficult between you. And they might want to talk to you about the litigation.'

'I can't see why.'

'You say you didn't get to speak to Leon at all last week?'

'He wouldn't take any of my calls.'

'You didn't think of just rolling up and knocking on the door?'

'No. I had no interest in being snubbed in person.'

North sipped his sherry and looked thoughtfully at his client. He'd often found the man edgy and awkward. He seemed more so today. He didn't think it was down to the dust.

'You seem very tense, Humphrey. Is it just the litigation that's playing on your mind?'

'Of course. I'm worried that, contrary to your expectations, the children might be persuaded by their advisers to continue with the suit. I shall remain so until we have the right answer back.'

'I would remind you again that they've always been very close to Audrey. I'm sure that relationship will work in your favour.'

'Let's hope so.' Butterfield rose abruptly. 'I may as well take my leave.'

'Going straight back to the country, are you?'

'Not straight back, no. I've got a little book shopping in mind, and I . . . I have an appointment with a friend later.'

'I presume you'll be back for the funeral?'

'I don't know about that.'

'I'm sure the children will want both of you there. It might be a while yet, though, before the police are in a position to release the body.'

A short while later, North stood by the window and watched his client striding across the square, head down. 'Rum fellow,' he muttered to himself. When he turned away, he noticed Butterfield's umbrella still hanging on the coat rack. He hurried back to the window and banged on the pane, but it was too late. The man was out of sight. North guessed there'd be a call later. Butterfield was one of those Englishmen who could never be without his umbrella, come rain or shine.

Merlin loosened his tie as he swung his feet up onto the desk. 'So we need to speak to Katz again?'

'Definitely. I had the feeling he was holding something back. If the solicitor hadn't turned up, I might have wheedled it out of him.'

'We'll try and see him first thing tomorrow.'

'Don't forget Micallef, sir.'

'No. And Robert Van Buren. Another busy day beckons.'

243

Bridges stifled a yawn. 'D'you think you got the whole truth from Grishin, sir?'

'Who knows, Sam? Those sorts of people spend their working lives bound up in a cocoon of lies. For what it's worth, Swanton believed most of what he told us.'

'And what's his opinion now regarding the Merino and Vermeulen murders?'

'He seems inclined to pin everything on the Germans.'

'And you, sir?'

'Keeping an open mind, as always.'

'We still can't bring the Americans into the loop?'

'No. Swanton's bosses won't budge.'

'So Virgil Lewis is being left to go down the plug-hole. The trial is still due to proceed tomorrow?'

'It is. I've got Bernie Goldberg working to delay it, but he's not hopeful at all. What else?'

Bridges told him what he'd got Cole and Robinson working on.

'Good. Also let's not forget we've got Van Buren's papers to look at. Anything on the tie pin yet?'

'No word from forensics.'

'Johnson's been tied up on the Hammersmith case all day?'

'Yes. The officer asked to cover for Robinson in court has apparently not been much use, and the prosecution wanted the inspector close at hand. He rang not long ago to say he was still stuck going over things with the prosecution lawyers at their chambers. He'll have to be in court tomorrow too, but is hopeful of being able to get away by lunchtime.'

'Unfortunate timing this going to trial now, but we shouldn't complain. What happened in Hammersmith was appalling, and we owe it to the victims to ensure convictions.'

'Oh, one more thing. I called Miss Van Buren when I got back, hoping to ask her about that Harley Street appointment. She was in a bit of a hurry, so I couldn't get to that, but she did mention that she was moving to a new flat tomorrow morning and that Micallef would be with her. Gave me the address.'

'So we can see him there?

'Yes.'

It was Merlin's turn to stifle a yawn. 'I don't know about you, Sam, but I've hardly eaten today. I'm going to go home, get a good meal and a good night's sleep. I suggest you do the same.'

Robinson and Cole drew a blank at the boat mooring. No one had seen anything unusual that Friday night. One of the residents was absent but likely to be back in a few days, according to a neighbour, and they made a note to follow up with him, then went their separate ways.

From the little she'd heard of Frances Walters, Robinson's expectations weren't high. Van Buren's children seemed to regard her as nothing more than a tart, according to the sergeant. The woman who opened the door of the quaint blue-washed terrace house to her, however, looked more like a school-mistress than a scarlet woman. Dressed in an old-fashioned tweed jacket and skirt, with short brown hair speckled with grey, she was not exactly pretty, but she had something about her. A small but full-lipped mouth sat beneath a long, narrow nose. Her bright blue eyes widened in surprise as Robinson presented her warrant card.

'I don't know why your arrival has startled me. I always knew the police would get to me at some point. Please come in.'

She led Robinson through a dark, narrow hallway into a small living room looking out onto a tiny garden. They sat down in matching floral-patterned armchairs. A large Bush radio resting on a sideboard was blaring out the BBC evening news.

'I'm sorry. I'm a little deaf.' Miss Walters reached out to turn it off. 'The walls of these houses are quite thin and the neighbours sometimes complain.'

'I'm sorry about Mr Van Buren, Miss Walters. I understand you were close.'

245

'We were, yes. Poor Leon.' There was a little sigh, but she seemed quite calm. Robinson got the impression she was a person capable of keeping a tight rein on her emotions. As if reading the constable's mind, she said, 'I've cried my tears, young lady.'

'Sorry. I'm sure you have.' There was an awkward silence before Robinson asked, 'How did you hear of his death? From his children?'

'Of course not. I'd seen the story about the body being found, and Leon's lawyers got in touch to tell me it was him. Have you made any progress yet in discovering how it happened?'

'Our investigations are continuing.'

'You can't say. I understand.' A small tabby cat appeared from nowhere and launched itself onto its owner's lap. 'There you are, Primrose. I've been wondering where you'd got to.' The animal glared angrily at Robinson as Miss Walters stroked it. 'Surprisingly for the unsentimental man Leon was, he had a soft spot for Primrose. She senses he's not coming back, I think, and is not quite herself.' She set the cat down carefully beside her chair, where it nestled against her legs.

'So, Constable, what do you want to know?'

'I understand Mr Van Buren came to see you last Friday night?'

'He did. Just after ten.'

'Rather late in the evening for a visit?'

'Oh, he liked to visit at all hours. The particulars of Friday night, though, were that he had originally planned to take me out to dinner before I went away for the weekend. Then he struck a deal for those drawings . . . I presume you know all about that?'

Robinson nodded.

'Quite understandably, he wanted to share his good news with the children and decided to invite them to dinner. He felt guilty about calling off our evening out, so promised to start the meal early so that he had time to join me for a nightcap.'

'He never thought of inviting you to the meal?'

246

'Oh no. His children won't have anything to do with me, I'm afraid.'

'I'm sorry to hear that. Could you tell me a little more about your relationship with Mr Van Buren?'

'I was a childhood friend of Leon's wife, Mary. She and I kept in touch over the years and would meet up on her visits back to England. She was luckier in the marriage stakes than I. As a young woman, I came into a decent inheritance, but I married a scoundrel who spent all my money. We divorced. Luckily there were no children. I was obliged to earn my living as a secretary in an advertising agency. When Mary returned to England for cancer treatment in the early days of the war, naturally I visited her. Her condition gradually deteriorated and she was moved into a nursing home. Inevitably I bumped into Leon every so often. We had met before, of course, and been on friendly terms. By the time his wife died, our friendship had deepened into something else. When the children became aware of our relationship, they took against me. They told Leon I was a fortune-hunter. That was not the case, I should say, but Leon asked me to give up my job and provided me with some financial support.'

'This house?'

'Yes, he rented it for me. He wanted me to be close at hand.'

'Do you know anything about Mr Van Buren's financial situation?'

'I know the history of his travails in Holland. I know that he retained enough of his wealth to live in reasonable comfort here, and indeed to look after me.'

'What about the art?'

'Yes, I knew he'd managed to sneak a few choice items out of Holland. Initially he was dead set against selling any of them, but he got into debt and his children were also quite demanding financially. Thus he decided recently to sell the da Vinci drawings if he could get a decent price.'

'The price he was offered was certainly a good one.'

'Yes, he was very pleased when he came to see me that Friday, although he made the point that he'd have got an even better one after the war. Anyway, he was lucky with this Mr Gulbenkian.'

'But then his luck ran out.'

'Yes. In spades.' Robinson thought she saw a little moisture in the woman's eyes as she looked down at the cat.

'Will the children be hard-pressed financially now, assuming the drawings are not recovered?'

'They'll be fine. Leon settled some money and assets on their mother before the war, and she had some private wealth of her own. Under her will, they get substantial bequests on reaching the age of twenty-six, or earlier in the event of Leon's death.'

'What about you?'

'My lease is paid up for another three months. Leon's informal allowance will stop, obviously, but his solicitor led me to believe some provision had been made in the will. He didn't say how much, but it will probably be a small amount. I still have my sec-retarial skills, so if needs must I can return to work.'

'Can you tell me more about Mr Van Buren's last visit?'

'There's not much to tell. As I said, he got here just after ten. I keep a supply of liquor for him here. He likes . . . sorry . . .' Her eyes closed briefly. 'Sorry, he liked a nip of Armagnac late at night. Said it helped him sleep. He sat where you are sitting now. I poured a glass for him and a glass of Benedictine for myself. Then we had a nice relaxed chat.'

'What did you talk about?'

'Mostly about the drawings. He was naturally in an excellent mood. He spoke about what he'd do with the money. Said that perhaps, after sorting out his debts, he might set up in business again.'

'Was he particularly anxious about anything?'

'Far from it. He was exhilarated. The only negative comments I can recall were about his children. He'd met with them both privately after the meal to tell them the full details of Gulbenkian's deal. He wasn't very happy with their reaction. Described it as "grasping".'

'They were thinking about what was in it for them?'

'Yes.'

'Isn't that only natural?'

'That's what I said to him.'

'What plans did they have for their portion of his new-found wealth?'

'Robert has this magazine he wanted his father to fund. Elizabeth just generally has expensive tastes. They tend to get jealous of each other, and with more money floating around, Leon thought that was only going to get worse.'

Primrose suddenly roused herself and looked up at her owner, purring loudly. Miss Walters lifted the cat back onto her lap.

'Did he have anything else to say?'

'Not on the subject of money, as I recall. He wasn't very impressed with his children's partners. He said that Elizabeth's young man seemed to spend a lot of time running his eyes over the contents of the house, though that seemed understandable to me if, as he told me, the man was involved in the antiques business. The girl he didn't take to as she was rather frumpy and part of Robert's literary set.'

'We understand Mr Van Buren had fallen out with his wife's family.'

'Oh, the litigation, you mean. You know about that, do you?'

'A little. He was suing his wife's sister and her husband, I understand?'

'Yes.'

'Mr Van Buren's housekeeper said his brother-in-law was trying desperately to get hold of him at the end of last week.'

'Yes, Leon told me. Said the matter was better left to the solicitors.'

'What do you know about the litigation?'

'The bulk of Mary Van Buren's personal estate consisted of a substantial farming property in Wiltshire, which she'd inherited from her father. Her younger sister Audrey and her husband, Butterfield, had the running of it. Originally it was understood that the farm would go to Leon when she died, but she changed the will in the last few months of her life, making Audrey the beneficiary. Leon believed that Audrey and Humphrey exerted undue influence on Mary when she wasn't of sound mind.'

'Had Mr Van Buren lost his Dutch business to the Nazis when his wife made the new will?'

'He had, but he'd not wanted to worry her with the details when she was so ill. He told her that he'd received proper compensation and all was well financially.

'So as far as she was concerned, leaving the farm to her sister wouldn't matter to him?'

'Yes, but Leon didn't see the matter like that. Said she'd have left it to him anyway if Audrey and Humphrey hadn't got their claws into her when she was dying.'

'Do you think he would have continued the litigation if he'd survived and the art sale had gone through?'

Miss Walters thought for a moment. 'I don't really know. He could be determined and ruthless when he had a bee in his bonnet.'

Robinson paused to write in her notebook. Then, 'Mr Van Buren left after your chat?'

'No. After we'd finished our drinks, we listened to some music on the radio for fifteen minutes or so. Then he went home.'

'Can you remember what time that was?'

'No, but . . .' Frances Walters unloaded the cat and reached down to a magazine rack beside her chair. 'I have last week's *Radio Times*.' She flicked through the pages. 'I remember we were listening to Henry Hall. Ah, here it is. On Friday, the Henry Hall Band programme finished at eleven thirty. Leon left immediately afterwards, so there's your answer.

'There was no question of him . . . of him staying the night?'

'Why, I do believe you're blushing, Constable.' Miss Walters smiled. 'No. He wouldn't consider it that night as he had the drawings and a large sum of cash in the safe. He wanted to be in his own house. With good reason, it now seems.'

'What sort of state was he in when he left?'

'Was he drunk, d'you mean? I suppose he'd had quite a lot of alcohol at his little party, followed by a nightcap at mine. However, he didn't seem particularly drunk. He could always handle his drink. I would say he was a little tipsy but perfectly capable of making his way home.'

'Was Mr Van Buren in good health?'

'As far as I'm aware.'

'It's just that he apparently had an appointment in Harley Street last week.'

Miss Walters looked surprised. 'That's news to me.'

Robinson paused again to run her eye over her notebook.

'One last question, Miss Walters. Did you notice whether Mr Van Buren was wearing a tie pin that night.'

'No, and I've never seen him wear such a thing.'

'I see. Thank you, Miss Walters. I think that will be all for now.'

Primrose jumped back onto her owner's lap. She stroked the animal thoughtfully, then asked, 'You have no idea at all how Leon met his death?'

'We have some theories, but I can't really discuss them with you at the moment.'

'I see.'

'May I ask what you think happened?'

Miss Walters considered for a moment. 'I'd say the burglar or burglars killed him. I think he must have returned to the house and found the burglary in progress. Knowing Leon, he won't have thought twice about taking them on. If the burglars ran away, he'd have given chase. He might have followed them to the Embankment where they turned on him and pushed him into the water. Something like that.'

'That's definitely one possibility.' Robinson nodded, then looked at the cat. It was nodding too.

Cole had managed to get hold of Butterfield's home phone number and been told by his wife that her husband had been in London to see his solicitor. She'd given him the solicitor's details and he'd immediately called, only to be told Butterfield was long gone. At a loss about what to do next, he went to the cubbyhole and made himself a cup of tea. Then he tried to find Sergeant Mason to see how the burglary investigation was going, but the sergeant had gone home already.

He was on the point of calling it a day when the telephone rang. The desk sergeant told him Wilfred North was on the line and put him through. 'I gather you're looking for Humphrey Butterfield, Constable. He's still in London and I have an address for him. He forgot his umbrella earlier and just called to ask that I send it to a hotel in Paddington. The Gloucester Hotel on Praed Street.'

'Thank you, sir. Does he know I'm looking for him?'

'He does now, as I told him. He asked me to say that he'll be there until eight fifteen, when he has an appointment.'

Cole checked his watch. It was ten past seven. There was time if he got his skates on.

The Gloucester was one of the scores of small hotels located within spitting distance of Paddington station. It was clearly at the cheaper end of the range. The shabby reception area had a good deal of peeling wallpaper, and the linoleum floor was encrusted with dirt. The clerk at the desk wore a faded green jacket, the right breast of which sported the hotel's name with the 'o' and 'r' missing. His hair was oozing oil, drips of which were falling onto the ledger in front of him.

He ignored Cole until the constable thrust his warrant card in front of him. 'Mr Butterfield?'

The clerk bared a mouthful of brown and black teeth and said, 'Room Eight.'

The room was on the second floor. When Cole got there, Butterfield greeted him coolly. 'This is very inconvenient, Constable. You won't be long, will you? I have a pressing engagement in . . .' he looked at his watch, 'twenty-five minutes.'

'I'll bear that in mind, sir.' There were two chairs and a bed in the spare, white-walled room. 'May I sit down?'

'If you must.'

Cole took the more solid-looking of the chairs. Butterfield reluctantly sat in the other.

'This a regular haunt of yours, sir?'

'I stay here from time to time when I'm in town. It serves its purpose for a reasonable price. I'm not in a position to throw money around, Constable, not that it's any of your business.'

'No offence intended, sir. Well, let's get down to it, shall we. You are aware of the death of your brother-in-law, Mr Leon Van Buren, I presume?'

'I am.'

'We understand you tried to get hold of him on the telephone last week. Several times.'

Butterfield pushed a couple of straggling hairs back onto his thinning scalp. 'Yes. Several times because he wouldn't take my calls.'

'So I understand. And what exactly did you want to talk to him about?'

'As you're probably aware by now, Leon was suing me and my wife. At my solicitor's urging, I was trying to see him in person without lawyers to discover if some sensible accommodation might be reached. Evidently he had no interest in doing that.'

'And these calls. You made them from where?'

'London telephone boxes.'

'Why didn't you just go to his house and try your luck?'

'I . . . I didn't want to take the risk of facing any unpleasantness.'

'So you never went anywhere near Van Buren's house last week?'

Butterfield took a moment before shaking his head.

'You seem a little doubtful, sir.'

'It depends on your definition of "near", Constable. I did go walking in Battersea Park last Friday afternoon. I toyed with the idea of crossing the river and knocking on his door, but rejected it. I made a couple of my calls from a box in the park.'

'So now that Mr Van Buren is dead, will the litigation end?'

'I am advised that is the likeliest outcome. There was an element of . . . um . . . personal venom in Leon's actions. His heirs, I'm assured, are likely to take a more reasonable approach.'

'If your advice is correct, you would appear to be a major beneficiary of Mr Van Buren's death.'

Butterfield's eyes narrowed. 'What are you suggesting, Constable?'

'I'm not suggesting anything, sir, just making an observation.'

Butterfield looked pointedly at his watch.

'After your failed attempts to speak to Mr Van Buren last Friday, did you return home to the country?'

'No. I made my last attempt to speak to him somewhere between eight and nine. I decided I couldn't face hurrying to catch the last train, so I caught an early train on Saturday morning.'

'You stayed here on Friday night?'

'I did.'

'So you would have been in London when Mr Van Buren met his death.'

'I don't know when he died, but if you say so. What of it?'

'Just another observation, sir.'

'I don't think I care for your observations, Constable.' Butterfield tapped his watch. 'Time is moving on.'

'One last question, sir. Do you have any thoughts on how Mr Van Buren died?'

'None at all.'

'Are you aware of any enemies he had?'

'I know very little of Mr Van Buren's affairs, Constable.'

'Very good, sir. It may well be that my superiors want a word at some point. Meanwhile, thank you for your time.'

Once he was out of the hotel, Cole ducked into a nearby alley and waited. The date he'd originally had with Shona had been called off because her mother was ill, and he was free for the evening. Free to take a closer look at Butterfield. There was something fishy about the man, he'd decided. What was this urgent appointment he had? Was there an appointment at all? He was going to find out. When Butterfield appeared on the street a few minutes later and headed off down Praed Street, Cole followed him.

Chapter Eighteen

Friday August 21st 1942

Elizabeth Van Buren's new apartment building looked a cut above her previous one, Merlin thought, as Bridges greeted him outside. 'They've just gone in, sir. The gentleman accompanying the young lady didn't seem too happy when she told him who I was. Good-looking young fellow, if you like that sort of Valentino Latin look.'

They took the lift to the third floor. The Van Buren residence was two doors down on the left. They found the door wide open and followed the sound of voices to a half-furnished room offering a panoramic view of the river. The young couple were standing by the window, deep in discussion. Bridges cleared his throat loudly.

'Ah, the chief inspector is here now, is he, Sergeant? Good morning, Mr Merlin.'

'Good morning, miss. Lovely outlook you've got here.'

'Thank you. I can't wait to get it properly furnished.' She nodded to her companion. 'Can I introduce my friend Teddy. Teddy Micallef.'

'Pleased to meet you, officers.' The young man extended a limp hand.

Miss Van Buren was holding a tape measure and some swatches of material. 'You want to speak to Teddy, I believe. I do hope you're not going to be too long with him. There's a lot that needs doing, and I require his advice.'

'We'll try not to detain him too long.'

'Good. Then I'll just go and take some measurements while you're chatting.'

'We shall need a few words with you too before we go.'

'Really? Oh, very well.' She shrugged, then disappeared down a corridor.

Merlin turned to Micallef. 'Now, sir.'

'What is it exactly you want, Chief Inspector?' Micallef asked brusquely.

'You were one of the last people to see Mr Van Buren alive. We are obliged to ask you some questions.'

'Ask away then.'

'Could you give me your impressions of the dinner party last Friday evening?'

'An enjoyable occasion and Mr Van Buren was a congenial host.'

'You'd met him before?'

'Once or twice.'

'How did he seem to you on Friday?'

'Happy. Why wouldn't he be after closing such a fantastic deal?'

'You know the finer details of the art sale?'

'I didn't hear them from him, but Elizabeth told me later.'

'So the entire party was in good spirits? No upsets at all?'

'Not that I'm aware.'

'I understand you came here from Malta quite recently?'

'I did.'

'When exactly?'

'January.'

'How did you break through the German cordon?'

'Under cover of night in a small boat. Clearly the Nazis can't cover every inch of sea. We benefitted from a bit of luck, and the weather was propitious. The onward journey was difficult as well. Not all of the group made it.'

Merlin glanced at Bridges. 'Sounds to me as if Mr Micallef is a very brave man.'

'Must be, sir.'

Micallef said nothing.

'I believe you've done quite well for yourself since getting here.'

'I do all right, Chief Inspector.' The young man shrugged.

'Miss Van Buren says you have some sort of dealership?'

'Yes. Cars, antiques, that sort of thing.'

'That kind of business would require a fair amount of start-up capital, wouldn't it?'

'I had the advantage of some family capital in this country.'

'You mean money held in a bank?'

'No. Cash. Looked after by some friends of my father.'

'Your father is currently in Malta?'

'He is.'

'What does he do there?'

'He has various business interests. Property, insurance, finance.'

'Presumably he's successful, if he has sent substantial funds over here?'

Micallef shrugged again. 'He does all right. Things are difficult at the moment, of course.'

'Of course.' Merlin rubbed his chin thoughtfully. 'Going back to the Friday party, where did you spend the evening?'

'Why in the rooms in which Mr Van Buren entertained us.'

'On the ground floor?'

'Yes.'

'You saw no more of the house?'

'No . . . apart from the upstairs bathroom.'

'That is on the first floor, I believe?'

'Yes.'

'As a dealer in *objets d'art* and the like, you weren't tempted to see whether Mr Van Buren had any interesting items elsewhere in his home?'

'No.'

'Were you aware of the presence of a safe in the drawing room?'

'I was not.'

'Miss Van Buren never mentioned it?'

'Why would she?'

'So the dinner proceeded on its jolly way. What happened when it finished?'

'Elizabeth and I went back to the flat. The one she's moving out of.'

'You spent the night there?'

'I did.'

'She mentioned you went out for a short while.'

'Did she? Well, it was a warm night and her flat was stuffy. I'd had quite a few glasses of wine. I went out to clear my head.'

'Around what time?'

'I don't know. Eleven, perhaps. Maybe a little later.'

'And where did you go?'

'I . . . I think I just wandered up to the King's Road and back.'

'A breeze off the river might have helped clear your head.'

'It might,' Micallef snapped, 'but I didn't go to the river. And what does it matter anyway? I went for a walk. Nothing happened.'

'The flat was only a short distance from the house in Cheyne Walk. If you'd walked towards the river, you might have bumped into Mr Van Buren.'

Micallef looked away, then pulled out a cigarette packet and lit up. Merlin saw that his hand was unsteady. 'You think I wouldn't have already told you if I had?' He took a few puffs, then sent a trail of smoke spiralling up to the ceiling. The cigarette seemed to calm him. 'Look, Mr Merlin, I can assure you I had absolutely nothing to do with Mr Van Buren's death, on my mother's life. Please believe me.'

'What about the burglary?' asked Bridges.

'I am not a thief, and even if I was, I'd be a pretty poor individual if I stole from the father of the woman I love.'

The object of his affections suddenly reappeared. 'I hope you're all finished now. I really would like to have Teddy's opinion on a few things.'

'I think we've just about covered enough ground for the moment.' Merlin looked hard at Micallef and nodded. 'I'd be grateful for a little more of your time, though, Miss Van Buren, as I mentioned earlier.'

'All right, as long as it doesn't take long.'

'If you could give us a moment, Mr Micallef?'

Sergeant Mason and the robbery and burglary team occupied three rooms at the rear of Scotland Yard. The head of the department was Chief Inspector Cecil Guthrie, the over-promoted nephew of the Police Commissioner, but Mason was the real boss. As he made his way over, Cole hoped he wouldn't have to deal with Guthrie.

'It's all right, son. He's off shooting grouse' said Mason, who was waiting for him outside Guthrie's office.

'Poor birds.'

'They'll be all right. I understand he's as useless at shooting as he is at everything else.' Mason was an East Ender like Cole, and was fond of the young man. 'Come on.'

They went in and settled themselves at Guthrie's desk. 'Are those bags I see under your eyes, son? Frank Merlin working you all hours as usual?'

'It's all right, Sarge. I like my job.'

Mason nodded approvingly. Cole looked around the office. He'd never been in it before. It seemed much grander than Merlin's, with its heavy ornate furniture and its proliferation of paintings on the walls.

'Fancy set-up, sir.'

'Guthrie looks after himself all right.' Mason pointed towards a large wooden box on his right. 'Probably got as good a collection of cigars in there as old Winston. And you should see the booze he's got tucked away in those cupboards behind you.' He leaned forward over the desk. 'I presume you're here to find out how I'm doing with the Cheyne Walk job?'

'Yes, sir.'

'It's clear we're dealing with professionals. They left a few small traces of their presence but generally the place was pretty clean. I say "they", but the footprints suggest there was only one. There are bound to be accomplices, but for the moment I'm concentrating on the main man, the safebreaker.'

'I understand.'

'One must always be prepared for the emergence of newcomers in the burgling world, but my bones tell me this is most likely the work of an old lag. Of the old lags in my little book, there are a limited number capable of a job like this. Four, to be exact. Of those, two are currently banged up in Pentonville and the Scrubs. The two at liberty are Bert Doyle and Jake Penny. Doyle mostly operates by himself, very occasionally assisted by a couple of trusted cronies. Penny is more of a team player. Often works for the Hill gang. One of those two is our man, I'm sure. My current information is that they've both been seen recently in town. I'm hoping to hear more shortly.'

'Does either man have a reputation for violence?'

'You're thinking the burglar might have attacked Van Buren?'

'Yes, sir. It must be a strong possibility.'

'Doyle has a conviction for GBH on his record. Penny is clean on that score, but he's no angel. Your man was a big fellow in his fifties, yes?'

Cole nodded.

'Doyle and Penny aren't spring chickens, but I'd be surprised if they couldn't outrun a man like Van Buren if he gave chase.'

'The burglar would have been slowed down by his loot, remember. Or perhaps there was an accomplice waiting who decided to go on the offensive.'

'Very possibly, I grant you. But that's for you and Merlin's team to work out. I'm just going to get on and pin down our burglar.'

Elizabeth Van Buren had dragged Micallef on a shopping expedition to Harrods after reviewing the new flat. When he finally managed to get away, he headed straight to the club. He found the boss munching a sandwich at his desk and counting a large pile of cash.

Hill gave him a cool reception. 'Thought I told you to make yourself scarce.'

'Sorry, Billy. It's just that I . . . I had an important question to ask.'

Hill finished his lunch and wiped his mouth. 'What is it?'

'Couple of lads said you had some strings you could pull at the Met.'

'My tame coppers, you mean?'

Micallef toyed nervously with his tie. 'So, I was interviewed by Merlin this morning.'

'I've got no influence over Mr Incorruptible.'

'No?'

Hill shrugged. 'How'd it go?'

'They . . . they seemed a bit suspicious.'

'A man's been killed and some very valuable art stolen. They're going to be suspicious of everyone connected in any way with Van Buren.'

'I . . . I think I handled them well.'

'I hope so. Did Merlin accept your answers?'

'I think so, but . . . he didn't . . .'

'Ah. I get it. He didn't like the cut of your jib?'

'No.'

'I wouldn't take it too personal. You're good-looking, smartly dressed, foreign. You probably fit his idea of a spiv. As long as he didn't catch you out in any way.'

'He didn't.'

'You haven't been acting flash, throwing money around in an obvious way since the job, have you?'

'No, Billy.'

Hill picked up a letter-opener and started using it to clean his fingernails. 'Anything else you need to tell me?'

There was a moment of silence before Micallef said, 'Well . . . it's just . . . on the night of the job, after the dinner party, I went back to Elizabeth's. Her place isn't far from her father's house. 'When I was there, I went out for a little walk after eleven, and she happened to mention that to Merlin.'

The letter-opener came down hard on the desk. 'For Christ's sake, Teddy! And no doubt that's when the coppers think Van Buren bought it. Am I right?'

Micallef shrugged.

Hill picked up the cash on the desk and put it away in the safe behind him. He settled back in his chair and studied Micallef carefully. 'You're not holding anything back from me, are you, Teddy?'

'No, Billy. Honest.'

'You didn't perhaps decide to go past Van Buren's house and check whether Jake had encountered any problems? You didn't perhaps bump into Van Buren when you did so?'

'No, and I told Merlin that.'

Hill became thoughtful. Eventually he said, in a calmer tone, 'All right. The police don't like your face and we can't do anything about that. You need to lie low – and properly low this time.'

'Should I get a brief?'

'Absolutely not. No lawyering up. They'll only think they're on to something if you do that. If things take a turn for the worse, we can think again. Now, I think you should skedaddle. And on your way out, tell Jimmy I need a word.'

Jimmy Miles arrived a minute after Micallef's departure and joined Hill at his desk.

'Our young Maltese friend may be about to become a bit of a problem, Jimmy. The police have interviewed him. Seems Merlin's taken against him.'

'Not surprised. Never liked the smarmy git myself.'

Hill waved a hand in irritation. 'Yeah, I know, but the fact is he has useful skills and he did put us on to a nice earner at Cheyne Walk.'

'Might have been a big payday, boss, but it's causing big problems. With this man Van Buren dead . . .'

'I know, I know. Merlin's men will be like flies on a turd.'

'And I don't trust the kid. Don't think he'll be good under police pressure.'

'I agree. I've told him to stay low and I'm relying on you to make sure he does.'

'All right, boss.'

'Have a word with Penny too. Ask him again about the night of the burglary. Make sure he's telling the truth when he says it all went smoothly. You know he loves the sauce. I can imagine him helping himself to a few snorts from the house drinks cabinet then getting himself into trouble.'

'Yeah. He can get pretty crazy when he's had a few.'

Johnson was waiting with the two constables when Merlin and Bridges got back.

'Finished at the Bailey, Peter?'

'Think so, sir.'

'The solicitors called to tell me the inspector did a great job,' said Robinson.

Johnson coloured and stroked the area above his upper lip. For a while in the early days of the war, he'd sported a moustache in the style of Ronald Colman, one of his favourite actors. Unfortunately it reminded the AC more of the Führer, and he'd been obliged to remove it. His hand occasionally returned to the spot now in fond remembrance.

Merlin addressed the room and gave a summary of where all the cases stood. He ended with the morning's developments. 'The sergeant and I didn't much take to Micallef. Flash and shifty, we both thought. He denies any wrongdoing, but I'd like to keep an eye on him. We also touched on a couple of points of detail with Miss Van Buren. She knew nothing of her father's Harley Street appointment and can't remember him ever wearing a tie pin.'

'Frances Walters said the same,' Robinson added

'Did she? So it looks like the pin's got nothing to do with the case or else belongs to a suspect. Unfortunately forensics can't help us there; they rang this morning to say they can't pull any prints from it. After Miss Van Buren, we had no luck again seeing her brother, so he's still on the list.' Merlin looked at Robinson. 'Your turn, Constable.'

'Nothing at all doing at the pier, sir. One boat was empty, though, and the owner should be back in a day or two.'

'All right. Let's not forget to follow up there. Miss Walters?'

The constable opened her notebook and summarised the interview.

'The will stuff is very interesting,' observed Merlin when she'd finished. 'You found her credible?'

'I did.'

'Suicide and accident have never been at the top of my list of possibilities, and they're even more unlikely on her evidence.'

'I forgot to mention that Miss Walters provided final confirmation about the contents of the safe.'

'Van Buren told her the drawings and cash were definitely in there?'

'He did.'

'Thank you, Constable. Your turn now, Cole.'

'In short, sir, Butterfield admitted all those phone calls, but says Van Buren wouldn't speak to him and they never met.'

'You believed him?'

'I don't know, sir. He's a rather awkward character. Answered all my questions, but grudgingly. And then there's what happened after.'

'After?'

'For some reason I decided to follow him after our interview. Because I had reservations, I suppose. He'd claimed to have an urgent appointment and I was interested in seeing who he was meeting. I tracked him to a pub, hung around outside for a while, then saw him leave with a young lady. They crossed the Euston Road and entered a house in a street behind the station. There was quite a bit of traffic in and out while I watched. I'm sure it was a brothel.'

'He never saw you?'

'No.'

'You waited for him to come out?'

'No, I called it a day after about an hour. Seemed he might be settled for the night.'

'Interesting, Constable. The fact that Butterfield frequents brothels tells us something about his character. Whether that has any relevance to our case, we shall see. Anything else?'

'Not on Butterfield, sir, but as requested, I did have a word with Sergeant Mason about the burglary. He's narrowed the potential culprits down to two, Doyle and Penny.'

'If that's Jake Penny, I had a run-in with him when I was a sergeant. Not heard of Doyle, though.'

'Penny is a known accomplice of the Hill gang.'

'Yes, I remember. Is that it?'

'Yes, sir, but I have one question. The sergeant told us to stop following up on Pablo Merino. Does that mean we've given up our interest in the case?'

'No. What it means is I think you went as far as reasonably possible on the streets. I'm still very keen that we find Merino's killer.'

The inspector raised a hand. 'A question from me too, regarding the Vermeulen case. Talk of the canvassing of the boat residents reminded me. Was the canvass of Vermeulen's neighbours ever fully completed? Weren't there also absentees in that situation?'

'Good point, Peter. We left it to the local bobbies and they discovered nothing. However, I'm sure there was mention of a few people not being around.' Merlin looked at the constables. 'Another job for you two, I think.'

★

It was time to see Nathan Katz. Bridges called the bank to say they were on their way. However, an operator told him that Katz had called in sick and was at home. The sergeant asked for his address, and within minutes, he, Merlin and Johnson were on their way to Hammersmith.

Traffic was sparse and the journey didn't take long. Katz's bedsit was in a terraced house just off the river, not far from the bridge. The street appeared to have suffered a good deal of bomb damage, but only on one side. Katz lived on the lucky side. A smiling white-haired man in dirty overalls answered the door. The smile disappeared when Merlin displayed his warrant card. 'Not in any trouble, am I?' he said, wiping his dirt-encrusted hands on a rag.

'We'd like a word with one of your lodgers. A Mr Katz.'

'Oh.' The man breathed a sigh of relief. 'What's Nathan done then? Nice quiet lad, 'e is.'

'Look, Mr . . .'

'Shuttleworth. Bill Shuttleworth. Excuse the appearance. Been working on the vegetable patch out back.'

'Can you just tell us if he's in?'

''Fraid not. Went out about fifteen minutes ago.'

'Any idea where?'

''E was in his suit. Thought it was a bit late in the morning but assumed 'e was going to work.'

'His office says he called in sick.'

'Did they? Looked right as rain to me. Well, if 'e's not gone to work, 'e might have gone for a walk down by the river. The lad often likes to take a turn down there.'

The officers hurried down to the Thames towpath. Merlin decided to head westwards. 'This way's a pleasanter walk. Let's hope he thinks the same. Come on. We'll go as far as Chiswick Mall and see if we can spot him. We're relying on you, of course, Sam, as the only one who's met him.'

'Righto, sir.'

267

The path was crowded with people enjoying the August sun. They'd just walked past a string of gaily-coloured barges moored up against the bank when Bridges saw their man. He was leaning against the river wall twenty yards ahead, seemingly lost in thought.

'Mr Katz!' the sergeant shouted.

The moment he recognised Bridges, Katz turned on his heel and raced off down the pathway. The officers were caught by surprise and slow to react. Katz had another twenty yards on them by the time they got going. They just about managed to keep track of him as he weaved through the crowd, but after rounding the corner into Chiswick Mall, they came to a halt as they realised they'd lost him.

'I'd gained a little on him, sir' said Johnson, who'd been closest. 'Then a couple of kids ran into me, and next I looked, he was nowhere to be seen.'

'Maybe he's nipped into someone's garden,' said Bridges.

Most of the houses on the Mall had small riverside gardens across the road. 'All right,' said Merlin. 'Let's take a look.'

There were twenty or so gardens. They checked them all without success. Then they turned round and proceeded to check again. About halfway back, an elderly woman came out of one of the houses and asked what they were up to. When Merlin explained, she said, 'My eyes may have been deceiving me, but I thought I saw someone in the water a moment ago.'

'Where exactly?'

'Just by the Eyot. Over there.' She pointed, and the officers followed her hand.

Chiswick Eyot was an odd little boat-shaped island of scrub and bushes that sat a short distance out in the river. If there'd been someone in the water, there was no more, but Johnson said excitedly, 'Something's moving out there in the bushes, I think. Can you see?'

'No, but I'll trust your eyes. Can one of you shout across?'

Bridges called out Katz's name, but there was no response.

Merlin had walked along Chiswick Mall many times. It was usually possible at low tide to walk across to the Eyot over the mud, but it was currently high tide. He sighed. 'There's nothing for it, gentlemen. We're going to have to get wet. I'd say it's about three or four feet deep at the worst point. We don't all need to go. Peter, you stay here and keep an eye out.'

'Katz might cut up rough, sir. I'm coming as well.'

Merlin smiled. 'Insubordination, eh, Inspector? Very well, we'll all have a wade. Best keep our shoes on, I think. The Met can buy us new ones if they're ruined.'

'Some chance,' said Bridges.

The old lady took care of the officers' discarded jackets, ties and watches, then they rolled up their trousers and stepped out into the relatively calm water.

Johnson was the first ashore. As Merlin and Bridges followed him up the bank, there was a crackling sound to the left. They followed it, making their way with difficulty through the prickly undergrowth. Johnson had just disappeared from sight when Merlin heard a splash, followed moments later by another. When he reached the end of the island, he could see two swimmers out in the main stream of the river. Bridges joined him. 'Blimey, sir. What was the inspector thinking? It looks decidedly choppy out there.'

The main part of the river was indeed much rougher than the little channel they'd crossed, and it looked like there was a strong current running. The two men were only a few yards from each other, some thirty yards out, and both were clearly starting to struggle.

Merlin was beginning to fear the worst when he heard the sound of an engine. A small motorboat was nearby, making its way upriver. He and Bridges started waving and shouting and pointing towards the men in the water. The message got through and the boat altered course and made for Katz and Johnson. It

269

didn't take long for them to haul the pair aboard then the boat turned and came over to the island. The crew turned out to be two young Wrens. Mooring was impossible, so there was a shouted conversation from a distance. The result was that the girls agreed to take the men on to St Thomas's Hospital, a couple of miles upriver. They reported that the younger man seemed to have taken in a lot of water and wasn't so good. The other was in better shape.

As they were departing, Merlin said, 'Please make sure the hospital knows that the young man is wanted and must be kept under guard. We'll arrange for a policeman to be there as soon as possible.'

As the boat moved away, the sergeant shook his head. 'All very strange, sir. I wonder why he ran?'

'Let's hope he survives to tell us.'

Merlin and Bridges parted and went to their respective homes for a change of clothes. As he was in Chelsea, Merlin decided to have another go at seeing Robert Van Buren. Finally he was in luck.

'He's in his study on the telephone,' said Caroline Mitchum after she'd let him in. 'He shouldn't be long. Please come and sit down.'

Almost immediately, an agitated Van Buren burst into the room. 'Damn it, Caroline, Roderick can be a right royal pain in the backside sometimes. I . . .' He suddenly realised they were not alone.

'This is Chief Inspector Merlin, Robert.'

'Ah yes, Chief Inspector. Good to meet you. Has Caroline offered you any refreshment?'

'I have, and Mr Merlin has declined.'

'I hope you don't mind if I partake? It's a little early in the day, but it's been rather a trying one so far.'

'Not at all, sir.' From his flushed cheeks, Merlin doubted that the whisky he was now pouring would be his first of the day.

270

Van Buren joined him on the sofa. 'So, how's it going, Chief Inspector? Getting anywhere with this damnable mess?'

'We're making some progress, sir.'

'Slow but steady, eh?'

'I think I'd prefer the word "meticulous". We have narrowed things down on the burglary. Your father's death is presenting greater problems.'

'If you have a suspect for the burglary, isn't there a good chance the same man did for my father? Find the burglar and you kill two birds with one stone, so to speak.'

'That is of course very possible.'

'Think there's any chance we'll get the drawings back?'

'We can hope. The Yard has a reasonable record of recovering valuable stolen goods.'

'Hmm.' Van Buren helped himself to more whisky. 'So. What is it you want from me?'

'I'd be interested in your observations about the dinner party and about your father generally.'

'Fine.' They ran over the events of Friday evening from the young man's perspective. He was unable to add much to what Merlin already knew. The evening had passed pleasantly enough. Everyone had been on their best behaviour. He did not have a high opinion of Micallef, but seldom did of Elizabeth's boyfriends. He'd not been aware of anyone prowling around the house that evening. Yes, he and his father had touched on the subject of magazine funding, and it was his understanding that, despite misgivings, his father would stump up the money. He shared his sister's distaste for Frances Walters. He remembered seeing a carnation in his father's button-hole but had no recollection of a pin on his tie. He himself occasionally wore tie pins, but the one Merlin showed him was not his. News of a possible fight on the Embankment was not a surprise, as it confirmed his suspicion that the burglar or burglars had been responsible for his father's death. After the dinner, he had gone straight home with Caroline and to bed.

Merlin moved on to a new subject. 'When was the last time you saw or spoke to your uncle, Mr Butterfield?'

'He called me last Thursday or Friday. Said my father wouldn't take his calls. Asked me to intervene. I said I might, but I didn't. I knew to keep well away from my father on a matter like that.'

'He was touchy on the subject of the litigation?'

'You bet.'

'Will you be dropping it now?'

Van Buren frowned. 'Do you know, with the shock of everything, I've yet to give it any thought. My uncle is a stuffed shirt for whom I do not care overmuch, but Aunt Audrey was good to us when we were young. I'm pretty sure Elizabeth won't want to carry on.'

'I understand your father's death accelerates some substantial bequests from your mother's will?'

Van Buren pursed his lips. 'You have been a busy bee, Mr Merlin, haven't you? It does. I suppose it'll take a while for the lawyers to sort everything out, but in due course I should receive a tidy sum, which will be welcome as I doubt we'll be getting much from our father. Unless the stolen goods are recovered, of course.

'How much is a tidy sum?'

'I'm not sure it's any of your business, but around forty grand.'

'So, no disrespect intended, in one way your father's death has done you a favour.'

Van Buren bristled. 'I don't think that remark's in very good taste, Chief Inspector.' He went to pour himself another whisky.

'I should have worded my observation better. My apologies.'

Van Buren returned to his seat. 'My father's death is a huge blow. And on top of that, there is the loss of the drawings, the value of which makes the sum of forty thousand pounds seem piffling.'

'Indeed.'

'I don't like to be rude, Mr Merlin, but we've been at this for quite a while. 'Will we be much longer?'

'I think your sister has answered a number of my other

questions already. One last question about your uncle, though. Could he be capable of violence?'

'Uncle Humphrey? Why, you can't think . . .'

'By all accounts he was distraught about the litigation. He faced personal ruin. As your father remained determined to proceed, perhaps Mr Butterfield decided there was only one way to get rid of his problem.'

'Well, you know, now I think about it, I . . . I did see him lose his temper quite violently a few times when I was younger. He once took a whip to one of the farmhands. He might not look it, but he's pretty strong. I saw him bring an out-of-control horse to heel a couple of times. Took some doing. Then there's his drink problem. I don't know all the details, but I understand he was out of order on a few occasions. He almost got arrested for affray in the local pub once. I understand my aunt pulled some strings to get him out of the mess. Still, Uncle Humphrey a murderer? I suppose stranger things have happened.'

Virgil Lewis was jerked sharply to his feet by the two guards. Goldberg watched unhappily as sentence was passed. The presiding officer, a bulging-eyed martinet, stared sternly at the prisoner. 'Airman Virgil Lewis, this court has found you guilty of the robbery and murder of Pablo Merino, also known as Tomas Barboza. The sentence is death by hanging. The execution will take place on Tuesday morning next. May God have mercy on your soul. Take him away.'

As he was hauled from the dock, Lewis started shouting 'I'm an innocent man. An innocent man!' His repeated cries could be heard until long after he'd disappeared from sight.

As the detective made his way to the door, Max Pearce stepped forward to bar his way. 'Justice done, eh?' he sneered.

Goldberg remained calm. 'Does Lewis have any right of appeal?'

'If there are grounds, but there are none. He's as good as dead

273

already. Murdered a man and must pay the price. Now scuttle off and tell your pal Merlin that his attempts to halt the course of American justice have failed.'

Pearce disappeared through the courtroom door. Goldberg decided to linger for a moment in the hope of a word with Captain Stein, the defence counsel. As the room emptied, he saw the dark-haired young man collecting his papers together and went over to introduce himself.

'Pleased to meet you, Detective, though I'd have wished for better circumstances.'

Goldberg shrugged. 'You sound like a fellow New Yorker, Captain.'

'The Bronx, born and bred. You?'

'Lower East Side.'

'I hear you've been handed the thorny task of dealing with the locals. They're not going to be very happy about this, are they? I understand Chief Inspector Merlin believes we tried the wrong man.'

'He does. I don't understand why he wasn't allowed to give evidence.'

'When we were in judge's chambers earlier, I argued he should be allowed to do so, but the court was in the palm of Pearce's hand, as you no doubt saw.'

'Can nothing more be done?'

'The military judicial system is brutally efficient. Or should I say efficiently brutal? I was shamefully given only twenty-four hours notice of this assignment. I shall apply for an appeal, but won't get one.'

'Do you think things would have gone differently if Lewis had been a white man?'

'I think you know the answer to that, Detective.' Stein closed his briefcase. 'Well, good luck. I hope that when we meet again, it will be on a happier occasion.'

'You're going to see Lewis now?'

274

'Yes.'

'May I join you?'

'Are you sure about that?'

'He may be beyond saving, but if there are any repercussions, I'd like to be able to say I had an opportunity to meet the man in person.'

'Very well, Detective. Follow me.'

Chapter Nineteen

Saturday August 22nd 1942

Merlin consulted his Saturday to-do list.

> *Check in with Bernie about Lewis*
> *Interview Butterfield*
> *Pull in Micallef*
> *Interview Katz (if fit)*
> *Speak to Charlie Mason*

He'd already telephoned Goldberg and heard the bad news. He'd expected it, but it was still not a great start to the day.

Cole had been in touch with Butterfield, who luckily was still in town. He would be coming to the Yard at ten. Merlin was just thinking of the questions to be put to him when the telephone rang. It was the AC.

'Frank, I'm glad I've caught you. The reason I'm calling is that I met with the commissioner yesterday. He had breakfasted with Sir Kenneth Clark earlier. You know who Sir Kenneth is?'

'I do. His name has cropped up in connection with the Van Buren case. It was he who advised on the authenticity of the da Vinci drawings.'

'That's what I wanted to talk about. Sir Kenneth told the commissioner that His Majesty the King has expressed concern about the fate of those works. The Royal Collection has several da Vinci pieces and His Majesty is a great admirer of the artist.'

'Very interesting, sir, but I'm not quite sure how that is relevant to my investigation. Naturally we are hoping to identify the thieves and retrieve the drawings, and I have Charlie Mason and his people working hard to that end.'

'I know, I know. I spoke to Mason myself yesterday. He told me where he'd got to.'

Merlin could feel the heat as the blood rushed to his cheeks. He could not hide his irritation. 'You shouldn't have done that. I should be your principal point of communication.'

'Oh fiddle-de-dee, Frank. Don't be so touchy. You were out and the commissioner was anxious I get back to him as soon as possible.'

Merlin's irritation gave way to a greater concern.

'You didn't give him details about Mason's two suspects?'

'Yes, I did.'

Merlin became so angry he couldn't speak.

'Frank? Are you there? Frank?'

Through gritted teeth Merlin said, 'That was a mistake, sir.'

'How so?'

'You know why.'

'Damn it all, Chief Inspector.' The line suddenly went dead.

Corruption was a fact of police life in London. Merlin did his best to avoid contact with officers suspected of having too close a relationship with the criminal community. A couple of suspect officers were known to have the ear of the commissioner. Merlin had raised the subject many times with the AC, but he refused to take the concerns seriously. The chief inspector's job was difficult enough without the progress of his investigations being leaked to men like Billy Hill by the force's rotten apples.

His team, save for Bridges, appeared at the door and he waved them in.

'You're alive then, Peter?'

'I must have swallowed half the River Thames, but I've lived to tell the tale.'

'Let's be grateful for that. How is Katz?'

'Not great, but he'll live. We might be able to speak to him later today. The sergeant is at the hospital now, reorganising the security arrangements. Oh, and Constable Robinson has something to tell you.'

'Let's hear it, then.'

'We did the follow-up canvassing of Vermeulen's neighbours yesterday, sir. I spoke to a sweet elderly lady four doors down on the other side of the street – a Miss Wheeler, a retired dance teacher. She'd gone to hospital for a foot operation the morning Vermeulen's body was found, but she was there in the days running up to his death. Moreover, she'd been housebound because she couldn't walk properly. She said she spent most of her waking hours in her front room reading or watching the world go by.'

'She knew Vermeulen?'

'They were on neighbourly nodding terms. She'd seen him in the mews recently.'

'Did she see any visitors?'

'She saw two. The first was a woman matching Mrs Dunne's description. The other was a middle-aged man who knocked on the door last Thursday, when no one was in. She also mentioned a couple of men she saw in the mews. As it's a cul-de-sac, the pedestrian traffic is made up mainly of residents and delivery men. These men were neither, and she thought their movements suspicious.'

'What were they doing?'

'"Loitering" was the word she used. She also saw one of them hanging around in Montpellier Square when a friend took her out in a wheelchair.'

'She saw these men how many times?'

'Three or four.'

'Were they ever together?'

'Not that she saw.'

'Descriptions?'

'Not particularly helpful. Suits, ties, hats. Never got much of a look at their faces. All she could say was that one was shorter and younger than the other.'

'And what about the man who knocked on Vermeulen's door?'

'Tall, smartly-dressed was the best she could do.'

Merlin found his tin of Everton mints and popped one in his mouth. 'The younger man must have been Pablo. Perhaps the second loiterer was Swanton's German spy.'

'What about the third man?'

'Your guess is as good as mine, Cole. Could have been an insurance salesman. Could have been a killer.' He looked at Robinson. 'She's got all her marbles, this Miss Wheeler?'

'Definitely, sir.'

'Did she hear any of the men speak?'

'No.'

'Hmm. More food for thought. Good work, Constable Robinson.'

Billy Hill kept a bedroom at the club for his occasional use and had spent the night there after a lively party. Dressed in a silk robe, he was sitting in an armchair sipping his favourite hangover cure of raw eggs, tomato juice and pepper when the bedside telephone rang. He recognised the voice at once and listened carefully to the fascinating information it imparted.

After he'd bathed and dressed, he went down to his office, where he found Jimmy Miles waiting for him. 'You look rough, Jimmy boy.'

'Mixed my drinks again last night. Never learn, do I?'

'I'll make you one of my special cures in a minute.' Billy sat at his desk. 'First, though, I've got news. I heard from one of our friends at the Met. The fat one.'

'Yeah?'

'Said Merlin's got Charlie Mason working the Cheyne Walk job. Mason's already got Jake in the frame.'

'That's fast work. What's their evidence?'

'Ain't got none. They're fingering him on the basis that there are only a few people they think could pull off a job like that, and most of them are banged up. Only ones out are Jake and that tosser Bert Doyle.'

'Well, that's no evidence at all, is it?'

'No, but obviously Jake is going to get some heat.'

'He can handle himself.'

'I know, but I'm worried they may try and finger him for Van Buren's death as well. He still claims he had nothing to do with that?'

'Swears blind.'

'You've got someone keeping an eye on Micallef? No more contact with the police?'

'No.'

'It's only a matter of time.' Hill examined his hands thoughtfully. 'Those drawings are too hot, you know. The fat man said the theft has attracted a lot of attention in the wrong places. Places like Buck House, for starters. His Majesty's hot for da Vinci, apparently. He's taking a "keen interest" in developments.'

Miles wasn't sure whether to be impressed or not.

'I can't see any way we're going to be able to shift them for a while, if ever. I've half a mind to turn them in. We still got a good haul in ready cash.'

'Well, I did say I thought Micallef was trouble, if you remember.'

'Shut it, Jimmy,' snarled Hill. 'I'm not in the mood.'

'Sorry, boss.'

'We are where we are and we need to work out where we go from here. That safe house in Harrow? Anyone using it at the moment?'

'I don't think so.'

'Good. Grab the two of them, Penny and Micallef, and stash them away there for a few days.'

'Won't Merlin and his lot get suspicious if they both disappear?'

'They're suspicious enough as it is already. Anyway, it's the weekend. People go away at the weekend, don't they?'

'Yes, boss.'

'So give them a weekend in the country. Buys us a little time. I'll give the matter further consideration on Monday.'

Butterfield's face was a picture of misery as Cole introduced him to Merlin and Johnson in the interview room.

'Haven't you people got better things to do? I've already told the constable everything I know, which is not a lot.' He made a show of checking his watch. 'There's a train I need to catch in forty-five minutes.'

'I suggest we get on then, sir,' said Merlin. 'I understand you and your brother-in-law were not on the best of terms?'

'Yes, yes. I discussed all that with this young man. I'm sure he's reported back. Must you really cover old ground?'

'Please bear with me, sir. It's always best to hear things from the horse's mouth, so to speak. So Mr Van Buren was trying to overturn his wife's will?'

'Yes, and kick us out of our home. My wife Audrey's father perversely left it to Mary when he died, despite the fact that Audrey and I have lived in and run the house and estate for nearly thirty years now. My sister-in-law made up for that injustice by leaving it to us. The idea that she was of unsound mind is ridiculous.'

'She was unwell, though, when she made the change to her will?'

'Physically, yes. Mentally, no. But what has all that got to do with Van Buren's death?'

'You would appear to be a major beneficiary of his demise. As such, your views and actions are of interest to us.'

'Are you seriously suggesting I had something to do with what happened to him?' Butterfield's tone suddenly became less belligerent.

'Naturally, given the circumstances, you must have harboured considerable resentment against the man. At the end of last week you had a frustrating time trying to contact him. By Friday night you must have been feeling very angry.'

'I may have been angry, but that doesn't mean I decided to push him into the river. Any such suggestion is . . . is . . . preposterous. To raise such an idea with me is—'

'Forgive me, but it is my job to explore all possibilities without fear or favour. Calm yourself, please. Now what I don't really understand about your efforts last week is why you didn't just take the bull by the horns and knock on the man's door. It's not as if you didn't know where he lived.'

'Constable Cole already asked me that and I told him I didn't want to risk an embarrassing scene.'

'What's a little embarrassment when your home and livelihood are at stake? And I understand you made some of your calls from a phone box in Battersea Park, a mere stone's throw from Cheyne Walk.'

'I . . . I could not bring myself to visit without an invitation.'

'I see. Now you returned home on the Saturday morning, didn't you?'

'Yes.'

'What did you do with yourself on the Friday night? At some point you gave up on telephoning, didn't you?'

'Yes. I made my last call somewhere between eight and nine from a box near my hotel. Then I went back to my room. I realised I hadn't eaten all day and was very hungry, so I went out for a meal.'

'Alone?'

'Yes, of course.'

'Where did you go to eat?'

'An Italian place in Kensington. Gennaro's, it's called.'

'And after the restaurant?'

'I went back to the hotel.'

Merlin looked away briefly then stood. 'If you don't mind, sir, I think I'd like a quick word with my colleagues outside.'

'What about my train?'

He ignored the question and led his men along the corridor to another interview room, which wasn't being used.

'I understand why you didn't quite trust this fellow, Constable. I'm sure he's not telling us everything. Peter?'

'I agree.'

'I have an idea how we might open him up. Your discovery the other night could be the key, Constable.'

'His visit to the brothel, you mean, sir?'

'I do. I'd like to confront him with what you saw. See if that provides leverage.'

They were all in agreement and returned to Butterfield, who immediately asked querulously about his train again.

'There are plenty of trains to your neck of the woods,' Merlin snapped. 'We'll talk about trains only when you've answered all our questions satisfactorily.'

Butterfield's mouth gaped open, but no words emerged.

'I'd like you to listen to what Constable Cole has to say. Constable?'

Butterfield went pale, then seemed to shrink, as Cole's story was told in all its unedifying detail. When it was finished, Merlin waited a moment before asking whether Butterfield had anything to say.

His voice was subdued. 'That's not the way it was . . . The girl was not . . .'

'You're suggesting the constable isn't telling the truth? It wouldn't be difficult to track down the prostitute you went off with and obtain confirmation of his report.'

Butterfield thought for a while, then, with a deep breath,

decided to pursue a different tack. 'All right. What of it? I saw a prostitute. Paying for sex isn't against the law, so whatever I did is none of your business.'

'Strictly speaking that's correct, sir. Solicitation for custom by a woman is, however, illegal, as is the maintenance of a brothel. With the constable's evidence, we could prosecute the woman you were with, and the brothel operator. Naturally we'd call you as a witness.'

'I'd refuse.'

'Then a subpoena would be issued and you'd have no choice. Once under way, of course, your involvement in the case would become public knowledge. It would be hard to keep from your wife.'

This provoked an angry shout of 'No!' Then, however, the difficulty of his position slowly sank in. 'What do you require of me to avoid such an outcome?' he eventually asked quietly.

'My colleagues and I feel you are not telling us the whole story. What are you hiding?'

Butterfield looked away and took a while to answer. Eventually he nodded. 'I did not kill Leon Van Buren, but you're right. There is more. You . . . you should know, Chief Inspector, that I have had a drink problem for some time. In the past year, I've made good progress, but I am still prone to occasional relapses, usually when I am under severe pressure. Recently I'm afraid I had not just one, but two such relapses. The second was on the night the constable followed me. The first occurred the Friday night of the week before. That evening, as I said, I went to an Italian restaurant for a late dinner. I walked from the hotel and got there around nine thirty. I hadn't booked, but there was a table free. I ordered just one course – the food is good, the service not so. As I waited for it, I weakened and ordered some wine. First just a glass, but then a bottle. I had some liqueurs towards the end as well. By the time I left, I was . . . well . . . sloshed.'

'At what hour did you leave?' asked Johnson.

284

'They close at eleven, so just after that. Inevitably I had spent the entire meal thinking about the litigation and its possible disastrous consequences. When I came out of the restaurant, I was in . . . in a febrile emotional state as well as drunk. A bus pulled up at a stop right in front of me. It was going to Chelsea, and on the spur of the moment, I jumped aboard. I was determined to see Leon and sort things out once and for all.'

'You went to his house?' asked Merlin.

'Yes. I'm not sure what time I got there but I suppose it was around eleven twenty five or thirty. I knocked on the door several times. No answer. The place was in darkness as far as I could see. I presumed he was out. I decided to wait around in case he returned. It was a lovely warm summer's night and I wandered across the road to have a look at the river.' Butterfield paused to recover his breath. 'I'm sorry. I'm a little asthmatic.' He took another breath, then resumed. 'A while later, as I was gazing out to the water, I heard a noise from somewhere to my left. I turned, but the moon had just gone behind some clouds and it was difficult to make out anything in the darkness. I took a few steps forward and the noise became clearer. There was some sort of scuffle going on. I'd sobered up a bit by now and realised I might be in danger. I turned away and went to the roadside hoping to see a taxi. My luck was in. In the distance I saw a faint light heading my way from the direction of the Royal Hospital. I thought I ought to cross over the road to get further away from the fight, and was about to do so when the moon suddenly reappeared and lit up the face of one of the protagonists. It . . . it was Leon. I was shocked, obviously, but before I could react, the taxi was at hand. I waved, the driver pulled up and I jumped in. I know . . . I know I should have tried to help Leon out, but there it is.'

'And the taxi pulled away?'

'Yes, Chief Inspector. I said "Paddington" to the driver and he chose to make a U-turn. As he did, I saw someone run across the road. I assumed he – I'm pretty sure it was a man – was going to somehow stop the fight.'

Merlin took a moment to mull over what he'd just heard, then looked at Johnson and Cole. 'Quite a story, eh, gentlemen?'

'If it's true,' said Johnson.

'It is, I swear,' exclaimed Butterfield.

Merlin studied his face carefully. 'These other men. The man fighting Van Buren and the supposed rescuer. Can you describe them?'

'I'm sorry, Chief Inspector. As regards the man in the fight, I only ever saw his back. I think I can say that he was shorter than Leon. That's about all. The other fellow . . . Well, it was very dark.'

'Weren't the taxi's head-lights on?' asked Cole.

'They were, but muted for the blackout, as you'd expect. I only saw a shadowy figure. I'm sorry.'

'I hope this isn't some bizarre cover-up story, Mr Butterfield.'

Butterfield sighed and shook his head. 'No, Mr Merlin. You asked for the truth and that's what I've given you.'

'It would help if we had some corroboration.'

'I wish—'

'What about the taxi driver?' interrupted Cole. 'Did you get his number?'

'I'm afraid I didn't.' Butterfield's face suddenly brightened. 'However, there is something. At the end of the journey, he lit a cigarette as he was waiting for payment. This allowed me a proper look at his face. He had a large birthmark, a purple one, on his left cheek. There can't be many London taxi drivers with a mark like that. If you can track him down, he'll be able to confirm my story.'

Charles Dunne had no Saturday-morning golf game for once, and accordingly was sharing a late breakfast with his wife in the kitchen of their London flat. It was, Ursula realised, their first meal together since Vermeulen's death. Her husband had been keeping late hours at the Home Office, and had chosen to stay several nights during the week at the Reform Club. He'd not had much opportunity to observe her grief. She wasn't even sure he'd noticed anything awry at all. Now, a week after the murder, she'd got herself onto a relatively even keel and, adept as the couple were at putting on a good front, a calm, civilised atmosphere prevailed at the breakfast table. Ursula had long ago fallen out of love with her husband, but she could still on occasion enjoy his company. He was a brilliant and well-informed man.

Charles had shared his inside information on the progress of the war with her over the meal. Afterwards, while Ursula cleared away, he went to get the newspapers that had been delivered earlier. Back at the table, he opened *The Times*, and his wife picked up the *Daily Mail*. After ten minutes, finding little of interest in her own paper, Ursula's eye alighted on a headline in his.

'There's something in your paper about the Americans hanging one of their soldiers. That sort of thing's in your bailiwick, isn't it?'

'It is. I know all about it. A black fellow robbed and killed some Portuguese chap. He's going to get his just desserts.'

'The headline mentions a hasty trial. How hasty?'

'I think by the time of the hanging, the whole thing will have been done and dusted in just over a week.'

'That's ridiculously quick, isn't it, to do proper justice?'

'The Americans don't mess around. The man was clearly guilty, and they're dealing with it fairly but swiftly.'

'As you know, Charles, I don't hold with capital punishment. There have been too many mistakes.'

Dunne shrugged and returned to his paper. Ursula rose from the table. 'I've got one of my migraines coming on, I think. I'm going to take a couple of aspirin and lie down for an hour.'

'All right, dear.'

She looked for the aspirin without success in her bathroom and bedroom. When she went back to the kitchen to ask Charles if he had any, he'd disappeared. Guessing that he'd gone down to the lobby to collect the mail, she decided to check out his bathroom. No luck there, nor in his bedroom. His study remained a final possibility. There she was relieved to find a pill box in one of the desk drawers. As she was removing it, something caught her eye. A sheet of paper – an invoice, in fact, from a Mr Desmond Roberts. Another name was mentioned on it, and it was this that had drawn her attention. The name was Vermeulen.

Micallef complained loudly as Jimmy Miles and Mal Jones, another Hill heavy, bundled him into the back of the car. 'Hell, Jimmy, what are you doing? What's going on?'

Miles made no reply as he slid in beside him and tapped Jones on the shoulder. The car pulled away sharply.

'Where the hell are we going?'

Miles looked at him menacingly. 'Shut your bleeding trap! Thanks to you, we're likely to have the Old Bill crawling all over us shortly. I never liked you, nor your Cheyne Walk idea, but you managed to smarm your idea past Billy when he wasn't thinking straight. Well he's thinking straight now. He wants you tucked up nice and safe somewhere Merlin and Co. can't get at you.'

'But I was lying low anyway, like I was told.'

'Well he wants you lying lower still. We've got a pleasant country cottage to hide you away in. You can enjoy a nice little holiday there. Now sit back and enjoy the ride.'

Micallef had got the message that he'd best do as he was told. As they drove through the London streets, he thought about the suitcase Miles had allowed him to bring. There was a secret compartment in it where he normally kept a gun. In the rush, he'd forgotten to check if it was still in place. Something told him he might need it.

Miles interrupted his thoughts. 'You'll be having some company.'

'Oh?'

'Billy thought it best to take Jake Penny out of circulation too

288

for the moment. The man can be quite entertaining if he's in the right mood. Good cards player, too.'

Micallef made no comment. Then a thought came to him. 'Look, I can handle the police all right. I'll have to see them again at some point, won't I? Why not just get on with it?'

'Billy needs some time to think.'

They drove past a number of bomb sites. This part of London had taken a real battering in the Blitz. 'Will there be a phone where I'm going?' asked Micallef.

'Nope.'

'Telephone box nearby?'

'You won't be going out, so it makes no odds.'

'Thing is, I need to get a message to Elizabeth. She'll be in a state if she doesn't know where I am. With her father's death and all, she's in a pretty fragile condition.'

'All right. I'll check with Billy. If he don't mind, I'll get Mal here to drop off a note. You write it and give some sort of believable excuse for your absence.'

'But—'

'Now shut it. I had a late night and need a little nap. Won't be long until we're there.

'I tracked down Bert Doyle,' said Mason on the phone to Bridges. 'Turns out he broke his arm a couple of weeks ago when he fell into a bomb crater in King's Cross.'

'He's not our man then.'

'No. It all boils down to Jake Penny. I've an address for him in Islington and I sent a couple of my men round, but he's slung his hook. According to a neighbour, Penny said something about going off to enjoy country pursuits. Can't quite see him as the shooting and fishing type.'

'Reckon he was tipped off?'

'Smells like it to me.'

'Damn. You'll keep us posted, Charlie?'

'Of course. There's one other thing concerning this fellow Micallef. I was chatting to an old mate of mine, a sergeant out in Walthamstow. He has a constable under him who's half Maltese. I asked him to find out if the constable recognised Micallef's name. He's a well-spoken lad, isn't he?'

'Yes. Sounds educated.'

'So I understood. I passed that on. Anyway, it turns out the constable didn't know anything, but when he mentioned it to his mum she remembered a young man called Edward Micallef who'd been to the best English private school on the island. Said he was quite a looker.'

'Sounds like our man. So expensive school – rich parents?'

'Rich and crooked. The father's a hotshot local gangster. Runs protection rackets and has a variety of other criminal enterprises.'

'The chief inspector's going to love this,' Bridges said. 'Any chance your men could haul Micallef in? We're a bit stretched.'

'Of course. Give me his address and I'll get onto it now.'

Merlin came in and heard Mason's news with evident satisfaction.

'I knew he was a wrong'un, Sam. We both did. He has to have been the inside man on the burglary. Now let me tell you about Mr Butterfield.'

'You believe him, sir?' asked Bridges when Merlin had repeated the key points of Butterfield's story,

'I think it may be down to the taxi-driver. The inspector and Cole have gone looking for him.'

'You let Butterfield go?'

'Yes, but I asked him to remain in London.' Merlin loosened his collar. 'What news of Katz?'

'Being discharged at three, then brought here by one of the Lambeth officers watching over him at the hospital.'

The telephone rang. Bridges picked up and listened carefully. When he put the phone down, there was a half-smile on his lips. 'It's all happening today, sir. That was the desk sergeant. A woman called earlier. The Soho barmaid Cole interviewed. Left a message to say she thinks she's seen the woman who was drinking with Pablo. Works in a shop just off Cambridge Circus called Evelyn Fashions.'

'Katz'll be a while yet. Let's go. We can take Robinson with us. A female touch might be helpful.'

'She's not here, sir. She had to go to that charity do last night with the AC out in the country, remember? Won't be in until this afternoon.'

'The AC and his damned charity events. Just we two then. Come on.'

Charles Dunne had been a very long time collecting the mail. When he came through the door, he apologised. 'Bumped into Colonel Hunt from downstairs. He invited me in for a chat that went on a lot longer than I'd intended.'

Ursula's anger had had almost an hour to stew. She waved the invoice furiously in his face. 'What the hell is this, Charles?'

'I've no idea. You know I can't see a thing without my glasses.'

'I suggest you go and get them. And be quick about it.'

Back at the kitchen table, he groaned when he saw what his wife had discovered. 'You've been rummaging through my private papers, have you?'

'Not with intent. I couldn't find any aspirin and looked in your desk. The invoice was under the pill box and I couldn't help noticing the name on it. Why on earth did you set a private eye on him?'

Charles loosened his cravat. 'It's damnably hot in here. Let's adjourn to a bigger room.'

In the drawing room, he opened the French windows wide before joining his wife on the settee. 'I'm sorry, Ursula. I know we like to avoid certain subjects. We roll along leaving many things unsaid. But now that you've discovered this piece of paper, I have no option but to delve into some of those things.' He fidgeted with his cravat again. 'The fact is for a long time we have allowed

291

each other leeway in matters of the heart. You may think, as we no longer sleep together, that I have no problem with your . . . your external relationships. Sadly, that is not the case. I was aware of your affair with Vermeulen almost from its beginning. It hurt me, but I chose, as usual, not to make a fuss. After a while, I began to sense that the attachment you had formed with him was stronger than most of your other flings, and I worried that it would threaten our marriage. Our marriage means a great deal to me, and not just because of the boy.'

Ursula was finding it difficult to look her husband in the face. She glanced away to the window.

'Because of my concern, I engaged a private investigator so that I might know more about the man who posed this threat. I learned quite a lot about Mr Vermeulen. I learned that he led an active and complicated life. I learned that he spent most of his time in Portugal and could only be with you for the odd week. I learned that his complicated business affairs meant this situation was unlikely to change. Mr Roberts even informed me that he suspected Vermeulen was engaged in secret work for the Allies. Naturally I told him not to pursue that any further. In the end, it seemed most unlikely to me that you would run off to Lisbon with this man. He posed no threat to our marriage. Accordingly, I ended the arrangement with Roberts. You will have noticed no doubt that the date on this invoice is over five months ago. It was his final invoice.'

Ursula forced herself at last to look her husband in the eye. A tear slid down her cheek. She had found what he had said surprising, disturbing and, in a strange way, commendable.

Sonia had been working in the ladies' fashion department of Swan & Edgar when Merlin had first met her, and he was knowledge-able enough about ladies' wear now to know that the dresses on show in the shop window were the expensive kind.

There were no customers in Evelyn Fashions, just the two

assistants standing behind the counter. One was a middle-aged woman with bouffant brown hair and a lot of make-up. The other, a pretty young girl with short dark hair, was busily wrapping a parcel.

'*Bonjour, messieurs.* 'Ow may I 'elp you?' said the older woman in a transparently fake French accent.

Merlin produced his warrant card. 'I'd be grateful for a word with your colleague, please.'

The woman's hands flew up theatrically into the air. '*Mon Dieu!* Ze police. What 'ave you been doing, Barbara?'

Barbara put down her parcel and looked nervously at Merlin. 'I don't know as I've done anything, *madame.*'

'The young lady is not in any trouble,' said Merlin. 'We need to talk to her about someone she may have met recently.'

Madame pouted. 'We are very busy zis morning. It is not vair convenient.'

Merlin looked behind him at the empty shop and raised an eyebrow. Madame sighed. 'Vair well. You may take ze policemen into the back room, Barbara. I shall do my best to man ze fort on my own.'

The two officers followed the young woman along a narrow corridor to a room piled high with garments and rolls of cloth. She invited them to sit at a small table at the back.

'May I know your full name?' Merlin asked.

'You're here to see me but you don't know my name. Isn't that a little odd?'

'We are acting on a description, miss.'

'My name is Freeman. Barbara Freeman.'

'A young lady was seen having a drink with a man in a pub. We think you might have been that young lady.'

'It's not against the law to meet a man in a pub, is it? Or is there some new wartime regulation I'm not aware of?'

Merlin smiled. 'Of course not. We're just interested in this man's movements at the time.'

'I'm prepared to admit that I've been known to enjoy a drink with a gentleman in a pub. Which pub? When?'

'The King's Head. Just around the corner from Soho Square. Wednesday the 12th.'

'Can you describe the gentleman?'

'A young foreigner. Might have claimed to be Portuguese but was in fact Spanish. I have a photograph with me. I can show it to you, though it's a little dark in here.'

Barbara got up and switched on a light, then took the photo and studied it. As she did so, Merlin examined her face. She had large green eyes and Cupid's bow lips. She seemed to be wearing as much make-up as her boss. Under the thick layer of face powder on her right cheek, he thought he could discern signs of bruising.

'I remember him. Tomas. Yes, that Wednesday. I'd been with some friends but they went off somewhere else, leaving me on my own. He struck up conversation, then bought me a port and lemon.'

'What did you talk about?'

'This and that. He told me about Lisbon, which was where he said he was from. A nice enough chap.'

'The pub landlady said she thought she saw you leave together.'

'Did she now, nosy cow.'

'Where did you go?'

'He said he'd not had much chance to see the sights. Asked if we could walk down to the river, have a look at Big Ben and the Houses of Parliament. He seemed a proper gentleman, so I agreed. We chatted a little more, then said goodbye.'

'Was that the last you saw of him?' asked Bridges.

The young woman seemed to hesitate before she said, 'Yes.'

'What did he tell you he was doing in London?'

'He said he was a salesman visiting customers. Leather goods.'

'Did he talk about anything else?'

'He mentioned the bombing. Said he'd seen more damage than he'd expected. Called the Germans nasty names.'

'Did he seem worried or nervous about anything?'

She shook her head. 'He seemed perfectly relaxed.'

Merlin nodded. 'Well, thank you, miss. Here's my card if anything else occurs to you. I couldn't help noticing that you seem to have taken a bit of a knock to the face. What happened, if you don't mind my asking?'

'Oh . . . a silly accident. Walked into a door.'

'Done that a few times myself. Here in the shop?'

'No. Somewhere else. I . . . I can be a little absent-minded. My sister says my head is too often in the clouds.'

They all got up and headed back down the corridor. Halfway along, Merlin tapped Barbara Freeman on the shoulder. She stopped and turned.

'I was just wondering, miss. You never asked us what our interest was in Mr Barboza.'

'I . . . I assumed it was a private police matter.'

'Not at all. I'm afraid Mr Barboza was murdered. Knifed in Soho, not so far from where you met.'

It was too dark in the corridor for Merlin to properly gauge the young woman's reaction. He did note, however, that there was no gasp of surprise or horror before she set off again towards the shop.

Lisbon

The ceiling fans in Gulbenkian's suite still weren't working properly. The windows and French doors were all open, but it was uncomfortably hot. He could feel a headache coming on. His mood was not improved by the latest correspondence. There was another cable from Tatar asking where his money was, and a letter from his London solicitors saying they were still encountering difficulties in getting his enemy alien status revoked. They had no news on the progress of the Van Buren investigation. Neither, it appeared, did anyone else among his contacts.

His secretary appeared at the door. 'More correspondence, sir.'

He groaned. 'And more punishment, no doubt.'

'Most of it can wait, but there's one letter I think you'll want now.' She passed him a sealed envelope.

'You've not opened it?'

'I . . . I thought you'd better open it yourself. Look at the handwriting.'

Gulbenkian put his spectacles on, then recoiled in shock. 'But . . . but this is Frederick's hand, isn't it?'

'I believe so. It seems he arranged for the letter to be dispatched in a British diplomatic bag the week he died. Somehow it got overlooked, and the embassy finally sent it today with their apologies.'

Gulbenkian weighed the letter in his hand. 'A communication from beyond the grave. Pass me the letter opener, my dear. Let's see what poor Frederick has to say.'

London

'I don't think that girl was being entirely straight with us, Sam.' Merlin said as they arrived at the Yard.

'I was thinking the same, sir.'

'Why did she never ask us why we were interested in Pablo?'

'She also didn't seem put out in any way by the news of his death. Almost as if she already knew.'

'I thought that too. Am I right in thinking neither name, Barboza nor Merino, has yet been released to the newspapers?'

'You are, sir.'

'Very odd.'

They found Johnson and Cole waiting for them upstairs in a state of some excitement.

'Found him, sir. Or rather, Cole did. The taxi driver. The constable tracked him down at Victoria station.'

'Got a corker of a birth-mark, sir,' added Cole. 'Just as Butter-field said. Not surprisingly, he's well-known, and I was tipped off that Victoria is his favourite haunt.'

'Has he confirmed Butterfield's story?'

'Says he picked up a man matching Butterfield's description by Cheyne Walk at approximately eleven fifty nine that night.. He records details of all his fares.'

'Did he see the fight?'

'Became aware of some sort of disturbance as he picked up his passenger, then saw someone running across the road in front of the car before he drove off. A man, he thought, though he can't say more.'

'So Butterfield has his corroboration. Any other developments?'

'Charlie Mason called to say that his men drew a blank with Micallef. No sign of him at his flat.'

'Did they try Elizabeth Van Buren's place?'

'They didn't know to, sir, but I rang her just now to see if she knew where he was. She didn't, and was ticked off with him as he was meant to have been taking her shopping.'

'You asked her to let us know when he does turn up?'

'Of course.'

Merlin looked over at the cuckoo clock. It was nearly 3.15. 'Katz is here?'

'Interview Room Two.'

'Come on then.'

The Harrow safe-house was a dilapidated cottage on a single-track lane a couple of miles outside town. As they pulled up, Micallef remembered a teacher in Valletta bragging about his attendance at the famous local school.

The driver started to unload some groceries from the car boot while Miles led Micallef into the house. The ground-floor rooms were sparsely furnished but reasonably clean. There was a very basic little kitchen at the back, which looked out on an overgrown garden. Beyond the garden was a paddock, and beyond that an endless vista of farmland.

'Not quite the Ritz, I grant you,' said Miles, 'but it'll do you for a couple of days. Penny'll be here in a bit.'

Micallef had one more go at making Miles see reason. 'Look, Jimmy, it's got to be nuts having the two of us holed up together. If we're found by the police, their case will be made there and then.'

'The police ain't got a clue about this place. It's only me, Mal, Billy and Jacky Lane who know you're here, so stop griping.'

'Jacky Lane?'

'Your babysitter. It's him that's bringing Jake.'

'Christ, this is all so damned stupid!' Micallef shouted.

Miles lurched forward and grabbed him by the collar. 'Look, you little Maltese prick, this is what Billy wants, and what he wants he gets. Just shut up and get on with it.'

They heard an engine in the driveway and Miles let go. 'That'll be Jacky now.'

They went to the front door. Jake Penny was a short, wiry man with a drinker's nose. Lane was younger and plumper, with unkempt fair hair and hands like shovels.

''Ow do, gents,' said Penny, as Lane pushed past him with some bags. 'Any grub going? I'm starving.'

'Mal's made some spam sandwiches.'

'What about beer to wash it down with?'

'I think there's some Worthington's in the cellar, said Miles. 'I'll go and see.'

He reappeared after a moment carrying a crate of beer bottles.

'Ta, Jimmy. That'll do for starters anyway.'

Miles turned towards the door. 'Mal and I'll leave you to it then, boys.'

'What about the message to Elizabeth?' Micallef called after him.

'You'd better scribble something, Teddy, hadn't you?' Miles produced pencil and paper from his pocket.

A short while later, Micallef and Penny were sitting on a bench in the garden. The older man chewed his sandwich pensively. 'Rum do, eh?'

'Plain stupid is what it is, Jake.'

'Billy Hill's a clever bloke. Must have thought it through.'

'Is he really that clever?'

'Cleverer'n you and me, that's for sure. He's still a pretty young fella, and there 'e is, sitting close to the top of the criminal world.'

'If you say so.'

'And you gotta remember his inside track with the Met. Billy'll use that to good advantage and we'll soon be home free. You'll see.' Penny polished off his beer and opened a second.

'He may have an inside track, but I'm not sure that's going to get us anywhere. Frank Merlin's as clean as a whistle by all accounts. I think . . .' Micallef's words were drowned out by the roar of a passing low-flying aircraft. As it sped away, he asked, 'Spitfire?'

' 'Urricane more like. Northolt aerodrome's not far from 'ere.'

'We never had a chance to talk properly about the job.'

'Not much to talk about. Went as smooth as could be, I told you.'

'Can you give me a little more detail?'

'You want detail? All right, I'll give you detail. I parked the car halfway up Chelsea Manor Street. Found the alley and got to the garden. Went up the tree. A doddle. Got into the house through the window you left open. Crept downstairs and checked the place was empty. Entered the main room downstairs, made sure the blackout curtains were drawn tight. Switched on my torch. The safe was an old model I've dealt with before. Took me about twenty minutes to crack it. Cleared everything out into my bag. Had a quick look around the room and found a few other valuables. 'Elped myself to a glass of one of the geezer's fancy brandies, then zipped back upstairs, down the tree and over the wall. Went back to the car and scarpered.'

'And you're sure no one saw you?'

'Positive.' Penny's eyes narrowed. 'But what about you?'

'What do you mean?'

'A few of the lads at Billy's were talking 'bout you when I was in last week. Some thought that as you'd set up the job, you might have returned to Cheyne Walk to check on me. And if you had, you might have bumped into Van Buren and got involved in a barney.'

Micallef picked up a stone and threw it angrily at a nearby tree. 'Why the hell would I be so stupid as to do something like that? The police were trying that angle. It's bollocks. Whoever killed Van Buren, it wasn't me.'

Penny shrugged. 'All right, keep your 'air on. Just so you know what's bein' said.'

'Is that what Billy thinks?'

'Never spoke to Billy.' He finished off his second drink. 'You ain't touched your beer, Teddy. If it's not to your taste I'll 'ave it.'

'Sure. Here you are.' As he watched Penny pour more beer down his throat, it occurred to Micallef that if Hill really suspected him of Van Buren's murder, he'd better get away from Harrow as soon as possible.

'How are you now?' Merlin asked a sullen Katz.

'Not so great,' replied the young man hoarsely.

'But well enough to speak to us, I believe. I see the hospital were good enough to clean and dry your clothes.'

'They were.'

'Does your uncle know what happened yet?'

'I . . . I don't think so.'

'I'm guessing he won't be too happy. I hope you don't try and excuse yourself by blaming police harassment.'

'No. I won't do that.'

'We'd really like to know why you took off as you did.'

Katz's eyes flickered nervously. 'When . . . when I saw the

sergeant, I presumed you were coming to arrest me. I panicked and ran.'

'Why would you think we were about to arrest you? Have you done something for which you ought to be arrested?'

'Well, no . . . I . . . You must be aware that police in other countries are not as they are here. In my panic, I forgot that was the case.'

'That doesn't answer my question, Mr Katz.'

'I . . . haven't been well recently. Hardly sleeping, anxiety. Drinking a little too much.'

'I'm sorry to hear that, but it's still no explanation. I'll ask the question again. Did you run because you've committed an offence?'

'No.'

'Then why? Has it anything to do with Leon Van Buren?'

Katz took a deep breath. 'You know about the drawings stolen from my family?'

'We are aware of your belief that Mr Van Buren acquired them illicitly.'

Katz glanced at Bridges. 'I told the sergeant I saw Van Buren just the once. That is not quite true.'

'Oh?'

'I just couldn't get the drawings out of my mind. I decided I had to see Van Buren again. I went to his house after work on the Friday of the same week. Before knocking, I peeped through one of the windows and saw there was a party of some kind in progress. This obviously presented a problem. Disappointed, I went for a long walk through Chelsea. After a while, I felt hungry and went into a pub. I bought a pie and had a few drinks.'

'And then . . .?'

'I was determined to tackle him again that night. By now, I'd spent a few hours in the pub. I thought there was a chance the party might be over. I walked back to the house.'

'What time would this have been?'

301

'It was ten fifteen. I remember looking at my watch. The curtains were drawn and the house appeared to be in darkness. There was no answer to my knock. It seemed I was to be disappointed again. There's a patch of greenery across from Van Buren's house. I went to sit on the grass and think again. I was very tired and had drunk three or four pints of beer. I must have dozed off. When I came to, I checked the time. It was around eleven forty. I tried the house again, without success. At this point I had pretty much given up, but I decided to have a cigarette before going home. I crossed the road and leaned against the river wall. It was then . . .' Katz fell silent.

'Yes, Mr Katz?'

'I . . . I realised I didn't have a light. It was dark, but there was a bright moon dipping in and out of the clouds. I saw someone else smoking further along the wall and I went to ask for a light. As the person turned, the moonlight caught his face. It was Van Buren.'

'He recognised you?'

'Immediately. He said, 'Ah, it's the da Vinci Jew.' He seemed a little unsteady on his feet, as if, like me, he'd had too much to drink. He asked what I was doing there, and I told him I'd been anxious to speak to him once more about the drawings. I tried to make my case again. His response was the same as before, except ruder and harsher. He said the drawings were going to make him a fortune. Said he didn't care if he'd got them from the Nazis, and didn't care if *they'd* got them from my stinking Jewish family. I hadn't a legal leg to stand on. Then he barged me away and told me to clear off.

'My frustrations came to the boil and I'm afraid I punched him in the face. He retaliated, and we tussled for a minute or two. As I pulled away, I saw something glint in the moonlight. He had a knife. He swung at me and caught my hand.' He paused to show the scab of a cut beneath his right thumb. 'I used to box when I was at the Sorbonne so am not without fighting skill, and Van Buren, while a powerful man, was older than me. After a few feints, I managed to grasp his knife hand and push it back towards his throat. Then I saw a trickle of blood on his neck, and pulled away again. The knife fell to the ground. A car suddenly pulled up. A taxi, I think. Van Buren came at me, and we were grappling again when I heard shouting. It was getting closer and I thought it might be the police. I managed to disengage and ran off into the darkness, then made my way home.'

'Anyone give chase?' asked Johnson.

'If they did, they must have given up very quickly.'

'And how about the taxi? Did anyone get in? Did you see who-ever it was?'

'I didn't see anything. I was too concerned with getting away.'

'Were you aware of any other bystanders?' asked Merlin. 'Apart from whoever was shouting?'

'No . . . but . . .but now I think about it, when I began to run, I think a torch flashed somewhere across the road.'

'Where exactly?'

'Somewhere around where I'd been resting on the grass.'

'Any idea what happened to the knife?' asked Bridges.

'The last I knew of it was when it fell to the ground. Maybe it's still there.'

'It's not,' said Merlin, 'but . . .' he reached into his pocket, 'we did find this. Recognise it?'

Katz shook his head. 'Never worn a tie pin in my life.'

Merlin leaned forward. 'Do I take it, therefore, that you ran away from us because you were afraid that if this story came to light, you would end up in serious trouble?'

'Yes. But I swear, Mr Merlin, by all that is holy, my story is true. I did not kill Leon Van Buren.'

'For Christ's sake, Robert. Our father has just been burgled and killed, and all you can think about is money. Please can we save all that until he's buried.'

They were standing in the living room of Elizabeth's new flat. Packing cases were strewn all around. It was the first time brother

303

and sister had been alone together since the discovery of their father's body.

'It's easy for you to say that, Lizzie. You've got your rent paid up for a long time, and I bet Father dished you a nice little chunk of that cash deposit before the rest was pinched.'

'Now you're being silly. And really, you've got nothing to worry about. You know that we are very well provided for by Mummy's will, whatever the condition of Daddy's estate.'

'But it's going to take ages for the wills to be sorted out. I need money now.'

'For your stupid magazine?'

Red spots appeared on Robert's cheeks. 'It is not a stupid magazine!' He sat down in the one available chair and attempted to recover his equilibrium. A sheepish smile eventually appeared on his lips. 'Look, Lizzie. I could use a little help to keep the show on the road. A couple of hundred would do nicely. You'll have it back in a week or so, I promise.'

She sighed. 'I suppose I could manage a hundred.'

'A hundred and fifty?'

'Oh, all right.'

'You're an angel.' He got up to kiss her lightly on the nose, then fell back into the chair. 'There's always a chance, of course, that we'll get the drawings back.'

'A slim chance, I'd say.'

'I can't say I was impressed with the policemen I met.'

'DCI Merlin is meant to be one of Scotland Yard's best.'

'Doesn't reflect well on Scotland Yard if he is.'

'All I really care about is them finding Daddy's killer. The burglary is secondary.'

'A very important secondary. We get the drawings back, we'll have a real fortune in our hands.'

'Not everything is about money.'

'Oh Lizzie, stop it. You say that because the old man always made sure you never lacked for anything.'

'And what about you? There was the polo, the travel, the social whirl he was happy to finance. There was the expensive education you did your best to muck up. And that fiasco cost him a pretty penny, didn't it?'

'There's no need to rake up that old stuff.'

'You started it, dear.' Elizabeth smoothed her dress. 'Look, I'm busy. What else did you want to discuss?'

'Father's funeral?'

'We can't do anything until we get his body back from the police.'

'When will that be, do you think?'

'I haven't a clue. Presumably once they know exactly what happened to him. I'll have a word with Merlin and see what he has to say. Now, are we finished?'

'I suppose so.' Robert stood up and looked down awkwardly at his feet. 'Do you . . . do you think I could have that hundred and fifty now? Cash would be preferable.'

Chapter Twenty

Merlin sat on a bench watching Sonia push Harry back and forth on a swing. He'd faithfully promised her a family Sunday and was living up to his word. This, of course, didn't mean that his mind was taking a rest from work.

On Saturday afternoon, he had pulled Butterfield and Katz back into the Yard and tested their stories again. It was clear they fitted neatly together. He had decided for the present, with some reservations, to believe them.

Van Buren's knife was one new element in the story. It would explain the neck wound identified by Spilsbury. Merlin would check with Van Buren's children whether they were aware he carried one. And if it had fallen in the fight, what had happened to it? Forensics would have found it if it was still on the Embankment. Someone must have picked it up. Was that someone the murderer?'

The torchlight seen across the road was another interesting new element. If there was another witness, would they be able to track that person down?

His thoughts were interrupted by a burst of loud giggles. Harry's playground excitement had boiled over. Merlin walked across to the swings and offered to take over.

'Remember, Frank, push him gently. He's only a baby.'

As he took hold of the swing, his son twisted round to give him an ecstatic smile. It was good to be reminded that there were things in life other than murderers and thieves.

They lunched at Lyons Tea House on the King's Road. Harry's parents were proud to note that he behaved perfectly. When they got home, the little boy was fast asleep in his pram. Sonia lifted him carefully and transferred him to his cot. She turned to Merlin and stifled a yawn. 'I think I'll have a nap too, Frank. I'm worn out.'

'You do that, dear. I'm going to read.'

He was just about to settle down in his armchair with a bottle of pale ale and his Quiller-Couch poetry collection when the telephone rang. Johnson and Robinson were manning the office today and he guessed it would be one of them.

'Sorry to disturb you, sir, but you did ask me to let you know if there were any developments.'

Merlin kept his voice down. 'Of course, Peter.'

'Baby having a siesta, sir?'

'And the wife. What's up?'

'Three things. I had a call from Ursula Dunne. Sounded fraught. Said she'd something important to tell me but didn't want to speak on the telephone. She's going to come and see me this afternoon.'

'No indication what she wants to talk about?'

'No, sir. Secondly, the sergeant rang.'

'I told him to take it easy today.'

'Some hope. He says he happened to go for a walk with the family along the Embankment. When he went past that boat mooring near Cheyne Walk, there was a man on the pier and Sam asked him about the resident the constables had missed. The man said he'd seen him heading off somewhere at lunchtime. Sam thought we'd like to know the fellow's back.'

'We'll see him tomorrow.'

'Finally, the duty sergeant downstairs took a call from St Thomas's Hospital. A young woman was brought in this morning, badly beaten. When one of the nurses went through her clothes, she found your card.'

'My card? Is it . . .Barbara Freeman?'

'Yes, sir. She's under sedation and they're keeping her in overnight. She's not fit for interview today, but hopefully tomorrow.'

Merlin returned to his armchair. He closed his eyes for a moment and smiled. Events were on the move and he was beginning to buzz.

Billy Hill had lunched with his family too, but had headed straight back to the club afterwards. In the office, he went to the safe and removed the da Vinci drawings. He unwrapped them and had another good look. 'Bloody bonkers,' he muttered under his breath. He really couldn't understand why anyone in their right mind would pay hundreds of thousands of pounds for a couple of miserable little religious sketches. It was a funny old world. Overvalued or not, though, they were causing him a load of worry. Jimmy'd been right, much as he hated to admit it. He should never have given the Maltese chancer his head. With even the King of England taking an interest, the heat from the police was only going to grow and grow.

Miles appeared at the door looking out of sorts.

'You look like you've swallowed a frog. What's up?'

'Micallef's done a bunk, Billy. I just got a call from Jacky.'

Hill picked up a glass from his desk and hurled it against the wall. 'What the fuck! How did that happen?'

'Jacky had gone to get a paper and cigarettes. When he got back, Penny told him Micallef had said it was a nice day for a walk and headed out. Jacky was immediately suspicious. Looked in the git's bedroom and realised his bag had gone. Jumped in the car and drove around for a couple of hours, but nothing doing.'

'Bleeding idiot.'

'He must've snagged a lift, or caught a bus.'

'Did you give that message to his girlfriend?' Hill demanded.

'Yes.'

'Maybe she came looking for him?'

'How could she do that? Message didn't say nothing about where he was. Just that he'd gone on business somewhere. Nah. He got away under his own steam.'

'Get Jacky in here tomorrow. Tell him that if he's not already shitting himself, he can start now.'

'Yes, boss.'

'Penny still safely under wraps?'

'He is.'

Hill loosened his tie. 'Well, whatever. We'll find the little bastard again. Where can he go? Not as if he can hike it back to Malta, is it? Put someone on his flat and someone else on the girl's.'

Left alone, he examined the drawings again. All of a sudden, his mind was made up. One simple act could relieve the pressure. Or two. He hurried to the door.

Ursula Dunne was looking a little unkempt, and her lipstick had been carelessly applied and overran her mouth. Johnson wondered if she might have been drinking. She set her handbag down on Merlin's desk and eyed the inspector and Robinson nervously. 'I'm very sorry not to have told you a little more over the telephone, but I couldn't speak freely. My husband . . . my husband was there and . . . Well, anyway, it's about Frederick. I found something.' She took a small brown paper package from the handbag and pushed it across the desk.

Johnson removed the packaging to reveal a gun. A revolver. It was a familiar model. The Enfield No. 2 was the gun he'd used on his police firearms courses.

'I found the thing in one of my husband's cupboards.'

'You didn't know about it?'

'No.'

'Have you asked him about it?'

'No. I'm too afraid.'

'What prompted you to search your husband's cupboards?' asked Robinson.

'I . . . I discovered something yesterday that I found . . . well, quite shocking. It made me want to investigate further, so I did so when he went off to his club.'

'What did you discover yesterday?'

'That apparently he engaged a private investigator to look into . . . into Frederick.'

'So he did know about your affair?'

'Yes, Inspector. It appears I underestimated his . . . attachment to me. After finding out about my relationship with Frederick, he says he became concerned that it posed a threat to our marriage. As it happens, the investigator's report persuaded him that it did not. Or so he says.'

'But your discovery of the gun suggests . . . what?'

Mrs Dunne took a breath before answering. 'I realised when we talked that I didn't really know him very well any more. His emotions ran much deeper than I'd thought. In the circumstances, it seemed quite possible that he might have gone to see Frederick in person to warn him off. And that if he'd done so, he might have taken this gun.'

'So,' said Robinson, 'you suspect your husband of Mr Vermeulen's murder?'

'Well . . . it seems to me he had motive and means. Isn't that what detectives in crime novels are always searching for?'

'We're not in a crime novel, Mrs Dunne, but of course we shall need to investigate your suspicion. You say you've not mentioned your discovery of the gun to your husband?'

'No, Inspector. If he had killed Frederick and I challenged him, what might he do to me? I couldn't sleep at all last night, and I knew I had to come to you. I thought your scientists would be able to tell whether his gun was used in the killing.'

'Unfortunately, the forensics situation may not be quite so

straightforward. We have been unable to find the bullet that . . . that passed through Mr Vermeulen's head. Most likely the killer removed it.'

Ursula Dunne paled. 'But what's to be done then?'

'Where is your husband now?'

'Out playing golf.'

'When will he be back?'

'He's playing in Oxfordshire. Said he'd probably stay the night in the country, then return to London tomorrow.

'Is he likely to come home before going to work?'

'He usually goes straight in from the station. What am I to do if he does come home?'

'Couldn't you arrange to be elsewhere tomorrow?' suggested Robinson.

She considered for a moment. 'Occasionally I go and stay with a friend in Guildford. I can give her a call.' She became tearful. 'I do hope I've done the right thing. How will Charles react if he turns out to be innocent? Oh dear. What a mess!'

The luck Micallef had enjoyed in quickly finding a lift soon deserted him. Once back in town, he'd been sensible enough to stay well away from his flat, but had felt obliged to call Elizabeth Van Buren from a phone box. After she'd accepted his profuse apologies, they'd agreed to meet at one of their favourite Italian restaurants, in Knightsbridge. There he had managed to put on a calm front despite the anxiety bubbling just beneath the surface. They'd eaten pasta and drunk far too much red wine. Unwisely, and against his better judgement, he had given in to her request that they return to her new apartment. Her bedroom there was now fully furnished and she was determined to christen it. They'd done so, then napped for a while before deciding on an early-evening walk down by the river. This was a mistake.

They'd gone no more than thirty yards when a large black car screeched to a halt beside them. The doors flew open and two men

311

emerged, grabbing Micallef and bundling him roughly inside. It was all over very quickly. Elizabeth was left screaming on the pavement, not quite sure of what had happened.

Micallef found himself yet again in the back seat of a car with Jimmy Miles. He was welcomed with a clip on the ear. 'Stupid move, Teddy. Billy's going bonkers. What were you thinking?'

Emboldened by the large amount of alcohol still in his system, Micallef wasn't prepared to be contrite. 'I told you it was a bloody stupid idea to box us up there in that dump. Billy wasn't thinking straight. I'm alibi'd on the burglary and on Van Buren's death. Merlin and his pals can't touch me.'

'Full of yourself, ain't you?' growled Miles.

'And why not? When's the last time anyone pulled off as big a job as mine? I can't understand why Billy's treating me like this. What's he going to do now?'

'Don't worry, my friend. You'll find out soon enough.'

Chapter Twenty-One

Monday August 24th 1942

Merlin had suffered nightmares about hanging before. This morning he'd awoken with an image of Virgil Lewis on the gallows, and it was with him still as he rode in the taxi to St Thomas's Hospital.

Arriving at Barbara Freeman's ward, he saw that she was involved in some sort of commotion. She was standing fully dressed by her bed while a man tugged at her arm and argued loudly with two nurses. As he approached, Merlin heard him say, 'I don't care what you two cows think. She don't need to be here. Come on, Babs. Let's be off.'

The young woman looked rough. Her face was swollen and she had two purple shiners. She'd obviously taken a severe beating.

Merlin patted the man's back. 'What's going on here?'

'What bloody business is it of yours, mate?' said the man, squaring up to him.

Merlin produced his warrant card.

The man was unabashed. 'There's nothing to interest you here, copper. My girlfriend had an accident on her bike yesterday and now she wants to go home. I'm here to take her. Ain't that right, Babs?'

There was a half-nod.

Merlin thought there seemed something familiar about the man. Of medium height, with slicked-back brown hair, saturnine features and a pencil moustache, he wore an expensive-looking wide-lapelled brown check suit, and sported several gold rings on his hands. He was a good deal older than his supposed girlfriend. Merlin had come across hundreds of wide boys like him in his career, and presumed this was one of them.

'It appears the nurses don't think Miss Freeman's departure a good idea.'

The elder of the two women chipped in. 'Miss Freeman is severely bruised all over and has been concussed. She should remain at the very least until the doctor does his rounds. That will be in an hour or so.'

Merlin smiled at the patient. 'Best follow the medical advice, don't you think, Miss Freeman?'

'Well, it's probably best if—'

'Look, pal, she's coming with me, all right.' The man started pulling on the young woman's arm again.

Merlin grabbed him by the shoulder. 'The lady should make up her own mind, I think, don't you? How about it, Miss Freeman?'

'If . . . if the nurses say to wait a little, Vince, I think I should.'

The man let go of her arm with a snort of disgust. 'All right then. Suit yourself, but remember what I said.' He glared at Merlin then hurried off.

The nurses helped Barbara Freeman back onto the bed.

'Shall I get back into my nightie?'

'No, dear. You might as well stay dressed for now,' said the older woman. 'Until we know what the doctor thinks.'

'Is it all right if I speak to Miss Freeman?' Merlin asked.

'If she's happy, we've no problem.'

Barbara Freeman nodded and the nurses moved off down the ward. Merlin took one of the bedside chairs.

'Is that gentleman really your boyfriend?'

'Sort of.'

'What's his name?'

'He won't like my telling.'

'I can find out one way or another.'

'It's Vince. Vince White.'

Merlin recognised the name. He'd nicked him for pickpocketing and petty larceny years before.

'Still a thief, is he?'

'He's a businessman. In the car trade.'

'Is he now?' Merlin examined her face carefully. 'He said you got these injuries in a bike accident?'

She nodded.

'What did you cycle into? A bus?'

'No. It was a . . . a wall.'

Merlin frowned. 'You went into a door last time, now a wall. I don't believe you. Care to tell me what really happened?'

She folded her arms protectively. 'I'm sorry, I can't . . . I can't tell you. He'll . . .' She left the sentence unfinished.

Merlin reached out and patted her hand. 'If you're worried about Mr White, be assured we can protect you if necessary. I'm sure you'd like him off your back.'

He watched as fear slowly gave way to resolve. She began to talk.

'Any progress, Frank?'

'Some, Harold. How about you?'

'I really shouldn't be saying this over the phone . . .'

'The Yard sweepers came in on their routine monthly visit early this morning, I'm told. The line is clear.'

'Well all right then. We know our German agent is still somewhere in Ireland. Our people picked up a couple of messages he sent.'

'To Germany?'

'Yes. Nothing terribly interesting, just him touching base.'

'You're still going with the theory that this man killed both Pablo and Vermeulen?'

'Unless and until you come up with something more compelling.'

'I know I'm flogging a dead horse, but I'll ask again. There's still no question of sharing your belief with the Yanks?'

'No. Too embarrassing for them to know we had a German agent at large and let him give us the slip.'

'Meaning an innocent man goes to the gallows so MI5 can save face.'

'I'm sorry, Frank.' Swanton sighed. 'I tried hard again to persuade them, but they wouldn't budge. Quoted some poetry at me. Something about reasoning why.'

'"Theirs not to reason why, theirs but to do and die." Alfred, Lord Tennyson.'

'If you say so. You're the expert.' Another sigh. 'You said you'd made some progress?'

'Some new lines of enquiry have opened up, but I'd rather pursue them a little further before discussing them. You should know, however, that I haven't given up yet on Virgil Lewis. One of the leads may yet save him.'

'Glad to hear it, Frank. You just fill me in when you're good and ready.'

Fifteen minutes later, Merlin gathered his team together for an update and briefing on his hospital visit.

'Miss Freeman was taken into St Thomas's yesterday by her sister. She was heavily bruised and partly concussed. Told the medical staff she'd been in a bicycle accident. That was not true. She eventually revealed that she'd been beaten up on Saturday night by her boyfriend, a thug named Vince White. It had happened before, but this beating was the worst. Another beating had taken place just over a week before. The reason for both was Pablo Merino.' There were a few shocked gasps. 'There was more to Barbara's encounter with Pablo than she'd previously admitted. They really hit it off in the pub, and some kissing and cuddling ensued down by the river. Unfortunately, as she learned later, one of White's sidekicks saw them. They met again the following night, the Thursday, and went to the pictures. A third meeting had been arranged for the Friday, but that of course never happened.

'In the early hours of that Friday morning, Vince White burst into

Barbara's flat, dragged her out of bed and started hitting her. He told her he knew she'd been cheating on him. Said he'd followed her and Pablo to the cinema. Fortunately, Barbara's sister woke and intervened, and the beating stopped. Soon after that, Vince cleared off.'

'Why on earth do women fall for men like that?' asked Robinson in disgust.

'I'd guess he established some hold over her when she was younger and more impressionable, but I'm no psychiatrist. Perhaps you'll be able to get the full story from her, Constable, in due course? Meanwhile, we urgently need to get hold of White.'

'Did he tell Miss Freeman what he did after she and Pablo parted after the cinema?'

'No, Inspector, but I think the presumption is clear, and we know the man is capable of serious violence.'

'I remember a Vince White,' said Bridges. 'Small-time crook in Seven Dials.'

'I remember him too. He was at the hospital trying to drag Miss Freeman away. Looked as if he'd come up a little in the world.'

'Got an address, sir? If so, I'm happy to go and pick him up.'

'I'll come with you, Sarge,' said Cole.

Merlin pulled a page out of his notebook. 'That's the address Miss Freeman gave me. I'd go with you, but I need to speak to Bernie about Lewis. And Inspector, you and Robinson should go and see Charles Dunne.'

Bridges raised a hand. 'One other development, sir. I picked up a message from the front desk this morning. Miss Van Buren called last night to report that Micallef had been . . . well, the word she used was "abducted" yesterday in front of her eyes.'

'Abducted. Really? Well, we'll have to follow up later. There's only so much we can do at one time.'

Bridges and Cole headed for the door.

'Hang on a second,' said Merlin. 'It might be sensible to grab more hands from downstairs. White might prove a bit of a tough nut to crack.'

'We'll be all right as we are, sir. We've dealt with plenty of tough nuts in our time, eh, Tommy?'

'If you're sure. If it looks like turning nasty, back off and call in reinforcements.'

Once he was on his own again, Merlin tried to get hold of Goldberg. Frustratingly, it took him half an hour to get through.

'Sorry, Frank. I've been chasing around like a headless chicken trying to delay the execution. No luck, I'm afraid. Pearce won't budge, of course, and McCluskey appears to have become just as stubborn. I've tried some other high-ups, but nothing doing. It's proved impossible to speak to the general. Things are looking bleak.'

'I have one piece of potentially good news. We have another suspect. Pablo picked up a girl in a pub. Her thug of a boyfriend saw them together and followed them the night of Pablo's death.'

'The real killer?'

'Maybe. He had motive and opportunity.'

'Who is he?'

'A criminal called White. We only have what the girl told us but let's wait and see.'

'Might need a little more in a court of law, but it's obviously helpful. I'll try and throw it in the mix. Have you arrested White yet?'

'Bridges and Cole are on their way.'

'Let me know what you get out of him.'

Inspector and constable were escorted by a male secretary into a sombre wood-panelled room and guided to a highly-polished mahogany table. Charles Dunne joined them soon afterwards and greeted them with a thin smile as he took his seat. 'I gather you have something urgent to discuss. Is it some police administrative matter?'

'No, sir,' replied Johnson. 'It's a criminal one.'

'Criminal, eh?' He smiled. 'If it concerns my exceeding the office biscuit allowance, I'm afraid I have to plead guilty.'

'This is not a laughing matter, sir. We're here to talk to you about Mr Frederick Vermeulen.'

Dunne's face darkened. 'Vermeulen?'

'He was conducting an affair with your wife.'

'I'm not sure what business that is of yours.'

'It is our business, sir, because Mr Vermeulen was found shot a week ago Saturday. We are investigating his murder.'

Dunne sighed. 'Oh, very well. Ask your questions.'

'When did you first become aware of your wife's relationship with Mr Vermeulen?'

'Soon after it started, just over a year ago. I happened by chance to see them in Piccadilly Circus. They were holding hands.'

'How did you feel about the affair?'

'My wife and I are grown-ups. It is not the first time she's had a fling with another man.'

'You were unhappy?'

'Naturally I was. I love my wife.'

'Mrs Dunne told us you employed a private investigator to report on Vermeulen.'

'Did she now? Well, yes, I did. I wanted to know what sort of man he was and whether he threatened our marriage.'

'And what did your investigator discover?'

'That he was a very busy man. That he spent more time in Portugal than London. That there was no evidence of him mis-treating or misleading Ursula in any way. That his way of living was unlikely to accommodate marriage. His report, coupled with my belief that it would take quite a lot for Ursula to give up the trappings of life as a top civil servant's wife, reassured me.'

'Was he seeing other women apart from your wife?'

'My investigator said not, though I stopped using his services months ago.'

'Did you discuss Vermeulen with your wife?' asked Robinson.

'Never until this weekend. Her discovery about the investigator prompted something of a heart-to-heart, in which I explained my motives and concern. I thought my answers had satisfied her, but I presume from your presence that they did not.'

'It was something else that led her to contact us.'

'Oh yes?'

'She found a revolver in your room.'

'Ah . . . I see. So she now thinks I used it to kill Vermeulen? The silly woman.'

'Did you shoot him, Mr Dunne?'

'Of course not.'

'Did you ever harbour violent thoughts against him?'

Dunne smiled wryly. 'No, Inspector. I'm not that sort of man.'

'Your wife says she had no idea you possessed a gun. Have you had it long?'

'I bought it at Purdey's the year before last. January 1940, to be exact. As you will no doubt recall, the prospect of a German invasion was very real at the time. Some of my colleagues and I discussed the threat and decided to take the precaution of arming ourselves.'

'But you didn't tell your wife?'

'No. She has a morbid fear of guns. Her brother died in a shooting accident when she was young.'

'You had no purpose for the gun other than self-defence?'

'No, Inspector. If you think I bought it just to take a pot shot at Mr Vermeulen, you've got your dates wrong. His relationship with my wife didn't commence until a long time after.'

'You have a record of purchase?'

'Somewhere in my desk at home, I think. If not, Purdey's will be able to back me up.'

'We have taken the gun into our possession for the moment, sir.'

'Have you now? Then I'd be grateful for its swift return.'

'We're going to carry out a few tests. Has the gun been fired at all?'

'It has. There is a shooting gallery available to civil servants. I attend every so often to practise and ensure the gun is in good working order. Hitler's invasion prospects may have diminished, but these are still dangerous times.'

320

'When did you last go there?'

'I think it would have been the Wednesday of the week before last. You can confirm with the gallery. Visitors have to sign in and out. I can give you their telephone number.'

'Thank you.'

'And how long will it take you to carry out your tests?'

'A few days.'

'Very well, I—' There was a knock on the door. The secretary appeared and asked Dunne to step out.

When he'd gone, Johnson asked for Robinson's thoughts.

'Seemed pretty credible to me.'

'To me too. Even if we were wrong, we both know the gun's not going to tell us anything in the absence of the shell.'

Dunne reappeared at the door. 'I'm afraid I'm required urgently on important Home Office business. Have you got what you need?'

'I think so, sir.' They followed him out.

In the corridor, he said, 'I'm sorry if you've been sent on a wild goose chase, but my wife is clearly not herself at the moment. By the way, does the name Frank Merlin mean anything to you?'

'He's our boss, sir.'

'Really? Well he's making himself distinctly unpopular with our American cousins. The call I took just now concerned him. Some case he's causing trouble about. I've been asked to intervene.'

'They're about to hang an innocent man. The chief inspector is trying to prevent that.'

'Is he? Well I'm sorry, but the rights and wrongs of the matter are nothing to do with me.'

'The rights and wrongs of the matter are everything to Mr Merlin, sir,' said Johnson.

'I'll be contacting his superiors regardless. We can't have Anglo–American relations damaged in this way. Now, let me get you the number of that gallery before you go.'

★

Above the half-open garage doors in the Knightsbridge mews was a sign: *White Motors*. The policemen entered cautiously. Ahead were two vehicle service ramps with cars on top. Another partially dismantled car was parked on their right, and tools, spare parts and machinery were scattered all around. A small table covered in paperwork stood by the door, but there was no sign of any people.

Bridges noticed a light in the back beyond the ramps and signalled to Cole. As they got closer, they could see it was coming from a desk-lamp behind a glass-partition. They found the door and went in. In addition to the desk, the small office contained a couple of battered armchairs and several cardboard boxes. Cole reached into one of the boxes and took out what looked like a petrol ration book. He showed it to the sergeant.

'He's in the forgery game,' whispered Bridges.

The photograph of a solid-looking, cheerful man in a three-piece suit beamed down at them from the wall. It was Herbert Chapman, the famed Arsenal football manager. Bridges detested Arsenal. He grimaced at Cole, who nodded. He hated Arsenal too.

They heard the sound of footsteps above and became still. There was music and the tinkle of laughter. Behind the desk was another door, and they went through it into a dark corridor. A flight of stairs led up from it. Bridges led the way, cautiously. The noise was coming from a room to the left of the landing.

As they were bracing themselves to enter, the door burst open and a half-dressed man tumbled out onto the floor. He was clearly very drunk. He looked up at Bridges. 'And who the bloody hell . . .?'

'Vince White?'

'Maybe. What's it to you?'

Bridges grasped White's arm and pulled him to his feet. 'We are police officers, here to arrest you in connection with the murder of Pablo Merino. You must be aware that anything you—'
White lurched violently out of the sergeant's grip, twisted round and started flailing punches. Bridges was caught in the face and

stomach before he managed to shove White back into the room. Both officers followed him in, and were confronted by two naked young women cowering together on a large bed.

Cole noticed White reaching for something on a side-table. 'Watch out, Sarge! I think he's got a gun.' The thug did indeed have a gun, which was now levelled at Bridges' back. In a fury, Cole rushed White and knocked him to the bed. As he fell onto the girls, there was an explosion. The gun smoke took a while to clear. When it did, Bridges saw that Cole had slumped to the floor. The girls started shrieking manically. Oblivious to further danger, Bridges bent down to his partner. 'Are you hit, Tommy?'

'He just winged me, Sarge,' Cole croaked. 'Nothing serious.'

He had fallen awkwardly and Bridges found it difficult to find the location of the wound. Cole's eyes widened. 'He's doing a runner, Sarge. I'll . . . I'll be all right.'

'Are you sure?'

'Yes. Go . . . go get him!'

Bridges decided to take Cole at his word and stood up. White had thrown on a shirt and jacket and was halfway out of the door. The sergeant turned to the girls. 'You're responsible for my colleague. One of you attend to the wound and staunch the blood. The other call 999 and get medical help here as soon as possible. If anything bad happens to him, I'll be coming after you.'

He bent to squeeze Cole's hand before racing out and down the stairs.

Merlin had started to worry about his men. He felt he should have held Bridges and Cole back until he'd spoken to Goldberg, then accompanied them. White was a nasty piece of work and could well resist arrest. He had a terrible feeling that something would go wrong. As he paced the floor by the window, a duty sergeant appeared at the door.

'Letter for you, sir. Sent over from the Foreign Office. Apparently it was in a diplomatic bag from Lisbon.'

'Lisbon, eh? Thank you, Sergeant.'

Merlin rooted out Bridges' silver letter opener and sliced open the envelope. He found two letters inside, one short and one a little longer. He read the short one first.

Chief Inspector Merlin,

I understand you are the officer investigating the death of my dear friend Frederick Vermeulen. I belatedly received the enclosed letter from Frederick the other day. While he was mostly busy with other matters on his recent and sadly last trip to England, he was always vigilant about my best interests in all quarters. His letter is self-explanatory and may be of value to your investigation.

I am, sir, your obedient servant,
Calouste Gulbenkian

He turned to the other letter. It was dated Thursday August 13th, two days before Vermeulen's body was discovered.

My dear Calouste,

There is something I wanted to communicate to you and I didn't want to risk sending the information by cable. It could, I suppose, have waited until my return, but as there is a chance of my being delayed in London while the da Vinci purchase is completed, and possibly for other items of business, I decided to put pen to paper and send it to you via the British diplomatic pouch. The subject is Cedric Calvert. I know the man has been with Warwick Petroleum for a long time and is someone you have always considered reliable. I also know he was a decorated hero in the last war and has a reputation for probity in British business circles. You are aware that he and I have never got on. Please be assured that my dislike of the man has no bearing on what I have to tell you.'

· The fact is that Calvert is a thief and a fraud. You know I have excellent sources within the British government. I have learned that there has been a secret investigation into manipulations of the petroleum market deemed detrimental to the war effort. This investigation looked, inter alia, into Calvert's business activities. They discovered clear evidence that he has been embezzling Warwick Petroleum. I have been shown this evidence. My sources also believe he has been consorting with the enemy. I will not set out all the details in this letter, but trust me, the case against him is incontrovertible. The motives for his illegal activity are not fully clear, but he is rumoured to have accumulated significant stock market losses over the years.

Yesterday I took it upon myself to confront Calvert about his wrongdoing. He denied everything and roused himself into a fine old temper, but was unable to refute the evidence I presented. At the end of our meeting I told him that I would be apprising you of the situation as soon as practicable.

I am very sorry to be the bearer of such bad news. I had not the authority myself to relieve the man of his position, but suggest you take such action immediately. I did take the liberty of warning the finance director to ignore any financial instructions issued by Calvert until he had heard from you.

I look forward to seeing you shortly, when I shall provide you with chapter and verse.

With, as always, my deepest regards,
Frederick

Merlin took a deep breath, then read the letter a second time.

Merlin was catching up with Johnson and Robinson an hour later when the call from St Mary's Hospital was put through.

'Chief Inspector Merlin? Dr Jameson at St Mary's here. I'm afraid I've got two of your officers in my care, both suffering from gunshot wounds. One is in a rather serious condition, the other less so. It was the latter, Sergeant Bridges, who asked me to contact you.'

His heart sank. He had been right to worry. The doctor continued to speak, but the words did not sink in. Eventually Merlin just shouted, 'I'm on my way!' and banged the phone down. After pausing briefly to inform his two subordinates, he ran out of the door.

When he got to the hospital, he found Bridges sitting up in bed in a private room, his right arm in a sling.

'Are you all right, Sam?'

'I'm fine, but Tommy's not so good. He took a shot in the stomach.'

'Where is he?'

'In the operating room.'

Merlin slumped into the bedside chair. 'I knew we should've gone in greater numbers. If anything happens to him, I'll never forgive myself. What exactly happened?'

'White was there at his garage having a party with a couple of pros in an upstairs room. I told him we were taking him in and he began throwing punches. Then he pulled a gun on me. I'd have been a goner if Tommy hadn't rushed him. Unfortunately, he ran straight into a bullet. I was trying to find out how bad the wound was when Cole told me White was scarpering. He said he'd only been winged and that I should go. I told the two girls to call for help and went off in pursuit.' Bridges looked away. 'It's me who'll never be able to forgive myself if the worst happens, sir. I should've stayed with him.' He sighed. 'At least those girls did well by him. I didn't know, but there's a doctor's surgery right next door to the garage. They got the doc to come straight away and he took care of Tommy until the ambulance arrived.'

'And you could've done nothing more. What happened after you went off in pursuit?

'White was still just in sight when I came out of the mews. I set off after him and followed him over Sloane Street and on towards

Belgrave Square. He had a jump of about fifty yards on me to start with. I'm not the fastest runner, as you know, but I found myself gaining on him. The skinful he'd had with those girls was slowing him down. Anyway, I'd got to within twenty yards or so of him when he decided to stop and take a pot shot at me. Jammy bastard hit my arm. It's only a flesh wound, but obviously it stopped me in my tracks. He took off again, looking back to make sure I was out of the game. That was his mistake. A few yards ahead of him a group of workmen were lowering a crate from the top floor of a building. He barged into one of them. That was enough for them to lose control of the crate, and it fell down almost right on top of him.

'He's dead?'

'No, he's here too somewhere. Very badly injured.'

'So no chance of getting a confession to Pablo's murder out of him any time soon?'

'No, sir.'

Johnson and Robinson were on their way to the City. The news of Cole's shooting made for a subdued journey. Johnson could tell that Robinson was on the edge of tears. When he pulled the car to a halt outside Warwick Petroleum, he patted her arm. 'I'm sure Tommy wouldn't like us to mope when there's important work to be done. Come on, let's snap out of it and see what this fellow Calvert has to say for himself.'

On arrival at reception, they asked for Calvert. Moments later, a plump, anxious little man came to greet them.. 'I'm sorry, but Mr Calvert's not in today. My name is Rufus Milton. I'm his deputy. Can I help?'

'Sorry, but it's Mr Calvert we need to see. Is he unwell?'

Milton glanced at the lady receptionist, who was playing close attention. 'I . . . I think it might be best if you come along with me.'

The policemen followed him along a thickly-carpeted corridor to his large office. The room was made to seem smaller by the boxes and files that littered the desk, table and floor.

'I'm sorry for the mess. Something came up and I . . . I'm obliged to do some research.' He cleared his desk as best he could and they sat down. 'This is a little awkward. The thing is, Mr Calvert has been suspended. That's why he's not here.'

'May we ask why?'

'I don't believe I'm at liberty to discuss the reason. It's highly confidential.'

'We are investigating a very serious crime, Mr Milton. Your full cooperation would be appreciated.'

'A very serious crime? Goodness.' Milton's eyes darted nervously around the room. 'You're . . . you're not financial police by any chance, are you?'

'No.'

He seemed to relax a little. 'Very well. On Saturday, I received a cable from our principal shareholder, Mr Calouste Gulbenkian, saying that he was suspending Mr Calvert forthwith for suspected financial misfeasance and that Calvert had been informed and barred from the office. I was to assume responsibility for the management of the company pro tem. Mr Gulbenkian then instructed me to carry out a thorough review of our books for the past two years and search out discrepancies. The finance director and his assistant have also been suspended, so the task falls entirely to me. Hence . . .' he waved a hand, 'this huge mound of paperwork.'

'Have you found anything yet?'

'No. I've only just started.'

'Where is Mr Calvert now?' asked Robinson.

'At home, I expect, though I've not spoken to him since receiving the cable.'

'And home is where?'

'Hill Street. Just off Berkeley Square. My secretary can give you the address if you want.'

'Thank you,' said Johnson. 'You've worked with Mr Calvert long?'

'About four years.'

'What sort of man is he?'

'Until this shocking news from Mr Gulbenkian, I'd have said a perfectly decent, hard-working businessman of the utmost integrity. He's rather serious and austere and we've never been close on a personal level, but we worked well together. He has an admirable background. He won a Military Cross at Ypres and was an accomplished sportsman. Played tennis at Wimbledon. County cricket. A keen horseman and hunter. Excellent shot. A man of many achievements. The very last person I'd think of as a fraudster.'

'You say he was an excellent shot?' said Robinson.

'A champion marksman, by all accounts. He's got trophies in his office from Bisley.'

'He still shoots?'

'I believe so.'

'He owns a gun, then.'

'Several, I should think.'

'Family man?' asked Johnson.

'Widower. One son — something of an embarrassment to his father. Got into some financial scrapes, I believe. His father never discusses him.'

'The son lives with Mr Calvert?'

'No. He was called up a few months back. I believe he's already overseas.'

Johnson glanced towards the window, which had an unprepossessing view of the back end of the Bank of England. 'You knew Mr Frederick Vermeulen?'

Milton looked a little surprised at the change of subject. 'Why yes, I did. I was very shocked and saddened to hear of his demise.'

'You had dealings with him?'

'Limited dealings. Mr Calvert was his principal point of reference here. I was told he ran important errands for the company, though I'm afraid I couldn't tell you what those errands were. Calvert asked me to entertain him to lunch once. A pleasant chap, who was certainly very knowledgeable about the oil industry.'

'Did Vermeulen and Calvert get on?'

'Well . . .' Milton frowned. 'It was my impression that their relations were quite cool. I heard Mr Calvert make several disparaging remarks about Vermeulen. I think he regarded him as Mr Gulbenkian's . . . well, spy.'

'Did he say anything about Vermeulen's death?'

'Not much. He just made a brief passing reference to it in a meeting. He showed no emotion about the event.'

'That's interesting.'

'My God, Frank. That's terrible. I really like that kid,' said Goldberg when Merlin called him with the latest from the hospital.

'He's a tough one. I'm sure he'll pull through. Meanwhile, I thought you could add this latest information into the pot.'

'Of course, but the powers-that-be remain stubborn. I passed on the development regarding the girl and White. McCluskey brusquely rejected it as circumstantial. This latest certainly makes the story more compelling, and obviously I'll go and try again.'

'If you can't move McCluskey, what about Ike?'

'I can't get through to him. Perhaps if you were with me, I'd have better luck.'

'I thought I was *persona non grata* there.'

'With the American police officers, yes, but not necessarily with General Eisenhower.'

'I'll come over then, but I've got one important errand to run first. I'll try and get to you as soon as I can but I'll be at least an hour.'

'I'll be waiting for you in the embassy lobby.'

★

The Shelley was the boat he wanted. It was moored at the far end of the pier, on the right. Merlin stepped aboard and tapped a window. Nothing happened, and he tapped again, harder. The barge moved under his feet and a door creaked open. A head of snowy white hair appeared from below. When it rose to face him, Merlin saw there was a matching beard.

'I say, old chap, you'll break the glass if you bang it like that.' The voice was deep and educated. 'May I ask whom I have the honour of addressing?'

'DCI Merlin. Scotland Yard.'

'Ah yes. My next-door neighbour told me to expect a visit. I'm Matthew Fielding. Please come in.'

Merlin stepped down and bent to follow his host inside the cabin, which was much more roomy and comfortable than he would have expected. There was plenty of bench seating, a decent-sized table and a well-equipped galley. Books, magazines and bric-a-brac were scattered everywhere.

Fielding shook Merlin's hand firmly and guided him to the table.

'Your neighbour told you why we wanted a word?'

He nodded. 'Someone went in the drink a few days ago and you're looking for witnesses.' He reached for the pipe smouldering in an ashtray and relit it. The tobacco had the same sweet, sickly smell as the brand Merlin's father had favoured. He remembered Harry Merlin smoking it the day he'd been blown to pieces in a Zeppelin raid in 1917.

'As you say, we're looking for witnesses. The night in question is that of Friday August the fourteenth. Do you remember seeing anything untoward?'

A small furry white dog of indeterminate breed appeared at the cabin door. It bore an uncanny resemblance to its owner. 'There you are, Coleridge,' Fielding said. 'What mischief have you been up to, I wonder? Say hello to the chief inspector, why don't you?'

Coleridge growled at Merlin, then scuttled over to settle at

Fielding's feet. 'He is getting on, I'm afraid, and his temper is not improving with age. He also takes a while to recover from travel. We returned yesterday from a brief sojourn in Oxford. I used to work there, you know. As an academic.' Fielding smiled. 'Academic is rather a grand word for a teacher, I always think. I taught at the English faculty. Packed it in a while ago.' He took two puffs of his pipe. 'I still have many friends there. Been staying with one of them. Went a week ago Saturday. So we're talking about the evening before I left?'

'Yes.'

'Did I see any funny business?'

'Yes.'

'You'll not be surprised to know, Chief Inspector, that night-time funny business is quite common here on the Embankment. We are blessed with a plethora of pubs in this part of London, and the river always seems to act as a magnet to drunks after closing time.'

'I'm not surprised in the least, but can you remember anything particular about that night?'

Fielding puffed thoughtfully on his pipe. 'Now that I apply my mind to it, I do recall some activity. I live a life of routine, Mr Merlin, but that night there was a little variance. I had to prepare for our holiday. Normally I take Coleridge out for his evening constitutional around nine thirty, but I was packing then. When I finished, I remember getting caught up in a book: the Moncrieff translation of Proust's great masterpiece. Have you read it, Chief Inspector?'

'*Remembrance of Things Past*? No, sir. Unfortunately I haven't the time.'

'Very few people do, sadly. A wonderful book. Anyway, as I say, the book distracted me. Eventually the dog barked to remind me of my duties. It was quite late. After eleven, I think. I have a standard circuit for the evening dog walk. Across the Embankment, up Royal Hospital Road, left on Tite Street, through various

332

back streets up to the King's Road, back down Chelsea Manor Street to Cheyne Walk, then past the Embankment Gardens, across the road and home.'

Fielding was taking his time, but Merlin had the feeling they were getting somewhere worthwhile. He nodded.

'It was when I reached the Gardens – rather a grand name, I've always thought, for a small agglomeration of grass, foliage and one or two benches – that I became aware of some sort of altercation in progress on the other side of the road. On occasion at night I have been rudely accosted by drunks when making my way to the boat. I decided to wait behind a bush until the coast cleared. These inebriated encounters don't usually go on too long.' He drew again on his pipe. 'The moon provided pretty good visibility that night.'

'So what did you see?'

'I saw two men brawling. I couldn't see their faces, but one was taller and broader than the other. After a few minutes, a taxi pulled up and picked someone up. I couldn't see whom. At the same time, as the fight continued, I heard some unintelligible shouting from off to my left, and a man ran across the road towards the combatants. Before he could reach them, the smaller man withdrew from the fight and ran off.'

'Did anyone give chase?'

'No. The two remaining men struck up a conversation. I was beginning to think it was safe for me to walk home when things began to become heated. Voices were raised.'

'Could you hear what they were saying?'

'Not really, but I did catch the odd word. A couple of names. I could swear I heard one or other of them say "da Vinci". Not a name you'd really expect to hear in those circumstances.'

'And the second name?'

'"Jacob" or "Jake" I'm not sure which.'

Merlin made a note. 'And then?'

'It looked like fisticuffs began, but at this point Coleridge decided to start barking. He'd had enough of hiding in the bushes. Naturally I didn't want to attract the attention of the brawlers, so I hurried off with the dog towards Flood Street and went round the block. When we returned to the Embankment, all was quiet and there was no sign of the men. We crossed over and went to bed.'

'You heard nothing else?'

'No.'

'Can you help us at all with descriptions?'

'Apart from the difference in size of the first two combatants, no, I'm afraid not.'

'And the man who ran across the road?'

'Sorry. The moon had gone back behind the clouds when he came on the scene.'

'I wonder, did you have a torch on you?'

'Why yes, I did.' Fielding reached down to stroke the dog. 'Coleridge's sight is not so good these days, and I use it sometimes – sparingly, of course, in the blackout – to light his way. I think it was on when we settled in the bushes. No doubt I turned it off at some point, but I couldn't say exactly when.'

Goldberg was waiting in the embassy lobby as arranged. He had good news. The general had agreed to meet them. He led the way upstairs and into the room Merlin recognised from his first meeting with Max Pearce.

A relaxed-looking Dwight D. Eisenhower sat at the table with Colonel McCluskey next to him. The colonel looked far from relaxed.

'You're late, gentlemen!' he complained.

'Apologies,' said Merlin. 'My fault. I've a number of murder cases on the go and was interviewing a key witness. It's been a rather hectic day.'

'More hectic than that of the commander of the American forces in Great Britain?'

Eisenhower, who was smaller than Merlin had expected, moved to lighten the atmosphere. He smiled and extended a hand. 'Frank Merlin, I presume? Glad to make your acquaintance. Mr Churchill speaks highly of you.' He glanced at McCluskey. 'You must forgive the colonel. They teach better manners in my home state, Kansas, than in Massachusetts, or so it seems.'

McCluskey's face darkened.

'The colonel has briefed me on this case you and Goldberg are all riled up about. I've also had the benefit of Captain Pearce's views. They both tell me Virgil Lewis had a fair trial and is guilty. For the sake of Anglo–American harmony, I've agreed to listen to your concerns. Against their advice, I should say. Now tell me, why shouldn't American justice be allowed to take its course?'

Goldberg signalled that Merlin should answer. 'I'll take it as read, General, that you know the details of how the case developed and fell under American jurisdiction. I would only point out that I was the first person to interview Lewis, and from the outset, I sensed that he was not a murderer.'

'Sensed? Is that what they call policeman's intuition?'

'Intuition is an important part of a policeman's arsenal, sir.'

'You can hardly expect me to overturn the verdict of a duly constituted American military court purely on the basis of your intuition.'

'I am not asking you to do that. We have acquired new information that strongly supports that intuition.'

'The victim was some sort of relative of yours, I understand?'

'A distant one, yes.'

'So I guess you might be keener than normal to find his killer?'

'I hope I deal with all my cases even-handedly and without prejudice, sir.'

'I'm sure you do. Carry on.'

'I am currently investigating two other murders. It so happens that in one of those cases, clear links to the Merino case emerged. Naturally, I was bound to follow up on them.'

335

'And step on Captain Pearce's toes in the process.'

'My apologies.'

'Accepted.'

'In following up those links, we identified a clear suspect for Merino's murder.'

'You have a better candidate than Lewis?'

'We do.'

Eisenhower turned to McCluskey. 'You know all about this?'

'Yes, sir. I didn't think it worth troubling you with the details. It's all highly circumstantial.'

The general's eyebrows rose. He looked back at Merlin. 'Feel free to trouble me with the details, Mr Merlin.'

'The man is a known criminal called Vince White.' Merlin continued with the full story of White's connection to Pablo and the disastrous arrest attempt.'

Eisenhower was shocked at the news of the policemen's injuries. 'I am so sorry. What is the prognosis for the young man?'

'All I know, sir, is that he was being operated on. I haven't heard anything more.'

'Dear me. And this White fellow? He's in bad shape too?'

'Last I heard, he was yet to regain consciousness.'

'So chances are it'll be some time before you have an opportunity to squeeze a confession out of him? If you have an opportunity at all, that is.'

'Yes, sir, but I'd argue that everything we now know points to him being the guilty party.'

'You say the man's a known criminal,' interjected McCluskey, 'so he might have any number of reasons to run away from the police. Besides, there's no physical evidence linking him to Merino, while there's plenty linking Lewis. It's all circumstantial, like I said, General. And don't forget, we have Lewis's confession.'

'Lewis retracted the confession at his trial,' said Goldberg. 'He told his lawyer it was beaten out of him.'

336

McCluskey's face went puce. He banged the table with his fist. 'That's a goddam lie! I . . . I . . .'

'Calm yourself, Colonel,' said Eisenhower, patting McCluskey's shoulder. 'There's no need for tempers to be lost. I asked to hear the case in support of Lewis, and now I've heard it. That is it, I presume, Chief Inspector?'

'Yes, sir.'

'What time is the execution scheduled for tomorrow, Colonel?'

'Seven a.m., sir.'

'Not much time, then.' Eisenhower looked at his watch. 'I must get on. I've a working dinner tonight with General Alan Brook and his people.' He got to his feet. 'I'll give the matter my consideration, Chief Inspector, when I get a chance later this evening, and relay my decision to you via the colonel. Thank you, gentlemen.'

'How'd it go, sir?' asked Johnson, as Merlin settled behind his desk.

'I'm not sure. The general gave us a good hearing, but he's a difficult man to read. As his officers are clearly dead set against us, I'm inclined to expect the worst. Any news from the hospital, Constable?'

'Tommy's had his operation,' said Robinson. 'The doctors are being very cagey. Wouldn't say whether it went well or not.'

'I don't like the sound of that. How about White?'

'Still out of it. However, there is one development. A knife was found in his jacket.'

Merlin felt excitement rise. 'We'd better get it to the scientists straight away.'

'The sergeant is being discharged shortly. He'll bring it here with him and hand it to forensics.'

'I don't think we should get our hopes up too much, sir,' said Johnson. 'It's quite a long time since the murder.'

'I know, Peter, but there must be an outside chance we'll find blood on it. Can you go and see if someone in forensics could do an overnight job, Constable?'

Robinson disappeared, and Merlin asked Johnson to sit down and brief him on his visit to Calvert.

'He wasn't there, sir.'

'Damn.'

'But we did get some useful information.' Johnson told Merlin what they'd learned from Calvert's deputy.'

'Did you go on to Calvert's place after?'

'He wasn't there either, but we quickly organised a search warrant. The next-door neighbour had a spare key, so we were saved the bother of bashing the door down. When we got in, there were clear signs of recent occupation. An open bottle of whisky and a half-full glass on a table, a full ashtray, dirty plates piled in the sink, an unmade bed. I saw several shooting trophies on display in his study confirming what the deputy had said about him being a good marksman. Most importantly . . .' he reached into a briefcase and took out a file, 'I found this in his desk. Take a look at the handwritten cover note.'

Merlin felt a jolt of adrenaline as he read it: *Dear Frederick, as promised, here's the main file covering Calvert's illicit activities. This is a summary of everything. I have access to other files of underlying detail if required. We are unable for various reasons to act directly against Calvert ourselves, but you are free to use the information as you see fit.* He held the note up to the light. The watermark was one he'd seen before on MI5 correspondence.'

'*Madre de Dios!* This is a turn-up for the book. So the question is, did Vermeulen give this file to Calvert, or did Calvert take it?'

One of the desk sergeants appeared at the door before Johnson could answer. He had a brown paper package in his hands.

'A young lad dropped this off for you ten minutes ago, Chief Inspector. We also took a call earlier from a lady called Van Buren. Sounded a bit upset. Asked that you get in touch.'

'Put it on the desk, please, Sergeant, and thanks.'

The package contained a leather folder of foolscap size. With a lurch of his heart, Merlin suddenly guessed what was inside. He opened it.

'The drawings!' He carefully removed the works and set them down side by side on the desk. Johnson moved round to join him. 'What do you think, Peter? Worth four hundred grand?'

'Not sure about that, sir. I can see a lot of artistry has gone into them, but I don't think I'd have them hanging on my walls. A bit depressing.'

'I think they're pretty impressive, but each to his own taste.'

'Astonishing that these little sketches have caused so much trouble. They are the originals, d'you think, sir?'

'We'll have to get Kenneth Clark to check, of course. But I can't see any point in the thieves returning fakes when an expert would spot them a mile off.'

'They must have decided the drawings were too hot to handle.'

'Someone like Billy Hill, if he's our man, is clever enough to know when to cut his losses. Doubt we'll get the cash back as well, though. 'We'd better find somewhere very secure to store these. Where do you reckon?

'The AC has a pretty solid safe.'

'So he does.' Merlin looked at the clock. 'He'll have cleared off by now, but his secretary will probably be there. She always works late. You can take them upstairs in a minute, but let's finish our discussion on Calvert. Do we have a photo of him?'

'I picked up a couple of what looked likely to be recent photographs in his house. I can call his deputy to ask if he has any distinguishing features.'

'Do that, then send a wanted person notification to all London stations. As he's supposed to be handy with guns, you'd better include a warning that he might be dangerous.'

A short while later, Robinson returned. 'No luck with forensics, sir. There's no one on duty. I tried Inspector Armstrong at home, but his wife said he's gone out to a formal dinner somewhere. She didn't know where.'

Merlin looked again at the clock. Seven thirty. Too early yet to expect a response from Eisenhower. Long shot or not, the knife analysis was clearly going to come too late. Was there anything more he could do on Lewis's behalf?

'Perhaps I should go and wait at the hospital in case White comes round?'

'With respect, sir,' said Robinson, 'you look bushed. I think you should go home and get a good night's sleep. I'll speak to the hospital and make sure they telephone me at home if White comes to life. I'll call you if he does.'

'That's very good of you. But I suppose I'd better deal with Miss Van Buren before I go.'

'I'm pretty sure that could wait until morning.'

After a moment's further thought, Merlin conceded 'All right, Constable. You win.' He stifled a yawn. 'In the words of Sir Philip Sidney, "Come Sleep! O Sleep, the certain knot of peace, the baiting-place of . . ."' Oh, I must be tired. I've forgotten how it ends.'

'". . . of wit, the balm of woe."'

Merlin grinned. 'Impressive, Constable. I didn't know you were a poetry lover.'

'I'm not in your league, sir, but I studied Sidney for School Certificate. Now off you go.'

Chapter Twenty-Two

It was still early, but the phone was ringing. Through bleary eyes, Merlin saw from the bedside clock that it was ten to six. He left Sonia snoring gently in bed and hurried to the hall. Heart in mouth, he picked up the receiver.

'The execution is delayed for twelve hours,' said Goldberg. 'The general requires firmer evidence of White's guilt and has given us that long to provide it.'

'Twelve hours isn't much.'

'It's better than nothing, Frank. Any news of White?'

'I would have been notified during the night if there was. There is one new item of information. A knife was found in White's clothes. I didn't think we had time to test it, but now we do.'

'Let me know.'

Bridges greeted Merlin in the office. His sling had disappeared. 'The knife is already with forensics, sir.

'Well done. How do you feel?'

'The odd twinge, but not too bad.'

'Good. We've got a lifeline on Lewis.' Merlin reported Goldberg's call.

'I have to say, there's nothing to be seen on the knife with the naked eye, sir.'

'Let's just hope there's some trace, however minuscule, that we can match. It occurs to me that I don't know where Pablo's body is.'

'Still in the Victoria mortuary, I believe. I'll make sure forensics know.'

'What news of Cole?'

'The doctors continue to be tight-lipped. He's sedated at the moment. They've allowed his mum to sit with him, and his friend Shona's been allowed a short visit.'

'You saw his mother?'

'I did.'

'In a bad state?'

'Not so you could tell, sir. She's a tough old bird.'

'She's been through it before, of course.' Merlin was thinking of the time Cole had taken a bullet in the shoulder in a Piccadilly shootout during the Blitz. 'Let's hope things turn out as they did then, eh, Sam? Now, I'd better bring you up to date.'

When Merlin was done, Bridges observed, 'Calvert could have been the third man that dance teacher, Miss Wheeler, saw in Vermeulen's mews.'

'That had occurred to me.'

'As for the Van Buren case, with Fielding's evidence, it all seems now to boil down to identifying the man running across the road.'

'And all we have going for us there, Sam, is the tie pin and Jacob or Jake.'

'Jake Penny's name naturally comes to mind, but how the hell would his name be known to Van Buren?'

'What if the third man was Micallef, and he was shouting for help, knowing Penny was at hand?' Merlin thought for a moment. 'But why would Micallef want to take on Van Buren? None of our three witnesses of the night – Butterfield, Katz, Fielding – have said anything about Van Buren running in pursuit of anyone. He was just having a quiet cigarette by the river, according to Katz, and seemingly oblivious to what had been going on in his house.'

'Any sign of Micallef or Penny, sir?'

'None of Penny. Miss Van Buren left an interesting message to say that Micallef had been abducted in front of her eyes. I owe her a call regarding that.'

'Did you ask about her father's knife?'

'I'll do so when I call her. If the knife wasn't Van Buren's but Katz's, it could put a different perspective on the story, but if we believe Fielding, Katz definitely isn't the killer.'

Seconds later, the desk sergeant rang. 'A Miss Van Buren for you, sir.'

'Speak of the devil . . . Yes, put her through, please. Good morning, miss. I'm sorry not to have got back to you.'

'I'm sure you're very busy, Mr Merlin. I had a message from the commissioner that you'd recovered the drawings.'

Merlin guessed the AC hadn't been able to resist telling the commissioner, who'd wanted in turn to grab a little of the glory. 'To say we recovered them may be a bit of a stretch. Someone handed them in yesterday. It appears the thieves decided they were never going to be able to fence them.'

'Well, however you got them, I'm very grateful.' There was a brief pause. 'You received my message about Teddy?'

Merlin heard the catch in her throat. 'I did.'

'I've heard nothing from him since. I'm very worried.'

'Can you tell me exactly what happened?'

When she'd done so, Merlin asked, 'Did Mr Micallef give any indication of knowing these men?'

'Not that I saw, but they certainly knew him. I heard one of them call out his name.'

'Descriptions?'

'Big and rough is all I can really say. It all happened so quickly.'

Merlin took a moment to think. It might be cruel in the circumstances, but he decided the young woman deserved to be told the truth. 'I'm sorry, Miss Van Buren, but you ought to know that we suspect Mr Micallef of involvement in the burglary of your father's house and perhaps even in his death.

He heard a gasp, then sobbing. Eventually she got a grip. 'Are you . . . are you out of your mind? Teddy's a well-respected businessman, not a murderer or a thief.'

'Apparently he comes from a family of hardened criminals.'

'You're talking rubbish, Mr Merlin. His father owns a string of successful companies in Malta. He and his family live on a large estate in the best part of Valletta.'

'He runs a major criminal enterprise. If he owns a large estate, it was crime that paid for it.'

'I don't believe you . . .' There was a long pause. 'I don't believe you, but even if that were true, it doesn't mean Teddy is himself a criminal. He makes his money trading in valuable artefacts. He's a gentleman. Besides . . . hell, on the night of the burglary, he was with me all night, during the party and after.'

'That would not have stopped him from being the inside man. He knew there were valuables on the property and knew the layout of the house. He'd been told that the house would be empty after ten and was in a position to leave a window open.'

'But—'

'Furthermore, it's not accurate to say he was with you all night. What about that late-night walk of his that you both acknowledged? He could have made a rendezvous with his accomplices during that time. Or he could have been involved in a confrontation with your father.'

'This is ridiculous! He is the least violent man I know. Maybe you're right about his family, but you shouldn't allow that to prejudice you about Teddy.'

'For your sake, miss, I hope our suspicions turn out to be wrong. However, if he's to clear himself, I need to see him and get the truth. The fact that he's been forcibly removed from the scene suggests to me that someone isn't keen we do so.'

Miss Van Buren began to cry again. Between sobs she said, 'I hope whoever has him doesn't hurt him. I couldn't bear the idea of him being hurt.'

'Can I ask, miss, was your father in the habit of carrying a knife on his person? A small pocket knife.'

'What does that have to do with anything?'

'Could you just tell me, please?'

'Well, yes. He loved to eat apples but didn't like the skin. He always kept an old penknife on him to peel the fruit. Why are you asking?'

'A man has admitted to getting into a fight with your father on the Embankment that night.'

'Why . . . why, you've got his murderer, then.' Her voice rose a couple of registers. 'Why all this idiotic rubbish about Teddy?'

'There is reliable evidence that this man left the scene before your father was killed. Another man was then seen fighting with your father later. However, the first man claimed your father pulled a knife on him. In the light of what you say, this seems quite credible.'

The voice that replied a good minute later was calmer. 'Look . . . look, I'm afraid this is all getting too much for me, Chief Inspector. The idea of Daddy being involved in not one, but two public brawls and drawing a knife is simply . . . simply too bizarre for me to contemplate at the moment. I think I'd better go.'

'I understand, miss, but I have one last question. Did your father have any acquaintances called Jacob or Jake?'

'He had a friend in Holland called Jacob De Vries. Another businessman.'

'Any idea of this gentleman's whereabouts now?'

'In Holland, I should think. I remember Daddy saying he was well in with the Nazis.'

'That's it?'

'Yes. I have one question for *you*, Mr Merlin. When will we be able to bury our father?'

'Soon, I hope Miss Van Buren. Soon.'

★

345

Mattie Bryant liked to get down to his riverside allotment in Chiswick early on bright summer mornings. He'd started at eight today and had already done three hours' work on his vegetable patch. A little more, then he'd move on to Terry's allotment. His mate had been ill for a few days and Bryant was happy to help him out.

Time for a breather, he thought, and went to his shed. He made a pot of tea, then relaxed back into his deckchair. Moments later, a loud bang made him jump and lose half his cup. The allotments were separated from the river by a narrow lane, and his first thought was that a passing car had backfired. Curious, however, he bolted the remains of his tea and wandered down to the main allotment entrance. His heart rose as he looked out at the glorious spectacle of the river shimmering in the strong morning sunlight. About thirty yards down the lane to his right, towards Chiswick Bridge, a car was parked on a patch of scrub ground bordering the river. He recognised it as a smart Austin saloon of some sort. A nice car. It looked like someone was sitting behind the wheel.

There was no one else working the allotments today. Bryant was a widower living a solitary life in a small Hammersmith council flat, and he'd not spoken to a soul for at least twenty-four hours. He felt the need for human contact so he passed through the gate and set off for the car. As the driver came into closer view, it looked like his head was hanging down. Thinking he was most likely taking a nap, Mattie paused and contemplated turning on his heel. Then it occurred to him that rather than napping, the driver might have become unwell. He ought to check. If he got a mouthful for disturbing the fellow's sleep, so be it.

His tap on the window produced no response. The driver was facing in the opposite direction. He tapped again without result, then turned the door handle and leaned in. 'Here, mate are you all . . .' He recoiled in horror. Mattie Bryant had done his bit for king and country in the Boer War and knew a dead man when he saw one. There was a neat bullet hole in the man's forehead. Blood was trickling down his cheeks and onto the gearstick. Mattie pulled out of the car and stood in shock for a moment before slamming the door. Then he ran as fast as he could to his shed, jumped on his bicycle and pedalled off towards Hammersmith.

The AC had asked Merlin upstairs for a chat. He'd been delighted with the return of the drawings and would have gone on forever about them if Merlin hadn't cut him short. 'I need to get on, sir. I'd be grateful if you could contact Sir Kenneth Clark and ask him to authenticate them.'

'Of course, Chief Inspector,' the AC replied with an irritable twitch of the lips. 'And heaven forfend that I should waste your valuable time.'

Back in his office, Merlin felt like he was sitting on hot coals. Forensics were taking their time working on the knife, and nothing seemed to be happening on other fronts. Then Johnson burst into the room.

'Two dead body reports, sir. One in the East India Docks. Bloke pulled out of the water. Red marks on his neck. The local bobbies think he's been strangled. I've sent Robinson off to take a look.'

'Any ID on him?'

'None discovered so far.'

'And the second body?'

'Male again. Bullet hole in the head. Found in a parked car by Chiswick Bridge. No further detail as yet. I thought I'd go and check him out myself. Do you want to come?'

'No. I should, but I'd rather wait on forensics here.'

Johnson and Bridges crossed at the door.

'Knife clean as a whistle, sir. Nothing to match,' the sergeant reported.

'Bugger.'

'However, they did think the blade was a match for Pablo's wound. Can't say definitively, though."

347

'That's something, I suppose. I'll pass it on to Bernie. Have you heard about the two bodies?'

'Yes. Billy Hill cleaning up?'

'We'll see.'

'I thought I might go to the hospital and check on Cole and White.'

Merlin looked distracted. 'Oh. Right. Good idea. Call me if there's anything.'

'I'd like to have a look in my father's study, Mrs Macdonald. Is it open?'

'I don't think so. I'll go and get the key.'

'Has anyone been in there apart from the police since . . . since Daddy disappeared?'

'No one apart from Mr Robert. He was here yesterday with Miss Mitchum. I was busy upstairs, but I saw the door open at one point. He had his key with him, of course. Sergeant Bridges said he was going to come and look at your father's papers, but he hasn't done so yet.'

After the housekeeper had let Elizabeth in, she remained hovering at the door.

'Can I help you, Mrs Macdonald?'

'Well, yes, miss. I'd appreciate a word about the house. I need to know for how long you might be requiring my services.'

'I'm sorry. You need to know where you stand, of course. Robert and I should have discussed it, but what with everything else . . . The lease has a few more months to run, doesn't it?'

'Six months.'

'I'll speak to Robert. I doubt he's given it any thought yet.'

'I think you'll find he has. I couldn't help overhearing him tell his young lady yesterday that there was a possibility he might move in here.'

Elizabeth looked puzzled. 'Really? You do surprise me. Well, I'll speak to him today if I can.'

The housekeeper departed and Elizabeth sat down at her father's desk. Her upsetting conversation with Merlin had prompted her to do some investigating of her own. It had occurred to her that there might be some clue to recent events in her father's papers that had escaped the attention of the police. She was going to take a look for herself.

She knew the police had boxed the papers to take away, and when she looked around the room, she spotted the returned boxes by the window.She went over to them and saw one labelled *Reviewed Desk Contents 1*, the other *R D 2*. She knelt down beside them and opened the first box.

Either her father had been more organised than she'd thought, or the policemen had done a good job compartmentalising everything. Either way, her task proved easier than expected. The first file she withdrew was headed *Family Litigation*. Having acquired only a superficial understanding of her father's suit against the Butterfields, she was surprised to learn from the correspondence how vicious and complex the legal wrangling had become.

Dutch Business was the heading of the second file. The majority of these papers were in Dutch. She doubted a translator had been hired to help and guessed they'd gone unread by the police. She spoke perfect Dutch and went through them meticulously. It was always possible that something from her father's past in Holland had had a bearing on his death. Robert had told her recently that MI5 contacts of his friend Havering had said England was swarming with German agents. The idea of a man like Havering having friends in MI5 was ridiculous, but she couldn't quite dismiss the thought that there might be Nazis in the country who'd had some motive to kill her father. However, the papers disclosed no clues that she could discern.

The da Vinci folder was next. It filled in most gaps in her knowledge about the fated transaction, but otherwise was no use. The file on her mother prompted tears but yielded no information to the point.

In the second box, there were reams and reams of banking and stock market papers providing clear evidence that her father hadn't been exaggerating the extent of his financial problems.

Finally, after almost three hours, she got to the last file, *Miscellaneous Bills*. She was quite fed up by now, and doubted it would be illuminating, but ploughed through every item anyway. Her determination was finally rewarded when she came to the final item, a bill from her father's tailor. There were two pages to the invoice, which had somehow become stuck together. She would not give up without seeing both pages properly. Eventually she managed to prise the papers apart, only to discover that a separate invoice had been trapped inside. She looked hard at the name at the top. It rang a bell. As she read on, she began to feel distinctly uncomfortable.

Merlin's growing anxiety as the time for Lewis's execution approached was made worse by the fact that he was on his own. He received two telephone calls, both disheartening. One, from Goldberg, told him that the limited forensic results on the knife were making no impact at the embassy. In the second, he learned from Bridges that there were no improvements to report on either White or Cole. At just after four, his painful solitude ended as Johnson and Robinson reappeared, looking excited.

'The Chiswick body is Calvert, sir,' said Johnson. 'I thought I recognised him from his photograph, and to make sure, we made a call and found the car was registered to him. Killed by one shot to the head.'

'Suicide or murder?'

'Not certain. The local police and medics are continuing to investigate. A very clean shot either way.'

'Anyone seen in the vicinity when he was first found?'

'No.'

'I see. And your news, Constable?'

'It was Micallef, sir. Had his business card on him.'

'Can't say I'm surprised. Hill has obviously had enough.'

'Why not just make the body disappear? Why put him unweighted in the river, where he's bound to wash up?'

'Sending us a message probably. "You've got the drawings back, coppers, and here's one of the burglars. Now lay off."'

'So we'll be finding Penny's corpse next?'

'I think not. Penny's a long-term gang member. Respected in his own crooked world. I doubt it would go down well with the troops if Hill did him in for nothing more than doing his job. Besides, he's got a proven track record of keeping his trap shut when caught. Micallef was a new recruit. An outsider. Could Hill trust him not to blab? Clearly he decided not.'

'Do you think the Vermeulen case can be closed with Calvert's death?'

'I'm loath to say that yet, Inspector. Let's wait until the picture is clearer.'

'Would you like me to notify Miss Van Buren about Micallef, sir?'

'Not yet, Constable. The body should be formally identified first. Perhaps I can do it. I'd prefer not to impose that duty on the poor lady.'

Merlin glanced at the clock for the umpteenth time. 'Things are looking bleak for Lewis. We're going to need a miracle.'

The telephone rang. He snatched up the receiver. 'Yes . . . Who? Yes, yes. Please bring her up right away.'

No one spoke until the door opened and Barbara Freeman stepped nervously into the room. Merlin greeted her and bade her sit.

'How can we help?' He noticed that the young woman's hands were trembling.

'I heard Vince was in hospital. What's his condition?'

'Pretty bad.'

'Rumour is he shot one of your men.'

'Two. One of them's seriously hurt.'

'I wanted to know . . . I wanted to know whether I need worry about him any more. I mean, can he . . . can he be a threat to me if I tell you something?'

'Not a hope. If he survives his injuries, he'll be facing the rope or a lifetime in prison.'

'God's honour?'

'God's honour.'

'Then I have more to tell you. New information.'

Merlin leaned forward eagerly. 'I'm listening.'

Barbara Freeman took a deep breath. 'Vince . . . he gets me to do his washing sometimes. Like an idiot, I do it. Anyway, I hadn't realised, but he left some dirty clothes behind the night he beat me up.'

'This weekend, you mean?'

'No. The time before. After . . . after I'd been to the pictures with Tomas.'

'The early hours of Friday August the fourteenth?'

'Yes. So . . . so there's a cupboard at my place where he keeps a few spare clothes. I hadn't looked in it for a while, but I was having a bit of a tidy-up after getting out of hospital yesterday. It's a good way of forgetting problems, or at least so I find. At the bottom of this cupboard was a grubby suit, along with a shirt and underwear. I remembered when he'd worn it last. It was one I'd helped him pick out in Savile Row. He must've changed into a new outfit after bashing me that first time and left the dirty stuff for me to launder.'

'You're sure it was left that evening? The evening of the fourteenth?'

'Positive. He didn't visit at all between the first beating and the second. Didn't change his clothes the second time, I know.'

'So he left dirty clothes. What about them?'

'Two things. There's blood on the shirt cuffs. Pretty sure it's not mine. He bruised me more than cut me that time. Might be his. Might be . . .'

'Tomas's?'

She nodded. 'Then I found something in the suit pocket. Here. Take a look.' She handed over a business card. It was in the name of Tomas Barboza, Sales Representative. Merlin turned it over. There was a bloody stain on the back.

'I'm afraid Robert's not here, Elizabeth,' Caroline Mitchum said at the door. 'He's meeting with the bank manager. I don't think he'll be long, though.'

'I'll wait then, if you don't mind.'

'Of course I don't. Can I offer you something? Tea? Something stronger?'

'A sherry would be nice.'

'Good idea. I'll have one too.'

The women were on to their second glass when Robert got back.

'Drinks time, I see. Good!' He poured himself a large Scotch.

'How'd it go?' asked Caroline.

'Well, I think. The fellow's eyes lit up when I told him the good news about the drawings. He wants some more information, but fingers crossed. Any news about your friend, Lizzie?'

Elizabeth sighed and shook her head.

Robert resisted the temptation to say 'Good riddance.' 'You're sure he hasn't just gone off on a business trip?'

'He was dragged off by two thugs in front of my eyes.'

'You've told the police?'

'Yes. They . . . they're looking for him.' She grasped the arm of her chair tightly, feeling the tears welling up.

Caroline reached out to pat her hand. 'You poor dear.'

'Buck up. Top up her sherry, Caroline. I'm sure he'll reappear.'

'No . . . no thank you. This is fine.' Elizabeth put a hand to her forehead. 'You know, I think I've got a bit of a headache coming on.'

'We've some pills somewhere. Try the bathroom cupboard, Caroline.'

'You're out of aspirin, Robert. I noticed yesterday. I can pop up the road to the chemist if you like, Elizabeth?'

'Oh no. Don't trouble yourself.'

'No bother. I'll be back in a jiffy.'

When Caroline had gone, Robert said, 'I've provisionally fixed a meeting with the lawyers for tomorrow morning, to go over everything. Eleven thirty. Is that all right?'

'I . . . I think so. But we need to have a proper chat before we see them. There are several things we need to decide. For example, what do we want to do with Cheyne Walk? Mrs Macdonald seems to be under the impression that you want to keep it on and move in there yourself. She overheard you talking to Caroline.'

'Would it be a problem for you if I did?'

'No, but you should be discussing things like that with me first.'

'Sorry. You're right, of course.' He took a gulp of whisky. 'Did you get anywhere with Merlin as regards Father's funeral?'

'He said he hoped they could release the body soon.'

'Really? That must mean they're getting somewhere in their investigation.'

'He said they have witnesses who saw Daddy in a fight on the Embankment that night. Two fights, in fact. They're looking for a man who was involved.'

'One of the burglars, I bet. Do they have a description, or anything else to go on?'

'I don't know. Merlin asked me whether Daddy knew a man called Jake or Jacob. By the way, Daddy's papers have now been returned by the police, and I had a look through them. Mrs Macdonald said you were in the study yesterday. Did you look at them too?'

'Me? No.'

'It took me a few hours to go through them all. The litigation file was illuminating. Daddy certainly gave Uncle Humphrey a hard time. I don't think we should extend his agony further, do you?'

354

'I suppose not, but I'd like to hear from the lawyers first. What else did you find?'

'All sorts of things, but not what I was looking for. I had hoped to find something that gave some pointer as to why Daddy was killed.'

'It's the burglars who did for him. Trust me.'

'Maybe. However, I did find one thing that surprised me. Right at the end.'

'What was that?'

'An invoice, from a doctor in Harley Street.'

Merlin sent Pablo's bloodied card straight off to forensics and Robinson to Barbara's flat to get White's discarded clothing. But he knew there wasn't enough time to get the blood analysed and produce incontrovertible physical evidence to the Americans. Everything now rested on Eisenhower's reaction to the girl's story alone. He reached the embassy at just after six. The execution was less than an hour away. Goldberg had bad news. Eisenhower was incommunicado until at least 6.30, and Pearce and McCluskey were nowhere to be found. 'Oh, yes, and the location of the execution has been switched. The executioner they brought over from the States became ill. They turned to the British authorities for help, and now it's one of your guys who will do the dirty deed, in Wormwood Scrubs prison.'

Merlin saw a ray of hope. 'The governor of the Scrubs is a friend of mine. We were in the last war together. I may be able to buy a little time from him if I get over there.'

'Hurry then, and I'll go and park myself outside Ike's office.'

'Do you have the Scrubs telephone number?'

'I can get it.'

'Ask for Cleverly. He's the governor. Fine fellow. Used to play rugby for England.'

'Still haven't had a chance to see that game. Harriman told me it beat the pants off American football.'

355

'British is always best, Bernie. You should know that.'

'I took a call regarding Calvert, sir,' Robinson told Johnson. 'They found the weapon in the car, under the seat. Somehow it had lodged in the metal underpinnings and fallen out of sight. It'll be checked for prints shortly.'

Johnson was at Merlin's desk, reviewing his notebook. 'Suicide, then?'

'Seems so.'

'No sign of a suicide note, though?'

'No, sir. They're going round to Calvert's house to see if they can find one there. If you want me to go with them . . .'

They were interrupted by the duty sergeant on the phone. 'Lady just called, sir. Seemed a bit disturbed. Wouldn't wait to be put through but said someone needed to get round to where she was straight away. Name of Caroline Mitchum. I've got the address here.'

Cleverly was completing the formal execution papers when Merlin barged in. He could hear his secretary, Miss Kendall, remonstrating loudly in the background.

'Frank? You startled me. What the devil are you doing here?' He looked down to add a final signature. 'This isn't a very good time, I'm afraid. I've an execution on the go.'

'I know. That's why I'm here. You have to delay it.'

'Delay it? I'm sorry, Frank, but that's impossible. Once these things are set in motion by the powers-that-be, the procedure is carved in stone. There's already been some disruption in the process, I understand. The system won't tolerate any more.' He looked at his watch. 'Six thirty-eight. Mr Pierrepoint will be completing his final checks now and the prisoner will be leaving his holding cell in a few minutes. I need to be there ahead of him.' He stood up, smiled apologetically and started for the door.

Merlin grasped his arm. 'Gordon, I swear on the lives of my

356

wife and son, Virgil Lewis is not guilty of murder. I've near as dammit established that another man committed the crime. The American authorities know but are being extraordinarily stubborn. You must believe me. You are about to hang an innocent man.'

'But Frank, it's really quite impossible to intervene at this stage.'

'Please, Gordon. I have someone waiting at the American embassy to present the latest crucial evidence to Eisenhower. The general is in a meeting but is due out any minute. Once he hears our new information, I'm sure he'll want to halt the execution. A delay of half an hour could save an innocent man's life.'

'You are utterly convinced of his innocence?'

'I am.'

'And this latest evidence is conclusive?'

'Ninety per cent conclusive.'

'I'd rather you said one hundred per cent, Frank.' Cleverly returned frowning to his desk. 'The Home Office will probably have my guts for garters for this, but . . .' He sighed and pressed a switch on his intercom. 'Miss Kendall, please let Mr Pierrepoint know that I've been unavoidably detained. I'll be there as soon as I can. Also make sure Lewis remains in his cell until I give the word.'

'Very good, sir.'

The governor leaned back in his chair. 'Now, Frank, tell me all and make it quick.'

Elizabeth Van Buren was sitting in the living room with a bandage around her head and her feet up on a stool. She looked utterly drained. The officers were shocked.

'Thank God you've come,' she said. 'Sit down, please. This is all very difficult, but . . . I suggest Caroline tells you first what she found on her return from the chemist.'

Caroline Mitchum looked bewildered. 'Yes, all right . . . if that's what you want, Elizabeth. So we . . . that's we two and

357

Elizabeth's brother . . . were chatting here when Elizabeth suddenly felt poorly. I volunteered to go and get some aspirin from the local Boots. As it happens, my expedition took longer than expected, as the Boots was closed and I had to find another chemist. I arrived back here forty or forty five minutes later. When I got to the door, I realised I'd forgotten to take my key, so had to knock. No one answered. I knocked and shouted out for what seemed like ages. Then the door suddenly burst open and Robert rushed past me without so much as a by-your-leave. He looked to be in a foul temper. I called out to him as he raced down the stairs, but he ignored me. There was no sign of Elizabeth when I entered the flat, so I went looking, and found her in Robert's bedroom. She was groaning and flat out on her back on the carpet. I saw blood. I hurried out to get a bowl of hot water and a bandage. And . . . well, that's it. She wouldn't tell me what happened, just told me to call Scotland Yard.'

'Thank you, dear,' Elizabeth said. Now if you don't mind, I'd like to speak to the officers in private.'

'Oh.'

'There's no need to look put out. You'll find out soon enough. It's just best if I do this alone. Look outside. The sun is still shining. Why don't you go and have a nice walk down by the river?'

'But . . .'

'Please, Caroline.'

'If you insist.'

When they heard the front door shut, Elizabeth said, 'It's going to be hard enough telling you what happened without having to cope with that poor girl's reaction.' She fiddled with her bandage for a moment, then took a deep breath. 'I came here to discuss various practical matters arising from my father's death. I also wanted to discuss something I discovered in Daddy's papers earlier today. After Caroline had gone out, I was introducing that subject when . . .' she blushed, 'when I was obliged to answer a call of nature. I told Robert, and he suggested I use the bathroom in his bedroom.'

She looked down at her hands. 'I had a headache, but when I got to the bathroom, I also began to feel a little faint. I suppose the pressure of all these awful events is beginning to have a physical impact. I left the bathroom and sat down on the bed, waiting for the feeling to pass. As I did so, I looked around me. On one of the bedside tables were some photographs I'd never seen before. There was one of an all-male dinner party. A colour photograph. The group included Robert and a couple of university friends of his. I remembered him mentioning this get-together at the beginning of the summer, so it hadn't been so long ago. He was looking very smart in a pinstripe suit and wearing the blue tie I bought him for his birthday.' She clasped her hands tightly together and her voice fell almost to a whisper. 'On the tie . . . on the tie was a pin. It was the pin you found on the Embankment.'

Robinson gasped. 'Are you sure?' she asked.

'I'm absolutely sure. You can have a look at the photograph yourself. The blue arrow design, or whatever you call it, is quite clear. I suppose there might be other pins with that design, but in the circumstances . . .'

'The coincidence is too great,' said Johnson.

'Quite. So after this shock, I decided to have a general rummage around in the room, and found an interesting file. I was reading through it when Robert came in. When he saw what I was doing, he went purple with anger. He started shouting wildly, then pushed me to the floor. My head hit one of the bedposts pretty hard, and blood began to flow. The sight seemed to bring him partially to his senses. He helped me back up onto the bed and sat down beside me. I said we needed to have a calm discussion about what I'd found.'

'You asked him about the tie pin?' asked Robinson.

'No, that was not the first question. I went back to the item I'd discovered in my father's papers.'

'Which was?'

'A doctor's invoice, or to be more precise, a psychiatrist's invoice. You see, when Robert was in his teens, he had an unfortunate experience with another boy at school. There was a fight, and Robert stabbed the boy with a knife. He has always had a fearful temper. The boy was seriously injured, but recovered eventually. My father had to pay the school and the parents of the boy a considerable sum to hush the matter up. He was extremely wealthy then, so the money was not a problem, but he was naturally distraught at what Robert had done. He paid out more money to persuade another school to take him, but that school insisted Robert have regular psychiatric care and assessment. Daddy arranged for this and Robert attended a practice in Harley Street for several years until he went to university. He saw the same psychiatrist throughout. The invoice in my father's papers was from that psychiatrist. It was dated last month. And the name of the psychiatrist is Jacob. Arnold Jacob.'

'Jake or Jacob.' Johnson muttered to himself.

'And there's more. The file I found in Robert's room contains Jacob's latest assessment, done in July. In it, he strongly advised Daddy that Robert should at the very least resume regular psychiatric sessions. His opinion was that Robert's mental problems were as profound as when he'd first seen him. He described him as a "psychopath". I've heard the word, but I'm not sure exactly what it means. It can't be good, though.'

'So you asked Robert about the report?'

'Yes. He was silent for a while. Then it all came out in a torrent. Daddy had insisted as a precondition to financing the magazine that he go for a mental check-up. Just, he told Robert, to satisfy himself that he was up to the pressures of running a business. Robert agreed to go. After the appointment, he was under the impression that all had gone well. Daddy implied as much, he said, but asked him to continue seeing Jacob. He wasn't very happy, but if it meant the money coming in, he knew he had to agree. Another appointment had been scheduled. Then, yesterday, he decided to take a look at Daddy's papers, and one of the first things he found was the report. Naturally, he disagreed with its conclusions, but he knew it should be removed in case anyone else came across it.'

'What exactly did he say about the report?' asked Robinson.

'That any suggestion he was mentally ill was complete poppycock. He just had a bit of a short fuse when dealing with idiots.'

'I see.'

'It was then that I asked him about the tie pin. He denied it was the one found by the police. I said I wasn't sure I believed him, and he became agitated. Grabbed my shoulders and shook me. I said, "You were the unknown man on the Embankment, weren't you?" He completely lost control. He put his hands around my neck and squeezed. Said, "And what if I was?" Then he suddenly pulled away. "All right," he whispered. "I'll tell you, but if you breathe a word, I'll kill you."'

The strain was beginning to tell on Elizabeth. Her shoulders had begun to shake and her hands were trembling. Robinson reached out a consoling hand, and after a moment, Elizabeth continued. 'He told me that after the dinner party, he came back here. Caroline went straight to bed. He wasn't feeling sleepy and drank some brandy. After a while, he decided he'd like to top off the evening with a cigar. He was out of supplies but knew there were plenty at Daddy's. It wasn't far, and he had his key, so he decided to go and grab a couple of Daddy's best Cubans. When he got to Cheyne Walk, he heard a noise and became aware of a scuffle across the road. To his surprise, he heard his father's voice. Naturally, he ran over and scared off the man attacking him. He asked Daddy if he was all right, but was roughly pushed away. Then for some reason Daddy said something vile about Caroline. He was drunk, I suppose. Robert responded by asking whether he'd had a nice time with his whore down the road. Daddy suddenly threw a punch at him, and Robert fought back. Eventually they disengaged. Daddy said something about the money he was going to get for the drawings and how Robert was never going to see a penny. He also referred to Dr Jacob's assessment and said that if Robert didn't start doing what he was told, he'd have him locked in a mental asylum. This triggered Robert into another physical attack on Daddy, which culminated in him going over the river wall.'

'But why in heaven's name didn't your brother call for help when your father fell in?'

'Perhaps . . . perhaps that's what being a psychopath means. I asked him that question and he just shrugged and smiled. It's almost like he'd become a different person. Like Jekyll and Hyde.' She looked down at her hands. 'I said I would have to tell the police. He threatened me, then suddenly jumped up and threw me to the floor again. I got another bang on the head and was knocked out. The next thing I remember is Caroline mopping my head with a hot towel.'

'Any idea where Robert might be now?'

Elizabeth wiped her eyes with her handkerchief. 'I suppose there's a chance he went to Daddy's house. If not there, then I've no idea.'

'We'll give that a go then. Will you be all right on your own?'

'I'll be fine, and anyway, Caroline will be back in a minute.'

'I'm very sorry you've had such a terrible ordeal.'

'Just remember, Inspector. Robert is not a criminal. He is ill and needs treatment.'

As they left the building, Robinson asked, 'Shouldn't we have told her about Micallef, sir?'

'Not the time, Claire. Not the time.'

'You've convinced me, Frank, but unfortunately I'm not the one who needs convincing.' Cleverly looked at his watch. It was 7.16. 'Your friend at the embassy hasn't called. I'll allow you one attempt to contact him. If there's nothing new or you can't get hold of him, I'm afraid I'll have to proceed.'

A call was put through to Grosvenor Square, but Goldberg

could not be found. Merlin asked for Eisenhower's office, but was told that all lines were busy. His shoulders slumped. 'Perhaps I could try again in five minutes, Gordon?'

'Sorry, Frank. You've had more than half an hour. We have to get on.' Cleverly got to his feet.

'Can . . . can I come with you, Gordon?'

'Are you sure? These are grisly affairs.'

'I think it's my duty.'

'Very well.'

Merlin followed Cleverly up a staircase and along a labyrinth of corridors to the place of execution. The noose hung down in the centre of a small, crowded room. Virgil Lewis was sandwiched between a burly British prison warder and a burlier American military policeman. He was clearly trying to put a brave face on things, but was unable to prevent his cuffed hands from shaking. Albert Pierrepoint, who looked more like a small-town bank manager than an executioner, was fiddling with the rope, an assistant at his side. The prison padre had taken up position to the right of Lewis. On the left were a cheerful-looking Max Pearce and two other American military policemen.

'Come to see justice done, eh, Merlin?' said Pearce. 'Surprised you've got the stomach for it.'

Merlin didn't bother to reply.

'I'm very sorry for the delay,' said the governor, looking at Lewis. 'Is there anything you'd like to say before sentence is carried out?'

Lewis glowered at Pearce, then turned to Cleverly. 'I am an innocent man, sir, as God is my witness.'

Merlin found it impossible to remain silent. 'The British police know it, Virgil. I'm sorry I couldn't persuade your people to see it our way.'

Pearce bristled. 'Damnation, Merlin, shut your trap. This is an American judicial proceeding. You have no standing here, and no voice.'

Cleverly pursed his lips and nodded to the padre who proceeded to recite the time-honoured verses. When he got to the final words, 'And may God have mercy on your soul', the guards moved Lewis closer to the rope. As they positioned him, he looked up at Merlin. 'Thanks for trying, Chief Inspector. I'll ask the good Lord to look out for you when I get to the other side.'

The noose was placed around his neck and a hood was pulled over his head. The assistant stepped away, and Pierrepoint reached for the lever. He was just about to pull it back when the door crashed open. A breathless Miss Kendall burst in, followed by two prison officers. 'Stop! We've had a communication from the embassy, Governor. The sentence is not to be carried out. General Eisenhower has decided to review Lewis's case. Formal paperwork is being messengered now.'

The shock of this late reprieve was too much for Lewis, who collapsed in a faint. The guards hastily pulled him to his feet to ensure he didn't hang himself under his own steam. Noose and hood were quickly removed, and as he came to, his lips formed themselves into an ecstatic grin. Captain Max Pearce, however, looked apoplectic. He couldn't bring himself to look at either Lewis or Merlin, and turned on his heel. As Merlin listened to his steel-tipped boots stomping down the corridor, he put an arm around Lewis's shoulders and breathed a huge sigh of relief.

No one answered when the officers knocked at the house, but when she peered through the letter box, Robinson thought she could hear music. Classical music of some sort. 'If the housekeeper was in, she'd come to the door, sir. There must be someone else playing the radio or gramophone.'

'Let's go and find out.' Johnson opened the door with Elizabeth Van Buren's key. The music was coming from somewhere above. He pointed to the stairs and led the way.

The source of the sound was a room to the right of the first-floor landing. The door was slightly ajar and the officers cautiously edged in. There was a thick fug of cigar smoke and a strong smell of alcohol. After a moment, they were able to make out the figure of a young man clad in pyjamas and dressing gown sitting up in bed, drink and cigar to hand. Robert Van Buren seemed little disturbed by the arrival of two police officers in his bedroom. He greeted them with an airy wave of the hand and a smile, but said nothing. 'I think he's sloshed,' whispered Johnson.

The loud music was coming from a gramophone by the window. Johnson had to shout to make himself heard. 'Mr Van Buren! We are police officers. We need to talk to you about your father's death.'

Van Buren remained silent. There was a welcome pause in the music, which Robinson now recognised to be a Mozart piano sonata. Van Buren reached for the whisky bottle on his bedside table and poured a refill. Finally he spoke. 'I have to give it to the old boy. Tightwad that he was, he kept a good supply of fine liquor. This is a vintage Islay malt. I highly recommend it. Would you care for a dram?'

'No thank you, sir,' said Johnson.

Van Buren leered at Robinson. 'What about you, sweetheart? Fancy some?'

The music started again. More Mozart.

'Lovely record, isn't it. I love Wolfgang Amadeus, don't you?'

'It would be preferable if we carried on this conversation downstairs, sir,' said Johnson.

'Preferable? Preferable for who? Not bloody preferable for me. I'm very comfy here, as it happens.' Van Buren fell back onto the plump pillows behind him. 'And who said we're going to have a conversation anyway? You're on private property. *My* private property now.' He took a puff of his cigar. 'So you can both bugger off.'

Johnson walked over to the gramophone and turned it off.

'Hey! That's not on, pal. Mozart soothes the soul, don't you know?' Van Buren swung his legs down abruptly from the bed and stared blearily at Johnson.

365

'Your sister has been talking to us, sir.'

'Has she now? And what did dear Lizzie tell you?'

'That it was you who pushed your father into the river.'

Van Buren took a large slug of whisky. 'She said that, did she?' He tapped his forehead. 'Mental problems, you know. My father had a few as well. Fortunately, I take after my mother. Mind as sound as a bell until almost the very end.'

'You deny killing your father?'

'I most certainly do!'

'I'm sorry, but we're going to have to ask you to accompany us to the Yard. We can discuss this matter properly there. Could you get dressed, please?'

After a moment's consideration, and rather to Johnson's surprise, Van Buren agreed. 'Very well, let's do that. I'm sure it won't take long to clear this up. I presume, however, that you don't expect me to get dressed in the presence of a lady?'

'No. Of course not. We'll await you downstairs.'

'Toodle-pip!'

They went down to the hallway and waited. Five minutes passed. Van Buren was taking his time, Johnson thought. After a minute or two more, he called loudly up the stairs a couple of times. There was no reply. 'Bugger, Claire, I think he's done a runner.'

They ran up to the bedroom, which was indeed empty. 'He's taken us for complete mugs. I bet he's gone to the top of the house and scarpered down that tree.'

'Which way shall we go, sir? Up or down?'

'He's probably out on the street by now. Down.'

Once outside, they checked the back lane, but there was no sign of him. Johnson thought it best they stay together rather than split up, and it was a toss of the coin whether to go east or west along the Embankment. He decided on west and they ran off towards Fulham. Assuming they were going the right way, they had one advantage. Van Buren was very drunk.

A hundred yards on, they saw a car screech to a halt ahead of them. When they reached it, the driver seemed shaken. 'Did you see that? I almost killed that idiot. He ran right out in front of me.'

The officers looked down the Embankment. To make life more difficult, the light was beginning to go, but Robinson thought she could see something. 'There, sir. Just before the bend in the road. I think that's him.'

Johnson could just make out a man weaving wildly along the pavement. Chelsea Power Station loomed beyond. They resumed their pursuit, and began to gain on him. When Van Buren turned into Lots Road, they were only about fifty yards behind. He reached the power station gates, then pulled up. He bent down, and it looked as if he was vomiting. They were only yards away when he straightened and ran through the open gates. As they followed, a lorry suddenly pulled in front of them and they lost sight of him. When the lorry pulled away, he had disappeared.

Suddenly they heard someone shout out to their left. 'Geddown from there, you pillock! It's dangerous!' They looked up and saw their man climbing the towering metal staircase that zig-zagged its way up the facing side of the power station. He paid no attention to the warning and kept on going.

The officers ran over to the workman who'd been shouting. Johnson showed his warrant card. 'We're after that man. What's wrong with the stairs?'

'The structure's awaiting repairs. Some parts, like the gangway at the top, are very dodgy. You'll be taking your lives in your hands if you follow him.'

'We may have no choice. Where do they lead?'

'There's a door into the upper part of the main power room at the top. I'm not sure if it's open. If it is, and he gets in, he'll have a good chance of giving you the slip. There are a lot of other entrances and exits.'

'Then we definitely have no choice. There's no point both of us risking it, Claire. You stay down here and I'll go up.'

367

'With respect, sir, not on your nelly.'

'That's an order, Constable.'

'Then you'll have to put me up on charges later, sir. Meanwhile, Van Buren is already halfway up the stairs.' Without further argument, she turned, ran to the stairs and started up. Johnson followed.

They climbed as fast as they could, heads down. Van Buren's feet clattered above them, but it was difficult to gauge whether they were gaining on him. When they were about halfway up, Johnson stopped and reached out to grasp Robinson's arm. 'Wait a second, Claire. I can't hear him any more. He must be at the top.'

There was a rattling sound above.

'Trying the door, sir?'

'I think so. Sounds like it won't open.' Johnson called out. 'It's no use, Van Buren. You're not going to get away.' They resumed their climb. The clattering above resumed briefly, before they heard a tremendous metallic groan. They stopped again and looked up. What had been a groan suddenly became a roar, and they saw the top gangway swing free of the superstructure. 'Come on, Claire. We'd better run for it.' Johnson grabbed Robinson's hand and pulled her down and ahead of him. The whole framework of the staircase was now shuddering violently, and they hurtled down as fast as they could. They only had two flights to go when they heard a blood-curdling scream and watched as Van Buren plummeted to the ground. They heard a sickening thud. Then the gangway followed him down.

As they reached the bottom, they saw several workmen waving at them frantically to get away from the staircase as fast as they could. They did so then waited breathlessly by one of the outbuildings until it appeared the structure had finally settled. Then they and the workmen made their way to the body. Van Buren's torso and legs lay mangled and crushed under the fallen gangway, and his head lolled to the side, split in two. Robinson had to turn aside, but Johnson couldn't tear his eyes away. He remembered reading that the ancient Roman punishment for parricide was to be sewn in a sack with a dog, snake, chicken and monkey and thrown into the Tiber. Van Buren's death had been horrible, but at least it had been quicker than that.

'You look like you could do with a stiff drink, Frank,' said Sonia at the door.

'I've already had a couple of whiskies with Gordon Cleverly at the Scrubs. I'd better get some grub inside me before I have any more.'

'You can explain later. I've been keeping a cottage pie warm for you in the oven.'

'Wonderful.'

'Before you settle down, though, I have to tell you that Peter Johnson called. He sounded excited.'

'Was there a message?'

'Only that everything was under control, and as it was late, he could wait until the morning to brief you.'

'I wonder what under control means?'

'Save your wondering for tomorrow. You've clearly had enough for today.' They moved to the kitchen. 'My briefing can wait until tomorrow too.'

'I'll just tell you the last bit, shall I?'

'If you insist, but let me dish up your dinner first.'

With an overflowing plate in front of him, Merlin proceeded to tell his wife about Virgil Lewis's last-minute reprieve.

'Does that mean he's a free man?' asked Sonia when he'd finished.

'Not quite. Eisenhower said he was going to review the case. He may order a retrial. But we now have time to analyse the blood on the business card and White's shirt. If it's Pablo's, then Lewis is home free. If the blood analysis proves inconclusive, the evidence we've put together still ought to be more than enough to get him off.'

369

When he had finished the last of the cottage pie, he couldn't stop yawning.

'Come on then, Frank. Bedtime for you.'

'Is the lad all right?'

'He's had a busy day and is now sleeping the sleep of the just . . . isn't that the phrase?'

'It is.'

'The very same sleep of the just that now awaits you.'

Postscript

Thursday August 27th 1942

Memorandum DCI Merlin to AC Gatehouse

Sir, a note summarising recent developments. Robert Van Buren fell to his death on Tuesday having admitted to killing his father. Attached is the recent psychiatric report prepared by Dr Arnold Jacob that Van Buren removed from his father's papers. You will note that the doctor refers back to his earlier assessments of Robert when he knifed a boy at school. He warned then that he thought more violent episodes were very likely and recommended institutionalisation. Robert's father ignored this advice to his ultimate cost.

Despite my officers saying she was very distraught when telling her story, I do wonder at the relative ease with which Elizabeth Van Buren turned her brother in. My guess is there was little love lost between them and that there may be a more mercenary side to Elizabeth than previously credited. The net result is that she is going to be an extraordinarily wealthy young lady.

Forensics confirmed that the blood found on Vince White's shirt and the card he had in his possession belonged to Pablo Merino. Detective Goldberg has passed this information on to the American authorities, who have confirmed that Virgil Lewis will be completely exonerated without the need for a retrial.

I attach a copy of the handwritten note found at Cedric Calvert's residence. In summary, he admits to fraud and murder. Driven by very large stock market losses, he embezzled funds from his company and sold oil trade secrets to the enemy. Having been confronted by Vermeulen, he went to his house to try and persuade him to back off. Vermeulen refused and Calvert shot him. He took with him the file Vermeulen had shown him in the belief, mistaken as it turns out, that it was the only copy. When he learned we were on to him, he took what he saw as the only way out. His chosen suicide spot was apparently a favourite courting spot of his and his late wife's.

Micallef's body has now been formally identified and Miss Van Buren has been informed. There is still no sign of Jake Penny. As ever, there is no evidential link to Billy Hill, but I'm sure he was behind it all.

Sir Kenneth Clark has now authenticated the drawings, as you know, and they have been returned to Miss Van Buren.

Miss Van Buren informs me she has issued instructions to end her father's litigation against the Butterfields.

I have brought Harold Swanton up to date on developments. He is naturally pleased that his rogue German agent had nothing to do with the murders. The agent is still at large in Ireland, he believes.

In case you haven't yet heard, we had good news yesterday when a guilty verdict was returned in the Hammersmith bomb shelter case. I have congratulated Johnson and Robinson for their sterling work.

You asked to be kept posted on the case my wife is involved with at the Polish legation. There has been no progress and the Russians continue to stonewall. It seems certain that evil has been done. Notwithstanding they are now our allies, I am heartily sorry they managed to inveigle poor Pablo into working for them.

DC Cole remains in a serious condition in hospital. We continue to pray for him. He is a very brave young man. I should mention that all my other officers also showed great bravery and risked life and limb in the investigation of these cases. A direct word of commendation from you would be much appreciated.

Monday September 14th 1942

News column in *Apollo* art magazine

The pending sale of two recently discovered da Vinci drawings to Mr Calouste Gulbenkian may have encountered a hitch. It is understood that a court injunction has been issued at the behest of Benjamin Katz, a City banker, on grounds that the drawings were stolen from his family in Vienna before the war.

Tuesday September 22nd 1942

Cable to Field Marshal Goering

REGRET INFORM YOU THAT LIEUTENANT
COLONEL VON WALD HAS BEEN DETACHED
FROM HIS ABWEHR POST STOP I HAVE DIS-
COVERED GROSS INSUBORDINATION ON HIS
PART STOP WAS RUNNING ROGUE OPER-
ATION IN ENGLAND STOP ALSO GUILTY OF
UNDERMINING MORALE WITH FALSE THE-
ORIES RE SUCCESS OF OUR ENGLISH
NETWORKS STOP HE HAS BEEN SENT EAST
STOP FÜHRER INFORMED AND IN AGREE-
MENT STOP CANARIS

Thursday October 1st 1942

Police Gazette

It is reported that DC Thomas Cole is to be recommended for
the Police Gallantry Medal. The constable showed outstand-
ing bravery in the course of an arrest in August. With scant
regard for his own safety, he tackled a violent armed criminal,
Vincent White, thereby protecting his colleague, DS Samuel
Bridges, from serious injury. Unfortunately, the gunshot
wounds sustained in the course of this action proved fatal.
Cole, 25, was buried in Hackney Cemetery on September
18th, with full police honours.